JOSIE'S JOURNEY

Scooter Tramp
Scotty

AUTHOR'S NOTE

Although Josie's Journey is often based on actual historical places and events, many of the details depicted are fictional. Yet Josie's is not a history book meant for the benefit of scholarly research, but rather the story of one spirit's steady journey across time, and the ultimate destination that awaits.

This is a work of fiction. Names, characters, businesses, places, events, locales, and incidents are either the products of the author's imagination or used in a fictitious manner. Any resemblance to actual persons, living or dead, or actual events is purely coincidental. No Part of this book may be reproduced in any form or by any electronic or mechanical means, including information storage and retrieval systems, without written permission from the author, except for the use of brief quotations in a book review. Copyright © Scotty Kerekes

CHAPTER 1	7
CHAPTER 2	13
CHAPTER 3	31
CHAPTER 4	33
CHAPTER 5	71
CHAPTER 6	73
CHAPTER 7	97
CHAPTER 8	130
CHAPTER 9	140
CHAPTER 10	154
CHAPTER 11	175
CHAPTER 12	187
CHAPTER 13	200
CHAPTER 14	229
CHAPTER 15	259
CHAPTER 16	311
CHAPTER 17	323

THE END OF THE BEGINNING
Chapter 1

1

At the age of 78, Josie found himself on his deathbed and reflected that he had enjoyed a long and good life. After all, had he not been a competent provider, husband, and father; been fair and honest in his dealings with friends and co-workers; considerate of God's earth and the animals while taking no more from the world's abundance than needed to support his family? But then, Josie had spent his entire life in a small village where this was the norm and simply what had been expected of him.

Yes, Josie had lived a good life and fully expected to meet God soon, who would then guide him to the *Pearly Gates* of Heaven. After all, he had been an avid churchgoer who had spent a lifetime trying to avoid the temptations of sin. Falling short of this perfect ideal on more than one occasion, Josie reflected that he had done his very best and that was all anyone, even God, could ask. But, had he been honest with himself Josie would have had to admit he was a fearful man. He had learned of God's wrath in Sunday school and, fearing for his immortal soul more so than by any act of true virtue, had tried to comply with the ways of Church and God.

Once standing before the Gates Josie would listen quietly as Saint Peter read him the rules of God's glory. But this would be only a formality since Josie had already spent a lifetime studying these things in Sunday school.

Yes, Josie reflected, he had served his sentence well and now it was time to receive his just reward. Besides, he missed his wife Adrienne who had passed on some years before and surely, through her beauty and her virtue, awaited his arrival beyond the *Pearly Gates*.

With that, Josie closed his eyes and died.

It was then that a curious thing happened and Josie found himself seemingly floating above his deathbed. But this oddity did not seem strange or unusual. In fact, it felt quite natural as he looked down upon the face of the haggard old man that now lay pale and quiet beneath the sheets of the straw-filled mattress. Was this really him? From his lofty perch Josie watched his daughter Rachel begin to weep as his two grandchildren, Mosaic and Jacob—both almost adults themselves—stood quietly beside her.

They all seemed so sad, but Josie did not feel sad and in this odd new state of being he wondered at Rachel's tears and wished to go comfort her; for they had been very close. But it seemed he could not. And so, he only observed this sad affair from his lofty exile.

The minutes passed slowly.

Eventually Josie's attention was interrupted by a light that seemed to have been switched on to his right and was of an intensity that could not be ignored. As Josie turned to look, a most curious sight startled him. Seemingly hanging in the air was a tunnel of some sort. Its sides were lined with pink cotton-candy textured fuzz and Josie noted that this intense light was emanating from inside, or at the other end of, this strange tunnel. What should have been the most disturbing thing was that the mouth of this cavern was moving toward him at an alarming rate. But, far from being frightening, this strange phenomenon seemed perfectly normal, if not familiar. With no choice in the matter anyway, Josie simply allowed himself to become engulfed inside. For a time, the light seemed to be blinding but, as Josie moved closer, he noted that the brightness was becoming ringed with an aura of light blue. Josie concluded, and rightly so, that what he saw was only the sun against a background of clear sky. Eventually the tunnel ended and, since its mouth was only a few feet above the ground, Josie floated easily down until his feet met with green grass and he felt the weight of his body once more.

The tunnel instantly forgotten, Josie craned his neck to survey the magnificent view. He stood at the top of a hill that overlooked a great meadow that stretched across the valley below. Beautiful wildflowers peppered the knee-high grass with yellow and purple hues of moving color as a gentle breeze blew silently across the land. Honeybees worked busily over the flowers as various birds weaved through the air. At the meadow's edge, Josie noted a wall of oak, pine, and other trees. This timber-barrier stood sentry to the seemingly endless forest that rolled across the small mountains for many miles before disappearing into the distance. The air was warm and, looking up, Josie noted only a few small and hazy clouds lumbering lazily across the sky and one magnificent hawk that soared high above the earth—if this was earth. For a long moment Josie only basked in the distant beauty of it all. Gradually though, his attention was drawn back to the valley and he looked more closely at the green grasses below. He saw that a wide creek babbled through the canyon's center as smooth rocks lined much of its shore and protruded from the flowing water. Beside the creek stood two large oak trees—the only trees in the clearing.

Looking more closely, Josie noticed a man who squatted at the water's edge beside the oaks and, with cupped hands, drank from its cool refreshment. Josie felt he knew this man and began moving in his direction. Before long he arrived beside the creek and the man slowly stood to face Josie as he wiped moist lips with the back of his hand. Josie looked more closely at the man's features. He was about 5'10" with skin that seemed light against a mane of such dark, straight, shoulder length hair. His face was clean-shaven and carried the faint lines of wisdom that gave the impression of one in his late 40s. But it was something about his eyes that lent this guy a sort of ominous presence, as their piercingly neon color was identical to that of the clear blue sky. Aside from this oddity there seemed nothing unusual about him. He was of lean yet muscular build and dressed in plain brown pants, a plaid shirt with sleeves cut short and, as was common in Josie's own village, sandals.

"How have you been God?"

"A little over worked these days I guess, but I'm not complaining any Josie. Come, let's go sit beneath the oaks; for you know I'm very old", and with that God threw a sly smile in Josie's direction. Josie agreed, and when each was comfortably seated against a tree facing partly toward the other and partly toward the water, God crossed his ankles, turned his magnificent eyes into Josie's and said, "Did you enjoy your experience?"

"It was a good life God. I did my best, went to church, took care of my family, and tried to treat others well. But then you already know all of this."

"I do."

"Then where is Saint Peter and the Pearly Gates? Did I not adhere well enough to the ways of Church and God? My sins have been few and, I had hoped, no more that could be expected of anyone that is human."

"You've done well Josie and I am very pleased. But you are not yet ready and would only hurt, or even destroy, that which is known as Heaven."

"But I thought…I mean…I tried so hard! And if you are pleased, then why can I not… And I miss Adrienne. I was so looking forward to seeing her again."

"Not to worry Josie, the Gates of Heaven will be waiting for you—I promise. And you will surely see Adrienne again as the love between you is forged of free will and has little to do with me anyway. Your partnership, you see, will simply last as long as you both agree upon it—although you may, at times, be apart for a little while."

"But…but God I…"

"You will just have to trust Josie, that I am God and have only your best interest in mind."

With that Josie fell silent, for he knew this was an argument he could not win. But as he watched his hard-earned dream slipping through his fingers, Josie began to stew at the injustice of it all. After all, had he not spent a lifetime in willing obedience for the promise of a great reward that would now only be denied him? Josie was pissed.

Then he began to worry.

"But what is to become of me now God?"

God noted the child's fearful tone as he spoke.

"There is a thing I need done," God tricked, "and it's something I cannot do for myself. But I have complete confidence in your abilities. Will you help me?"

Josie was floored at the idea that the Almighty could need his help for anything! After the moment of shock had passed, his chest puffed at the thought of helping and, although he would not have admitted it, even becoming God. Josie's heart filled with a new sense of pride and importance. His former anger was forgotten. So he said in a voice that betrayed more excitement than the tone of humility originally intended, "Of course I'll help you God. What is it you ask of me?"

"Will you allow me to think on the particulars of this for a few minutes Josie?"

"Of course, God. Take your time," Immediately Josie regretted these foolish words and wished to take them back. But God seemed not to notice, and he only turned the conversation to simple things. Minutes passed. A doe and her young fawn stepped cautiously from the forest to drink at the stream's edge only a stone's throw from where the two men sat.

When an hour had gone, and unable to contain himself any longer, Josie again inquired as to the task God needed him to perform

"Come," God said, "There is something I wish to show you." After standing to shake the grass from his backside, Josie followed his friend to the stream. Once there, he watched as God knelt to peer into the calm, clear water. This gesture seemed familiar, and Josie joined him. But as the old man caught sight of his reflection, Josie was momentarily shocked at the young man staring back. He wondered then, when this transformation had happened. The image began to change and again Josie saw the tunnel that had brought him to this place…and again it engulfed him. But this time the light at the end was not the sun of God's meadow. Josie began to feel himself being pushed, then pulled, through this strange crawlway. What the hell was going on? Soon, he was freed from the tunnel. Josie was in a very strange land now. Never before had he seen the likes of this. Everything seemed so…BIG! Was he in a land of giants? Then, like a fish or maybe a game animal, Josie was lifted abruptly into the air and suspended by only his ankles. Next, a very intrusive crime was dealt him with cold and calculated malice as something hit him. At this stinging injustice Josie began to cry and, as air filled his little lungs for the very first time, the memory of all that had gone on before left him.

Josie had been born again.

DEGRADATION
Chapter 2

1

As always, the kaleidoscope of living green hues that blanketed the surrounding Alabama countryside was complete. No man could dispute the natural beauty of this land.

The little homestead that sat in a small canyon beside Patsy Creek, where it received relative shelter from the winter winds, was neither extravagant nor was it neglected. The sky above was clear and although the air offered a crisp, clean chill, no sign of the occasional winter snow lay upon the earth. In the front yard four riders sat atop their mounts facing the log house as an older man stood his ground some 25-feet before them. His bearded face betrayed little emotion as the man's rifle remained trained upon the intruder's leader.

"We know ya got deserters held up on your place Bob," Daniel called down from his horse. "You know well as anyone that harborin' deserters of the Confederate Army is an act of treason and a hangin' offense. If you just turn 'em over nice and peaceful like, we'll consider ridin' out with our prisoners and just forgettin' we ever seen you today."

"Now look here Daniel, I side with you in this here war," the old man lied. At one time, Bob had backed "The Cause" with the same passion and confidence as every other Southerner worth his salt. They had put up a good fight too. But the war had lasted too long…too many had died. The South now lay in tatters of broken homes tended only by women, children and the very elderly who starved in desperate destitution without the strength of their menfolk to work the fields, tend livestock, and see to other essential chores. Most of the horses and other livestock, along with the men, were gone as well; commandeered by the army long ago. As word of the situation back home spread, desertion had run rampant among the ranks and hordes of hungry men set upon the perilous journey along roads or through the woods in attempt to avoid the Union Army or Home Guard and return to their families. Few cared about this war anymore, the years of suffering had seen to that. "But I'm a telling you now mister, ain't no deserters here. Now turn your asses around and get off my property before someone gets hurt!"

Daniel was a big, bearded man who wore a long oil-skin slicker beneath his black wide-brimmed hat, "Now, be reasonable old man," he continued, "We know you're lyin'. Might be your boys Billy 'n Travis in there, huh? Now hand 'em over or there's gonna be trouble."

From his mount at Daniel's left, Josie raised his eyes to the house as he noted some movement there. He saw only a small boy who stood at a windowsill he barely reached to observe a situation he could not understand. Josie deemed the boy harmless and returned his hard gaze to the old man.

"Now look here Bob," Daniel continued, "There's four of us and only one of you. You got no chance and one way or the other we're leaving here with our prisoners!"

Bob's eyes betrayed nothing, "I'm a peaceable man just tryin' to raise a family here. I got no stake in this war an' I'm tellin' you this much Daniel Waters, I might get only one shot before you fellas cut me down, but that bullet's a goin' right through your nasty old heathen hide!"

"You threatenin' me old man?"

"I'm sayin', leave my property now or die on it today Mr. Waters!"

"Now Bob, be reasonable," Emmett said. With gun still trained on Daniel Waters, Bob turned attention to the new speaker. "We got no quarrel with you…" A shot rang out and Bob fell, dead before he hit the ground. The horses stirred and Josie looked to the rider at his far right. It was Zeke, an older man of thin build with black hair and boney features. His gun still smoked. Zeke had raised a pistol to just above his saddle-horn and shot Bob when his attention had been diverted to Emmett.

Josie turned next to Emmett. He was a young man with dirty blond hair that hung shoulder length from beneath a tattered, tan, wide-brimmed hat. Emmett's boyish face betrayed nothing of his icy heart. Josie guessed the war had hardened him, as it had most everyone in recent years.

At the age of thirteen Josie himself was still too young for the army, but he had his late father's guns and, alongside these men, had figured to do his part for "The Cause".

Emmett stared at the dead man. His face revealed no emotion.

The little house's front door flew open, and a woman ran from inside, her long blue dress flying in the gale behind. Tears streamed from her aging face as she threw herself upon the man on the ground.

At the cabin's window the boy remained motionless.

The riders dismounted and moved into the yard. Zeke and Emmett pulled the hysterical wife from Bob's body and dragged her to a tall post that had been set to accommodate a clothesline. Both men pushed her against it and lashed both hands together at its other side. Using a large Bowie knife, Zeke cut the neckline of her dress then tore the cloth to expose her pale back. A broad grin crossed Zeke's lean, almost skeletal, face. The man was enjoying himself. So was Josie, as he observed this little show from the nearby fence upon which he leaned.

With the woman firmly bound, Zeke produced a bullwhip. He moved some paces from her, and the long whip whistled through the air before striking its target. The woman screamed and dropped to her knees. Zeke adjusted his aim and hit her again. Her cries were louder this time.

"Come out boys," Daniel yelled at the house, **"Your momma can't take much more!"**

There was no reply. Zeke raised the whip and continued his beating. The woman's cries subsided into whimpers.

Two boys, neither much older than Josie, finally stepped from the front door to assume a stance of surrender, and were immediately cut to pieces by the hail of bullets fired by every man present. For a time, there was only silence. Without a word, the riders moved toward their horses and remounted. Josie stared at the house; the woman still tied to the post, her husband lying upon his back in a pool of blood while two young men sprawled dead upon the little front porch. The place was quiet now. Chickens returned to the business of pecking and scratching as birdsong that had been momentarily quelled by the blasts began to resonate from the surrounding trees. A squirrel leapt from one high branch to another. All seemed peaceful again. For a moment Josie thought of home and the days of his own youth…

2

    It had been in a little two-story farmhouse, not unlike this, to which he had been born. Josie's mother had no longer been a young woman when she had given birth to him, but he had been her only child just the same. Memories of her long dark hair, often tired face creased with fine worry-lines, gentle caress, and caring coos for his well-being still haunted him. To date, she had offered the only real love he had ever known. But soon after his eighth birthday she had died of the sickness. It had been a crushing blow and Josie knew not if he would ever forgive her for leaving him, or the heathen God she had believed in so deeply for taking her.

    The boy had been left to live with his father. The man was a drunkard who was good for little else in this world. Life with only him had been an unsettling affair at best. Although not a violent man, his sometimes funny and more often tragic antics had amused Josie but little. There was scarce security to be found in him for a child. He was lazy, dirty, and seldom put food upon the table. Josie was forced to grow up much too fast and his spirit had grown hard. Having spent many hours beside his mother's side as she had performed the tasks necessary to sustain them, Josie took greater interest in these now. He began to feed and milk the family cow. He fed the chickens, collected their eggs, and sometimes butchered them for meat. He also took interest in cooking. Josie cut smaller rounds for the wood stove and fireplace with a bowsaw since he was still too little to handle an ax or maul. His hands grew callused. In gardening he took interest as well. But the boy despised cleaning or laundry and most often just went dirty.

    Josie would often secure his daddy's musket and hunt quail,

pheasant, duck, rabbit, squirrel, possum, or any other small game that could be found. Fishing was one of his favorite pastimes and, along with hunting and the collecting of wild foods and nuts, these activities had brought to him most all the pleasure he received from this life. The land had always been good to him. From it, he gained a sense of peace. The rolling hills, the magnificent Chattahoochee River, clear-watered creeks, beautiful trees, and gentle breezes that put the leaves to flutter, all calmed him. He loved the sound of birdsong, as their tone always brought life to his day—neutral life that neither judged nor brought burden upon his world. And although he sometimes killed them for food, often he did not, and only observe their habits instead. For by and large, they comprised the bulk of his companionship in this lonely world.

But Josie was still only a boy mostly alone in a man's world and it was not uncommon that he went hungry—especially in winter. Fortunately, there had been neighbors who knew of the boy's plight and insisted upon sharing their sometimes-slender resources with him. For these kindnesses Josie had been torn between gratitude and contempt of such charity.

Eventually the old man had also grown sick. The doc said it was his liver and Josie had been able only to watch with fear and disdain as his father grew yellow with the jaundice. When the old man finally died, Josie took his musket and 36-caliber revolving percussion-pistol for his own. Next, Josie had called upon his neighbors, Ed and Janice, who lived closer to the town of Irwinton. Upon their arrival, and with the help of a man called Preacher Mike, the couple had dug a grave behind the house. The boy had then watched with mixed emotions as the emaciated body of his father, wrapped only in an old gray blanket, had been carried to the hole then lowered into the earth. Once the dirt was replaced the Preacher said a few words, and without shedding so much as a tear, the boy bowed his head with the others in silent prayer.

Ed and Janice offered a place in their own home then, but the boy had refused it. In his slight ability and proud sense of independence, Josie had opted to shrug off the idea of such change. It has been said *the cause of all fear is the unknown*, and even at his young age Josie feared deeply that which was different. No, Josie would not leave the only home he had ever known. But that very night, for reasons he'd failed to understand, the child had cried himself to sleep.

For some months, the boy lived alone upon the little homestead of his upbringing. Janice sometimes worried and the couple might have removed him forcibly were it not for the coming of Josie's uncle Jeb in early summer.

Upon his arrival, Jeb stated flatly that he had come to stay upon the farm and help to raise the son of his late brother. To some extent this was true, but it was also true that Jeb had grown weary of his wandering in recent years and now sought a place to settle. The farm was his answer.

Josie had never met this man before and voiced his protestations loudly, "Nobody asked you to come here," he yelled, "an' you ain't welcome. How do I even know you're even my uncle? I never seen you before. So, I'm telling you mister, get off my property now! This ain't your place, an' you ain't stayin'. So, you best just…"

Had anyone been watching they would have laid witness to a powerfully comical sight. A dirty little boy of only ten years standing tall in the stunningly green beauty of his Alabama front yard, wearing only tattered boots and a pair of grimy coveralls, while yelling at the big bearded man before him. Jeb stood in his equally dirty tan-britches with black suspenders stretched over a large potbelly to cross his dingy blue button style shirt. With musket in one hand and gunnysack slung over the other shoulder, he stared down at the boy with cold amusement. As the boy's ranting continued, Jeb set down his burdens then turned to spit a dark stream of tobacco juice upon the ground. Then, in one smooth movement that seemed too quick for a man his size, the back of Jeb's left hand shot out and struck the boy solidly across the mouth. Josie hit the ground hard. He saw stars and wondered if his jaw had been broken. Rubbing his face in shock and disbelief, Josie stared up at this stubborn prick. He was quiet now.

"Now look here boy," Jeb began, "I'm your daddy's older brother by two years; you oughta see that just lookin' at me."

It was true. Jeb was a big man with powerful arms that hung from a barrel chest with potbelly below. His face was round and topped with short black hair and shaggy beard blended with streaks of gray. Jeb's nose was wide and blunt between dark eyes set far apart and when he grinned through thick, full, lips his perfect teeth showed the stains of heavy tobacco use. The resemblance to Josie's father and, although his own body still carried the leanness of youth, even to Josie himself, was undeniable. Jeb looked down at the boy with eyes that narrowed beneath the beads of sweat that glistened upon his broad forehead in the summer sun. "Now like it or not boy, I'm here to stay in the home of my late brother so you'd better just get used to it." With that, Jeb had retrieved his musket and gunnysack then walked to the house.

So it was that Josie's reign of solitude upon the farm came to an end.

But Jeb was not the drunkard his brother had been, nor was he lazy. In time, Josie would learn that although his uncle was strict and sometimes cruel, he was a fair man who seemed quite capable in his endeavors. Jeb was not one for affection and never again was Josie to know anything akin to the gentle caress of his mother's caring hand. Although Josie had at first resented the coming of this strange man, the presence of an adult, especially one in command of such great strength, brought a very comforting sense of safety.

In time, Jeb came upon the guns Josie had taken from his father. The boy feared the worst then. But Jeb did not raise a fuss, nor did he confiscate the firearms. Instead, he encouraged, and even instructed the boy in proper use of such weapons. Although Jeb was a hard man and clearly not prone to acts of kindness or generosity, he carried the conviction that he must educate the son of his late brother to the ways of this world. Jeb believed that a man's weapons were a necessary instrument to this ambition and, for better or worse, the boy would keep his.

Josie began to hunt openly. Upon seeing the small bounty of meat the boy often brought home, Jeb decided to take Josie on his first deer hunt.

So, it was at the age of ten that Josie killed his first doe.

His uncle taught the boy proper methods of gutting, cleaning, skinning, and eventually, smoking the sweet meat into long strips of dried jerky. Just as Josie had once taken unusual interest in the forages with his mother when they had collected wild foods, so he took keen interest now. The boy's fascination was most uncommon.

Seeing this only fueled Jeb's natural desire to share his own wisdom with one so interested. Jeb allowed the boy to try his hand at the job. Although Josie fumbled, Jeb patiently corrected him and noted that the boy learned unusually fast.

3

Originally it had been mostly families of sustenance, farmers like Josie's, who had come to build their homesteads upon the unusually fertile land of this region. Later, came the grand cotton plantations as well. And it had been upon the backs of so many slaves who worked the fields that the state of Alabama, along with much of the South, had grown to such ornate riches. Although this wealth had, to some extent, trickled throughout the community, most of the plantation owners exercised their considerable influence over local governments to keep taxes low so the money might instead be diverted to personal interests. To this end, public schools had yet to be established throughout the south. And because most of the cotton was moved by riverboat, federally maintained roads were uncommon—as were railways. In the end, the rich grew richer while the poor, along with the niggers, enjoyed little change.

Jeb took work as overseer on a nearby cotton plantation. For the black man he felt only contempt. This was a white man's world and there was no place in it for the likes of such ignorant and stupid savages imported through virtue of madness from the stinking jungles of some far-off land. *Hell*, Jeb thought, *If God had wanted the niggers to live among the finer fruits of a civilization created by the white man's superior intellect, He wouldn't have banished those black bastards to the far reaches of the world in the first fucking place.*

Accordingly, Jeb treated the black man with obvious disdain. His only real restraint was a warning from his employer that to damage the rich man's property to the extent at which the nigger could not work would bring swift consequences. Jeb adhered to this restraint, if only grudgingly.

From the tidings of his meager pay and profits from some livestock raised upon the farm and sold, Jeb spent a percentage upon the son of his late brother. Josie's ragged clothes and tattered boots were replaced. Jeb sometimes brought the boy powder, flint, and shot for his musket and occasionally gave him a little cash. Jeb said the clothes and money were Josie's fair share for the work he did around the farm.

It was true that Josie did his part, but it was also true that Jeb believed it important to the boy's upbringing that he learn the connection between work and money. If Josie did not learn this, his uncle believed, the boy would surely grow up to become a thief. And although he himself had not been above such conduct on occasion, Jeb hated thieves and believed it his job to teach better of the boy.

For Josie, life with Jeb had been better in some ways. But besides his marginal qualities, Jeb seemed a man haunted by his own demons. He was often grouchy, discontent, intolerant, angry and sometimes violent, seemingly for no reason. Josie had occasionally donned bruises or black eyes at the hand of his uncle. Other times Jeb was talkative and even moderately kind. There was just no way to figure at a glance what particular mood Jeb was entertaining. Josie had often kept his distance and sometimes retreated to the sanctity of the forest he loved when his uncle was in a foul mood. In these ways and others, Jeb became the only role model Josie had ever known. In time, as the lines between them had been defined, life within the boundaries of the small farm became reasonably comfortable for both occupants. Although on occasion Josie had thought Jeb to be almost likeable, more often he felt little more than contempt for the man.

It was the wee hours of morning when Josie had come awake to the quiet rustling of chickens in the hen house. A rooster crowing at this hour was not unusual, but this was different. From his bed beside the second story window Josie had lain awake in the dark and listened. Was it weasel or coyote? His ears strained for an answer. Next came the faint squeak of a loose floorboard in the adjacent bedroom and he knew Jeb had heard it too. Ever so faintly, Josie heard his uncle slink down the stairs then slip out through the back door. In slow quiet movements the boy had raised up to peer stealthily through his open window to the scene below.

    The sky offered only a half-moon that illuminated the yard in dark shadows. Josie saw the side of the coop some twenty feet from the garden. It had been fenced with rusty chicken-wire long ago. The disturbance grew louder. Josie's head turned towards the dark figure of his uncle who, musket in hand, had moved from the house to stalk quietly upon the coop from its backside. Josie's gaze returned to the coop. Something was backing away from the hen-house door. What sort of varmint was it? Josie's eyes strained through the dark. Suddenly he saw. It was a man! In his right hand he carried one limp hen as he backed cautiously toward the surrounding forest. Jeb stepped swiftly from the shadows and was upon him, musket trained on the man's gut.

    "What ya got there mister? What ya doin' in our yard at this ungodly hour o' the night?"

    From the window Josie heard the words as clearly as if Jeb were standing beside him. There was no excuse for the chicken-thief. He had been caught red-handed.

    "I didn't mean no harm sir," the man quivered, "It's just that, well, I haven't 'et nothin' for better 'n three days and I'm mighty hungry." The stranger paused to note any sign of compassion in his aggressor's eyes. There was none, so he resumed, "It's only one chicken sir and I'd be glad to oblige if you'd allow me the dignity to work it off…"

    Jeb shot him.

    The blast startled Josie and he jumped, banging his head loudly against the sill. Jeb did not look up. The remaining chickens stirred and clucked noisily. Although the shot had been fired point blank, the man was not dead. He writhed on the ground clawing at his gut and, drawing back a bloody hand, screamed in shock and disbelief, "You shot me! I can't believe you shot me! Hell, it was only one darn chicken!" His voice trailed into weak moans as strength began to desert him. To Josie's amazement, the man's voice fell to whimpering sobs.

    Jeb seemed unaffected by the man's plight as he began to reload the musket. Then he started talking, "Naw mister, I ain't mad about you stealin' my chicken. Hell, it ain't no thing. I see you're a starving man, an' sure you can come on in, have breakfast with us, then work the grub off uh pullin' weeds in my garden…." When the gun was reloaded, Jeb leveled it at the dying man's chest—his babbling never missed a beat. "…Hell, we'd be happy to have ya. Might even share my wife with you if I had one…" The second shot put the man quickly out of his misery. Jeb finally shut up. For a time, the cackle of chickens also subsided and the little valley again lay quiet and peaceful as if nothing had happened. Josie looked through eyes wet with queasy emotion at the silhouetted vision of his uncle, musket held loosely in one hand, standing motionless in the night with head bent in silent contemplation of the dead man at his feet.

Jeb looked up to the window then, and as their eyes met Josie's heart froze. Jeb was a murderer!

"Get your ass down here boy. An' fetch some shovels on the way. Come on now, **move!**"

Josie did as he was told.

Using one hand, as he held the musket in the other, Jeb had dragged the thin body some distance from the house before the two began to dig in mutual silence. When the hole was deep enough, Jeb threw the chicken-thief in and again reached for his shovel. For a long moment Josie stared down upon the old wretch who now lay still upon the dirt. *It ain't so bad*, he thought then. After all, he had seen plenty of animals die and that never bothered him none. Then came the recollection of his father as he had lain in a hole not so unlike this one. But it was not Josie's father down there—just some scrawny chicken-thief. *Who gives a shit*, Josie decided, *I never seen this guy before anyway and, by the looks of him, he's better off dead!* Something changed in Josie that night, or maybe it was something that had always been there and he'd just never let loose of before. Either way, Josie decided he was glad the chicken-thief was dead. Never had Josie enjoyed the handling of a shovel before. He did now.

The boy slept well that night.

Neither Jeb nor Josie ever spoke of the chicken-thief again, and the memory of that night had faded quickly as life returned to its tedious normality.

Time passed.

4

Word of the war came and, although certainly past his prime, Jeb had rallied enthusiastically in the streets with the others before all had marched off to crush the insolent North. It was an exciting time and few worried for it was common knowledge that, when met with the Southern man's superior spirit, intellect, and capability, the North would crumble quickly. The war would last no more than a month…maybe two.

They were wrong.

Although Josie had wished to fight for the Cause, he had been too young and was made to stay and tend the farm instead. For this injustice he was angry. Besides, and although there was also a political agenda unknown to Josie and his uncle, for them this war was about freeing the niggers. And regardless of what Josie's feelings were toward Jeb, the man was right about one thing— niggers did not belong as equal to whites! Anyone could see that. Although having experienced only minimal contact with them, Josie had seen the black man. He was different. Different in his appearance. Different in his manner of speech. And certainly different in his way of thinking. *Obviously*, Josie had concluded, *this creature is stupid.* And this judgment granted even a simple farmer a comfortable feeling of superiority.

There were those dumb enough to side with the niggers, but Josie was not among them. If, this war was lost the Negro might obtain freedom to roam at will and live in any manner he chose. His difference might grow and spread. Josie's own world might be changed forever! What would become of him then? To this question the young man had no answer, but the very idea terrified him, and this fear spawned anger. And in his anger Josie began to hate *all* that is different.

In Jeb's absence, loneliness might have beset him again were it not for a position gained in the Home Guard. Convened in the wake of so many gone to war, the Home Guard had been comprised mostly of remaining local men. Their job would be to defend any woman, children and elderly left behind while the young soldiers were away, and also brought justice to any deserters that might pass through or hold up in the area. But the job description had rarely resembled services rendered. As more men were lost to the war and those who remained knew few would return, the Home Guard found itself in an unusual position of power and its integrity had often deteriorated.

The war had lasted years rather than months, with the South eventually taking a heavy beating. At home, as on the front lines, the tremendous impoverishment that followed changed men. In time, the whole affair seemed less about "The Cause" and leaned more toward the rapid ascension of a world gone completely mad. White man killed white as well as black. Homes of those left behind were pillaged for food and valuables and sometimes even commandeered in the name of war. Death became a common sight. Although less frequent, there were remarkable acts of kindness and heroism as well.

Josie's own farm, having been located some distance from town, had been set upon on two occasions. The first had been three men claiming to be confederate troops, but Josie knew them for deserters. Two of these he had shot forthright through the front window as the third ran for the woods. One of the downed men, a boy not too much older than himself, had survived and Josie had walked up and shot him point blank in the face even as the young man had pleaded for his life. Both were buried almost beside the place at which they had fallen because the men were too heavy for a young boy to drag far. On the second assault there had been more men and, after hastily grabbing only what possessions could easily be carried, Josie had slid out the back to retreat into the forest. For if he had chosen to fight they would surely have killed him and taken all anyway. Besides, there was not much to take.

But Josie's place among the Home Guard had been set, and it was in this way that he had come to the little farmhouse to stare upon the face of a small boy who stood at the windowsill to witness the rapid destruction of all he had ever known.

Josie looked at him now. The boy scowled back. He seemed to be studying Josie's face with his smug little stare. *Must be frozen with shock,* Josie thought. "Tough luck kid," he whispered under his breath, "But get used to it. It's a fucked-up world," and with that

Josie turned his horse and started after the others.

5

Four years after it had begun, the war ended with the South in bitter defeat. Jeb would never return for the battle at Picket's Mill had been his last. For this Josie was not sure how to feel. Although he had never thought highly of the man, Jeb was, after all, the last of his known kin. He was alone now.

The country had just torn itself apart from the inside out. The military onslaught had caused unprecedented billions in damage and the South now lay in a hideous shamble of devastation and ruin. The daily needs of those who remained went painfully unmet and starvation prevailed. Desperation was everywhere.

With the war lost to the victorious North, the South's justice system collapsed completely. Thieves, petty crooks, and bands of outlaws roamed freely. Rape, theft, and murder were common practice, and most crimes went unpunished.

Lawlessness prevailed. Countless suffered.

The recent implementation of the thirteenth amendment guaranteed the freedom of former slaves, but most southern men were severely opposed to the idea of accepting blacks living among them as equals and they rebelled harshly against the notion.

In time, the north imposed a period of *"Reconstruction"* upon all former Confederate states. Until its end, any remaining Southern whites would lose the right to vote, hold public office, or appeal for legal assistance against any injustice that befell them. Also, mobilized under the Reconstruction Act, Northern armies moved south to occupy many of the ex-Confederate towns and cities. And although the so-called "Carpetbaggers", along with military personnel, had been officially sent south to help rebuild infrastructure, more often than not corruption prevailed as these men stole the allotted funds, and anything else that could be taken from the southern man. Their terrible crimes were widespread.

Along with almost every other Southerner left alive, Josie seethed with anger at their defeat, loss of power, property, position, prosperity and, worst of all, the release of former slaves who were now free to roam at will. Resistance groups formed quickly. Many of their members were tough, well seasoned veterans of the recent war, and some had been Indian fighters before it. Although all these organizations were white supremacist in nature, the most notorious was the *Ku Klux Klan*.

Along with white robes, these new Klansmen (to which Josie quickly counted himself a member) often wore white hats and veils to hide their faces because anonymity was imperative lest they later face the death penalty for such crimes. Horses were likewise covered with white sheets and their hoofs muffled with heavy cloth wrappings to help silence the approach of these armed men who often came by torchlight procession on their ominous and terrifying night-rides.

At first the Klan directed its efforts to locating the meetings of Carpetbaggers and disbanding them. They destroyed Union League counsels, broke up bands of roaming Negroes, whipped black militiamen and forced them to pledge non-allegiance to the Union. The KKK also brought its brand of justice to anyone committing perceived crimes against a Southern white.

There were those in the Klan who carried noble intention— for many wished only for an answer that would bring the return of security and normality to their lives and families. But hate was everywhere. It could not be avoided. And for each who brought good intention, there were more who did not, and Josie took his place among the latter. His seemingly natural ability to leadership, ferocity, and unflinching willingness to act in the most extreme circumstance granted him quick rise to leadership there. For it was over the course of his short time in this cruel world that Josie had come to take his place among the most ruthless and violent of men. To all human life, even his own, Josie assigned little value. And if the end should come today, he really didn't give a shit.

Josie was a Klansmen feared by other Klansmen.

With the southern man having been disfranchised while blacks had since gained the right to vote, a second battle was born between North and South for control of the black man's ballot. For each wanted only those who shared their own interests to hold office in the South. While the North used deceit and manipulation to achieve such ends, the South soon reacted with acts of extreme violence against both black and white—though these actions were generally more extreme towards the Niggers.

The tactics of these resistance groups were *extremely* affective.

As the Klan's power grew, their crimes escalated accordingly. Killing became commonplace. Josie led his men to kill the livestock belonging to black farmers. Negroes who engaged in any business other than farming were beaten and tortured. Homes of black families were fired upon then burned with occupants still inside. Josie felt nothing for the murder of women and children. He was glad to do it. During one incident he kicked a six-year-old Negro girl to death then forced the girl's mother to hold her severed head even as he shot her.

The Klan killed Negroes and left their bodies alongside the roads. They attacked and frequently killed any armed forces assigned to the duty of protecting Negroes and brought more of the same upon those who sought to further the ideal of racial equality. Negro political leaders, heads of families, leaders of churches, and community groups, were killed as well. Crimes orchestrated by the Klan against the Negro were so numerous and widespread that it would require an entire volume to list them all.

All over the South white resistance groups rallied to similar activities. Guerilla warfare killed thousands.

6

The sky lay clear above the opposing walls of thick forest that lined either side of the narrow road's dirt surface. It was dark and he was alone. As Josie's horse rounded a slight bend the half-moon illuminated a mounted figure from behind. To Josie, the man's features appeared as dark silhouette. *It seems strange,* Josie thought, *how he just sits there.* Thinking little more of it, Josie continued. As his horse came alongside the other, Josie touched the brim of his hat in due pleasantry and said, "Evenin'."

"Evenin'," the man returned this gesture, "Remember me?"

Josie reined his horse and peered harder into the darkness. He saw little. "Don't reckon I do," he said, "Have we met?"

"It's been a long time," the man replied as he lifted a double-barreled shotgun to center upon Josie's chest.

Alarm flooded Josie's veins. "Now look here mister, if it's money you want you sure picked the wrong man."

"I don't want your money."

"What do you want? Don't believe I got no quarrel with any white man I know of."

"Don't reckon you do, but I certainly got one with you."

"Do I know you?"

"Really don't remember do ya? Well let me freshen your recollection some. Last time I seen you I was standing knee high to a windowsill watching you an' three others have some fun in my pa's front yard."

Josie's heart leapt with recognition.

"Just wanted you to know why you're dyin'," and the man pulled both triggers.

Tunnel
Chapter 3

1

Again, Josie found himself in the tunnel. But today it did not lead to the meadow for God knew his words would only bounce off such a thickheaded hard case as the child had become. And since it no longer seemed wise to allow the boy to remain among the general population, God decided to send him to live among his own kind—in HELL. And although hell may come in any number of forms, God knowingly chose the right one for Josie. *At least*, the Almighty mused, *he will not be lonely there.*

HELL
Chapter 4

1

The world was excruciatingly hot, the land a barren waste of rocks, dirt, and desert mountains. Little grew here and food was scarce. In this place religion was law—and the law religion, and both dictated that many of the things worthwhile in life were illegal and the practice of them would bring swift and dire consequence. Life was often hard and offered little to live for. For this, many of the people were just as hateful as Josie. In this place Josie—or Yusuf, as he was known to this land—lived among his own kind and together, from the convictions of intolerance, hatred, anger, violence, fear and greed, they would forge a place known throughout the ages as **Hell.**

Like most structures of the region, Yusuf's home had been built of adobe-mud reinforced with grass and constructed over a floor of dirt before being covered with old corrugated steel that leaked in the almost nonexistent seasonal rains. The house stood at the edge of a vast and decaying city also constructed mostly of brick and adobe. Heir to a household of eight children, his mother was a thin woman of dark complexion—as were all the people of this arid land. Her features were blunt with shoulder length hair of jet-black streaked with gray. For the virtues of motherhood, she appeared oblivious and her caring for the children seemed granted more as an act of duty rather than any real sense of caring. But then, aside from the pressure of her own precarious life, the woman's time was stretched very thin. From her, Yusuf took little love. His father, Hosea, was an angry, overbearing, and deeply religious man. He was prone to fits of violence and Yusuf's mother often carried the bruises of his truculent wrath.

Almost as soon as he could walk, Yusuf was made to work in

the factory. It was a dirty place of foul smells and long hours of hot and tedious monotony at the controls of a sewing machine. The child knew little joy.

The years passed and he grew into a young man.

Of the never-ending holy-war, Hosea had always been a part. But now, as his son came to maturity, the aging man solicited the boy's effort.

Regardless of faith, almost all the men of this land seemed exceedingly anxious to die in the service of God and country. For many it was, at least in part, a true sense of duty to which they owed this uncommon loyalty. For a culture that had survived the sands of 4,000-years, custom and belief was virtually unchanged and for just as long, it had cemented the nucleus of this extraordinary ideal into the very core of its citizens. Yet, it was also true that with such scarcity of kindness, compassion, nourishment, and pleasure in this desolate land, many simply had little to live for. But at least, as was promised by all holy men, there would be compensation, reward, and peace in measures beyond imagination, only *after* one had given his life in the service of God and country.

Some could hardly wait.

With a seemingly natural hatred of all that is different, Yusuf's pain had brought him to rage. Following the lead of his sometimes-fanatic peers, this rage would further convince him that, since theirs was the only true avenue ordained by God, they must seek to convert those of unholy belief, or punish them for their acts of insolence against the Great One. With all his being Yusuf believed this to be God's ordained purpose for him. So, his father's pleas had made little difference, even had there been another path, Yusuf would not have chosen it. And it was in the holy name of God and country that he would fight. A noble cause indeed. So, it was that the young man went to war.

A seemingly natural soldier, Yusuf excelled quickly in the military. It was through his willingness to follow orders regardless of risk, intelligence of planning when granted such responsibility, and ability to win at any cost, that called the young man's extraordinary service to the attention of his superiors. Yusuf gained notoriety and position quickly and it was in this capacity that he soon found purpose and meaning for his life.

Yusuf also found more excitement than he had ever known, and the intensity of conflict often brought an exhilarating clarity of mind, and the rush of overcoming those who opposed him. These things produced a great sense of power and purpose. Best of all, as Yusuf killed, no longer did he feel anger. Yet, when he stopped, it was always back again. In many ways he loved this life.

At first, Yusuf was not without humanity, but it did not last. War offered little room for such sentiment. Not infrequently were the times his men moved into a small village filled with common farmers, sheep or goat herders, and the like. Simple families of men, woman, and children. Yusuf wished to harm none, yet it was also usually true that at least one or more was in consorts with the enemy. Emotion cried, *"Let them live!"* while logic dictated, *"Kill them all."* Many were the times Yusuf and his men had pushed an entire village's population into a circle and gunned them down. Once, in a heavy firefight, Yusuf's best friend lay mortally wounded at his side. Emotion had shrieked, *"I must help him!"* But again, logic demanded, *"There is no time. Keep fighting or die with him."*

No. Sentiment held no place in battle.

In time, all emotion, along with any other feelings, were pushed away until, finally, they ceased to exist. Yusuf felt nothing then. It was a terrible, hollow, and seemingly inhuman emptiness that filled him, and this was far worse than those steadily less frequent moments of pain, or even fear—for at least these were things of the living. On occasion Yusuf found amusement in burning small cigarette holes in his arm and feeling nothing. For many soldiers it was the same.

Each new battle only deepened this quandary.

Still, he fought.

It was in this way that Yusuf died before reaching the age of 35. But even death did not bring the exalted liberation of which he had been promised, and only returned him instead to the place from which he had just come. For him there was no escape.

And again, it was the same.

Three times Yusuf was born to this place, always dying on the battlefield—then living again. Sometimes he led, and sometimes he followed, but always he fought and killed for his cause. And with each return, his terrible anguish grew.

2

It was an unusually cool morning in the tattered streets of a small and distant city to which Yusuf and his men had been sent on their holy mission. The fighting had been heavy, and he was tired. It seemed Yusuf was always tired these days. But the conflict had ended in victory with the opposition, what remained of them, was driven from the city. All lay quiet now as Yusuf walked alone. To either side of him tall adobe buildings, some partially destroyed by mortar and rocket fire, and all showing the scars of misspent bullets, lined the virtually deserted streets of hard packed dirt. In doorways, and scattered sporadically along the roadside, lay the bodies of those who had fallen. Far ahead, he noted a drab-yellow military transport truck that sat parked at roadside as its occupants, Yusuf's own men, raided a small market of its meager contents. Beyond, smoke could be seen rising from the many fires that still burned throughout the city.

Yusuf's left thumb was hooked into the strap of a rucksack that hung from one slender shoulder as he carried a rifle at his right. Through bitter inner-turmoil and physical exhaustion he plodded on. Ahead, the tall rock and mortar wall at his left fell away and, as he passed its ragged edge, Yusuf noted a large clearing that had obviously once been a beautiful park. An exceptionally large and circular fountain, which had undoubtedly served as the little city's main water supply, still remained there. From its center, had once stood the magnificent statue of a maiden, baby held at one hip, as she balanced a cauldron atop her meticulously crafted head. Fed from an underground spring, the life-giving water had been pumped steadily to fill the large pool that was rimmed with a stone wall one-meter high. The park occupied an entire city block. Through it, cobblestone pathways meandered past once green gardens and the sparse trees that had shaded a few scattered bench seats. Yusuf thought of how the people had once come to rest in the shade and talk with one another amid their gardens before returning to the chore of carrying the water filled cauldrons home to their families.

That was gone now.

Amid the fight, the statue had been struck by a rocket and it now lay bent grotesquely at the knees as the maiden's head lay half submerged in the muddy shallows of remaining water. Beyond, the trees were mostly dead, and one burned corpse lay amid an equally charred garden. Some of the benches were destroyed and parts of the short stone wall surrounding the entire park was blown apart, riddled with bullets, or blackened by fire.

Turning attention ahead, Yusuf saw a girl sitting atop the park's short stone wall with elbows set upon small knees and face buried in little hands. She could not have been no more than 10-years old, maybe less. Her tattered black shoes hung some distance from the ground. From ankles up, she wore a dark green dress pleated with white material that covered only her flat chest and narrow shoulders. Its sleeves flowed to her wrists, and the waistline was tied snugly with pale twine. As was tradition, her head was covered with a white '*khimar*', or headscarf.

Thoughts of sexual assault filled Yusuf's mind; to this he was no stranger. She heard his footsteps and looked to see what manor of fate encroached upon her now. Although neither tall nor short, the soldier's imposing stance granted an air of great power. He wore tan army-boots. Tucked into them were the cuffs of gray khaki trousers with large pockets stitched to the legs. The collared shirt had its sleeves rolled up to the elbows. He carried a rifle with long clip protruding from its underside. At the man's other shoulder hung a rucksack. Tied around his waist was a belt that carried a pistol, canteen, and ammunition. His dark hair and beard were unkempt. The young face was steely hard with eyes that warned of danger.

As Yusuf returned her gaze, all former thought vanished, and he was taken aback. It was her eyes! For they sparkled with the same neon blue as that of the cloudless sky; a most unusual thing in this land of darkly colored people. As Yusuf looked more deeply, the truth of her tortured and broken spirit poured powerfully through those little eyes and bore deep into his own. Yusuf drew a shallow breath as, unknowingly, her stare breached the stone wall that had encased his being for so long—*and pierced his heart*. For it was in those strangely pretty eyes that Yusuf saw the reflection of his own tormented soul.

But, the sight of him brought her only fear and she turned nervously to stare at the ground.

Unable to help himself, Yusuf set his rifle against the wall and took a seat beside her. She trembled. Then, in a momentary twist of character, and without so much as a word, Yusuf removed the metal canteen from his belt and placed it in the girl's hand. But, she did not drink and only continued to stare motionless at the ground. Beside her, Yusuf sat thoughtfully, but said nothing. Taking the pack from his shoulder, Yusuf began rummaging through it and soon retrieved a portion of flat-bread stuffed with half-dried goat-meat and smelly cheese. He reached forward and placed the offering in the girl's other hand before again returning to his position of silence beside her.

For a time, she remained motionless. Then, slowly, she set his gifts atop the wall and turned to face him. As he was again sucked into the abyss of her gaze, Yusuf saw only pain there. He tried to smile. A feeble attempt at best but it was enough, for in that instant she too saw herself within him. The child's face contorted then, and she threw little arms around his neck and began to cry. Much moved by her display, Yusuf, slowly at first, returned the gesture then held the girl as she convulsed within his embrace.

It took a long time for the tears to end, but once they had, the two drew apart to again sit in silence. She looked a little embarrassed and stared down at the wall unable to hold his gaze again. He was, after all, a stranger. Thoughtfully, Yusuf retrieved another portion of the bread, meat, and cheese. After showing it to the girl he flashed a smile so radiant that she could not help but smile back. After taking a bite, he motioned to the food still atop the wall. She looked at him thoughtfully. Yes, he was a stranger, but it mattered little anymore, for with him she felt safe. She reached for her food, gave him a bashful smile, and began to eat.

So it was that through Yusuf's uncommon kindness that the two children of God shared a moment of heaven in this living hell. This was a thing that did not go unnoticed by the soldier.

When the meal was finished, Yusuf spoke the first words between them, "What is your name?"

"Hooriya. And yours?"

"Yusuf."

"Thank you, Yusuf. I was very hungry."

"Then why didn't you eat all the food?"

"My grandmother is also hungry, and I must save some for her."

Yusuf contemplated this. Then, changing the subject, he asked, "What are you doing out here?"

"I came to get water, my grandmother is very sick, but the water is bad now and...and..." again she began to cry.

Not knowing what to do with the moment, Yusuf only observed the girl's display in silence. He knew the value of water well, for in this place it was often worth far more than gold. Nothing could live long without it. When the time had passed, he looked thoughtfully at her and said, "Come Hooriya, show me the bad water."

She looked up at him through puffy eyes that glittered above tear-streaked cheeks. "Okay," she said, "But I don't know what good it will do. The well is ruined," again she almost fell to tears. Paying no attention, Yusuf threw one leg over the wall to stand at its far side. Hooriya followed. He lifted the rucksack, picked up his rifle, and looked down at the girl. Her two plastic buckets had been set behind the wall and she bent to lift them. When she stood again, handle in each hand, Yusuf noted that she was an exceptionally small girl and the sight of her little frame standing between the large containers seemed almost comical. Yusuf hung the rifle-strap over his shoulder and, with a quick smirk that only puzzled her, reached for one of the pails. With the blind trust of a child, she handed it to him.

So it was that the man's long strides carried him across the ruined park of death and destruction as one small girl hurried to keep up.

At the fountain, both stopped to set their burdens on the ground. Yusuf peered over the wall at the shallow and murky water. It was filled with debris from the ruined statue. Algae had begun to form, and a few insects swam within its depths. Although it undoubtedly contained bacteria, the water could not be poisoned, or the bugs would not live. Yusuf submerged one hand then tasted a small sample. Next the young soldier removed his shirt then knelt to stretch it across the opening of Hooriya's bucket. "Hold this tightly," he instructed. With his left hand Yusuf swooshed debris from the water's surface before dipping her second container in with his right. He lifted the pail of cloudy liquid then poured its content through his outstretched shirt and into Hooriya's first container. When this was done, Yusuf removed the shirt to find the water much cleaner. He then folded the shirt double then instructed the girl to hold it across the other bucket. She did, and Yusuf filtered the water a second time. It came cleaner. A quick scouring of the area produced the empty tin can they used to fill the second bucket. Although they were unable to filter the water twice, it was still not too bad.

Yusuf wrung the excess liquid from his shirt and put it back on, since the day had grown warm anyway. The rucksack being lighter than either bucket, he handed it to the little girl. Next, Yusuf threw the rifle strap over his shoulder, hefted one container in each hand, looked down at the girl, and asked where she lived. Hooriya started forward, "It's not far."

3

As they approached the dwelling, Yusuf noted the charred cookpot set atop an old iron grill that rested on the loose rocks of a fire-pit near the rear entrance. The building was large, but the space in which Hooriya and her grandmother lived was not. They entered through a back door that still hung solidly upon its hinges. The room was dark, for the city's electric service, which had been inconsistent even before the bombardment, was now gone completely. Hooriya had no oil for the two lanterns that sat upon a small wooden table at the dwelling's center. The room was long and rectangular with a broken window at its front wall that was covered with by a brown blanket. All walls were bare. To the right of the rear entrance stood a doorway that led to a small kitchen and adjacent bathroom. Although many of the adobe huts in the poorer areas of this city offered no running water and electricity, this place had at one time. In the room's far corner, a single mattress and neatly spread blankets lay upon the floor. Undoubtedly Hooriya's bed. Against the wall at Yusuf's left, another mattress sat atop an iron frame. In it lay an old woman. She appeared pale and feverish.

Hooriya set down the rucksack, picked up a small square of cloth, and went to mop the sweat from her grandmother's forehead. The woman's eyes opened, and she called out the name of a man. After setting his things down, Yusuf placed one hand upon her forehead. Hooriya's grandmother was burning up and he guessed, rightly, that it was pneumonia from which she suffered. Yusuf took the cloth from the girl and dipped it into the pail of their dirtiest water then set it atop the old woman's brow.

Hooriya took a cup from the table, filled it with the cleanest water, and moved toward the old woman. "No," Yusuf scolded. "That water is not yet fit for drinking."

"But it's all we have."

"Yes, but soon it will be better. Come here," he commanded, and the child obeyed. After again rummaging through the rucksack, Yusuf produced a small bottle of iodine tablets. He opened it and, after showing them to the girl, dropped three pellets into the bucket. "You must wait one hour before you drink," he told her, "They will make the water taste funny, but when their job is finished it will no longer be poisoned and you may drink all you like. Will you do that?" he asked.

The girl nodded.

"Good. Give your grandmother all that she will take. Drink only of the good water and use the other for cleaning. Is that clear?"

Again, the girl nodded.

"Good," Yusuf repeated as he handed the bottle of tablets to the girl, "You may keep these."

Hooriya reached for the bottle, then stopped, and again turned her beautiful eyes into his as she said, "But what about you Yusuf? You will need good water too. I could not think of your suffering without it," she pushed the bottle back.

Yusuf looked at her. In the light of her own desperate need, Hooriya would not see him suffer…even at the cost of her own life. Yusuf was moved beyond words and he fought against the heat of his new emotion.

Although he knew it not, in that moment Yusuf fell in love

with her. It seemed strange that in the scorched land of hell a little girl should begin to teach a soldier of pain and suffering the virtue of love.

"It's okay Hooriya, we have more at camp."

He was a soldier. She had forgotten; for to her he had been only a man. She looked at him speculatively then. It was soldiers who had brought such destruction to her homeland and reduced her life to what it now was. But Yusuf was her friend, a kind and caring friend—she could not hate him.

Changing the subject Yusuf asked, "Where is the rest of your family?"

"It's a long story," Hooriya said, knowing not if she cared to relive the horrors of this tale.

"I've plenty of time, and I'd like to hear it."

"Well," she resigned herself, "it's been four years past and I was very little when other soldiers came to the city. There was a small room with a door that stood only this high," she extended a flattened hand to one meter from the ground. "It was used only for the storage of food and clothes. My parents took my older brother, grandmother, and myself there and closed us inside. They said that no matter what happened we were to remain quiet. The soldiers came to the door and my father answered," Hooriya spoke with forced courage now. "I could hear him talking with someone. Then there was yelling, the sound of scuffling feet, and quietness. I knew my parents had been taken. In the darkness we waited—for what, we did not know. Then came the distant sounds of many others also being assembled in the street. I heard more yelling then…" the little girl's courage deserted her as again tears began to fall. But this time her face remained rigidly emotionless as she spoke. "…then came the sound of gunfire and I knew…" Valiantly she looked at him squarely through moistened blue eyes, "…I knew they were dead. Killed for the faith they had chosen."

Those fucking infidels, Yusuf thought as his anger surged, *I will kill them all for these crimes!* More than ever, he hated them now.

Hooriya continued, "To offer his life in the service of God was my father's greatest wish, but it does not change the way I miss him now…and my mother too," Hooriya almost fell to tears again. When she had regained composure, the little girl continued, "We stayed in the storage room for many hours. It was very cramped, and I began to ache. The soldiers had come in early morning, but it was late afternoon when we heard their trucks leave. Eventually, we left the little room and wandered into the street. There we found a pile of bodies lying in the places they had fallen. My best friend was among them. She was ten, one year older than me. Along with the others who had survived, we began to search. At first, we did not find my parents and I hoped that somehow they had escaped. I was wrong.

"My brother dug two holes behind the house, and we buried them with little ceremony because the city's holy men had all been killed. We have moved since. That house is still at the edge of the city and sometimes I visit the graves."

"Where is your brother?"

"It's been almost two years since he left the house and never returned. I know nothing of what has happened to him and I pray for him every day."

Yusuf thought of the story he had just heard. Hooriya's life had brought no more contentment than his own, and her suffering was no less.

"And I pray also for the soldiers, Yusuf. Every day I pray that God will help them to know better of their ways. I can only hope that someday my prayers will be answered that they too may enjoy happy and useful lives."

It was with shock in his dark eyes that Yusuf stared at the girl. In him, the infidels brought feelings of rage and revenge, yet in her they only aroused pity. What manner of person was she? As he contemplated this, another thought occurred and he asked, "Of what faith were your parents?"

She regarded him with frightened eyes. He was a soldier! But he was also her friend; and some deep intuition told her that she must trust him now. As her lower lip trembled with fear, Hooriya told the truth.

Yusuf was aghast. He had been warned that, because of its often-transient population, and unlike much of the country, in this place varied faiths sometimes existed together and in peace. But this was the first he had actually seen such a thing. Hooriya was of a false faith! No wonder God had forsaken her. Anger arose in him. But it was short-lived as he looked into the beautiful eyes of the enemy and saw only a child. For in her he also saw himself; but more than that Yusuf saw a friend. He could not hate Hooriya.

Yusuf was torn.

The soldier picked up his things, "I have to go," he said.

"But…will I see you again?"

"I don't know." And with that Yusuf stormed down the street as the little girl stood in the doorway to watch him go.

The walk was a long walk, and it gave him time to think. His life had always been pain. Yusuf had known little else. But the time spent with this girl had been the best of his life. For a while he had known happiness…such an alien thing. But he was tired of pain, so very tired. Yet she was different! She was not of God; she was of those whom he was sworn against! Yusuf himself had been on many raids just like the one that had taken Hooriya's parents. Did she pray for him?

Yusuf's head swam with confusion.

He slept little that night. But even bad sleep may sometimes help those of quarreling emotion to reach decision. So it was with Yusuf. By morning's light the young soldier knew what he must do.

In the early quietness of the new day's dawn, and even as his colleagues slept, Yusuf arose in the dusty camp of canvas tents erected at the edge of town and amid the convoy of vehicles and weapons. As the sounds of light snoring carried on the early breeze, Yusuf gathered his rifle and slipped away.

The ruthlessness of his conduct and intelligence concerning strategies of war had granted Yusuf uncommon rank, and with the responsibility of his position also came certain liberties.

Quietly now, Yusuf climbed into the bed of the drab-yellow truck. The space was concealed by a tall metal frame covered with canvas. Passing the bench seats that stood on either side, Yusuf made his way to a large metal strongbox set against the cab. The young soldier slid his key into the lock and lifted the lid, then removed some things and stuffed them into his rucksack. When finished, Yusuf shouldered his bag, picked up his rifle, and strode silently away. The dim twilight that illuminated the dirt road leading him to the heart of the city brought a magnificent sunrise, but the troubled thoughts of what he must now do enveloped Yusuf's mind to such degree that he did not notice.

4

From the deepest of morning's slumber Hooriya came awake to the familiar sound of squeaky door hinges. Her heart leapt with terror as she sat up to see the silhouette of a soldier, rifle in hand, standing in her doorway. So, he had come to kill her! Terror stifled the cry that would have escaped had she been able. Clutching a blanket tightly against her breast, the little girl stared into the dark face of her fate. She thought of her grandmother then. Hooriya had done all she could for the old woman, but she was only a little girl after all. That was over now and, amazingly, she found herself accepting this fate. Soon she would see her parents again. Motionless as a rabbit caught in the snake's hypnotic gaze, she awaited the end.

The figure stepped forward—her breath stopped. "Hooriya," it was Yusuf's voice.

She did not move.

The soldier set his rifle against the wall, loosed the rucksack from his shoulder, and knelt beside her bed.

So, she thought, *he would do it silently with a knife. I will die at his hand even as I feel his breath upon my face!* Her heart leapt; now more than ever she did not wish to die. Hooriya's breath came back, "Please Yusuf," she pleaded, "I don't want to die."

"And so, you will not. Not today anyway, for that is not why I've come."

Hooriya took her first real breath, "Do you mean it?"

"I would not lie about such a thing little girl. I've come with gifts. I think you will like them."

Hooriya began to relax, and she lowered the blanket. The curiosity of a child overcame her then, and the girl leaned forward to see what he had brought. To her young mind the bag seemed made of magic as Yusuf began to pull things from within its depths.

First he produced a bottle of serum, a syringe, and container of pills. Antibiotics were extremely rare in this arid land. But no mater where they were found, soldiers always confiscated this valuable commodity. "This medicine will cure your grandmother. After the shot, you are to give her one pill three times a day until they are all gone. Do you understand? She must take them all."

The girl nodded, "Do you think the medicine will work?"

"It will," he said with feigned conviction; for the old woman was so weak, "In a few days you will see a difference and within a week I'm sure she will be up and around good as new."

Hooriya's smile glowed at him and Yusuf's heart warmed to beyond his understanding. Never before had he known the joy of giving. In a moment he continued, "This," he said producing a single burner field-stove and holding it out for her inspection "will run on either kerosene or gasoline. It uses very little fuel and, I hope, will serve you well." The girl took it from him to run small hands over its smooth surface. Her eyes glowed with wonder. Yusuf took the stove, set it upon the table, and began to instruct Hooriya on the intricacies of its use. When this was done, the soldier reached into his rucksack to retrieve a box of matches and set them also upon the table. He struck one, turned the handle that released the gas, and lit the burner. For a moment it flared yellow, but soon settled into a strong blue flame.

Hooriya was delighted.

"Do you have a cooking pot?" he asked.

The girl jumped to her feet and ran to the kitchen. When she returned, Hooriya carried a small cast iron pot in one hand and offered it to him. After setting it atop the stove, Yusuf stood to retrieve the girl's bucket of drinking water. Finding the pail one-third empty, he poured a portion of its remaining contents into the pot. When this was done, Yusuf settled back down to his knees and waited. The girl flopped atop her sleeping mattress and looked up at him rather sheepishly. Words seemed to elude her now. But it mattered not, for the radiance of her smile told him everything. In a moment she jumped forward, threw little arms around his neck, and buried her head into his shoulder. Yusuf smiled and hugged her back. A thought came to him then, *"how lonely it must be for her here; and with her only living relative delirious and close to death."*

When the moment had passed, she pulled back to study him with adulation glittering in those sky-blue eyes. Never before had anyone looked at him in that way. "Can we give the medicine to my grandmother now?" she asked.

"Of course," While Yusuf readied the serum into the needle, Hooriya, as instructed, cleansed the area to be penetrated. Yusuf looked down at the old woman. She was much too pale and weak. In attempt to ease the moment's tension, he offered Hooriya a warm smile then turned and inserted the needle. The old woman did not flinch. When this was done, he told Hooriya to bring the pills and a cup of water. The girl hurried off. When she returned with the things he had asked for, Yusuf raised the old woman's frail body to a seated position. He let her head of tangled white hair tilt partway back as, from beside him, Hooriya pulled her grandmother's mouth open and threw one pill as far back as she could, then lifted the water to wrinkled lips. The woman drank so greedily that she seemed not even to notice the pill. *Well,* Yusuf thought, *easier than I had hoped.* Slowly then, he laid her down and backed away.

Yusuf returned to the place beside Hooriya's bed, sat upon the floor, and leaned his back against the wall. The girl hurried to take a seat upon her mattress beside him. She seemed to glow. "Would you like some tea?" he asked.

An excited grin creased small lips as she nodded, "Yes please. Can my dolly come? Her name's Camellia"

Yusuf stared at her speculatively. She had often exhibited wisdom so far beyond her years that he had almost forgotten…Hooriya was a child. "Yes," he said finally, "Camellia can come. Do you have any cups?"

"Oh! I do." Hooriya jumped to her feet and bounded off to the kitchen. When she returned the girl carried two delicate cups of painted china with saucers to match, and a raggedy little cloth doll with frizzy black hair. She set these things beside the stove then arranged her blanket on the mattress so Camellia could have a good seat there. The water began to boil, and Yusuf reduced the flame. As the girl watched with intent interest, Yusuf again reached into the magic rucksack to retrieve a plastic bag filled with tealeaves and a few scraps of thin cloth. After carefully folding the fragrant leaves into the cloth and sealing it with a pin, Yusuf placed it into Hooriya's cup then added hot water. The child waited until the man had done the same for himself and, in a moment, both began to drink. Hooriya then poured tea into a thimble and offered it to Camellia.

"Are you hungry?" he asked.

"Yes. Are you?"

"Sure," he said, "And today I've brought food I think grandma…and even Camellia, will like." Maybe it was because he had been denied the playfulness of his own youth, or maybe he was just finally going mad; ether way, and much to the surprise of a soldier who dealt in the business of suffering and death, Yusuf found himself enjoying this little girl's game immensely. Again, he reached into the magic bag and this time produced a large can of stew. Yusuf poured the stew into the pot and turned the flame back up.

Both people, and even Camellia, relaxed with their tea to sit and chat of simple things for a time. Yusuf could not remember ever having enjoyed himself more.

When the stew was hot, Hooriya brought clay bowls, and both ate their fill. Once cooled, the remainder was given to the old woman who brought even more delight to Hooriya's little world as she took small slurps from the wooden spoon her granddaughter lifted with such concern to the old mouth.

When this was done Hooriya asked, "Would you do something for me please Yusuf?" the girl frowned, "It's not pleasant."

"What is it?" he inquired.

She looked at him sheepishly for a moment then stated flatly, "She has messed herself. She lies in her own filth and…" the girl's lower lip began to quiver as again she fell to tears. Hooriya made no attempt to hide them, "…and I'm not strong enough to move her," the child's voice broke. After a moment's pause, she regained composure, "You have been so kind, and I hate to ask for more, but would you please roll her onto her side for me? The rest I can do myself."

Kind? Him? Such strange words to hear. But her request was really not much to ask. Besides, if it would make her happy… "I'll help you," Yusuf found himself saying. And he did. Hooriya was right, she truly was a mess. But, of the many things Yusuf had seen in his lifetime, this was nothing. Thoughtfully, he retrieved a bar of soap from the rucksack and handed it to her. It had been for her anyway. She thanked him, and Yusuf moved to stand just outside the rear entry and wait.

The reddish clay building that held Hooriya's small dwelling in one corner was rough and pockmarked with the signs of age. It had been built at the edge of this mostly-deserted city and her back door opened onto the rocky desert of dirt and sporadic patches of brush. Tall mountains stood at either side, for the city had been built amid a wide valley. From his vantage, no sign of the recent battle could be seen. Yusuf gazed past Hooriya's fire-pit and across the silent land. The desert was neither friend nor foe, neither good nor bad, it simply was, and it enveloped him with the quiet calm that only nature can sometimes provide. In this moment, Yusuf felt deep inside himself…

    His former pain had vanished and in its place Yusuf found only a deep contentment. He was happy! For most, this is a thing that may come and go, but for Yusuf, a man who had previously known nothing beyond suffering, it was something entirely new—*a thing of unprecedented value.* So it was that through his unexpected effort to help another for no reason and without thought of personal gain, Yusuf again experienced something of heaven in this living hell. Through his own experience the young soldier had begun to learn that most inflexible of cosmic laws which states: *If one is to hurt another then he will always feel pain in return. Yet if he instead seeks an opposite intention, then he will just as assuredly receive an exact opposite compensation.*

    It is said that God exists within as well as without. If a part of God truly does reside within each human spirit, then it is only among the spirits of one's fellows that he may ultimately find God's peace, contentment, fulfillment, and personal ascension to a useful purpose, or, if you prefer—*to heaven.* Yet, to shun or willfully hurt the spirit of one's fellows, will obviously only move him farther from these ideals—*and closer to hell.* But, no one need to remind Yusuf of these things now. And no one, now or ever, could take this priceless truth from him.

    From behind, Yusuf heard Hooriya's voice announce that she had finished. After stepping back inside, Yusuf again took a seat on the bed beside his host then leaned against the wall.

5

For a while, few words passed between them and Yusuf did not mind, for he had always been a quiet man anyway. Finally, Hooriya asked if he would like to go for a walk. Yusuf agreed and, since an earlier explosion had jarred the front doorjamb, they exited through the rear.

Having left his rifle and rucksack behind, Yusuf walked freely with only a pistol upon his hip. A refreshing coolness still clung to the morning air as they strolled along the street of marred dirt amid the wreckage of this war-torn city. Buildings lined either side of their path broken, at times, by vacant lots of rubble that lay as specters to the memory of what once was. Most had left the city or died of disease or famine, but some had not. Although many still slept at this early hour, others milled around the streets or hastened to the business of rebuilding life's necessities from the ashes. However, the fighting was over now and Yusuf and Hooriya walked with the ease and comfort of bellies filled with food and tea and, for Hooriya, the knowledge that her last living relative now had a chance.

She put her hand in his.

This was a breach of custom and at first, Yusuf tensed, but it seemed he could not say no to her. When some minutes had passed, he relaxed and even found himself enjoying this small act of affection.

"Where are your parents?" the little girl's question was also a breach of custom, but Yusuf did not mind. So, he answered truthfully, "I'm an orphan. My parents died in an automobile accident when I was very little." He did not mention the car-bomb.

"I'm sorry," she said, "Do you have other relatives?"

"No. For a long time now the army has been the only family I've known."

The girl fell silent again. She tried to imagine the life he had led. The world held so much pain; but at least for a while she had known the love of a family. Yusuf had not. He had known only fighting. Looking down, she hid her sadness from him as she tightened her grip upon his hand.

For a time, they walked in silence.

The sight of other children playing in the streets lightened her mood and Hooriya began to speak of little girl thoughts…and dreams of becoming a woman, and eventually a mother. Yusuf only listened.

Before long they again came upon the fountain. A small crowd was gathered there. Men wore traditional loose-fitting cloth-leggings with long robes of light-blue, gray, or yellow. Heads were adorned with either a turban or small cap. All men wore beards. Some of the women were dressed much like Hooriya, while others chose long skirts and full-sleeved shirts sometimes with tunics or light coats over them. Some of these offered tapestry prints of two colors, or even flowers. All women wore khimars upon their heads.

Hooriya released Yusuf's hand.

With containers of various shapes and sizes, these people sought what was left of the murky water. Two camels stood nearby, as did an old pick-up truck. In this place the modern and the ancient often existed side by side. "Get your empty bucket," Yusuf said, "Then meet me at the fountain." The girl hurried off.

Yusuf made his way to the fountain. The water was almost gone. At the rear, men were working, and Yusuf moved closer to observe. Some were startled at his approach, for Yusuf still wore the garb of a soldier. But the fighting was over, they knew. Yusuf smiled to convey his benevolence and the people acknowledged him with indifference. Two men worked on a hand-pump that had stood at the fountain's edge before being torn from the ground by a truck that had careened off the fountain's low wall and now lay on its side nearby. Yusuf inquired of one seemingly ancient, yet talkative man and, after introductions and pleasantries, he was told…

"In the beginning this was a beautiful oasis and a magnificent pool lay where we stand. For many years the water was stable, and one could depend upon this place to provide for any size caravan. Since this oasis lay at the center of a trail that connects two large cities, all who made the long journey sought to rest here. In this way, many valuable goods were brought through and this became a place of business and trade. A town was born, and later a small city. The water supply was good; for as fast as it was taken, the pool refilled. Troughs and pipe were laid in to carry water to the gardens that many planted just beyond the city. Aside from that which was brought from far away then sold here, food for one's animals was also grown nearby, and it was no longer necessary that one remain nomadic in the endless search for grass needed to feed livestock—should he choose not to. As the modern world moved closer, in-the-house plumbing and even electricity was added to many homes. Prosperity was enjoyed in abundances."

"But in time, something within the earth changed and the water fell back into the ground. The men dug with pick and shovel, but it was no longer enough. The people panicked. A city council was called, and it was agreed that a crew should be hired. Before long, men arrived with a big truck made to drill holes deep into the earth. After some manner of testing, they told the council they believed a river flowed 180-meters below. They said that, although the gap that had allowed water to flow to the surface was no longer there, they believed the river still was. But no one could know for sure. They might drill for weeks and come up with nothing. A price was set. It was high but the people had no choice. It was the only hope.

"The drilling began.

"For days the men worked very hard. Some came to offer them food. But even with this new hope, fear came to the people as never before. Tempers burned and there was trouble.

"On the seventeenth day the men struck water and a celebration rang out. A hand pump was put in. In time, an electric pump was set to bring water in quantity from far below, and a generator house was also built that gave power to *only* this pump when the city's troublesome electric supply would not run. This pool was then built of rock and mortar so the people could enjoy something of what once was. The park was added later, and the people settled down because they again felt safe.

"Of the war we often heard news, but it seemed far away and for the longest time did not come here. The people prayed. But in time, the war did come. A few took sides and fought, but most hid or fled. Many died. Then the battles ended and we began to rebuild. For a while, all was well. But the soldiers returned. Then again. And still again. Men, women, and children were killed; families broken up; animals were stolen, and businesses looted. I guess all good things must eventually end, and what you see now is all that is left. As you know, the city no longer has electricity. We wanted to use the fountain's generator but have since learned it's been stolen..."

Yusuf cringed.

"...The hand pump that was the last hope for water has been torn from the ground. The situation is desperate."

A vision of Hooriya upon her little bed with cracked lips and parched skin, as she lay dying of dehydration near the decaying body of her grandmother, flashed through Yusuf's mind. He found the thought intolerable. It seemed strange that of all those who occupied this fucked up world, she should be the first he had truly cared for.

"Once the fountain has been emptied," the old man continued, "we will clean its inside then mortar the cracks and, if the water is returned, scrub the surface before refilling the pool. We can only pray that all goes well."

As Yusuf contemplated the situation, he felt a tug at his shirt and looked down to see that Hooriya had returned. They went to the fountain's edge. As before, both worked to retrieve as much of the murky water as possible. Its level was very low.

As they labored beside the others, some of the women greeted Hooriya. Many seemed to like the little girl. Yusuf had not previously thought of this. The child's blue eyes beamed radiantly from behind a dirty face as she told of her new friend the soldier and the kindness he had shown her. They were looking at him now and Yusuf cast a self-conscious gaze downward. He was a soldier in their midst, and always when given to such situation he and his men had commanded great power over the common people. But, he stood alone among them now and, for once, power was not his objective. It was truly a strange day after all. When Yusuf finally did venture a glance, he noted that many eyed him with curiosity—and maybe even approval. Hooriya was still talking, "...here are some pills for your water," she told a friend, "Put them in then wait an hour before you drink...."

She was giving the iodine away! Had she no sense? What would she use for herself? Water could be boiled of course; but there was little fuel and boiling was not as affective as iodine. He wished to tell her, but an interruption seemed inappropriate. So, as was often his way, Yusuf simply stayed quiet.

When their task was completed, Yusuf picked up the bucket

and the unlikely pair moved off. Once passed beyond hearing of the others, Yusuf stopped, set his burden down, and turned to scold the child, "Are you crazy? Why did you give the tablets away little girl? I have no more, and what will you use for your own drink?" His stance was unyielding.

"Do not think I am not grateful for all you have done Yusuf," she stood strong and tall at him and the soldier felt as though he were addressing a small woman rather than a child, "but these are my people, my friends. I would not have them become sick while the medicine sits on my table unused! If the fountain is fixed, the water will run clean, and I will no longer have need of the pills. I've kept enough for what we carry and if they do not get the well working again, what good will water pills do me without water?"

She was right of course; one could not drink iodine tablets. For a man who had always believed it necessary to serve himself first and foremost, Yusuf had simply not thought of this.

Take of your need before it is taken from you. Kill before you are killed.

A lifetime spent in such philosophy could not be reversed in a day. Yusuf did not even know he wished it changed at all. But of one thing he was sure: no longer could Yusuf bear the pain of his former existence. Today he felt better than ever in his life. Better, it seemed, than he had believed possible. This was because of the girl…he knew. Yusuf's mind was open now…pain had seen to that. For better or worse he would consider these new ideas, even if they did come from such a small and unlikely messiah.

6

Without a word, Yusuf hefted the pail and continued on.

After seeing to the old woman's needs, Yusuf asked if Hooriya would accompany him back to the fountain as he wished to observe the men's progress. The girl agreed and they started off.

The water was gone. The crowd had thinned. Only workers remained. Some labored over the hand-pump. A pick-up truck had been backed against the fountain and others stood within its wall as they worked with shovel, broom, and hammer to break the rock and debris that would be loaded into the truck for removal. Talk was minimal.

Yusuf had not observed for long when a strange compulsion came to him. Without a word he climbed into the fountain and began to work. All noted his presence, but none gave protest.

An hour passed and the day grew warmer. Women began to bring drink to their men. Yusuf heard his name and turned to see Hooriya standing at the fountain's edge, a clay mug held in one little hand. He went to her and took the container then sat upon the wall to drink greedily as sweat ran from his brow. Dust floated in the air. The work was hard and dirty, but he did not wish to stop. For what Yusuf wanted most now was to see a clear pool shimmering before the happy face of his little girl. When the cup was drained Yusuf handed it to Hooriya, voiced his appreciation, and returned to the job.

A break was soon called, and each man set a strip of rug upon the ground with which to kneel and pray. Yusuf joined them. Failure to do so was to demean God by insinuating that the toils of daily life were more important than He. And nothing held more importance than the honor of God. It was the way of the people.

When the time had passed, the men resumed their toil.

Howls erupted suddenly from the small crowd and Yusuf turned to see a thin man dancing across the wall on one foot like some crazed chicken. Beyond him clear water ran from the hand-pump as one man held a plastic container while another worked the lever. The people grinned and murmured words of approval. Yusuf beamed.

Before long, the gaiety mellowed, and men returned to their labor. News spread quickly and others arrived with varied containers to wait in a long line at the fountainhead.

An hour passed. Still the men worked.

Sweat furrowed lines through the dirt caked upon Yusuf's dark face as the muscles of he and three others strained to lift the statue's large head into the truck. The old vehicle sagged beneath its load. The men stood to catch their breath. The sun was approaching midday and air grew hot. As Yusuf lifted one weary arm to mop sweat from his brow, his eyes caught sight of the five women walking closer. Two carried a large cooking-pot suspended between them as steam rose from its uncovered surface to be quickly lost in the slight gale of their pace. The third carried a large ceramic bowl filled with thin wafers of flat-bread, while a fourth brought with her the length of white linen containing a variety of utensils wrapped within. Hooriya was the fifth and she waddled valiantly with the large clay vase held in her little hands. Soon, she broke from the others to work the well's pump-handle over her container.

Upon the fountain's low wall, a large bowl was set and Hooriya filled it from her vase. Beside it was placed a scrap of cloth that the men might wash their hands before the midday meal. A larger linen was spread upon the ground and the steaming caldron was set upon it. Bread was placed in a neat pile and an assortment of bowls laid beside. Not a word was uttered as the women worked.

With this task completed, the women brought clay mugs of the clear water first to their respective men, then the others. As was tradition, Hooriya found Yusuf first, handed him the mug, then bowed slightly and backed away having not once looked him in the eye. When finished, the women disappeared as quietly as they had come.

One of the men called a break and eight workers climbed from the fountain. As a guest, Yusuf was given first opportunity to wash as the others waited behind. With hands clean, each moved to kneel in a row upon the cloth he used only for prayer. Again, time was offered to God. When the moment had passed, the men took seats upon the ground and in a circle around the food. Yusuf was to serve himself first. It was a lentil-based soup with onions, spices, occasional chunks of mutton, and flat-bread at the side. Common fare of the poor.

It was those who could not afford to give that had provided the food. Yusuf knew it a custom of the poor (and sometimes the wealthy) to share generously of one's often slender resources when opportunity arose. But in his heart the young soldier had always believed this custom to be a lie conjured by the strong to weaken the masses. Yusuf himself had partaken in this insane courtesy only when the situation demanded. The idea that the doctrine of giving might be the foundation of heaven, and his own philosophy the very substance of hell, had never occurred to the soldier. There was a time when he would not have believed himself endowed with the power to create his own heaven or hell, but that was changing now. Still the young man could not yet grasp the idea that maybe, when faced with the opportunity to benefit another, the people simply gave without question of why. Had he inquired, most would probably have said, "God would ask no less."

Using only his right hand, each began to eat. For a time, silence fell upon the weary men as only food dominated their thoughts.

Minutes passed.

When hunger was sated, light conversation began. Although weary, all seemed in good spirits on this bright day.

Hospitality is held in high regard among all the desert people and the women served small cups of Turkish coffee. It was a flavorful drink prepared with meticulous care and held in high importance to properly conducted social endeavors. Yusuf was surprised the people had these precious beans…and he was grateful. As always, custom was held to great importance and such formality demanded that, whether a man hail from wealth or poverty, he was to be treated with respect and courtesy until the day, if ever, his actions deemed him unworthy of such credit. So, it was with Yusuf. Introductions went around and the soldier was asked if the food was to his liking, his thirst sufficient quenched, and the coffee flavored to his taste. Yusuf answered yes to all accounts then made great praise of the fare.

Conversation turned to common things. They talked of the fountain's condition and the good fortune that had allowed the pump to work again. Talk turned to livestock and the condition of a large communal garden that stood somewhere nearby. No man inquired of another's family. Such conversation was considered rude.

There was a deep camaraderie here. It was bound by the effort of unified labor as each sought the betterment of life for all. Yusuf had never experienced such a thing. He had often felt a closeness with his men; especially in situations fought side by side for their very lives. But this was different…much different. In the past, Yusuf and his men had always worked toward the ambition of destruction. Now, he labored with these men toward an opposite objective. The effect was astonishing.

A deep feeling of purpose and well-being enveloped him. It moved him to powerful emotion and made him giddy. Yusuf felt truly a part of something worthwhile at last. But his actions had inadvertently purchased another unexpected recompense; for the feeling of desperate loneliness that had always eclipsed his life was gone! He felt as one with the people! He had never known. The others felt this too; but for Yusuf, a man who had experienced only torment for so long as he could remember, the sensation was profound.

The men were very curious of him, Yusuf knew, and eventually, using gentle discretion as not to appear rude, they made delicate inquiry to the status of his troops. Yusuf was not offended and simply told the truth, "Our work here is done, but it was a very hard battle. Our fuel and munitions are exhausted, and we have lost many men. We will wait for the delivery of supplies, fuel, rearmament, replacement troops, and orders to our next destination. Relief will probably arrive within two to six weeks. Until then, we have no choice but to wait."

All seemed thoughtful then, and Yusuf knew they were considering how this might affect their own lives. But, to their credit, the men said nothing.

They worked for two hours more. Mortar was brought to patch cracks in the fountain wall. But the relentless afternoon heat would not permit anything that lived to remain in the open for long. In obedience to the ways of this harsh land, the men abandoned the project and moved off for the shade of their homes. There they would either sleep or simply relax through the afternoon hours. Yusuf returned to Hooriya's home where the two sat to talk and drink tea for the remaining daylight, and into the night. Another would probably have found the little girl's consistent talk improper, and she might have been silenced, but Yusuf did not mind. He enjoyed the sound of her voice. It pierced the loneliness that had held his heart in torment for so long, while also freeing his mind to new thoughts and ideas. Besides, for him, Hooriya could do no wrong. In the intimacy of her pleasing company, Yusuf's tongue loosened and he told of things, and feelings, he had never spoken of before.

The hour grew late and eventually Yusuf moved to leave. From his rucksack the soldier removed the remainder of his tealeaves, canned food, dates, and dried meat, then placed them upon the table. He said goodnight and, as he knelt before her, she stepped forward to hug him. With a passion that startled him, Yusuf returned the gesture. The man then lifted his things and started for the door. Momentarily he stopped, turned to her and, with an expression that furrowed the smooth lines of his young face, said, "If you come in contact with any of my men and they inquire as to the faith of either you or your family I want you to lie Hooriya."

"But Yusuf I…."

"Do not argue with me little girl. Just do as I say. I expect your word on this matter right now. Do you swear?"

"Yes sir," the words slipped through small lips in little more than a whisper, "I swear."

"Good. Now get some sleep and I'll see you in the morning."

She brightened, "You're coming again?"

"Yes, early. After we see to your grandmother, I wish to again tend the fountain. I have an idea."

"What is it?"

"You'll just have to wait and see." he offered only a grin, "But I'm sure you will approve." With that he slipped through the door and disappeared into the night.

Later, Yusuf enjoyed a peaceful slumber such as he had not known for many years.

7

The few stars that remained above the desert land were only beginning to fade as dawn's purplish glow slowly overtook them. In the newness of early morning most residents still slept, and the city of ruin lay still and silent. But the big diesel engine of a drab-yellow, flatbed truck with its windshield folded down soon broke the silence as it growled loudly along the city street. In the truck-bed sat an exceptionally large, and very controversial, payload carefully concealed from view with a thick canvas tarp.

Although the world below seemed almost as tranquil as the

misty stars above, Yusuf's nerves did not reflect this calm as he maneuvered the large vehicle. For, although very used to doing exactly as he pleased, Yusuf now pushed the limits of that liberty. Use of the truck was excusable, but when he returned without its cargo there would be suspicion among the men. Yet, aside from the considerable liberties that accompanied his rank, the men had also witnessed Yusuf's brutal cruelty toward *any* who opposed him. He was a man of steel nerves and cool malice who truly enjoyed his carnage. Yusuf was an insane anomaly who cared nothing of life or death—including his own. He would kill a man, even one under his command, at a moment's notice, and at times for only the slightest reason. For this they feared him. And it was a byproduct of this very thing that had granted his great power and freedom within the kingdom of hell.

    Hooriya had been awake for over an hour when she heard a large vehicle stop outside the door. She pushed a curious head through the opening in time to see Yusuf step from the truck. The horizon echoed only shadows of the day's first light. She turned to gather something from beside her bed then returned with the item clasped in one little hand and held it behind her back. Hooriya positioned herself some feet from the door that she might face him as he entered. As he did, she noted that today he carried no rifle.

    Outfitted in an immaculate lavender skirt that flowed snugly from waist to clean ankles, Hooriya's upper body was covered with a close-fitting chemise of fine cotton adorned with light flower print that complemented the skirt perfectly. Upon her head was an elaborate khimar that flowed ornately down her back. Its color matched exactly that of the skirt. She offered a radiant smile that shown through the magnificent eyes of, what seemed to him, one who must be very close to God. He could not remember anyone so beautiful having ever been so happy to see him. Somewhat taken aback, Yusuf stood to admire her small form. She moved forward two steps then stopped to hold the small bouquet of desert wildflowers high and wait hopefully for his approval. Yusuf had never been offered flowers and was not sure how to receive them. But, sensing the importance of her gift, Yusuf knelt to accept the flowers with notable praise. He smelled deeply of them then offered a satisfied smile—far more for the girl than the gift.

    Satisfied, her grin widened and Hooriya threw herself into his embrace. Next, she took his hand and led Yusuf to their sitting place of the day before. Beside them the pot of water already bubbled upon the field-stove. Yusuf was happy to note that the girl had been able to operate the device without incident. Painted cups were already set upon the table and strips of cloth filled with tealeaves while Camellia, the doll, held her seat nearby.

As the second unlikely meeting-over-teacups ensued between the Lucifer of a living hell and one small angel of God, conversation resumed as though the previous night's talk had never ended.

Yusuf's men had recently presented stolen goods to a local man in trade for a goat of which they had butchered at camp, and today, Yusuf brought a portion of this greasy meat for their breakfast. He also produced six eggs and more bread.

Delighted with the opportunity to prepare this meal, Hooriya moved happily to the task. She produced a tattered pan then took to the job of cooking the meat and scrambling eggs into its grease. Yusuf leaned against the wall to sip tea and enjoy the morning's early dawn as he watched the girl work. As was again a minor breach of custom, man and girl dined together and Yusuf did not mind. Besides, the home offered only one room for sitting and sleeping.

When the meal was finished, a can of broth was opened, and its contents set upon the stove. When this was done Hooriya cleared the table and the unlikely team again moved to attend the old woman. As Yusuf put one hand to her wrinkled forehead, two dark eyes opened to stare soberly into his. Terror: he saw it clearly. Her city was in ruin, her family dead or scattered to the winds, there was little food and she had been left without even the ability to care for herself or little granddaughter. All these things had come at the hands of soldiers; soldiers not unlike the one she saw now.

Yusuf tried to smile but he could not.

Hooriya set one hand on the woman's chest, but still the unblinking eyes remained fixed upon the soldier. Hooriya shook her, "Grandmother". Then louder, **"Grandmother!"** Finally, the old eyes focused upon the girl. "This is Yusuf. He is our friend and he has brought the medicine that would make you well," Hooriya glowed down at the old woman's return to consciousness. She put one hand to the wrinkled cheek. "How do you feel?" There was no reply. Grandmother was either too weak or too afraid.

"Her name is Athaliah," Hooriya said.

"Well, Athaliah, you look much better today," It was only a partial lie as the woman had gained some color and her delirium seemed gone, "I think you're going to be fine. Would you try to drink some of the broth Hooriya prepared for you?" he managed a slight smile, but the bedside manner of one who plundered in the name of God did little to ease the woman's foreboding. Athaliah remained silent. Turning to Hooriya, Yusuf said, "Her fever has broken, and I think the medicine is working. Call me when you are ready for the pill," and with that he went to sit in the doorway and take comfort in fresh morning air. When the old woman had taken most of the broth, Hooriya called for him and the two administered Athaliah's medicine. When done, Hooriya left her grandmother with words of comfort; slipped from her fine clothes into those more suitable, then followed Yusuf to the truck.

8

In effort to avoid midday heat, the men had arrived early and already labored within the fountain as the large vehicle approached. All stopped to wonder, or maybe worry, at this unnerving sight until they noted Yusuf and Hooriya in the cab. The truck stopped near the fountain, and its occupants stepped to the ground. Greetings were made. Although clearly curious, courtesy demanded that none make inquiry of the truck or its contents. Soon Hooriya wandered off to seek the company of women while Yusuf resumed his place among the men as the labor continued.

Within an hour the remaining debris was removed and the three holes from which clean water had once flowed into the fountain were cleared in the hope that, if electrical power was ever restored, the people might enjoy something of what once was. A small entourage of women and young girls arrived carrying buckets, rags, and any soaps available. Hooriya was among them. As women lifted their dress to enter the fountain, the men removed themselves at the other side then wondered off to sit beneath a shade-tree. While most of the women began to scour the fountain's floor and inner walls, two girls passed among the men offering cups and refills.

The men talked. Yusuf was again asked if anything could be done to improve his stay within the city. After offering thanks, he stated that all was fine, then added quite truthfully that he was enjoying his time here. The men looked approvingly at one another then. Although some remained skeptical of the soldier, most were beginning to really like Yusuf.

As before, conversation turned to the simple things life is so often made of. With much of the previous day's stress gone, the men were quick to smile and even quicker to laugh.

They are simple people, Yusuf thought. *They have no hope of wealth in this torn city, no cause for which to fight, no real hope for the future, and only family, friends, and the simple toils of everyday life as reward for their existence. Yet, even in the shadow of all that has happened they seem to enjoy more happiness than I have known.* In the weeks to come the soldier would give great thought to this observation, but for now he was content to just sit in the shade among these men. Yusuf felt relaxed today. He was part of something seemingly greater than his own ambitions. He felt freed somehow. This new feeling of belonging loosened the soldier's tongue and the normally quiet man talked more freely than he could remember having done before.

Abraham was an unusually tall yet thin man with long neck and large Adam's-apple that bobbled beneath a short beard of mottled black and white as he spoke. His robe and leggings were a dark gray while the small tuqiyah, on top of his head, barely covering shortly cropped hair, remained a simple white. Although the man seemed almost frail, his black eyes and confident manner reflected an air of remarkable kindness. As would many in turn, Abraham invited Yusuf to a meal at his home the following evening. Hooriya would be welcomed to dine among his wife and daughters. Yusuf thanked the man and made promise to attend.

When all were rested and the time seemed right, Yusuf asked if the men wished to view what lay in his truck beneath the tarp. Of course, they did.

As the small entourage moved toward the flatbed, Yusuf's stomach churned with worry; for he knew the object would bring as much animosity as approval…maybe more. Yusuf hoped it would not destroy what he had gained here, but believed this a risk he must take.

The soldier untied the rope that secured one edge of the tarp as three others released its remaining corners. Once the cover had been unfastened, Yusuf stood within the bed and gazed nervously at the faces now turned up to watch him. Then, with quick conviction, he grabbed the tarp and flung it to the ground. The men stared in stunned disbelief. It was a gasoline generator. Not just any generator, but the very machine that had recently been stolen from them! Silence befell. None knew what to say. Beads of sweat formed on Yusuf's brow. Seconds passed…each an eternity. It was Abraham who spoke first, "God has smiled on us, for he has sent a soldier to return the machine that would again bring water in abundance!" Abraham looked to the others then. Ten more seconds of silence. Then another spoke up, "Let us praise that God would send such a stranger in our time of need." All joined, and shouts of approval split the air as Yusuf looked down to the crowd that applauded below. Never had he experienced such a thing. As the power of this event overwhelmed him, the soldier struggled valiantly to conceal his surge of emotion.

The big generator was taken to the pump-house and a mechanic set to the task of its intricacies. Yusuf offered one jerry can of fuel with an apology that it was all he had. The men refused, with a statement that they had a small supply. Yusuf nodded and said no more.

The men's work at the fountain was finished and all began to disperse. Soon only Yusuf and Abraham remained. "Walk with me," Abraham gestured, "Let us see how the woman's work is coming." Yusuf agreed and the two began a slow stroll across what remained of the park.

"What will you do now?" Yusuf asked.

I will relax at home. In the morning I'll come to check the fountain. Even with the generator it will require much of the night to fill. If everything is okay, I will join those who work to remove the bodies from our streets. There are many as you know.

It was true what Yusuf had said: the battle had been fierce and in the enemy's retreat they had been forced to leave many of their dead.

Both men came upon the fountain. A glance inside confirmed the women had already completed most of the tedious cleaning, but the blistering midday heat was settling in and the females had already gone. "They will return at sunset to finish," Abraham said, "so the generator can run through the night.

"I'm sure you will agree that the city's electricity may never work again. The generator is not enough to run the bigger pumps that once took water through the city's plumbing, and even if it could, there are too many broken pipes. As it has been for a long time, this fountain will be our only source. Once it is filled, we will turn the pump to our crops and livestock. If it does not work, water will have to be carried by hand. But it's of small consequence now for our numbers are few and little is needed anymore. The city is dying and in time we may be forced to leave or perish. If this is the will of God, then I welcome the change."

Yusuf only listened. It was true what Abraham said: this was the will of God. But it was also true that Yusuf and his kind were the direct cause of the conflicts that had inflicted such destruction upon the lives of those who now brought happiness and meaning to his own life. A deep guilt gripped the young soldier. "Maybe I will see you in the morning Abraham," he almost whispered. With eyes that never left the ground, Yusuf turned to walk from the park. Abraham watched him go and, although the older man knew something deeply troubled his new friend, Abraham remained silent. *Sometimes a man must face his demons alone,* he thought. With that the tall, robed figure started for home.

Yusuf did not stop to see Hooriya that day and instead returned to the security of his men to brood quietly for the remaining daylight hours. Again, his thoughts and emotions swam in confusion and turmoil. And again, he did not sleep well.

On the other hand, never again would deep emotional pain be a common companion to Yusuf, and it was the promise of a different way that again drove him to the early morning light of Hooriya's door. Besides, he already missed her.

Strangely, it was that one powerful and highly decorated soldier spent yet another day laboring alongside the common people.

For three weeks more Yusuf stayed in this place and among these men. Many called him friend, and as his lust for carnage began to subside, so did small acts of kindness become a daily event for Yusuf. It was the best time of his life.

When the day arrived to leave, Yusuf brought many gifts to Hooriya and her grandmother and made promise that he would soon return to remove them from the dying city and into his own home. Hooriya's excitement filled the little room then, but Yusuf also felt the sorrow of her tears when he turned to leave.

It was the last he would ever see of her.

9

Shortly thereafter, Yusuf left the military and returned home. For a time, he was filled with a nagging emptiness and boredom, for the army was all he had ever known. Beneath its expansive blanket of authority, machinery, and men united to a common goal Yusuf had known much security and excitement. But most of all it had given him purpose. The only purpose he had ever known. But, that was gone now and in its place was only a feeling of emptiness and loss.

Still, he would not go back.

Thoughts of Hooriya and his new friends in the distant city followed Yusuf constantly. They gave him hope and happiness; yet alternately brought guilt and sadness too. How many cities had he ruined? How many maimed, crippled, or made destitute? How many homes broken? How many grieving grandmothers…and how many orphaned little girls? These thoughts haunted Yusuf's nightmares and even his waking moments. An inexorable transformation had begun.

Yusuf was becoming human.

There were those in his own town who had known such torment. In addition, whenever a young boy, grown man, *small girl*, or any other, limped past on shabby crutches that suspended a disfigured or crippled body of this war-torn land, Yusuf felt his shame. Sometimes he cried.

Yet it was from them that the former soldier would ultimately take his salvation; for it was to them that his acts of kindness continued. Yusuf's effort did not go unnoticed, and it was not long before a host of new friends grew around him. Among them were those who deeply valued the time he shared with them. Some even came to love him. Soon there would be more. Again, Yusuf's heart grew warm, and a generous degree of contentment returned.

The young soldier had come full circle.

Eventually Yusuf's new ambition brought him to the doorstep of a rundown orphanage operated by those who labored in the name of God. But the fate of his eternal soul meant little to Yusuf anymore, for what concerned him now was the quality of everyday life. Of the here and now. And it was to this objective that he had come to offer service—if they would have it. Of course, they would; for all orphanages, as well as every civic institution of this land, was understaffed, underfunded, and always struggling to survive.

It was at that junction, Yusuf made his beginning.

In time the young man was loaned a truck, had saved enough money, and set on his journey back to the dying city and his promise to Hooriya.

It was with terrific excitement and the news of salvation that Yusuf entered the home of his little friend and mentor. But the girl was not there and only the old woman greeted him. Although free of sickness, Athaliah appeared gaunt and undernourished. Her clothes were ragged. She took a seat upon the bed and Yusuf settled himself beside. Hooriya's bedding lay as it had upon the floor with Camellia the doll propped comfortably against the wall. Courtesy demanded a time of re-acquaintance and Yusuf did not mind for he was happy just to be here. Eventually he asked the question, "Where is Hooriya?"

For a moment, the old woman's gnarled fingers kneaded nervously together as she bowed her head downward. When half a minute had passed, she raised her eyes to meet his and said simply, "She's dead. Hooriya has stepped on a landmine more than two months ago. I…" her voice trailed off.

The words cut like a knife. Yusuf wished not to believe, but incidences such as this were common and Athaliah would not lie about such a thing. Yusuf's boyish grin fell apart. Without a word he rose to his feet. He paced the small floor twice, then collapsed to sit upon Hooriya's bed and sob profusely with face held in both hands. For a long time, he cried. It was the first he had ever loved…and the first love he had ever lost and a sadness unlike any he had known. When the moment had passed Yusuf lifted the doll, held it before him with both hands, and thought deeply of Hooriya. Her love had changed his life and he would never forget her.

What Yusuf did not know is that, for God's purpose, the little girl's time here was finished.

When the moment had passed, he looked at the old woman through blurred vision. Athaliah's gaze held only the floor. She had neither moved nor spoken.

The next morning Athaliah's few belongings were loaded into the truck. Yusuf set Hooriya's doll on the seat between them, nudged the truck into gear, and the long journey home began. Athaliah spoke little and Yusuf was grateful. For much of the three-day trip thoughts of Hooriya haunted him. Hers was a face he would never see again. To watch such loss in the lives of others had never bothered him before…*it did now*. He thought of those he had purified with bullets—and of those who had loved them. Their faces began to haunt him. Then, as though a dam had collapsed, waves of emotion unfelt before washed over him in a flood. Yusuf's breath caught and he fought for composure. Against a backdrop of empty desert, the young man stopped the truck to exit its cab then stand against the tailgate and cry uncontrollably as the old woman sat rigid in the passenger seat. It was a most embarrassing thing, but Yusuf could not stop. When the time had passed, he vowed to God that never again would he kill for *any* reason beyond the necessity of survival.

Yusuf meant it.

For the remainder of her life Athaliah lived in the home of Yusuf, and she grew to care for him as family.

Yusuf's ability for leadership had once brought uncommon notoriety. Now it was through those same qualities redirected that he became such an extraordinary asset to those in need. From donation raised through new and aggressive methods of solicitation, the orphanage gained a new wing, concrete was poured over the dirt floor, superior kitchen instruments were acquired, a much better supply of food, and other improvements as well. Through virtue of old connections, Yusuf was able to procure some funding, medicine, and surgical equipment for the local hospital. Next, he focused on the school.

Yusuf became a humanitarian.

It seemed a lot of work, but in short time Yusuf saw that for every ounce he gave, he received three in return. This was yet another *Cosmic Law*. In time Yusuf's own life grew to overflowing with the riches of contentment, belonging, and the byproduct of these which is—happiness.

Yusuf was truly a wealthy man at last.

Maybe, he gave more than was necessary to achieve any real feeling of worth in this crazy world, but he believed that in this life he had taken much more than could ever be re-payed.

Yusuf spent the remainder of his life in the service of a new, loving God, and his fellow man. When he eventually died hundreds came to morn. Many cried.

THE MEADOW
Chapter 5

1

Again, Josie came to the meadow, and again he met God. But all God had to say was, "Well done Josie," for nothing more need be said. And again, they spent time together in this place, laughed, and spoke of simple things. And again, each enjoyed the other's company immensely.

But eventually God led his child to the water's edge once more…

AN AVERAGE GUY
Chapter 6

1

Josie's dark eyes stared with misgiving through the window of his middle-class living room to the narrow middle-class street that ran through his likewise middle-class neighborhood.

The last time he had stared so grimly through this window it had been to watch the cops storm the house next door. Josie had known, as had most everyone in the neighborhood, that the quarrelsome couple who had previously occupied the place were drug dealers. He'd watched the steady flow of shady characters come and go through all hours of the day and night and had wondered why it took the police so long to catch on. But, that time, Josie's feelings had been lined with the taste of bitter relief. This time they were not.

Since then, the house had sat vacant and there had been peace. That was about to change.

Through suspicious eyes Josie observed the big U-Haul parked in the adjacent driveway. It was a family this time. Two parents who were obviously on the cusp of middle age, and three children. The little girl appeared no older than five while her two brothers were probably around eight and twelve. Josie watched as all, even the girl, helped to move boxes, furniture, and other belongings, inside.

It was not the idea of a family moving in that bothered Josie. No. It was the idea of a *Mexican* family living there that pissed him off.

The sight of Mexicans was nothing new, for the big city by the sea, in which Josie lived, was not far from the border and they were numerous here. It was a fact that the young man simply accepted and, as long as he need not interact too closely with them, he did not mind. For the Mexican, he knew, was different…different in his appearance, different in his language, different in his culture, and certainly different in his way of thinking; and different was something Josie had always been wary of. Although he had never really experienced any close contact with Mexicans, Josie had once made a short visit to a nearby border town. Through the wisdom of that short afternoon journey, coupled with the many rumors he'd heard, Josie had been able to pretty much figure it out. They came from a dirty land of desert, poverty, and lawlessness to pour over the border like flies in attempt to escape a place that surely, through their own ignorance and abuse, had been transformed into a living nightmare. Least that's how Josie saw it. Now, he suspected, they had come to his own neighborhood to start the problem anew. Right here, in his front yard! Adrienne would see things differently, he knew. So, for the sake of his wife and an honest desire to avoid ridicule, Josie would keep his feelings quiet…for now.

Initially though, Josie would at least make an attempt. For, although he might not approve of a people or their culture, it was not in his nature to hate. For the sake of his wife, 11-month-old daughter, and the new home of which he had worked so hard to acquire, Josie would at least test the water. And even if he found it not to his liking, he would do no more than keep his distance from the new neighbors.

As she held the baby and paced slowly around the room offering gentle cooing sounds, Adrienne's sparkling blue eyes peered from below her beautiful head of long brown hair to also keep watch through the living room window. Her thoughts differed much from those of her husband, and it was with high hopes that the small, shapely young woman (her body had recovered from childbirth almost instantly) observed. After all, she and Josie *were* buying their home and if the new family were found disagreeable there could be trouble for years to come. Unlike Josie however, Adrienne saw only people who might not brawl and peddle drugs like the previous occupants and, with luck, even become friends. Once the new family had a few days to settle in, Adrienne would put together a welcome basket with which she and Josie might mosey over to welcome the new arrivals. In this way she hoped to start off on a good note.

2

It was three days later, on a Saturday afternoon, that Josie stood upon the neighbor's little wooden porch beside his wife as she held a large plastic bowl covered with Saran wrap. With real apprehension, Josie reached for the doorbell then waited to see how they would be received.

A man answered. He was quite tall with overtones of gray in his otherwise black hair. Although certainly not fat, the rounded belly and fine lines that adorned dark eyes, told of middle age in one who was slightly past his prime.

It was Adrienne who, in her usual outgoing manner, spoke first, "I'm Adrienne," she held out her free hand, "and this is Josie. We're in the place next door and wanted to welcome you to the neighborhood."

As the corners of the man's lips curled upward Adrienne noted that the crow's feet at his eyes were really only smile-lines after all. From them came the warmth of kindness and Adrienne decided she liked him already. Accepting her hand, he said in perfect English, tinged with a slight accent that betrayed this as his second language, "Glad to meet you, Adrienne. I'm Albert". He turned then to take Josie's hand in both of his own, "It's a pleasure Josie. Come in. We've been wondering when we might get to meet you guys."

Albert led them inside. Although the furniture had been arranged and some necessities already put into place, unpacked boxes were still stacked about in disarray. At one corner of the room a small shrine had already been erected upon a little wooden table. Candles set into tall glasses with illustrations of the Virgin Mary pasted to their surface sat among a variety of other pictures and small plastic figures. Mounted on the wall above was a porcelain model of a man nailed to a cross. For a moment Josie stared at this strange display. It seemed so tacky. But it was not in Josie's nature to question the Gods of others, so he only observed in silence.

A long green couch, two matching lounge chairs, and one old wooden rocker were positioned around a glass-topped coffee table. Nearby sat a large console TV set with rabbit-ear antennas protruding from its top. The oldest boy was slouched lazily into the far chair while his younger brother lay sprawled upon the couch. Both were watching reruns of an old Roadrunner cartoon.

"This is Oscar," Albert motioned to the oldest boy, "and Louis," he looked at the other, "Boys, this is Josie and Adrienne, our neighbors from next door."

Oscar stood respectfully to shake hands with the newcomers while Louis, who was closer, simply reached up to do the same. "Pleased to meet you," each said in turn.

"Maria!" Albert called to the kitchen, "Come meet our new neighbors, Josie and Adrienne."

A small, dark, and slightly plump woman appeared from the kitchen. Maria's overtones of gray would surely have matched those of her husband were it not for the little bottle of hair-color still packed away somewhere. The lines that were beginning to form upon her round face only added to the air of motherhood that surrounded this woman. Beside her stood a little girl, one hand clinging onto her mother's light brown dress. Maria wiped wet hands on her white apron as she appraised the situation. Immediately she brightened, then moved forward to make introductions. "Glad to meet you two," Maria said as she took Josie's hand then turned attention to his wife, "Adrienne. It's a pleasure," again, good English with a slight accent. "It's a real relief to know there's another woman so close by. As you see, I'm surrounded with boys and sometimes it's enough to drive a person flat crazy."

"What about me Momma?" the girl tugged at her mother's dress and stared up into the faces of four grow-ups. She seemed anything but shy.

Maria patted her daughter's head affectionately, "Aw, you're a big help honey, and I'm sure I couldn't get along without you, but you're still a little girl and sometimes mommy would like to talk with someone closer to her own age." Maria turned back to her guests, "This is Nancy". Introductions were again made.

"Here," Maria smiled at Adrienne who had forgotten she still held the bowl of chocolate chip cookies, "Let me take that. Did you make these yourself?" Maria would not have asked had she not already known the answer.

"I did," Adrienne said, still feeling a little self conscious in these unfamiliar surroundings, "We'd hoped this might be a sort of special occasion."

"Me too," Maria agreed with kindness in her gentle smile. Adrienne relaxed a little. The prospect of having a good friend so close had not previously occurred to her. It did now. Adrienne became hopeful.

Maria took the bowl and set it on the glass tabletop. She then kicked Louise in the foot, and said, "Scoot your lazy butt over and make room for our guests." The boy jumped at his mother's command. "Please, sit down," she told the newcomers. "Make yourselves at home. Don't mind the mess". Josie and Adrienne sat rather stiffly onto the sofa, the boys stayed where they were, and Albert relaxed into the wooden rocker. Maria snapped something in Spanish and Oscar rose to shut off the television then returned to his seat.

"Would you like something to drink?" she asked, "Milk, soda pop, beer?"

Albert asked for beer, as did Josie. Adrienne and the boys went for soda, while Nancy requested milk. "Be right back," and Maria trotted off to the kitchen. Nancy followed.

For a moment it seemed no one knew what to say. It was Adrienne who broke the silence, "How do you like your new house?" the question was aimed at Albert.

"So far we love it," he replied, "We've always wanted to buy our own place but, as you can see, we have a few kids, and they can certainly be a financial drain. Little by little though, we've been saving, and it looks like our persistence has finally paid off," Alberto held both hands in the air and looked happily around. "Yes Adrienne, I think you could say we're pretty happy with the new place. It's our first. How about you two?"

"Oh, we're buying," Josie replied, "It's our first place as well." It seemed both families had at least some things in common. "It was the same as you. We had to save for a few years, but I guess we just managed a bit sooner because of the kid thing, like you said."

Adrienne noted that Josie was on his best behavior today.

Maria arrived carrying two cans of beer, cups, and milk while Nancy followed on her heals to help by carrying a two-liter bottle of soda pop. This big job earned the five-year-old a pleasing feeling of importance. Both set their burdens on the table before Maria divvied out drinks (milk for herself), removed the plastic from Adrienne's cookies, grabbed two, then took a seat upon the remaining lounge chair. Nancy also grabbed cookies and milk, then simply knelt at the glass table. All complimented the cookies.

"Will you have to go to a new school?" Adrienne asked the boys.

"Naw," Oscar replied, "Our old house was pretty close to here. Same school."

"That's one of the reasons we picked this place," Maria said, "Oh, the house needs a little work we know, but Albert's good with things like that. He loves projects. Besides, Oscar will help."

"Yeah," Josie said, "Our place is the same. I've had almost two years to work on it and there's still plenty to be done. Sometimes I wonder if it'll ever get finished. But I work full time and don't have a son to help so the going's kind of slow. Adrienne helped in the beginning but, since the baby's come, she's had her hands pretty full. It just seems like there's never enough hours in the day."

"Amen to that," Maria said, "Just think what it's like with three of them running around. And we just learned we're going to have another."

A little smile curled Alberto's full lips, and he puffed visibly with pride.

"You're pregnant?" Adrienne asked.

"Yeah," Maria told her, "But this is the last one. While at the hospital I'm having them fix that. I don't care what my mother or, sorry baby," Maria shot a sideways glance at her husband, "Albert says. I will have brought four babies into this world and that's enough."

"Where's *your* baby?" Nancy asked Adrienne, "I've seen you carrying it. Is it a boy?"

"Girl," Adrienne answered, "Her name's Rachel, and she's next door with my mother."

"Can we see her?" Nancy seemed excited.

Adrienne looked questioningly at Maria. "Oh please," Maria replied to this silent appeal, "We'd love to have her. And meet your mother too."

Adrienne brightened, as did Josie, "I doubt my mom will come. She's not really the sociable type. But I'm sure Rachel would like to meet you." With that, she looked at Josie, who only offered a nod, then stood to exit through the front door.

When she had gone Josie remarked, "You guys speak really good English. Were you born here?"

"No," Albert answered, "Maria and I are both first generation Americans. Maria's family immigrated when she was still very young. Mine came when I was not much older than Oscar. It was especially important to my father that we learn English, so we all studied together. For a while Spanish wasn't even allowed in our house. I think he just figured there would be no opportunity here if we did not speak the language. Our children are all second-generation Americans but speak Spanish as well. In contrast to my father, I want our kids to have the option of returning to Mexico, if they ever want too. It's a beautiful country you know."

Josie didn't know.

Adrienne returned through the front door then again sat on the couch, this time with Rachel in her lap, who was dressed in pink baby clothes and booties. Nancy was immediately at her side staring goo-goo eyed at the baby. With exception of Oscar, all seemed enraptured with the child and Rachel found that she had quite an audience as she stared silently at the new faces and chewed on one tiny fist. But Nancy's was the closest and, at the little Mexican girl's wide grin, Rachel had little choice but to smile back.

"She's beautiful," Maria said, and everyone agreed. Rachel's parents beamed with pride.

"Can I hold her?" Nancy asked.

"Sure honey," Adrienne said as she scooted over to make room for the little admirer upon the couch, "Climb up here and she can sit in your lap." Once in position, Adrienne gave her the baby. Rachel, who had always been an almost unnervingly easy toddler, did not complain and even seemed to enjoy the affections of one so close to her own age.

For a time, all admired the baby, and she was passed around a little. When the newness had finally subsided, conversation returned to things of a more adult nature. Bored with this talk, the boys stepped out to ride their bikes while Nancy brought in toys for her and Rachel to play with.

The young couple might have made an excuse to leave then but, to Josie's surprise, they found themselves genuinely enjoying the time and chose instead to hang around.

As the wives fell into an apparently seamless conversation of whatever it is women talk about, Albert asked if Josie would like to see the garage. This might have seemed an unusual request had it not been for the truth both men knew; this was really only an excuse to get away from the women and talk of things that interest men.
The guys bowed out quietly and the girls barely noticed. On the way, Albert stopped at the refrigerator to grab four cans of Budweiser that still hung in their plastic clasp. Albert's garage was attached to the house and they entered through a door at the kitchen's far end.

Although the single-car garage still lay in a state of boxed up disarray, one heavy workbench with large vice attached, a roll-away toolbox, and a display of wooden shelves had already been set into place along the walls. It was obvious that no car would ever park in here. Many other tools, some for woodworking and others automotive, lay scattered about the floor and shelves. At the room's center waited two white-plastic lawn-chairs and Albert relaxed into one while Josie took the other. The older man handed Josie a beer then popped the tab of his own and took a healthy pull. Albert let out a long burp, turned to his new amigo and said, "Welcome to my sanctuary good buddy. This is the one place in the whole damn house where a man can get a little peace."

"Yeah," Josie said, "you've got quite an entourage in there."

"Tell me about it. I don't know how I'd get along without my family but sometimes a man needs a place to get away and surround himself with the things of his own interests. Know what I mean?"

Josie contemplated this. "I guess so. But I'm an only child. I've never been part of such a big family." For a moment Josie fell to silent thought. There was no guidebook for parenting and, since Albert obviously had more experience, the younger father decided to ask, "Tell me Al, what's the secret?"

Albert pondered in silence for a moment before he turned his gaze into the eyes of his guest, "Well, I don't think there is a secret. But if I had to guess I'd probably say you've got to learn to let things ride. Try not to get your feathers ruffled every time one of them does something that really pisses you off, because if you do you'll never get any peace. There's always one of them's doing some damn thing he or she shouldn't be. Oh, and let your woman have her way whenever possible. No one can understand what goes on in the mind of a woman—not even another woman…"

"Amen to that," Josie said.

Albert shot a sideways glance at this interruption, "…so don't even try. It's important to choose your battles. I think it's often a lot easier to just let her do whatever crazy thing she's gotten into her funky female brain lately than it would be to try and stop her. Unless it's something really important to you, just *let it ride.* If there was a secret, I guess the answer would probably have to be *patience*—lots of *patience.* …And a good garage." With that Albert took another pull from his beer. "Well, now that you've heard the word of the master, that'll be five bucks. And Josie…"

"Yeah?"

"…We only accept cash."

"I'll get right on that, soon as I finish this beer."

Both men grinned and a moment of silence passed. Josie took another large swallow of his Bud.

"So, Al, with all the kids you've got already, how do you feel about one more?"

Again, Albert looked his new neighbor in the eye. Each man's personality already seemed to complement the other's unusually well. "I've always wanted a big family. My children are the bright spot of my life. You heard Maria, this will be our last and I look forward to its arrival with the same enthusiasm as each of the others. You should know Josie. You're a father."

Josie did know.

"So far you have one. But if you ever have a third or fourth then you'll also know that each kid is so different. A little extension of yourself maybe, but also an individual. A unique life that will add things to your own you never would have otherwise experienced; and probably also wreak a little havoc you could certainly live without. How can a man not be excited about a thing like that?"

Albert's candor surprised Josie. He'd always heard that Mexico was a place of great machismo and had just figured its men were probably something akin to arrogant pricks who kept their emotions well guarded. But Albert was not that way at all. If anything, he wore his feelings on his sleeve. His humanity seemed less guarded than many of the white men Josie had known. It was hard not to feel at ease with one so open.

Having run the gamut of talk concerning home and family, Josie changed the subject, "What do you do for a living?"

"I'm a welder."

"You like the Job?"

"Don't mind it, I guess. I've always liked building stuff. Besides, it pays the bills."

"Yeah. I know what you mean. I sell cars. Wanted to be a gigolo but Adrienne didn't think it was a good idea, so I settled for the nine-to-five rat-race. What can you do?"

"Hell, I wouldn't know," Albert's frown was halfhearted.

"Me neither I guess."

Albert grabbed another beer then handed Josie its twin. Both popped the tops and relaxed some more. Albert initiated a conversation about sports. A subject that, although neither was an avid fan, each at least had some interest. More Bud was retrieved from the fridge and the talk seemed to flow like the beer.

It was long after dark when Adrienne showed up to collect her man. Rachel slept in Josie's arms as the trio strolled across the manicured grass that separated the two middle-class American homes.

"Did you have a nice time?" Adrienne asked.

"I did."

"They're gonna have a housewarming party weekend after next. Maria figures it'll take that long to get the place settled. We're invited…if you'd like to go."

"That'd be great," Josie's words were slurred. He had never been much of a drinker and, since she had seldom seen him like this, Adrienne smiled to herself in the dark.

3

The days passed. Cars sold, babies cried, dinners were cooked, and lawns mowed. Adrienne, being home a lot anyway, spent some hours visiting with her new amiga. Even Josie, when he was home, not busy, or just too plain tired, took a few moments to shoot the bull with Al. But most often it was Nancy who initiated contact by dropping by to see if she could play with the baby. Before anyone knew where the time had gone, the housewarming party was upon them.

Josie gazed out the window to see another car pull up as yet another entourage of Mexicans, often carrying food, unloaded and sauntered inside. That made seven new vehicles parked on the street. It was Saturday again; the clock said 12:30pm.

Josie's attention was diverted from the window by a call from behind, "Josie. Are you ready? Rachel's dressed, and everything's set." He turned to look at her. She was dressed in an old pair of blue jeans that clung like paint to smooth curves, skimpy sandals, and a light gray halter-top with picture of a lion's head printed in black across her small, yet ample bust. Her dark hair was thrown loosely over slender shoulders to cascade halfway to her ass. For a moment Josie entertained thoughts of dragging her viciously to the bedroom for a hearty afternoon romp. It would be fun—for both of them. But the moment passed. He looked again. She was, after all, only dressed for a casual Barbeque with friends.

She seemed so relaxed, so at-ease, however, she had always been like that. Sometimes, he envied her genuine, seemingly natural easiness with people. The proficiency of her social skill was probably ten times his own; and many seemed drawn to her wherever she went. What a saleswoman she would make.

Although he did his best to hide it, Josie was nervous. They were going to a house filled with Mexicans. They would probably be the only white people there! Customs might be different, Spanish would most certainly be spoken often, if not exclusively, and there was a boatload of strangers to meet—Mexican strangers! Oh, what a chore it all seemed.

Sensing his unease, Adrienne said gently, "They're just people Josie. If it gets uncomfortable, even a little," he knew this meant if *he* got uncomfortable, "we'll just make an excuse and leave early. Okay?"

Josie looked at her. How could she know him so well in just the few years they had been together? "Okay," he replied.

With a large bowl of chips (again covered with plastic wrap) in one curled arm, and a dish filled with homemade guacamole dip piled atop that, Josie stood beside his wife and daughter on the small stoop. The neighbor's front door stood wide open, so he simply stared inside. The furniture was filled to capacity while four others sat upon plastic chairs added for the occasion. All were women. Among them, Josie saw Maria. The small crowd seemed happy in their endeavors and, just as Josie had feared, most of the talk was in Spanish. But he also heard English. It seemed the two languages were being melded at times. There were no other white people in sight.

Maria noticed them and her smile beamed as she came forward to escort her neighbors inside. Adrienne, and even Rachel, already seemed at home in these strange surroundings as Josie trailed nervously behind. Soon the newcomers stood as the center of attention among the little gathering while introductions went around. Most of the greetings were made in English and all seemed genuinely happy the make their acquaintance. To her obvious delight, mounds of attention were heaped upon Rachel. Adrienne kneeled beside the glass table to engage in happy small talk while Maria took the chips and dip from Josie's arms. "Albert's in the back yard with some of the boys," she told him, "In case the girl talk gets too much for you."

"Thanks Maria."

"No problem," she smiled at him, "I'm so glad you could make it. Most of the people here are family and others are their friends or ours. Make yourself at home amigo. Oh, and Josie, thanks for the chow."

"Thank Adrienne," he said. Then, after a thoughtful moment, "Most of these people are your family?"

"Yeah, both Albert's and mine. Many live here in town but some crossed the boarder to be here. But then, most cross every day for their jobs anyway."

"You have a big family."

"We do."

Maria kissed Josie on the cheek. It was a simple gesture that helped to ease his nagging sense of estrangement.

When three minutes of pleasantries had passed, Josie wandered off to find Albert. The young car-salesman stared through the open sliding-glass door to note a backyard that, like his own, was surrounded by a tall wooden fence. A patio roof—not unlike the one Josie wanted for his place—protruded from the house's eve. It had not been there two weeks ago. Although this new patio was not yet painted or roofed, the structure provided refuge from the summer sunshine. In the shade below—about where Josie hoped to place a concrete slab in his own yard—Albert had covered the dirt with an old slice of carpet. Atop this rug stood a handful of mismatched folding chairs. Most were filled with men and Albert sat among them. Nearby, a small patch of ground had been scraped to dirt and two old car-tire rims placed slightly apart then topped with what appeared to be a wire refrigerator shelf. A fire crackled below. On this makeshift "grill" two large fish, wrapped partially in tinfoil, simmered in their juices as a handful of onions roasted beside. Below, five potatoes, also rapped in tinfoil, sat directly in the coals. This trailer-trash-barbeque made Josie wonder if Albert had ever heard of K-Mart.

Nearby, a wooden picnic table rested somewhat crookedly while atop it sat two fish that had recently been removed from the grill then covered with a towel to retain heat. Beside these, a large bowl was beginning to fill with potatoes as they were brought from the fire. Next to that set bowls or pots filled with hot tortillas, salsa, salad, refried beans, paper plates, sliced limes, chopped onions, tomatoes, cilantro, and other condiments. Although Albert loved to barbeque, his cousin Fernando now tended the grill.

Josie's gaze wondered to the cheap plastic swimming pool filled from a hose and the five children who played in it. Louis was among them.

"Josie," Albert's voice called him back, "I've been wondering if you'd ever show up. Pull up a seat man. Stay a while."

Josie settled into a folding chair. Introductions went around and the young white man found himself staring into a small crowd of unusually dark faces. Assuming the role of a minority was something new and he did not like it. It was…disconcerting. Josie tried to hide his obvious discomfort.

"What would you like to drink," Albert asked, "Today we've got Corona, Tecate, or Bud. There's also Pepsi, Sprite, Root Beer, and I'm not sure what else." Albert opened the Styrofoam cooler beside his chair.

Josie went with Corona. He settled in and tried to relax as conversation began again. Possibly for his benefit, talk was kept primarily to English, lapsing at times, mostly by those less familiar with the language, into spurts of Spanish.

Fernando was an uncommonly flamboyant man. His relaxed manner was quick to laugh and blessed with extraordinary wit. Your typical life-of-the-party type. His constant banter of jokes and theatrics as he danced about the strange barbeque brought to the small crowd, Josie included, an almost seamless string of laughter. It seemed important to most that Josie be included in conversation, and obvious effort was made to this end. The young white man, helped by the consumption of a few beers, began to loosen up. Before long he was just one of the boys.

Eventually the food was ready, and Louis was called from the pool to notify those inside. People filtered into the yard and a line formed at the picnic table. Josie took a place beside his wife. He noted an easy cheerfulness among the crowd. Josie knew, as did all white people, of the assiduous importance of family in the Mexican culture, but never had he been invited to participate, to him, such a remarkable practice. There was a feeling that seemed natural, and even wonderful, about the whole thing.

"How you getting along?" Adrienne's voice whispered from his right side.

"Good," he replied to her questioning look. "Really," and she saw that his smile was genuine, "These guys are totally cool. How about you?" but he didn't really need to ask. She was, after all, an uncommonly social creature.

"Oh, we're having a grand time. As usual, Nancy's asked if she could *please* play with Rachel and I've hardly seen either of them since. Bless her little heart. You ever had a babysitter ask, 'Oh please, can I watch your kid?' It's certainly a new experience for me. Yeah, I think you could say we're doin' just fine."

As they moved closer to the table Josie noted that, after securing a plate, each person took a tortilla, placed it over the fish, then pinch off a portion of the meat to make the beginnings of a taco. Once they had secured four of five, each would squeeze lime across the meat then add the desired condiments. Having never witnessed this ritual before, plus the crude homemade barbeque, the carpet over the dirt thing, and a plethora of other discrepancies, Josie marveled at the differences in culture. It all seemed so alien.

Josie was not sure he liked it.

The crowd became more dispersed as women mingled among the men and children. Everyone took seats wherever they could be found. All chairs, including the picnic table's bench seats, became occupied. A few crouched against the wall and one man sat on a large beach ball while others returned to the living room.

The food was good, Josie had to admit, and the afternoon passed in a blur.

Much to his pleasure, every single adult and some of the children approached him and, regardless of their skill with the English language, attempted friendly conversation. This helped to quell the newcomer's feelings of estrangement even more and although Josie still felt his differences, the knowledge that he was valued brought a wonderful sense of belonging.

Although not yet dark, it was early evening when Josie returned home with his family. It had been an interesting day.

4

Time again passed as the days turned into weeks and the weeks into months. More contact was made between the neighbors and, although Albert seldom came to Josie's place, Josie began to visit him more often. Sometimes it was to borrow a tool or ask advice for some home project, but it was also becoming common for Josie to seek the company of his neighbor when he felt the need of companionship, or simply sought sanctuary in the man's world of Albert's garage.

While Maria grew fat with pregnancy, the men were becoming good friends.

It was 1 a.m. when Adrienne came groggily awake to the sound of car doors slamming and a vehicle speeding away. Through the fog of slumber, she thought little of it and fell back to sleep. Josie never stirred.

The morning's routine went as usual, and Josie sold three cars that day. Although he generally hated his stupid job, today had not been so bad. Josie whistled a little tune as he entered the house; but it was the long stare Adrienne shot from across the room that brought him up short. Josie knew that look. The little tune ran out like the whistle of a tea kettle removed from the heat, "What's wrong?" he stared at her and waited for the worst.

Adrienne stared back silently as she paused to savor some twisted pleasure from his discomfort. Finally, she let the corners of her mouth curl into a smile and said, "Maria had her baby last night. It's a girl. She's healthy and the doctors already released her. She's next door right now. I'm sure your amigo can't wait to show you."

Josie let out his breath, "Well that's great. Guess I'd better get right over there. Wanna come?"

"Sure. Let me grab Rachel."

The day was bright as Josie's little entourage climbed the three steps to the neighbor's front stoop. Since the door had again been left wide open, the trio could not help but see inside. There on the couch Maria sat contentedly as the baby suckled at her breast. Seated beside her, Albert beamed at the newborn. Nancy sat at Maria's other side seemingly sharing the same trance as her father. The boys occupied both chairs.

"Knock, knock," came Josie's voice through the doorway.

Albert looked up, smiled, then motioned them inside. Maria seemed neither embarrassed nor self-conscious of her breast that, although mostly covered by the little blanket, remained in the baby's mouth. She too smiled at the visitors. *Yet another cultural difference,* Josie thought, knowing full well that almost any mother of his own culture would hasten ashamedly to put that tit away; had she ever dared nurse a baby before an open doorway in the first place.

Adrienne, who had already seen the baby, sat with Rachel in the wooden rocker while Josie took the lounge chair closer to the couch.

Maria removed the infant from her breast, covered herself, and then turned the baby for Josie's inspection. Josie leaned down for a better view. Albert radiated delight. Regardless of whether one cared for the coming of a newborn or not, it was impossible for anyone who shared the room that day not to become caught up in the emotion of the moment.

Maria handed the baby to Albert who then handed her to Josie. "What's her name?" Josie asked as he pulled the child gently to his chest.

"Valeria," Nancy shouted from the other side of the couch.

"That's Valerie in English," Albert added.

"Beautiful name," Josie said. He took one hand and slowly moved the little blanket farther from the child's face. Josie knew that his approval was important to the man who had become his best friend. Today Al would not be disappointed.

Little hands wiggled in the air as the new face came clearly into Josie's view. She was dark, she was healthy and, Josie thought, uncommonly lovely. For a moment Valerie looked as though she would cry. Then, as her wide eyes seemed to stare into his own, the little face broadened into a grin. Vivid memories of his own daughter's birth leapt to the forefront of Josie's mind as little Valerie brought the emotion of that day back to him in a flood. And just as he had the first time his own daughter had been placed into his arms, Josie was moved to soft tears. Momentarily a tinge of embarrassment overcame him, and he handed the girl back to her father. "She's beautiful Al," was all he said.

In this way the young white man shared the emotion of a very important day in the life of a Mexican.

Louis was sent to the kitchen for refreshments and before anyone had noticed an hour and a half was gone. But there were things to be done at home and the visitors eventually said goodbye. They would be seeing plenty of the new baby in the coming months anyway.

Although Nancy still came to see Rachel, her visits were less frequent.

Adrienne, tired of being cooped up in the house playing 'mom' all the time, had begun to take Rachel on outings. The park was a favorite. It was there that the young woman had begun to meet other new moms with which to share a common bond. Her almost daily rendezvous with these new friends was rapidly becoming one of the bright spots of her life.

As for Josie, a nagging emptiness deep within him had begun

to grow and fester. To his credit, the young man had already achieved many goals. He had a steady job complete with medical and retirement; his own home, two cars, a beautiful wife and healthy daughter. The world was his. He should be happy—but sometimes he was not. What was the matter? Try as he might to fight it, Josie had begun to experience occasional bouts of depression.

5

As usual, the southern weather was pleasant. The air was neither hot nor cold. With exception of a few clouds lumbering lazily across the eastern horizon, the sky was blue and inviting. Just another day. Having put in his eight hours, Josie pulled his brand-new Toyota into the driveway beside Adrienne's Celica. Carrying a briefcase filled with papers he hoped to review that evening, Josie stepped through the front door. With eyes cast downward as he fumbled with the briefcase, Josie turned to face the living room. As his gaze lifted Josie was startled to see Adrienne standing there. But it was not the sight of her that gave surprise; it was the look on her face. Something had happened.

"What is it," he said.

"I don't know any other way to say this Josie, so I guess I'll just say it. Valerie died in her sleep last night. Al and Maria didn't know until after you left this morning. Maria said that Valerie liked to keep them up half the night then sleep late. Anyway, it's a classic case of crib death. I don't know what else to say. I think it might be a good idea if you went to see Albert."

Without a word Josie set down his briefcase and walked out the door. He crossed the lawn slowly for need of time to think of what to say, but found no words. Maybe he should have waited an hour before coming. Maybe he would be calmer then. He didn't know, so he just kept walking.

The neighbor's front door again stood open, and Josie stopped at the thresh-hold to peer inside. Seated upon the couch, he could see Maria with her mother and sister sitting at either side. The boys were in either chair, while Nancy had the wooden rocker.

Albert was nowhere in sight.

Knowing not what else to do, Josie just stood there. A long moment passed before Maria noticed him. "Please Josie, come in."

He walked forward and greetings were made. Josie looked Maria in the eye, "I'm sorry," was all he could manage.

"I know you are Josie. Listen," her voice was almost a whisper, "Albert's been in the garage all day. He's not letting anyone in. Why don't you give it a try?"

"Okay," Words, it seemed, were a hard thing to find today. Without another sound Josie turned and walked through the kitchen. When he arrived at the entrance the thought occurred to knock, but instead he simply opened the door, stepped inside, and closed it behind.

Josie surveyed the room. It was dimly lit. An old floor-jack sat in the corner. A V-8 engine sat atop a stand, while a few other unfinished projects lay against walls or were stuffed onto shelves. Most tools had been stacked neatly away. Aside from a bottle that lay broken on the floor, the place appeared as it always had. Both plastic chairs occupied the floor and in one Albert sat with elbows resting atop either armrest and a Pepsi bottle held loosely in one hand. Since both chairs were angled slightly away, Josie's view of the other man was mostly a profile. With the stillness of a mannequin Albert stared straight ahead. Knowing not what else to do, Josie just stood there.

"Get out," Albert's eyes never left the wall as he said these words.

Still, Josie stood there.

Slowly Al's head began to turn, **"I said get ou…"** As Al's gaze fell upon him, Josie saw a mixture of pain and anger. Albert closed his mouth and for a moment only stared at the intruder. He seemed unsure of what to do next. Finally, Al pointed to the chair at his side then returned attention to the wall.

Josie took a seat.

Still, he did not know what to say, for in fact no words befitting such a moment existed. Later Josie would realize that he had not come to talk this day. He had come only to convey a message: 'I have no words my friend, but here is my heart'.

Without taking his eyes from the wall Albert pointed to the other three bottles of Pepsi that lay on the floor. Josie took one and twisted the cap. Albert turned to look at him, opened his mouth as if to speak, then closed it again. As Al focused attention back to the wall, his face contorted into a mass of tortured flesh and he hung his head to cry. Harder his sobs came—then still harder. Finally, Albert rose to his feet and in a fit of rage hurled the bottle into the wall. He stood for only a moment then dropped into his chair to cry some more. Al's sobs grew weaker.

Albert's tears cut Josie. He thought of Rachel. What must it be like to have your own child die in the night? Unthinkable. But it had happened to Albert. *The pain,* Josie thought, *it must be beyond measure.*

It was in this way that the young white man shared yet another deeply emotional time in the life of a Mexican.

Al began to talk. He spoke of the dreams he'd had for the girl. Of how he would have bounced her on his knee and pushed her on the swings. High school graduation…he would have been so proud. Her quinceanera. To watch her ascension to womanhood. To see her start a family of her own. And his grandchildren… Al's face again contorted, but this time no sobs came.

Josie quietly allowed the man his dreams.

Albert said that nothing like this had ever happened to him before and it made him afraid for all his children. He didn't know if he could endure this again. His words came in a flood then and Albert began to ramble lapsing, at times, into bursts of Spanish.

Josie listened.

Sometimes he understood, and sometimes he did not, for besides the occasional reversions to Spanish, Albert also rambled in unintelligible English. The man was a mess. It was of little wonder he had hidden himself in here.

And still Josie listened….

It was past 1:00 a.m. when Josie finally flopped into bed. Physically drained and somewhere beyond exhaustion, Josie felt only a strange sensation of numbness. *Sleep,* he thought, *should come quickly now.* But it did not; and it wasn't until the wee hours that Josie finally succumbed to slumber.

The baby was buried in a nearby cemetery beside Albert's father who had died some years earlier. For Maria, the tragedy seemed less devastating, for it seemed she had always carried a natural acceptance of things she could not change. Not so for Albert. For a week he did not return to work. For a time, Josie came to see him everyday. If nothing else good ever came of it, the child's death would be the final cement of a bond that had been forming between the two men. That bond would last a lifetime.

Slowly Albert's attention was again drawn to the remainder of his family. They were, after all, still alive and in need of his attention. It is said that memory fades for a reason. In Al's case this cliche was a saving grace. In time the child's fate was banished to the recesses of history. Life resumed as it had before.

Years passed.

6

Rachel grew into a fine little girl and began riding the bus to school. Her absence freed Adrienne to think of other things. Her career came to mind. *Yes,* she thought, *the time has finally come.* And with that the 33-year-old woman dug out her diploma and began putting out applications.

It did not take long before Adrienne accepted an offer from a local elementary school and began teaching third grade. With a natural love of kids and genuine desire to be helpful, Adrienne threw herself into the job with real delight.

Josie's mysterious bouts of depression deepened. Finally, at his wife's request, Josie sought professional help. The doctor called the problem a 'chemical imbalance' before writing the prescription for an equally chemical cure. Josie would try better-living-through-chemistry.

Motherhood and her work with the third graders was the bright spot of Adrienne's life. As with so many other well-meaning teachers, it was more than just a job. The work, she had hoped, would offer opportunity to make some real difference in this crazy world—even if only in some small way. But it did not take long to see (as had many before her) that the system of teaching currently in use was flawed and seemed more to promote failure than success in students. Assuming that this system might have once worked (though she could not see how) but was simply outdated, Adrienne set out to resolve the problem. With real intelligence and, at times, slightly brilliant ideas, Adrienne prepared to take her solutions to the senior staff.

She was sure this effort would be met with approval.

Although Josie's depression ebbed considerably and he grew mellow behind the medication, he also began to experience some undesirable side affects. Much to his wife's dismay Josie's sex drive fell off like a ski jump. He also found his usually sharp mind often numb now. He seldom experienced the lows anymore, but neither did he experience life's highs. It seemed as if a fuzzy buffer had been placed between the inside of his head and the outside world. Try as he might to breach this hazy obstacle, he simply could not. Josie's performance at work suffered. But it was not until he began to experience bouts of nausea that the young man returned to his doctor who ran more tests before adjusting the prescription.

To her astonishment (also like many who had come before her), Adrienne's proposals were met with obstinate opposition. She began to realize that her workplace was not so much an institution of higher education as it was a breeding ground for staff-room power plays, ego trips, and snippy conflicts. Most of these were based upon who was kissing whose ass properly, or who simply did not like whom else. It seemed to Adrienne that the place was mostly one big soap opera with a bunch of kids running around to fund the production.

The entire thing disgusted her.

The new medication only brought a new set of side affects. Finally, Josie abandoned the ways of modern medicine entirely. For although this solution might be right for some, he was convinced it was not for him. Josie would have to seek his remedy elsewhere.

Josie changed his diet and began to take regular exercise. He joined a gym. With dedicated determination his body was strengthened to new heights. With this strength of body also came enhanced strength of mind and Josie's condition lessened considerably. *This is the solution,* he thought, *enhanced health.* Josie redoubled his effort.

Time passed.

With little choice in the matter, Adrienne began to view her job as only a way to earn (that word made her laugh these days) a paycheck. From this day forth she would do her work as best possible and, having grown tired of dodging dangerous accusations, keep her head low.

Josie's condition returned. Depression was such a debilitating thing. His enthusiasm for life, his passion, and his energy often evaporated into thin air. And no matter how he tried, no matter what he did, he could not regain it. Sometimes the sickness hit him so hard it took extreme effort just to get off the couch. When this happened his gym workouts suffered, or even stopped completely. When the pain became too much, Josie took long walks and often forced himself into jogging. This activity helped, but a cure it was not. Thankfully, these debilitating bouts came only in occasional waves and Josie was able to enjoy something like normal life more often than not.

Barbeques, and occasional sleepovers among the children, continued between the neighboring families. They took turns babysitting each other's kids, the men hung out, and the girls told each other everything. The bond tightened.

MISTY LAKE
Chapter 7

1

For the approaching-middle-age car salesman vacation time came once a year and he happily embarked upon one well-planned excursion or another at the side of his wife. They always left Rachel behind with Adrienne's parents. Once, they visited a distant and exotic city to see the great sights that attract so many tourists. Next, they rented a fine hotel that resided along one well-known beachfront. Then came the desert gambling town. And there were others.

It was one such year that Adrienne came up with an idea for something different and, after giving it some thought, Josie agreed…

The town of Misty was a small and relatively unknown place that resided in low mountains of heavy pine, oak, and scattered dogwood trees. The town was located near a smallish body of water know as Misty Lake, and at its far side a little cabin was rented for the duration of the two-week vacation. The place was nestled into heavy forest along the waterfront and sat quite some distance from the closest house—which was unoccupied anyway.

With no set plans or remarkable sights that must be seen, the couple took to sleeping late and often enjoyed long afternoon walks. Sometimes they grabbed two poles and tackle from the utility closet and went fishing in the aluminum canoe also provided with the house. Much to Adrienne's surprise this was an activity both enjoyed. Other times, as was the case one starry night when Josie found himself in awe of the clear mountain sky (he had not witnessed such a thing from his home amid the city lights), they just paddled around the lake. Sometimes they swam. Although cooking in the cabin was a common occurrence, the couple also took to having breakfast, and sometimes dinner, at a diner in town. They even made a few friends.

 Josie began to loosen up. In fact, it was not long before the *successful* middle-class man found himself in better spirits than he could remember having enjoyed for years…if ever. Something about the clean mountain air seemed to agree with him. The freshness of it all, the lack of traffic, the trees, the birdsong, squirrels and two deer Josie had seen drinking from the lake early one morning—they all told of a refreshingly simple world so far from the pressures of his own. Deep within Josie something wished, even needed, to become part of that world

 The second week passed to quickly and just about the time life in the city had begun to seem as a distant memory, Josie and Adrienne were driving back to it. Nothing had changed. The traffic was still there, as were the crowds. Josie returned to the car-lot and, in the fall, Adrienne went back to the classroom. Before long, this life again seemed the only real existence possible. Memories of the mountains and the way they had affected the spirits of both vacationers faded into something that felt more like a distant dream than reality. Josie's pain returned, as did his depression. And so this dance continued; for Josie had sold his soul to the machine long ago and it was to this race that he held. Josie knew no other way. *This*, he thought, *is just the way the real world is.*

 Never again was the couple to experience the high-dollar thrill of tourist places or amusement parks, as the two-week vacation would be spent only in the simple splendor of Mother Nature's mountains. Often Josie at first dreaded the thought of leaving the city even for such a short time, for there were always so many things that required his attention at home. But after two or three days in Misty, Josie's mind invariably calmed, and his spirit was uplifted again. And he remembered: He remembered what it was like to live without emotional pain, to relax, to play often, to be at ease. *Easy living*, it seemed such an unreal and useless ideal back in the real-world where there was always so much that must be gained in such short time. But just when his mind had pleasantly succumbed to this new way of being, the day to leave would arrive.

 It was their fourth vacation to Misty and Adrienne navigated the small two-lane highway that twisted through the familiar mountain forest. There were very few houses to interrupt the natural beauty of this place.

From the passenger seat Josie gazed silently through the side window that remained rolled up to better allow the air-conditioner its job. His mood was sullen with the burden of unusually heavy responsibility lately. The car-lot was involved in a messy lawsuit that stemmed from a deal for a small fleet of automobiles he himself had contracted with a large car-rental company in good faith—or so he had thought. His boss was not happy. Aside from the normal duties of his life, Josie had been forced to make multiple courtroom appearances. Josie's mouth was set into a deep frown as he gazed to the forest beyond without really seeing it. Today he wondered why God had banished him to a life so heavily laden with burden. And the muddy bog that is depression spread around him like some primordial quicksand.

Adrienne had assured him it was only a phase and things would lighten up soon. He believed her. Josie had faced hard times before and they had always passed. But he worried that the disease of depression would follow him to Misty and ruin the sanctity of their vacation time. He had often worried over this before and was always grateful when it did not happen. For invariably it seemed that this demon did not like the town of Misty.

It was just past 1:00 pm as the white economy car approached the small town. Josie gazed ahead with mild interest; for the place had long since become familiar.

The twisting blacktop of highway-42 straitened to become Main Street, which passed through town-center for ½-mile before resuming its lonely path through the mountains. Both sides of Main St. held most of Misty's businesses. First on the left was the old Philips-66 gas and auto repair station, owned and operated by a graying, pot-bellied man named Otis. Next came Emma's Bakery, and to the right a small Ace Hardware. After that was a couple of arts and crafts stores aimed mostly at the modest tourist industry, a tiny sheriff's station, Ida's Ice Cream Shop, a couple of saloons, and so on. Assorted trees grew through holes in the sidewalk, between buildings, or from the grassy yards of businesses. Sunshine beamed from above and the streets seemed alive as they basked in its warm glow. Cars were parked about as a variety of locals, some Josie recognized, and a moderate crowd of tourists went about their business. Some sat talking with one another upon the large wooden deck of the ice cream shop, or along the sidewalk in front of Wired Willies—the town's only espresso bar. Josie watched with keen interest at what he believed to be clean living in another world so different from his own. His spirits brightened. For to him the mountains held such a high quality of magic.

At Main Street's end the Copper Kettle Diner waited beside McGregor's Grocery. Adrienne pulled into the Kettle's roughly paved lot and shut the car off. Not bothering to lock the doors since they had become familiar with the country trust ethic, both exited the vehicle and strolled inside. The lunchtime rush was over, and the place held only a small handful of patrons. Once inside, they found a booth and plopped onto red-vinyl upholstery. A teenage waitress appeared.

"Josie, Adrienne. Coffee?" As always, the young girl was a bit shy, if not self-conscious, but she had an excellent memory and her familiarity with the couple helped to lessen this discomfiture some.

"Yes, please Joanne," Josie said as he slouched comfortably back to regard her, but before another word had time to reach his lips, he heard Adrienne's voice.

"How've you been Joanne?" the smile was radiant as she beamed at their hostess.

"Fine, thank you."

"Aren't you gonna be graduating pretty soon Joie?" It was a name only those who knew her used.

"Yeah. Next year I'll be a senior."

"Going to college after that?" Adrienne continued.

"Well…my parents don't really care if I do or not," she said shyly. Then, summoning more courage added, "Mom says it's up to me. If I wanna go they'll pay. But really, I don't want to. I mean, I never really liked school anyway."

"Well, what-the-hey then. If you don't wanna go why bother…right?"

Typical Adrienne, Josie thought, *always the diplomat*. In time she would probably take the same attitude with Rachel and it would be he who would have to lead the campaign to a better future for their daughter. Adrienne was just so soft all the time. So often it was that she would rather just let things ride than push to make them right. Such weakness. Good thing she had him.

"Hey," Adrienne continued, "you still goin' with that guy Donny?" Local kids often hung at the Copper Kettle and Adrienne had seen these two together.

"No. We broke up." As was so common among those who talked with Adrienne for even a few minutes, the girl was beginning to loosen up. Although Josie'd witnessed this phenomenon a thousand times, it never ceased to amaze him.

"To bad. Got another guy yet?"

"Well," Joanne continued, "I've kinda been seeing Steve."

"Steven Foster?" Adrienne's excitement escalated.

"Yeah."

"Oh-my-god, that guy is so hot!" Adrienne kept her voice low, but Josie noted that she had begun to sound like something of a teenager herself. "Are you really going out with him?"

Joanne's face lit up, "Well, yeah. He gave me this ring," she leaned forward to offer her hand for Adrienne's inspection.

"Wow," Adrienne beamed while fondling the ring with slender fingers, "There's a rumor he's the greatest kisser. Is it true?" she almost whispered as she gazed excitedly up into the other girl's deep-green eyes.

"Well," Joanne seemed to have lost herself now and she bent even lower as she prepared to divulge intimate details. But the girl caught herself and shot a sideways glance at Josie. Embarrassment flushed and Joanne quickly turned back to Adrienne and whispered, "I'll tell you later." Then she added as if by afterthought, "But the answer's yes," her tone was barley audible.

Joanne stood up strait and her manner became all business, "Would you like lunch or breakfast?" Josie and Adrienne often came in for a late breakfast when in town and, lucky for them, the Kettle served it all day.

"Breakfast," said Adrienne.

"Me too," Josie added.

"Okay." and she looked first at Adrienne, "Chilly cheese omelet then, or would you like a menu?"

"Chilly cheese will be fine Joie."

"And Josie, veggie omelet with Swiss and grits instead of hash browns, right?"

"Perfect," he answered.

"Okay then, I'll get your coffee, and the food'll be right up." With that the young girl hurried off.

When she had gone Josie regarded his wife thoughtfully. With people she often became so close so fast. How did she do that? Did she really think Steven Foster was hot? Maybe, but he knew from experience that Adrienne did not really care much about the topic in any such conversation. What mattered to her was the quality and closeness of interaction with the other person. At this she was a master. Seemingly aware of his thoughts Adrienne offered him a smile and Josie returned the gesture with a sparkle of love in his eye.

She was one hell of a woman.

The food arrived and they dug in. Aside from the low chime of clicking utensils the table became quiet.

Thirty minutes later Josie paid the bill, and they left the Copper Kettle.

Soon they were cruising one tiny road that passed through tall trees and a spattering of houses as it meandered along the water's edge to the lake's sparsely inhabited far side. For it was there that the familiar little hideaway waited. A checkerboard of shadows created by warm sunshine filtering through tall trees washed across the car as Adrienne drove slowly onward. Numerous squirrels seemed intent upon their work along the ground and in high trees today. Josie watched them with keen interest.

As Adrienne turned into the short dirt driveway, Josie gazed curiously ahead. The little place seemed very much alone as it sat among the numerous pines that dominated these hills and to the water's edge. As always, the stunning vision of such beauty and seeming serenity took him aback. Once again, a great mass of tension seemed lifted. Josie's body relaxed and his shoulders slumped visibly.

Within three days he was a new man.

The neighborhood was a quiet place and the city-sounds of traffic, sirens, and weed-whackers Josie missed but little. To him the world seemed right without them. The occasional passing of deer also held his attention. The couple loved long walks along lonely trails and dirt roads. Fishing and swimming were still favorite pastimes as were restaurants and an occasional drink at a local tavern. The friends they had made seemed so laid-back and before long Josie always found himself just as relaxed as they. None locked their doors. Josie always thought he felt the presence of God here, and the mountains themselves soothed him with a wonderful sense of contentment. It was never until this altered state had settled itself within him that the city-dwelling-car-salesman realized the depth of pain he had arrived in. After all, for most of the year mental and emotional discomfort was his normal way of being.

2

It was in the wee hours of the night that Josie found himself alone in a very strange place. He looked around the room. The furnishings were exquisite, and the comfort they offered undeniable. This was obvious even from where he stood upon the flawless carpet at room's center. Though the décor was unfamiliar, Josie knew he was at home. He felt pain here, a deep and nagging pain. But it was a familiar pain, a safe pain—a thing he could no longer remember having lived without. Yet there was something strange about this place. Looking closer he saw…no windows! He looked again and realized no other rooms connected to this small cubical and only one very solid looking door stood between him and the outside! Claustrophobia… just a little at first but soon the sensation grew. In a moment, he felt strangled by it. Quickly Josie walked to the door and reached for the handle. Ever so slowly he turned…it was not locked. For only a moment did he hesitate, then, with one powerful thrust, Josie flung the barrier open and stared in deep shock. **Bars!** The way was blocked with **steel bars! He was trapped!** Josie threw himself against the blockade of this gilded cage and, with face pressed firmly against the steel, looked with crazy eyes to the world beyond. What he saw took his breath away.

It was a great meadow, an unbelievable meadow of unprecedented power and beauty. The chatter of birdsong hit him in an onrush of twittering, and he noted spectacular skill as they darted this way and that. Vast groves of purple and yellow flowers moved with a gentle breeze that blew silently across the land as a thousand honeybees worked busily over them. Clear water babbled over smooth rocks as a wide creek passed gently through the meadow's center. Josie could see that this place rested in a wide valley. He looked to the rolling hills beyond and saw they were carpeted with a seemingly solid wall of forest that surrounded the meadow almost entirely. Looking to the sky Josie observed a few small and hazy clouds that lumbered lazily in the distance as one magnificent hawk soared high above. The sun was bright and the day good. There was something magical at work beyond those steel bars. Josie could feel it. The fulfillment that awaited him there, he knew, was beyond the limits of his comprehension. It called to him, and his need of it was complete. So complete in fact that Josie began to shake the bars violently. The effort gained nothing. Again, he threw himself against these constraints, pushed his face to the steel, and reached beyond to shake both fists angrily at the sky. "Why am I in here?" he yelled to the wind, "Let me out," and again, "Let me out!" and still louder, **"Somebody please, let me out!"** Josie pounded his fists, he stomped his feet, he screamed, he yelled, he ran across the room then turned to again throw himself at the bars. He must escape. Josie's rage escalated and he attacked the steel with the viciousness of a rabid animal. Like a wild man he screamed, kicked, pounded, and groped against the gate but for all his effort it would not move. Finally, weakened with exhaustion, Josie slumped to the floor and began to cry.

When this was done, a sort of calm settled in, and in his weakened state, a moment of clarity befell him. Josie looked inside himself and saw the truth. And that truth, strange as it seemed, was that he did not wish to go out. He was afraid. No, more than that, Josie was terrified. For that which lay beyond the gate truly was beyond comprehension, and that which was beyond comprehension was also beyond the comfort of that which is familiar. It was the unknown, and with it came a kind of fear Josie simply could not breach. In a moment of bitter surrender, the middle-aged car salesman got to his feet and, with eyes aimed only at the floor, walked to the safety of the familiar and dropped into the softness of one padded sofa. Instantly the pain returned. But it was a dull pain, a familiar pain, and he knew it well. The birdsong was gone, and in its place an eerie silence settled. Josie let his chin fall against his chest and closed his eyes.

It was then that a gentle voice came from somewhere beyond the gate and although he could not place it, the tone seemed vaguely familiar…if not soothing. Josie lifted his head to listen.

"It's okay Josie. You may remain inside the little prison you've built of fear for the rest of your life if you so choose. For like any other you have freedom of will. I am no puppet master who would see you dance at the end of a string. I am no slave keeper and would never insist you venture to a place you don't wish to go. But your heart calls for more, doesn't it my friend? It has been said that there is a greater calling for every person, yet the free will that is God's gift grants that anyone may choose *not* to follow that calling if he so wishes. The choice is yours. For it is true that many have chosen to follow their fears rather than their heart. You would not be the first.

"But if you ever decide to follow the small voice inside—the place from which I call—then know that I will stay with you for the entire journey. And although the road may become bumpy at times, as life often does, as we travel together you will come to know and love your true self such as never before. And I won't leave you; for is it not my job to be your guide in this life?"

Josie arose from the sofa and walked to the doorway. He wished to see the man who had spoken these words—words he would never forget. Josie wrapped both hands loosely around the steel and again pushed his face to the bars. There was no one; as he had known it would be. Only the meadow remained. At least the sound of birds was back. Josie stared ahead at the startling beauty and the image began to change, as did the sound. Colors swirled and ran together until finally fading into one solid wall of darkly stained wood shrouded in deep shadows. He listened then to the sound of a windless rain that fell gently upon the tin roof. Josie turned to see his wife still sleeping soundly under the patchwork quilt. He was awake now and, as it would for a long time, the dream haunted him.

Josie sat up and reached for his pants…then thought better of it. After another moment's thought he got to his feet and, still naked, left the bedroom, crossed the small living room, and opened the front door. Fresh air ran over his body; but it was only a light summer storm sent up from the south to bathe the mountains in warm tropical freshness. Josie stepped from the door and traversed the three steps that led first to the smooth concrete walkway, then to the pine needle carpet beyond. He was not cold. The rain bounced off his shoulders to trickle along his body while Josie listened to the soothing sound of drops as they hit the earth and trees. Once near the shoreline, he dropped to sit upon the dirt and lean against an oak tree. The ancient oak pressing against his back seemed almost as an old friend. Absently, he reached behind to stroke its rough surface.

    Josie looked across the calm black waters of Misty Lake. The far shore was a silhouette of trees against a dark, yet tranquil, canopy of clouds. To the east he could see the beginning of dawn's first light. The oak branches above held a million tiny leaves that let large drops fall upon his naked body as he watched gentle rain spatter across the water. Josie thought of the dream…of the meadow. It had been so beautiful, so alluring; it had taken his pain away. But now, as he looked across the small lake, Josie thought he saw something akin to the great meadow right here, right now. A thought occurred and Josie looked inside himself to find his pain gone! It had been replaced by only a relaxed sense of ease. He thought some more and realized that, as usual, it had been like this since their arrival in the mountains. He wished again that they would never go home. But one could not spend his entire life on vacation, could he? Would he return to the city? Of course he would. Responsibility demanded it.

    The rain had lessened to a drizzle and the sky was beginning to clear as early sunshine slowly overtook it.

    Josie's mind wandered back to the dream. What of the voice? Was it true? Did he create his own prison? But then, it was only a dream…or was it? Josie had never been one to remember his dreams. They came to him seldom and were usually vague and obscure, if not just plain weird. But this was so real, so startling, and so filled with truth…wasn't it? But it was *only* a dream after all.

    It was full light by the time Josie returned to the house. He went first to the bathroom to dry with a towel before returning to bed. Adrienne had not stirred. Josie slept soundly until 10 a.m.

    Vacation time passed, and the couple went home.

3

Dreams of abandoning all and returning to the mountains forever began to haunt the aging car salesmen and his wife. Of course, they would eventually retire there. But Misty offered no car-lots at which to apply. And even if he were to throw caution to the wind, and do so irresponsible a thing as to uproot his family and simply move (as Adrienne had repeatedly suggested), think of the consequences. They might starve! And surely there would be a need to reduce their belongings. Josie could not bear the thought of giving up the wonderful things they had worked so hard to acquire…of their good life in the city. What would become of him if he let go of this hard-earned security? Something terrible might happen! It was the unknown again and he simply could not go there.

Although Josie was not a religious man, he did believe in God. In conversation he had sometimes professed to have implicit trust in his guardian angels for, as can most anyone, Josie could easily recite a variety of life's incidents where some force beyond himself seemed to have been at work. Although Josie did trust in theory, real life was much too important to place in the hands of some mysterious myth. Although Josie talked of trusting God, what he really trusted was *money*; for it is not an easy proposal to truly trust something one cannot hold in the palm of his hand. Though he would never admit it, even to himself, the idea of truly trusting his Creator terrified Josie to the core of his being. Fear, it seemed, could be a very powerful master.

Josie and his wife began to concoct various ideas to conquer the many obstacles and maybe even escape into early retirement. *More money* seemed the most obvious answer as money could pay off mortgages, quell credit card debt, purchase early retirement, a cabin in the mountains, maybe even happiness—who knew? It was to this end that the most promising of plans were made.

Josie increased his hours at work. He also began to buy cars at auction, clean them up, and then sell them from his home through ads in the newspaper. His yard became occupied by the various automobiles that came and went.

A teacher's job can be very taxing, for in addition to a 40-

hour workweek there are always test preparations and grading that must be done at home and on the teacher's own time. As compensation, in years past Adrienne had always enjoyed the months of summer vacation when school was out. Now she began to take jobs teaching summer school as well. Adrienne did her part, and every little bit helped.

Their efforts brought in more cash.

As thoughts of the distant mountains again began to fade, the priorities of real life just seemed more important. It was in Josie's nature to care very much for the people he loved, and in his thoughtfulness the middle-aged father and husband had always wanted for the things that would make them happy. For his beautiful wife, a kitchen and bathroom remodel job had been purchased. It had been a two-month nightmare of trips to the temporarily overcrowded bathroom of Albert's house as the workers had ripped Josie's own shower and toilet from their pipes only to reinstall the large fiberglass shower and tub combination beside a modern sink and commode. The walls had been finished with beige wallpaper that depicted antiquated bathroom scenes above a floor now covered with deep red tile.

During that time Adrienne had sometimes cooked on the backyard's propane grill while the kitchen underwent a similar process; and Josie had grown sick of take-out pizza and Chinese. The kitchen job had brought even more inconvenience, especially with the daily routine of work and school that must carry on around it. But when finished the house offered both kitchen and bathroom as beautiful as any modern home could hope to achieve.

The effort to attain such luxury had seemed much greater than Josie or Adrienne had anticipated, and both still worked to pay the second mortgage required to fund these projects. But the workmen had done a fine job and Adrienne seemed quite pleased with the outcome.

For keeping her school grades up, Rachel was awarded a brand-new car upon the first day she earned a driver's license. Both Adrienne, and especially Josie, were delighted with their daughter's elation at this gift. A happy moment indeed. The exceptionally mobile family now owned three vehicles.

For Josie, it seemed a just reward that something be granted to enhance his hard-earned relaxation time. A fine home-entertainment system was soon purchased to replace the old; and although quite expensive, Josie felt no guilt. *Surely*, he thought, *this is a luxury I deserve.*

The rear patio was eventually finished, and it was a beautiful sight indeed. The new slab of concrete, nicely covered with indoor/outdoor carpet, now held a large round table and five chairs; all natural-wood-finished with thick varnish. Beside these stood an expensive propane grill and small refrigerator. All lay beneath a patio roof.

Adrienne had always enjoyed a seemingly natural love of botany and in her limited spare time she planted hedges along the wooden fence line. Other areas were filled with rose bushes and flowering plants that offered a riot of color when in bloom. The two orange trees she had planted years ago granted shade at either end. Neatly mowed grass connected it all. Adrienne insisted on watering by hand, and it was common to see her out tending her little piece of mother nature as Tetch, the shaggy family dog, kept watch from his lazy place upon the nearby carpet. As for the front-yard, Adrienne landscaped that too.

Over all, the new accommodations at Josie's were quite superior to the work done at Albert's house. Oh, there had been changes made to that old place, but most had been done by the residents themselves. Although always functional, most of these modifications and repairs seemed, to Josie, quite below standard. The nasty living room rug had been torn out, but unlike the new carpet Josie'd had professionally installed, Al and the boys had laid down inexpensive linoleum tile. Rather than replace an old toilet, water-heater or washing machine Albert usually just repaired them. Sure, his backyard now offered decent landscaping and an above-ground pool (tacky), but, although the patio roof had been shingled, no concrete slab was pored beneath it. In place of the old carpet previously covering the dirt, a deck had been constructed from recycled wood and only throw rugs covered its unpainted surface.

Josie sometimes felt a smug tinge of pride at his own obviously superior ability to meet the call and rise to a better life. Other times he wondered why Al had not utilized his own good credit for the funding necessary to make these changes properly. In the end, Josie chalked it up to the fact that the Mexicans had only one income since Maria spent most of her time with the children rather than take a day job as Adrienne had. Besides, Al only put in 40-hours a week—unlike Josie's 60 and sometimes 70—and surely the meager wage of a welder could not match the high commissions of a salesman. Poor Albert. But Al endured his lot proudly and Josie admired him for it.

  Then there was that nasty old Ford truck. Now there was a mystery. For although Al occasionally bought a rusty classic automobile which he and Oscar would fix up over the course of a year, he always sold the newly refurbished car and kept driving that goddamn truck! Why? How often Josie had offered a phenomenal deal on a good used ride, but Al always refused. Of what was he thinking?

  Once Josie had asked for the answer to this perplexity, but Albert had only offered two questions as answer. He had simply replied, "If I have all the things I need, and most of the things I want, then why would I want to get more?" and, "If something is working well for me then why would I want to replace it?"

  To both rather disturbing questions Josie had no answer.

  Josie often spent his days with a little cloud of seemingly endless problems hanging over his head and seldom noticed the generous quantities of laughter that could be heard within the walls of his neighbor's home. But he did see that Albert seldom, if ever, suffered pangs of depression, and for this Josie alternately envied, and sometimes almost hated the man. But at least, since the time of Josie's increased workload, he'd had little time to notice these episodes of despair. Workaholism; it seemed as good a therapy as any.

4

  Eventually, another mortgage was secured and a beautiful little fixer-upper purchased along the far shore of Misty Lake. Although many repairs would be needed to bring the house to standards, the place was what they could afford. But it did not matter, for plenty of time remained to make the needed repairs before the day of retirement arrived. Josie and Adrienne, both in their early 40s now, were ecstatic. The new cabin was affectionately named "Compensation".

The house was a cozy, two-story job, rectangular in shape and offering a small, single-car garage attached to its side. As was common in Misty, the roof was covered with dark-green corrugated metal from which protruded a chimney built of the same natural rock used in the fireplace below. The exterior walls were cedar siding painted a light brown that blended with the surrounding trees. Although three pines grew close to the house, the rest were back enough to allow the place its share of sunshine. A definite asset, for at this elevation the winter air could be quite crisp, and with the background of mountains and tall trees, dawn came later, and dusk earlier than in open lands.

Both front and rear entryways offered small wooden decks. The rear had five steps to the ground, then a short walk to the picturesque shoreline of Misty Lake and the home's little weather-beaten dock. The large front yard offered a dirt driveway covered with pine needles and a decaying cement birdbath at its center. Although quite rough, Josie could easily imagine the finished product. The driveway would be paved of course. Repair of the birdbath would bring pleasure to Adrienne as she watched summertime fowl splashing there. She would also see to landscaping and might even plant a garden. The two nearest houses stood some distance off and were mostly obscured by thick forest anyway.

To Josie, Compensation was a wonderland filled with only the things of his deepest desire. *Yes,* he thought, *with a little work….*

Misty was a sleepy un-crowded place with all its homes built some distance from each other and not a single yard was fenced. This openness brought a warm sense of ease and freedom to the area. Freedom! It was an idea—a very ideal—for which Josie's heart had come to cherish. For this single word would surely be his greatest reward; the light at the end of so long a tunnel. And with the purchase of this beautiful little house Josie could now not only imagine that light, he could see it with his own eyes! The reality brought a wealth of emotion and colorful fantasy.

Whenever time could be found, including the usual two-week

vacation, they visited the mountain to work on the new love nest, the place where they would spend their "golden years". The loan had allotted for some improvement money and new paint (the interior they did themselves), and electrical work was soon completed. The new carpet was placed on a credit card, as was the roof. New furniture would also be purchased. Everything had to be *just right*, for neither Josie nor Adrienne wished to screw up this hard-earned reward through negligence in preparation.

Parenting is an important responsibility and, knowing that the end of Rachel's youth was near, the couple wished to do more with her before this magic time vanished. Rachel, now a budding young woman, had acquired a love of water and often spent her free-time sunning, surfing, playing volleyball, and chasing boys at the nearby beach.

Her parents devised a plan.

Another loan was secured for the purchase of two Yamaha Wave Runners so the family could have more fun together. Besides, the now graying car-salesman had acquired a love of toys these days; for the tinkering with them offered some reward for the general monotony of his life. Josie lived, after all, mostly within the confines of a car lot.

Rachel loved her parents, dug the motorized water toys, and genuinely enjoyed family excursions to the ocean. But almost no young girl wants her parents present while engaged in teenage social duties. So, it did not bother Rachel that her folks seldom found the time or energy for beachside play. In the end, both wave runners spent most of their days in the garage beside three mountain bikes, two exercise machines, and a Harley Davidson motorcycle Josie had acquired as trade-in at the car lot. Then there were the boxes of other knick-knacks and toys seemingly too numerous to calculate.

Aside from the things Josie added to his plate voluntarily, there was also the everyday stuff that just came up. A vehicle broke down; a leaky faucet required a plumber; new school clothes; a check bounced unexpectedly; and there was Rachel's college education to consider. The list seemed endless.

The constant stress and pangs of emotional pain now dogged Josie daily and his dream of escape to the mountains escalated to a need. Yet for all his effort, the anticipated reward seemed no closer now than it had before. Sure, the couple earned a much larger income, but it seemed the more they made the more they spent. It was simply not enough. Redoubling his efforts, Josie threw himself harder into the job he was working so diligently to escape, but the effort extracted an alarming price both mentally and physically. The hard reality seemed to be that, in the name of a solution, increasing the quantity of that which was killing him only added more of the problem to the problem.

For the longest time Josie fought for his dream with admirable valor, but as the years passed, his efforts began to relax. He simply could not keep up the fight. One day, in a moment of defeat, Josie made the decision to accept his lot. And with this decision came relief. *Acceptance,* he thought, *that's the answer. After all, great dreams are for great people and I am only a common man.* But it did not take long for the ramifications of this decision to take root. For from that day forth, Josie spent his time as might a stallion with broken spirit. He only trudged from one day to the next, all the while hoping that something better waited on the other side. Depression continued to dog him. Josie developed an ulcer.

Again, the years passed…

5

Rachel knew not what she wanted to be when she grew up, but she did know that her folks believed in a formal education. Rachel also knew that a stint in college would offer opportunity to ride the parental dime a few more years therefore prolonging the dreaded plunge into the real world. After all, she had always liked school. It was a familiar place filled with friends and *boys*. Rachel had always earned good grades and was sure she could continue. For her parent's anxiety and pride at the coming of their little girl's ascension to impending adulthood, Rachel was sent off to a somewhat esteemed college.

Near the end of her second year Rachel met a boy and fell in love. Shortly thereafter she turned up pregnant. Rachel was elated at this new development, as was her guy, and they soon married.

It was an old story.

The courtship had been magical, but the first year of marriage seemed unusually trying. *Oh well,* Rachel thought, *everyone knows marriage isn't always easy. I'll try harder*. And she did. But in time things deteriorated and eventually the couple was divorced. Rachel's marriage had lasted only two years.

Josie reached the time of early retirement, but the relatively small pension was not enough to support their accustomed standard. Not knowing what else to do, Josie soon found himself at the front door of Central City Ford and was quickly hired on. It would be another 15-years before he would pull a second pension and put the car business behind him forever.

Adrienne made a similar move.

For some years Rachel lived alone in a small house with only her little boy as company. For Rachel it was enough, and although she dated on occasion, Rachel was a woman who genuinely enjoyed the trials and rewards of motherhood, and the men she met seemed only to complicate this.

Although her ex usually made good on his child support, it was not enough and Rachel took work with an insurance company. Her duties as secretary required only basic schooling. Although Rachel enjoyed the company of insurance salesmen almost as little as she did sitting behind a cluttered desk, she endured her lot valiantly. For had she not already seen that the way to make it in this world is to find something you hate doing, become good at it, then dedicate your life to it?

Eventually, Rachel would meet another guy. She would find Jim Stevenson genuinely kind and patient. For this, she would remarry then spend the remainder of her life in relative happiness with him.

As for Josie, early retirement was again considered; but the company had a sliding scale that offered a significantly larger sum if he waited until age 62. Adrienne's options differed very little. There was also an IRA account to consider. Besides, the couple wanted all their financial responsibilities and mortgages paid off completely before retirement. After all, surely there could be no bills in heaven. Yup, 62 was the magic number.

Yet, had Josie been honest with himself there would have been another truth to consider. Thus far he had been a consistent man, a responsible man, and through this stability Josie had also attained safety. Seldom had he found need to venture into the unknown and although he had often felt pain, Josie had rarely experienced fear and this single emotion was now so alien, that even a slight reference to it terrified him. No. Safety was his goal. After all, as he had often preached to his daughter, safety is certainly a responsible objective. In fantasy it might seem fine, but an *actual* move to Misty would change everything! Why, just the adjustment alone would be uncomfortable. New place…New friends…*New life*. Oh-my-god! What if it did not work out? There would no longer be a mental picture of paradise upon which to cling. Well, the time of reality was still some years off. Besides, maybe he could just keep getting ready forever. This was certainly a comfortable idea.

Along with the lines that crested more deeply into Josie's features with the passing of each year, his face had also become puffy beneath a rapidly receding hairline. His belly continued to grow as his ass shrunk and any vigorous exercise (a thing he seldom indulged in anymore) winded him quickly. Despite his best efforts at a controlled diet (generally weak and fleeting), Josie's stomach problems continued, and he became a Maalox junky. Arthritis had begun to creep into Josie's back and knees, and this condition was destined to slowly worsen for the duration of his life.

As for Adrienne, it seemed she would never lose her hourglass figure, but the years now marked her face, and the long dark hair offered streaks of gray.

Adrienne contracted high blood pressure.

Throughout her life Adrienne had sometimes been plagued with headaches, upset stomach, nausea, female ailments and, or, whatever cold or flu might be going around. Josie had long ago concluded that his wife had simply been born with a weak constitution. In times past this had been only a minor inconvenience, but in recent years the condition had grown steadily worse. Now it could bring cause for serious concern at times.

Although born with perfect vision, both required glasses to read.

Time carried on.

6

    The age of 50 had come and gone and as Josie peaked 60 an ancient truth settled. He was becoming an old man! Time was growing short—he could see that now. The time had finally come to reap his hard-earned reward, for if he waited longer they might plant him before his chance! Josie began to fear this even more than the change. But once the decision had been made the aging car salesman became excited. As the day of retirement drew near, it was with a frenzied anxiety that Josie began the final preparations. After all, at his age retirement was certainly the responsible thing to do. Besides, with all the years of preparation, the outcome was most certainly set and therefore safe.
    It was time.
    Originally purchased with only the needs of two retirees in mind, the cabin in Misty was much smaller than their place in the city. The city-house however, was practically overflowing with those wonderful things collected over the course of a lifetime. Now necessity demanded many be liquidated. Both Josie and Adrienne were livid at this thought. So much of their lives were stored in the garage, the attic, closets, drawers, cabinets, two plastic sheds in the backyard, and even those things that hung upon the walls of the house itself. No. The thinning of worldly possessions was not an appealing prospect. Yet, had Adrienne gotten her way in the first place this would have happened long ago, for she had always cared little for the city and wished to leave it since the days of girlhood. So, it was Adrienne who took the lead.
    Feeling that in this way she could eliminate things without actually giving them up, Adrienne loaded her daughter with everything that could possibly be heaped upon the girl. She did the same for Nancy, who's own two children were now teenagers, and also Maria, who still remained a good friend. Next, she held repeated garage sales; and even though the original price of her wonderful things had soared into the thousands, Adrienne now turned a modest profit of only several hundred dollars. But it no longer mattered, for

the object of her labor was to get rid of, rather than rich from, the selling of these items. For with the sale of the house, their pensions check, plus prudent saving and long-term investments, the couple would enjoy all the money two old people could hope to need.

For the things that were just too cherished to *ever* let go, a storage unit was rented so this special stuff might be neatly stored in a secure place until sometime probably after they were dead.

As the two watched the very material of their lives disappear, the reality of what was happening set in. Life as they had always known it was over. A chapter was about to end. Oh-my-god! But within the torrid emotions brought about by this event there was one feeling that surfaced to stand paramount against all others— excitement! After all these years they were actually going to do it! Oh-my-god!

Eventually a moving company was hired and those things that remained were packed off to Compensation. Not since the day they had first set eyes upon the city house some 40 years ago had it seemed so empty…so lifeless. It felt as though the couple was abandoning a huge part of themselves.

The place was put on the market and soon sold at a handsome profit. There was no turning back.

For retirement Josie kept only one car, a four-wheel-drive utility vehicle—a mountain car! Since he and Adrienne were now *unemployed* (he could no longer say the word without a giddy grin) there would no longer be need of multiple vehicles. The Jeep was a deep blue, it was new, it was paid for, and Josie hoped this would be the last car they ever owned; for he was so sick of dealing with fucking cars.

From the small, quiet road Josie pulled the Jeep onto the new pavement that capped the driveway of their little slice of heaven. He reached for the key and killed the motor. "Well baby, this is it" he smiled onto the wrinkled face seeing only the beauty of one who had stood beside him through all it had taken to achieve this moment.

"I can hardly believe it!" she grinned back as the light of a younger girl glittered through blue eyes.

Although both had seen the place a hundred times, today seemed much different; for from this day forth there would be no returning to the city for anything beyond short visits. They were home! Josie appraised the place through new and wondrous eyes. He was about to embark upon an entirely different journey. A new life! The old Josie was dead—what would the new Josie be like? Reality gripped him; excitement aroused him.

With a desire to enter through the front door rather than garage, Josie parked in the driveway of Compensation. After retrieving his cane from the back seat, he and Adrienne stepped out. The early Autumn air was crisp, clean, and a bit chilly. *Spring*, Josie thought, *the perfect time to start a new life.*

And with that, momentarily ignoring the pain in his back and knees, Josie carried his wife across the threshold.

For a long time, the couple reveled in the bliss of life on permanent vacation. They ate at least one meal out almost every day, fished until the baiting of a hook seemed almost monotonous; rented movies, took long drives, and walked as many trails as ailments would permit. Numerous friendships tightened and just as many began anew. Sometimes they visited people's homes, parties, and other social gatherings. But more often they frequented "Timber's Bar and Eatery" where, after dinner and a few drinks, the two would fall into lively conversation with some of their jovial and often half-lit friends. Oh yes, they'd talk it up, dance to the country tunes of "Bobby and The Barflys" or some other local band, then return to the table and talk it up some more. They could stay out all night if they wanted, then sleep till noon the following day! Oh, the freedom! Retirement was such a wonderful thing.

So, they slept late, ate out, walked, fished, partied, rented movies, and took Sunday drives. After that they slept late, ate out, walked, fished, partied, rented movies, and took Sunday drives. When this was done, they would sleep late, eat out, walk, fish, party, rent movies, and take Sunday drives.

Under this prescription for easy living Josie's stomach problems faded into oblivion, as did the ache in his lower back—at least to a large degree. The pain in his knees continued.

It had been a concern that the moderate mountain altitude (just over 4.000 feet) would adversely affect Adrienne's blood pressure and the drugs previously prescribed would no longer be effective, though they had offered only limited effectiveness to begin with. But it was found, to Josie's relief, that although the altitude brought her blood pressure up, the ease and richness of mountain life brought it down again. And although her occasional bouts of sickness still came and went, in the end Adrienne's blood pressure stayed about the same.

For both Josie and Adrienne, the severity of these afflictions varied from day to day and activities were often limited to how either was feeling. And although there were many good days when ailments abated in unison, there were just as many when they did not.

Josie began to wonder if the end of one's life was perhaps not the best time to *start living.*

The warm days of summer passed like a pleasant dream into the chill of fall.

Although Compensation offered an efficient forced-air heating system, Josie began to keep a hardy blaze going in the living-room fireplace. After all, when the two cords of oak that waited under a tarp alongside the house were depleted, he would buy more from a firewood business run by two local brothers. It was now true that he and Adrienne could afford the luxury of whatever they wanted.

Josie often sat upon the cushy deep-green sofa and gazed silently into the natural-rock fireplace. The ancient flames that licked skyward before turning magically into smoke always mesmerized his mind, and called almost violently to something seemingly primordial within him. Before long, this activity became a thing he could no longer imagine living without.

But the cold of winter limited the small cycle of activities they so enjoyed. Besides, and although he was not yet ready to admit it, Josie had grown weary of *life on permanent vacation.* It had been only nine short months since their arrival and already he was beginning to suffer feelings of idle uselessness and an unnerving lack of purpose. Boredom! He had never contemplated the idea that retirement could be boring. Always Josie had fantasized only of release from a life that required constant toil.

Josie's archenemy "depression" came to Misty. He was crushed. Never before had this demon tormented him here. *Oh-my-god*, he thought, *Will I truly be made to suffer the remainder of my existence even while surrounded with the perfect nirvana I've worked so hard to achieve? Is there no justice?* To the best of his knowledge, he had done everything expected of him. Everything responsible…everything right! What more did God want? Fear gripped him. Soon this fear grew into a seething hate. Josie turned his wrath to the heavens then, and in his loath and confusion he cursed the heathen God he had begun to barely believe in anymore.

7

Springtime came again and with its warmer days the squirrels returned, as did the tourists. Although the early spring air was still cool, bright sunshine again beamed through the trees to create an atmosphere of clean, sweet smelling mountain freshness.

Even though his knees had complained of it often, winter, with its bitter cold and occasional snowstorms, had been a new and exciting experience for Josie. But the novelty had soon worn off as the cold days dragged on, and now he was simply glad to see such a magnificent spring morning. So, it was with a notably happy face that Josie piloted the Jeep into town. Upon the passenger's seat sat the short shopping-list Adrienne had given him.

After parking the Jeep in the familiar lot, Josie ambled busily into McGregor's Grocery. It was mid-morning and, except for a single patron who stood in an isle of canned goods, and Pat McGregor at the register, the place was empty. After gathering the things he had come for into a plastic hand-basket, Josie approached the checkout counter. "Mornin' Josie," Pat said, "How's the misses today?"

Josie contemplated the guy. He was a thin man of medium height with mostly gray hair and a twinkle of kindness in his eye. "Mornin' Pat," Josie set his basket on the wooden counter, "She's hangin' pretty well. How's things at your place?" Josie knew that Pat's 22-year-old son Buddy, afflicted with Downs Syndrome, still lived at home. The boy could be a handful at times.

"Same as always Josie," Pat began taking things from the basket then ringing them up manually because the counter offered no automatic scanner, "You know, same shit different day." Josie cringed at that statement. He had grown to hate it long ago. "Hey Josie, you know Edith moved off the mountain," The old woman had worked at McGregor's seemingly forever, "Said she wasn't staying here one more stinkin' winter. Anyway, I find myself shorthanded and it seems like everyone I talk too around here's busy lately. Couldn't use a little work, could you? I mean, I know you have some time on your hands. What-do-ya-say?"

Josie's head bounced up and he stared into Pat's hazel eyes. Surly the man could not be serious. He was retired! Why in the hell would he want to work? But Pat's steady gaze said that he *was* serious. Josie opened his mouth to say no—then closed it again. Maybe he should think about this. Things had, after all, been a little stagnant lately.

Seeing his hesitation, Pat elaborated, "All you'd mostly have to do is sit behind the counter and take people's money. A few days a week would be fine." Josie still seemed unsure, so Pat continued, "You know I'm flexible Josie. There's a phone so you and the Missus won't be out of touch. The money's not great, but the work's good. Mostly you just sit around and shoot the breeze with people all day, then take their money. I know you enjoy talking to folks Josie, and sooner or later everyone in town passes through here. The social aspect's great…really keeps a person in touch," Pat's talk trailed off and he waited for a reply.

When a long moment had passed Josie said, "Okay if I mull it over till tomorrow?"

"That'd be fine." Pat scribbled something on the side of Josie's paper grocery bag. "That's my home phone plus the number here. Let me know soon as you can." Pat pushed a final button on the antiquated cash box and the money drawer popped opened with a *ching*. "That'll be twelve dollars and eighty-six cents."

The next day Josie gave his answer and the following morning the retired car salesman started his new career as grocery clerk.

The awkwardness of this new job passed quickly, and the inside of McGregor's soon became comfortable as an old shoe. People came and went. The locals said "Hi", and when things were slow some lingered to talk a while. On his breaks Josie often sat just outside the swinging glass doors and watched with real interest as the world, its people, and its life, passed before his attentive eyes. Even some of the tourists were interesting. Sometimes a man would stop and talk of his life beyond the mountains and Josie would remember. But always they talked of how beautiful Misty was and how lucky he was to live here.

It was true what Pat had said about the social aspect, and it had always been a seemingly natural attribute of Josie's nature to care for the people he loved or called friend. Besides, Josie felt productive again; and usefulness is a thing that holds great importance too many a human spirit—even if that spirit resides within the body of an old man.

It was six weeks later that Adrienne also accepted part time employment. Her duties were as helper at Helen's nursery. The only business of its kind on the mountain, Helen catered to local landscaping companies and those of surrounding communities as well as anyone who kept a garden or loved houseplants. As did most everyone, Helen loved Adrienne's outgoing personality and genuinely enjoyed having her around. Helen knew this woman, who was 20-years her senior, came retired and with a few health issues, so she cut the lady some slack. Besides, the pay was low enough to warrant a loose work atmosphere—which was how Helen liked it anyway. So, the job offered even more flexibility than Josie's, and Adrienne could always get time off with a quick phone call. But she seldom did, for Adrienne, enjoyed the caring-for, transplanting, trimming, etc. that the job required. There had always been something about working her own hands into the dirt that brought a sense of ease and satisfaction.

Seasons passed. Rachel came to visit from time to time and on occasion her parents made short jaunts to the city. Alberto had retired some years ago but harbored no intention of leaving his city home. Although his kids were grown and gone, they visited constantly. Josie noted that Al seemed happy amid his family and the many projects that still passed through the garage. But the city still grated on Josie's nerves and it was never more than a week before he longed for the return to Misty. For Adrienne it was the same.

Misty was their home now.

But for Josie, although the mountains certainly offered a greater quality of life, the pangs of depression still came and went.

For there had always been something fundamentally wrong with his life—he knew. Misty had not changed this. And as he had done before, again Josie accepted his lot as best he could, always hoping that something better awaited on the other side.

Three years had come and gone since the move to Misty.

8

It was December again. Christmas had just passed, and New Year's was only a few days away. Outside, the ground lay frozen amid the occasional tufts of week-old snow. Although only a few inches had fallen, it had been a white Christmas after all. Dressed in his new Santa Claus pajamas, and with bare feet crossed atop the low coffee table, Josie relaxed into his cushy sofa. With a steaming mug of coffee held in both hands he watched morning news on the big-screen which sat atop its polished-oak stand beside the fireplace. Large flames crackled from behind the spark-screen as warm air pored into the room. In the kitchen, Adrienne was busy whipping up a special breakfast of vegetarian omelets with Swiss cheese. Josie's favorite.

As Adrienne worked, she stopped occasionally to admire the new diamond recently set into her 45-year-old wedding ring. Although she seldom took the thing off, on one of the rare occasions when she had some three weeks ago, the ring had disappeared and, after secretly searching everywhere, she'd been forced to accept that it was gone. Then, on Christmas morning, Josie had presented her with a big box that rattled loudly when she had shaken it. Adrienne had opened the box to find a smaller one packed inside amid wadded newspaper. But the smaller box had contained nothing more that an old rock that produced a rattling sound when shaken. She had turned bewildered old eyes into his laughing ones then, but before she'd had time to speak, he said, "Look closer." So, after riffling farther through the newspaper, she had finally found the tiny box that contained her ring. Her delight upon seeing it again had filled the room with such a radiance that Josie's heart actually skipped a beat. But the ring was different now. Originally, it had been a simple platinum band with nine tiny diamond chips laid flush into its surface. But the diamond chips had been moved aside and a much larger diamond set between them now. Josie assured her that, aside from the new diamond, it was still the exact same ring. It seemed to Adrienne like a thing that should have accommodated their anniversary rather than Christmas, but she knew how unpredictable Josie could be about such things. And she did not care, for to her this gesture said that, after 45-years, he would marry her all over again. After putting the ring on she threw herself at him, knocked him onto the couch, and showered his face with sloppy kisses.

 Afterword's, when Adrienne had asked the significance of one large diamond being set between nine smaller ones, he had said it was because she was the best of nine. "Nine what?" she had questioned. And he had laughingly begun to recite the names of nine imaginary high school girlfriends. She had hit him with a couch-pillow and said, "Watch it old man or you might not get anymore pussy for the rest of your natural life!" But he had taken her to the bedroom just the same.

 With one savory plate held in each hand, Adrienne made her way from kitchen to living room so they might shut off the television and eat before the crackling fire. Josie would insist.

 Josie heard the crash of breaking dishes and, as he opened his mouth to offer comment of his wife's clumsiness, he heard a thud. This second sound was wrong, and a strange fear gripped him. Turning his head, Josie saw this instinct was correct, for there on the floor amid the slop of wasted food and broken china Adrienne lay face down with her long gray hair fanning in all directions.

 Fear gripped him! Josie leapt to his feet and ran to her. Kneeling at Adrienne's side he first checked for a pulse and was relieved to find one. Josie called to her but got no response. Tears ran freely from old eyes as he tried again—Still nothing. Rolling her over, he looked concernedly into Adrienne's face, but what he saw only disturbed him more. She was not unconscious, nor was she coherent. Adrienne's eyes rolled continuously back and forth seemingly unable to focus upon anything. Her mouth hung open and drool ran from one corner. "Oh-my-god!" he cried—almost whined.

 For a second fear overwhelmed him and Josie froze. An icy

calm befell him then—it was a reaction that had always come naturally to him in times of crises. All emotion receded as only a crystal-clarity of logical thought beset. Overriding all else, this instinct took control. Josie checked for breath—it was there. He walked to the phone and dialed 911. An ambulance was immediately dispatched from Mountain's Community Hospital. It was not far.

Josie laid Adrienne's body flat, then knelt beside to watch and wait. If her breathing stopped, he would perform CPR. But if she should die today, it also seemed of paramount importance, that he be there for those last breaths; that he might have stayed with her to the final end.

A degree of emotion abruptly returned, and he reached to brush the hair from her face. Josie ran one palm gently over Adrienne's cheek as he started to speak. In a surprisingly calm tone, he began to proclaim his love for her. He talked of all the warm days together and the wonderful ways in which she had brought such happiness to his life. Josie's voice cracked as he begged her not to die—his tears fell profusely. He said that she was the only one for him and that if she had to go, he would never, he promised, take another. Josie was sobbing uncontrollably now and, no longer able to speak, he simply took her hand in his own, hung his head over her chest, and cried shamelessly as his body shuddered in uncontrollable fits.

He heard the sirens then, but still did not leave her. When the paramedics knocked, Josie yelled for them to enter. As they approached, logic returned and Josie backed away to let the professionals do their job. As if in a dream he watched the men give oxygen, start an IV, and then lift the old woman onto a stretcher.

After being stabilized Adrienne was life-flighted to the nearest big city hospital as Mountain's Community was ill equipped to handle an emergency of such magnitude.

Adrienne had suffered a massive stroke.

Five weeks later Adrienne was released from the hospital and returned home in a wheelchair. Her left side was mostly paralyzed, and overall motor-skills were dishearteningly retarded. Immediately Josie had a wheelchair ramp added to the front porch and the bed moved downstairs that the couple might sleep in the den. The upper floor would seldom see use again. In times past Adrienne had always rejected the idea of hiring household help. Her home was her own and the care of it, and her man, had always brought a sense of usefulness. Now Josie hired a girl to keep up the chores and help with his handicapped wife.

When Adrienne had been lifted into the ambulance Josie had pleaded with God to let her live, but now that she had he began to feel like an ingrate. *"How could I have complained so about the things that are wrong in my life while forsaking those I've been blessed with?"* he thought. For a time, Josie again made peace with his Creator.

Although Adrienne's rehabilitation was slow, progress was made and in time a measure of clarity returned to the old eyes and speech became less slurred. In the Spring, Josie sometimes wheeled his wife onto the back porch that they might sit together and watch over the calm waters that lapped against the tranquil shores of their mountain paradise. On other occasions, when his own body permitted, the couple again took walks along the small country roads and Josie sometimes thought of what a sad affair it is to push the one you love through heaven in a wheelchair. They still fished, but Adrienne only sat on the dock to offer words of encouragement as Josie threw his line into the lake. Oh, she sounded optimistic enough, but Josie knew that, deep inside, the feisty spirit that had always driven this previously active woman suffered immensely in the face of such convalescence. But she never spoke of it…and he never brought it up.

Two years passed, and although Adrienne would never again be more than a shadow of her former self, she did regain the ability to walk (although shakily) and, to some extent, even take care of herself.

9

It was yet another winter morning as, sitting up to the mattress's edge, Josie placed his feet into furry slippers then paused to let sleep's gentle fog fade from his head. When the moment had passed, he turned sleepy eyes to regard the place upon which Adrienne slept at his side. She lay silently upon her back with gray hair cascading across the pillow. Something was wrong. As he looked closer the remainder of sleep's fog vanished in a rush. And he knew.

Adrienne was dead.

Putting one gnarled hand to her face he found the skin cold. He checked for a pulse—there was none. Sitting back slowly, Josie let out a muffled sigh. It was a kind of sound that cut to the very core of human agony.

She was gone. He was alone.

A sort of numbing calm settled upon him then and Josie arose and walked to the kitchen. When he returned, Josie positioned himself on the bed to sit against the headboard with forearms resting atop bent knees as he sipped slowly from the coffee cup held in both hands. Seeing nothing, his blank stare reached uselessly to the wall. For a long time, he stayed like that.

Eventually his eyes shifted to the face of his dead wife. Josie stifled a sob. When the moment had passed, he set the cup down and crawled beneath the sheets. Scooting to Adrienne's body, he reached to pull her close. He laid her head upon his chest and began to rock gently. "I'm gonna miss you so…" and his voice trailed off as the old man fell to an almost violent fit of weeping.

It was the saddest moment of Josie's life.

When a long time had passed, he placed her again as she had lain before and returned to his own side of the bed. Josie reached for his cup. But before the mug had touched his lips Josie's features contorted into a mask of rage and he threw the cup hard against the wall. Josie turned his wrath to the heavens as he rose to bent knees and threw one angry fist into the air. He yelled to the heathen entity that most assuredly presides over this back-assed world, **"Fuck you God…you cock-sucker! You can take this sick-assed world and shove it right up your fucking ass! There was a time when I thought you might be on my side, but I see now just what a dumb-ass wet-dream that was. Never again will I pay recognition of any kind to such a cruel and unjust motherfucker as you!"** And he meant it.

When he had finally screamed himself out, Josie sat again at the bed's edge and hung his balding, gray head into big hands. When ten minutes had passed, he arose and walked to the rear porch to gaze solemnly across the water. For the morning's remainder Josie called no one. He moped around the house, often returning to the bed. He talked to her, for Josie had hoped that, at least for a little while longer, it might be his final chance to spend time with his wife. But in the end, reality could not be breached—she was gone, and nothing could bring her back.

Finally, Josie went to the phone and called Rachel. His daughter left for the mountains immediately. Next Josie called the coroner's office.

The doctor said Adrienne had died of an aneurysm, but Josie believed only that the previously active woman simply could not go on living that way. No. She had died of a broken spirit. That was for sure. For this single added insult to his already troubled and often unsatisfied life he would never forget…and never forgive…God.

She was laid to rest on a Tuesday beneath the shade of an old oak tree at the Misty Hills cemetery. All of his family and, of course, Al and Maria (both now in their 80s), Nancy, and the boys were there on that cold yet sunny winter day. Much of the population of Misty was in attendance as well.

It was an impressive turnout.

Josie cried silently as they lowered the casket into the ground and this time there was nothing *Albert* could do but share his friend's pain.

Rachel came to visit her father more often and, taking note of his desperate plunge into depression, repeatedly implored him to come live with her. But he would not. Josie had worked hard for this place and would remain here until the day they finally planted him beside his wife.

Josie continued through the pain of Misty. Although the mountains would always remain dear to him, no longer did they represent heaven. The last flicker of that idea had died with Adrienne; for to him heaven could not exist without her.

Josie became a bitter old man. Children avoided him, as did many adults. Oh, there were those sympathetic to his lot, but in time his crabby attitude and sometimes cruel comments pushed even them away. 'I know it hurts Josie, but you're not the only one to ever endure a thing like this. You still have friends, family, and community. For Christ's sake, *move on man,*' became a common attitude.

But Josie did *not* move on.

In the end he too died in sleep, a bitter and often reclusive old man.

THE MEADOW
Chapter 8

1

Again, Josie found himself in the meadow. Soon he was sitting against the old oak quietly gazing beyond the trickling creek waters to the gentle foliage and strong forest that lay beyond. He seemed lost in sullen thought. A blue jay called from somewhere and Josie thought of how, even in Misty, he had always hated the high-pitched squawk of those damn birds. In a moment he heard a question. "Well Josie," the familiar voice brought no comfort today, "how was your experience?"

"What about my wife God?" Josie scowled. He seemed unaware of God's inquiry.

God's slight smile strained for a moment before the corners of his mouth turned down. He knew of Josie's great love for the woman, just as he knew of their toils together. But the smile soon returned as he said, "Don't sweat it too much Josie. You'll see her again very soon."

Josie's gaze shot up into the beautiful eyes of God. "You promise?" he said.

"I promise. And I'll do you one even better than that; for the next time you see her she'll be in perfect health. Will that be acceptable?"

Would God lie? Of course not. God did not lie. Despite his seething anger, Josie let out a long breath and his face relaxed visibly. "Thank you," the words came as a whisper.

Leaning back against the old oak, God turned his attention into the distance. Josie was grateful for the lull in conversation for he needed a moment with his thoughts. As for God…well…he had all the time in the world. And the gentle breeze that blew silently through the tall grass tugged affectionately at Josie's hair. For a time, all the world seemed calm and contented.

Josie barely noticed.

And again, the question came, "Well Josie, how was your experience?"

Slowly Josie drew the whole of his beaten spirit and angry gaze from the meadow and again turned to stare into the crystal blue eyes of God. He had long ago begun to wonder if this man was his friend. Still, since he was, after all, talking to God it only seemed right that he be honest. Josie lingered for only a moment before he began, "Well God…you know…I didn't get to do all the things I'd hoped for. And the endless toil for money just seemed like a lifelong prison sentence." Yes! Already it felt good just to say it. Besides God deserved to hear of all the trouble he had caused. "I mean, that screwed up job was such a nightmare, and it was almost impossible to get out of that damned city," the words came easier now, "I didn't get to catch nearly enough fish…or see enough sunsets…or take enough walks with my wife; she always loved that you know. And no matter how hard I worked it always seemed there was one more thing that needed to be done…something always came up. It was near impossible to get ahead, and it often took years! Yeah God, mostly I just worked a lot. It all just seemed like one big endless *grind*. Why'd you make it so hard?"

God's eyes twinkled with amusement as he listened. "You know Josie," he began, "I gave you the moon and the stars. The mountains, deserts, forests, and beaches. Beauty beyond compare…at least I like to think so. I gave you good health. I gave you as much intelligence as the next man. I put you in a place where you had the opportunity and freedom to go, be, and do, anything you wanted—anything at all! I gave you the best of all that is mine to give, and that's what you did with it? Why'd *you* make it so hard my friend?"

Josie opened his mouth to speak, then, realizing he had yet no words, shut it again. It all sounded real poetic he had to admit, but what a crock! He had just blamed God for an unsatisfactory life of toil and monotony and God had only returned the ball with a point-blank statement that this was only the road that Josie *himself* had chosen! How absurd. How infuriatingly ridiculous! "But God, if there really had been a choice, don't you think I'd have chosen it? I mean, don't try to pin this thing on me man. The stinkin' world was your idea after all. I don't know…"

"Remember the dream?"

Josie's jaw hung in mid sentence. He closed it. Josie's eyes left the other man's and dropped to the ground. *What dream? Oh…that dream.* He had not thought of it in years. Of course, he remembered it. It had haunted him for longer than he cared to remember. Josie thought of it again now. And the seconds seemed to pass slowly as he worked to file this information into some manner of sensible logic. It would require more time. "But God," the words ran from his mouth before he'd had time to check them, "what in the hell was all that fucked up depression about!" Immediately Josie cringed at the sound of his own voice. How could he have said such a thing in the presence of the Almighty himself? In the forthcoming moment of horror and shame Josie's anger abated and he actually forgot the question he had just asked.

But God did not forget; for always he appreciated truth above sugarcoated lies fabricated to mask insincerity and fear. For in the light of a child's spirit, education, and well-being, language itself meant even less than nothing. Besides, Josie had a perfect right to express himself if he were angry. So, God only offered his young friend an approving smile. It seemed such a small gesture, but with it came a great sense of relief for Josie saw that he might exercise the freedom to be only and completely himself whenever in the company of his Creator. Josie relaxed visibly, as God had known he would.

God began to speak, "Depression may result from any number of causes Josie, and the ways an individual reacts may vary just as widely. But for now, let's have a look at one common circumstance, shall we?"

Josie's nod was almost imperceptible.

"All the world's a spiritual experience my friend, and the body, mind, and spirit are far more connected than one might think. Ever notice the way you feel when the alarm clock hits you like a bullhorn early in the morning and you know you've gotta get up to go do something you really don't want to? Like a job you can't stand, or a life you're unhappy with. For all the times you hit that snooze button you can still hardly drag your ragged ass outta bed. It is compared to administering a small dose of poison to the spirit Josie, and if this ritual is repeated with regularity poison levels increase and the spirit will, of course, become dull and lifeless. It will wither and begin to die. How could it do anything else? Since the two are very much connected, the body will soon follow. As energy levels drop, sometimes dramatically, life will begin to seem futile and even useless. Under this circumstance a person may grow listless, bitter, angry and, of course, *depressed*. Often, rather than expend the necessary energy, or face the fear of a dramatic change, a person may just resign himself to his lot and muddle through as best as he can, all the while hoping something better waits on death's other side. As mid to later life approaches, the likelihood of acquiring any number of diseases, both mental and physical, is increased tenfold. How could it not? For neither the mind nor body have much to live for anyway.

"Now tell me where you find my fault in any of this?"

Josie shrugged. He had no answer.

In a moment God's easy manner resumed, "Now let's take this same scenario again. The alarm clock blasts you at some unholy hour of the morning. Difference is, this time you're getting up to do something you really like—to meet a life or a job you truly love. Maybe you're going to the mountains, fishing, a skiing trip, bicycling, spending time with friends or family. Could be something so simple as a long hike with your spouse, walking the dog, or even a few unfettered hours of working in your garden—**who cares**, so long as it's a thing in which your passion lies. Today that ol' alarm just doesn't seem so bad now does it? Hell, you probably don't even need it. You might already be up. You feel good, excited, and you're ready to go. Am I right?"

Josie nodded. It was a truth no one could deny.

God continued, "This, my friend, is as nourishment to the spirit. And just as poison will cause the body and spirit to become dull and lifeless, so then will nourishment bring about color and passion. The body's energy levels will rise—how could they not? Life will become a thing built mostly of pleasure and interest. In time a deep clarity-of-thought will often befall. With the tools of more energy and a mind now awake and hitting on all cylinders it will become much easier to do more, or even less, in this world depending upon the call of the individual heart's-desire. At this point that person may find that they've become something, or someone, they *truly* like. Maybe even their favorite person. Others will sense this and become attracted to them. Sounds pretty far out, huh? Well, to those who reside beyond the Pearly Gates Josie, this is very old news."

God grew quiet then as he relaxed against the old oak to turn his gaze back across the meadow and allow Josie a moment to digest all he had just heard.

But it was not really necessary, for to Josie the message seemed quite clear. So clear in fact that it pissed him off. For this meant that he himself had been the cause of his own troubles in life. So, he said in defense, "What about all my daily responsibilities? What would've happened had I neglected them? Hell, I'd have lost everything…become *destitute*."

Again, God turned his magnificent eyes into those of his friend. An amused smile furrowed the contours of his face and he said, "Destitute huh? So often when you look into your past you see that I've been with you all along don't you? But when you imagine your future Josie, I'm not there."

God's expression changed then, and he became more serious, "So then tell me my friend…did you really need all the things you worked so hard to get? Do you have them now? And do they still seem so important? Did you ever consider trading some, or even many, of the things you didn't really need for things, or times, you'd really enjoy? Besides Josie, when you think about it, going out to enjoy the life I've given you is probably one of the most responsible things you can do…and the greatest gift you can give me in return."

Trade his hard-earned stuff? The idea still somehow offended him. But it was true; for all his life's toil he had nothing to show for it now. In fact, it felt as though he had even less than nothing.

Though the heat of his argument was beginning to run thin, Josie still felt compelled to take another stab at it. "But what about Rachel," his tone carried less anger now. God would probably only offer another irrefutable rebuttal anyway. "Parenting is a big responsibility you know…" Josie's voice trailed off.

God's response came quickly, "Throughout history kids have most often lived under far more primitive circumstances than your own. Now I'm not suggesting you raise your child in a cave, but don't you agree that a happier home and more time spent with frequently joyful parents who like to do fun stuff can go a long way to help dispel a lack of computer games, big screen TVs, high dollar tennis shoes, or even an extravagant house? I mean, who's been suggesting you need all that stuff anyway—the people who want to sell it to you?"

Josie opened his mouth to rebut…then closed it again. That was a hard one to argue. In a moment another thought came, "But God, if I hadn't worked so hard to look out for her future then…"

"…Then what?" the Almighty interrupted, "Your effort has been of notable consequence to Rachel Josie. Truly it has. But let us remember that God has no grandchildren. And although she loves you, the guidance of Rachel's journey is far more my responsibility than it is yours. Let's not forget that you are not the only one who loves her."

Josie had not previously thought of this. He did now, and it made sense.

Josie said nothing more. His argument was beaten. It seemed clear that he was, after all, the only one to blame for his life's failings. His guts twisted at the way he had let himself and his family down. Josie felt hot tears begin to well behind his lids.

Once again God regarded him with that easy gaze as he said, "You know, I've had this same conversation with almost all who have come to talk with me over the millennia Josie. Don't worry about it man. You're right on schedule and I'm *very* proud of you," and with that he offered a bright smile.

Josie's spirits lightened. Being confused and unsure as to the ramifications of all this, Josie took simple comfort in the idea that God did know and, moreover, he seemed pleased.

God pulled a long weed from the ground and regarded it thoughtfully before placing one end between his teeth. The old oak held firmly from behind as he rested with legs outstretched and hands folded into his lap. After a moment God bent one knee to set his elbow atop that he might face more in Josie's direction. Again, he began to speak, "You know Josie, a very important part of your job in life is simply to go out and enjoy yourself; to play amid the wonders of the world. To find the things you love doing, then do them. To follow the calling of your own spirit; for in the end it is only there that you will ultimately find *yourself*."

"But," Josie rebutted with some frustration, "I have no idea what these things of which you speak are."

"Did you ever take the time to seek them?"

"Mostly I just worked a lot…remember?"

"Well, not to worry; in time you'll get a good grip on this one—I promise. Besides, I think you have some idea already."

After a moment's pause, God continued, "If a chunk of your job is to enjoy yourself, then as well a part of mine is to supply *all* you need to make this happen and oversee the journey as well. I drive the car; you sit back and enjoy the ride. And Josie…"

"Huh?"

"You do trust my driving, don't you?"

"I don't know. I've never seen you drive. Do you even have any roads around here?" In spite of himself Josie could not contain a rather stupid grin.

With feigned indigence God placed one hand over his chest and cried, "What, you think that I, the God of All Creation, needs driving lessons? Who's gonna give them to me? Could you suggest a good driving-school?" and with that both men broke into small fits of hilarity.

The laughter lasted a long time, and when it had subsided the mood seemed very much relaxed, and the air was somehow lighter.

2

In a moment God raised one arm and pointed to a large bird that seemed to float upon the wind some few hundred feet into the distance. "You see that Josie?"

"Yeah."

"Look close. See the white coloring around his head and tail? It's a bald eagle. Look even closer and you'll see a gopher clutched in his talons." Josie strained his eyes across the bright sky. "They have a nest in the top of that tree. Eagles mate for life you know, and he's returning home with food for the two chicks that await him. Their mother will be along in a few minutes, I'm sure."

With keen interest Josie watched as the magnificent bird

approached its destination. Yes! He could see the nest now. Even from this distance it seemed huge when compared to the twiggy homes of smaller birds. There were few twigs here, for this nest was made almost entirely of larger sticks and branches. He marveled at its construction. But Josie saw no movement there. Slowly now, wingtips twitching here, and making slight adjustment there, the great bird glided to land upon the nest's rim. Instantly, two little heads were up and raising a fuss. Although Josie could not make out their mouths from this distance, he was sure they were open and begging belligerently to be fed. With one sharp talon placed firmly over the dead rodent, the eagle began to tear strips of meat from the carcass and lower them into small, hungry mouths. Although he had not realized it, Josie's back no longer rested against the oak. His attention at peak, the young man's eyes strained to accommodate the distance of his interest. Minutes passed but he hardly noticed. Then he saw her—the mother! Yet she carried no food. Soon the female set down upon the rim beside her mate and began to feed the chicks from her own beak. Josie looked puzzled for a moment.

"Water… She's giving them water, isn't she?" Josie's eyes never left the nest.

"She is."

With unfaltering interest, Josie watched until the inevitable moment when both adults left their young. As they soared high above the tree-line intent upon the next order of business, Josie's gaze followed, and he wondered what the view must be like from the lofty set of their keen eyes.

Momentarily Josie realized his position and leaned gently back against the oak. The land seemed more interesting now and his gaze still reached out to ponder it.

Again, he heard God's voice.

"Josie,"

"Yeah."

"Do you believe freedom is a very important thing?"

This is an easy one, Josie thought, "Of course it is." He turned to look at the other man, "I mean, everyone wants to be free. Many wars have been fought over this subject. Yes, I think that freedom is probably one of the most important things there is."

"I agree. And is not your own individuality a thing you place high value upon? Would you give it up if you could? Would you want to? And would you ask as much of another?"

God paused as Josie contemplated.

He began again, "The world requires many different races and cultures so that man might learn not to hate that which is different from himself. When this ideal is engrained, and only then, may one pursue true freedom of individuality rather than become a sheep who would blindly follow the others for fear of ridicule or even exile if he does not. With this liberty each individual may enjoy true *freedom of his own will* to be, or become, absolutely anything he desires. Whether that person grows into a great leader, humanitarian, architect, athlete, doctor, carpenter, artist, teacher, mechanic, fishermen, philosopher, or even a gay poet, he may enjoy acceptance, and even worth, within the community. After all, individuality and freedom are some of heaven's greatest ideals.

"So, you see that man must learn to grant other men the same freedom I do. It's *more freedom* I seek for all my children Josie. For I do not want to serve only as shepherd to a herd of mindless sheep, but wish instead to be among the company of friends and share in the joy as they ascend to new heights of individual accomplishment.

"Besides, the many different peoples and cultures also offer a much larger variety of experiences. They also stand as evidence that there is *no one true and right way for everyone*; a seemingly impossible concept for many to grasp."

Josie thought of Albert. He had been a true friend after all. His boys were alright, and Nancy was probably still Rachel's best friend. Then there was Maria, so full of life, so kind, so strong and wise even in the face of hardship. Yes, they were different, and yet Josie had loved them all. God, he missed them already. Josie wiped at moist eyes then. Emotion could be such a trying thing. But the moment passed, and Josie found himself staring into the crystal water as it bubbled over smooth rocks protruding from the nearby creek. He felt a little sullen again.

"How about some fishing?", and with that God stood to his feet and started for the shoreline.

The finality of this statement told Josie the time for business was over. Josie rose from his place beneath the oak and followed his friend to the water. Once there, God produced two antiquated fishing poles. Before long, the two men sat atop large rocks with baited hooks dangling into the water. The sun warmed Josie to his core as sweet sounds of trickling water emanating through a background of the bee and birdsongs that gripped his spirit. The two men talked little now—and the day was good.

A bite took Josie's line, and his face broke into a grin as he rose to meet the challenge of one exceptionally large trout. *This guy's a fighter,* Josie thought as he focused concentration to the battle. The fish leaped from the water and Josie almost yelped with glee. *Easy now, don't wanna lose him.* Eventually the trout was brought to shore and it was with a radiant smile set upon a face now aglow with life that Josie held his line in the air and proudly displayed his catch to God. This warmed the Almighty's heart, for the child had come to the meadow in such a distraught state, and God mirrored Josie's excitement as he returned the gesture.

Josie hung his catch upon a twine stringer and carefully placed it into the water before re-baiting the hook and returning to his place upon the rock. Throughout the afternoon Josie's mind occasionally returned to the things God had spoken of. Although it had begun to sink in, Josie still seemed unable to grasp the entire meaning. Oh well, at least he felt much better now.

Both men caught many fish that day and before long they began letting the excess go.

It was late afternoon as Josie sat happily upon his rock, his bare feet resting on the sand six inches below the water's surface. Suddenly something caught his eye down there. Something was moving. With slight curiosity Josie tilted his head downward. *Probably just a small fish,* he thought casually. But it was neither—it looked more like a tunnel of some sort.

"God." Josie's eyes never left the water.

"Yeah."

"I just want to say that I think you're a magnificent person and tell you of how much I've enjoyed the time here."

"I love you too Josie."

And he was gone.

THE GREAT MAN
Chapter 9

1

It was 3 p.m. on a sunny Sunday as the old brown, half-ton, Chevy pickup bounced along the rough two-lane pavement of County Road 128. At the center of the vehicle's bench seat a woman straddled a gearshift lever that protruded from the floorboard between her legs. Of this annoyance she took little notice as she cradled the small white blanket wrapped around the newborn son held in her arms. Even though the boy was Rachel's second child, the instinct of her motherhood had always been unusually strong and her enthrallment at the arrival of this new life in which God had entrusted to her was complete. As the old truck continued, Rachel was unable to take her eyes from the newborn as she threw a constant echo of coos and gentle murmurings in the boy's direction; pausing at times only to kiss him affectionately on the forehead.

At her right Rachel's other son Jacob, or Jake for short, who had turned six in April, seemed quietly lost in thought as he gazed through the open window. He loved the window seat and always complained if denied this privilege, but today his mother had gladly relinquished this luxury that she might sit closer to her husband. *So, they can share the stupid baby*, he thought. And the tall, rolling hills of golden wheatgrass that lay dotted with oak trees beyond Jake's momentary confinement seemed to roll on forever across his little world. Truck rides had never ceased to amaze him. Today however, Jacob was uninterested in the view as he entertained only thoughts of his new 'little brother'. Jake was not yet sure if he liked the idea.

At Rachel's left, her husband Jim, or Jimmy as only she sometimes called him, handled the worn steering linkage of the family's old pickup with one skilled hand as his other elbow protruded from the open driver's window. A kind man, Jim Stevenson was 37, two years older than his wife, and, like her, was infatuated with the arrival of their new family member. With the stress and worries of pregnancy and childbirth behind, Jim was now free to adore his new son. Jim frequently allowed his attention to leave the road that he might shoot goofy grins and goo-goo eyes in the infant's direction. *And what a wonderful name*, Jim thought, "*Josie*"—he had picked it out himself.

For awhile the truck bounced past small dirt roads whose entrances were lined with tin mailboxes, and a spattering of driveways that led to the roadside houses of his many friends and neighbors. Eventually the truck began to slow, and Jim turned into the dirt driveway of his family's aging two-bedroom house. Although they had called this place home for only four years, both Jim and his wife were born to the area and had lived in close proximity for the entirety of their lives.

A tan-colored horse stared blankly from inside a corral whose wooden fence bordered the driveway's left side. To the right lay a square strip of mowed grass with a single giant oak tree at its center that offered a tire swing and littered the ground below with small dry leaves. At the driveway's center, Alley, the big shaggy family-dog, barked happily as he ran to meet the truck and escort his people for the last 50-feet of their journey.

The single-story house lay dead ahead and today Jim did not notice the chips of yellow paint pealing from its wooden surface. To the left of their home and across more dirt driveway sat his garage and workplace. Jim was a mechanic—and a good one. "If it has wheels and burns gas then Jim can fix it," many had said. Although he would never be rich, Jim's remarkable skill and reputation promised that as long as men needed cars and farm equipment, his own family would never go without.

It was also true that his wife had developed an interest in mystery writing some years earlier and, after what had seemed like an endless cyclone of work and rejection slips, she had recently received an advance check for the coming of her first novel. The book was even now at the printers. Although neither yet knew it, by the end of her life Rachel would have sold eight novels and even enjoyed a certain notoriety.

Just now though, two cars and a tractor sat outside the garage. One was an antique Mercedes, Model 190 that belonged to

Mike Parker. The thing was in for a motor rebuild and the hood compartment sat empty as the engine rested on Jim's workbench. Since it was an old car that Mike had bought for his wife because she '*just had to have it*', and the Mercedes needed plenty of restoration, Jim knew he would be dealing with Mike Parker for months to come. The other car, a Plymouth that belonged to Miss Hadley, was in for brakes. The tractor needed a clutch.

But this was a day of celebration and these responsibilities never crossed Jim's mind as he opened the truck door to ward off Alley's excited antics and make his way around to the passenger side. Although he tried, Jake always had trouble with the door handle. He never realized that Rachel had pushed the lock button down. Rachel stealthily unlatched the lock then waited for Jim to get the door. After lifting his eldest from the passenger seat to set him gently on the ground, Jim took Josie and cradled him in strong arms. Rachel then led Jake by the hand as Jim carried Josie up the four steps and opened the front door—which was never locked.

Although the place was modest and obviously put together on a budget, Rachel was a good homemaker and the old furnishings had been arranged to emit an air of optimum hominess. For now, Josie would sleep in a crib beside his parent's bed. When old enough, he would share Jake's room. It was a good home for a boy.

Under his parent's care and love, Josie grew like a weed.

Aside from occasional bickering with his brother, for Jake had been born with a slight mean streak and often teased his sibling, Josie was, for the most part, a good boy. He got along well with other children, tried to obey his father's wishes, and often helped his mother with the chores.

Because of his seemingly natural caring for others and wish to give of what he had, both Jim and Rachel favored Josie. And even though the boy's parents did their best not to play favorites, Jacob knew of their inconsistency and this would always be a source of contention for him. Although the boys spent time playing together (their father's refusal to allow a television in the house demanded this), for their differences they would never become truly close.

From the very start Josie had loved the land. As he aged and the constraints of childhood began to loosen, Josie spent much time roaming the fields and the thicker woods that began at the creek bed behind their house and continued for miles through the canyons.

Sometimes he went alone and sometimes he took the aging Alley-dog for whom he had a deep affection. But *always* Josie went to the land.

On weekends Jim often took his boys to the nearby Cactus Lake for a day of fishing. Both boys loved these outings and, although Jacob's natural sense of competitiveness and years of seniority quickly deemed him the better fisherman, Josie did not mind. For although he did love to fish, for him the best thing about these forays was the opportunity to spend time with his dad…and even his dumb brother. Also, since many others came here to fish, Jim and his boys usually ran into friends. On exceptionally hot days, and against Jacob's protestations that they would scare the fish, everyone sometimes laid down their poles and jumped in. Eventually, given to defeat, Jake always joined them.

Josie began to ride the school bus that picked him and Jake up at the end of their driveway and hauled them to the town of Bowden seven miles away, then brought them home in the evenings. Josie kept only average grades, but his social skills seemed naturally good and, to Jacob's envy, he made many friends. Although Josie appreciated the company of his peers, his love of the land ran much deeper, and he always returned to the solitude of the woods.

For his 13th birthday, Josie received an air rifle from his father. It was just what he had wanted. From that day forth, Josie's trips into the forest began to produce a bounty of cottontail rabbits, quail, and even an occasional pheasant, of which he would meticulously skin, clean, and deposited in the freezer. On occasion Rachel would thaw Josie's catch and prepare a family feast. Although the meat always tasted a bit gamey, Josie puffed with pride at his ability to provide for the family.

Josie spent time with friends, loved the land, and enjoyed his boyhood.

The years passed.

2

In time, outsiders began a steady migration to the area. The town grew at an alarming rate as houses and businesses started popping up everywhere. A new wing was added to Bowden Junior High (which Josie now attended) to accommodate the booming population. The people seemed to just to keep coming; and with them also came nicer clothes, fancier cars, expensive toys, and *money*. Although Josie still rode the bus to school, many of these new kids drove their *own* automobiles—almost all of which were nicer than the Stevenson's old family truck. This car thing grated on Josie's nerves. *Certainly*, he thought, *girls only want a guy who has his own ride. By the time I'm old enough for a license I'm gonna have me a car!*

Josie's mind was made up.

By the beginning of Josie's freshmen year there were many new riders aboard his school-bus. One of these, a girl who always boarded at the stop near Woodruff Road, sent shivers up his spine. An upcoming woman of 5'3", she wore a thick mane of dark brown hair that fell halfway down her back. Her eyes were a deep blue and when Josie looked into the depths of their sparkling abyss, breath always deserted him. The girl had a rather heavy jawline with uncommonly wide mouth and full lips that held back unusually white teeth. The effect was beyond beautiful, and on the one occasion when he had seen her flash that unbelievably radiant smile, Josie's heart had actually skipped a beat. Her build was amazingly slender, with firm bust, a strikingly small midsection, and an amazingly firm ass that did unbelievable things to his teenage brain. To him she was the most beautiful creature on earth. On the third morning of his second school week, it happened that the seat beside Josie's was vacant. Much to his surprise and excited embarrassment, the princess of his teenage dreams took that seat. Knowing not what one should say to an angel, Josie sat frozen in terror and stared at the setback ahead. But she soon turned the stunning face of a goddess upon him and said, "Who've you got for first period?"

Somehow Josie managed to liberate his desert-parched tongue and reply, "Mr. Rose…Social Studies."

"Oh, I've got Rose too…except for third period instead. With all that hair sticking out the sides of his head, and that chrome-dome melon on top, Rose always reminds me of Bozo the clown. Don't you think?"

"For sure," Josie said, "And yuh ever notice the way he hobbles around like he's got a stick up his ass? Hell, the other day I imagined him with a clown nose and figured even if he was wearing Bozo shoes he'd probably still walk the same." With that the girl burst out laughing and, after his initial shock, Josie joined her. The sweat on his brow seemed to dry some then.

"My name's Adrienne," she said holding out one slender hand.

"Josie," he replied accepting her offer. Silly as it seemed, he was just glad of the opportunity to actually touch her, "Pleased to meet-chu."

From there, conversation came easier and the two chattered on for the trip's duration. By the time they arrived, and although the ride had lasted only six short miles, Josie felt as though he had known this girl much longer. On the return trip they again sat together. From that day forth Josie always made sure the bus-seat beside his was vacant—and Adrienne always took it. They became inseparable. They spent lunch together, exchanged phone numbers, and rearranged classes that they might study in each other's company.

Adrienne openly spurned the attentions of other boys and it amazed Josie that such a girl would prefer him, a boy who hailed from '*poor white trash*' to that of the many wealthier suitors. *She deserves more and someday*, Josie promised, *I'll shower her with all the good things in lif*e.

Adrienne was not a shy girl. In her essence there seemed an unusual kind of caring and compassion for the lives of those around her. To her, if it were not for others and the ways their lives touched her own, then what would be the sense of living? Adrienne had few goals. Her natural ambition almost always centered in relationships and it was only there that, to date, she had found reward in this life. This was her nature and instinctively others sensed such genuine concern and friendships came faster to her than anyone Josie had ever known.

But this was not Josie's lot and, although he was genuinely fair, considerate, and giving (qualities that led Adrienne's heart to throb and eventually sealed her love for him), he would not forgo his own ambitions and would work hard to fulfill such dreams. For this she loved him all the more. It has been said that opposites attract, and although Josie and Adrienne were not complete opposites, each owned strengths the other lacked. And it was from the strength of one that the other often drew large profit.

That summer Josie took a job at a local dairy farm. His duties required much physical labor and, although Josie had always been a strong boy, his body now began to take on the stature of manhood.

Whenever she could barrow her mother's car (like Josie, Adrienne had recently acquired a driver's license), she would ride the four miles to Josie's place of employment to bring him lunch. Although Josie always bagged his own, Adrienne argued that it was not enough for a *man* (she would indulge his ego) that worked as hard as he. Josie always agreed with this excuse since he looked forward to these almost daily visits and any excuse to be near her was fine with him.

One day Adrienne arrived early and found she must wait ten minutes until his lunch break began. So, she watched through the open car window as Josie dug postholes to accommodate a new corral. First, he would loosen the earth with a heavy steel bar that he repeatedly lifted into the air, then plunged hard into the earth. Next, he repeated this movement with a posthole digger. It was man's work and Adrienne watched with increasing interest as Josie's muscles flexed and the sweat glistened upon his sun-darkened skin. A heat began to rise from within, and Adrienne felt a twitch between her legs.

Thereafter, Adrienne sometimes made a point of arriving early in hopes of catching her man at labor that she might spend a few minutes in admiration. After all, it was his rough handsomeness and rugged disposition that had attracted her in the first place. Many of the wealthier boys had attempted to win her affections and they often wondered why a prize such as she would hang with a lowlife like Josie. Most of these 'city slickers' however, seemed frail and inept to Adrienne. The money and status they sought to impress her with meant little as Adrienne's values in this life did not revolve around material gain. Sure, she wanted for her needs, but beyond that Adrienne had little interest in wealth. No. She wanted a man—a strong man—to complement her femininity.

Josie was the one.

Josie was delighted with the modest paychecks. On his days off, and if he were able to secure the use of his father's truck (which was often), Josie would pick Adrienne up at her house then drive to the malt shop, or dinner and a movie. With this new ability his pride and sense of worth as a provider swelled.

Adrienne was an only child and her father, Gregory Henderson, did not easily take to the idea of his little girl growing up and dating a boy! But the girl's mother didn't share Greg's sentiment and, caught between the scorn of two determined females, Gregory quickly learned to temper his protestations. So, it came to pass that, with Greg's reluctant consent, the boy was allowed to date his daughter openly (as if he'd ever possessed the power to prevent their courtship in the first place). Also, Greg found Josie hard to dislike and the boy's goodhearted nature eventually wore him down.

3

By season's end Josie had managed to save several hundred dollars and, with his father's help, was able to purchase a good running El Camino. From that day forth neither he nor Adrienne ever rode the school bus again. The trip was always made in Josie's car.

But status was quickly becoming the new God in Bowdon.

By most, Josie's Chevy was considered a 'junker' when compared with the late model BMWs, Toyotas, and fancy 4 by 4 pickup trucks those from much wealthier families drove, and Josie was sometimes held up to ridicule by his peers. Even those who did not say as much, Josie believed, considered him little more than a common dirt-farmer.

Yet for one to muster the strength required to resist the influence of those around him or her and simply follow their own heart and mind requires great character; for at first there is bound to be ridicule. Yet how can one learn who he truly is if he only imitates others, or seeks to become what he believes they wish him to be? For throughout history it is the single concept of individuality that, almost invariably, sets those of notable accomplishment and admiration apart from their fellows. Although Adrienne instinctively knew of this truth—Josie did not. For he was gravely influenced by the actions of others and, as it has been for so many throughout the ages, this single weakness would ultimately deny him the freedom to discover his own mind, passion, means, and ways—or, if you prefer, **himself**. And although the call of another man's deepest desire might very well be the road to riches, for Josie it was not.

      Josie began to stew at the injustice of it all. But at least he now had a new measuring tool with which to gauge success—he would use the yardstick of materialism sanctified by the masses. *Dirt farmer indeed!* he thought, *I'll show them, I'll win at this game. In time they'll have no choice but to acknowledge my accomplishments. I'll earn, no,* **command** *their respect and admiration! They'll see.* Josie meant these words.

Adrienne's father was a contractor. His business was to build spec houses then sell them at handsome profits. Gregory had moved his family to this area that he might take advantage of the recent construction boom to provide a better living for himself and his family.

      In his growing fondness for Josie and concern for his daughter's future, Gregory offered the young man a job. Josie was delighted with the new pay scale (considerably higher than the dairy farm) and the potential for advancement. So it was that in the summer after his junior year Josie became a carpenter's apprentice. Given his natural physical attributes and rugged country-boy upbringing, this job suited him well. In his excitement, Josie soaked up each new lesson like a dry sponge on spilled milk. He learned quickly. By summers end Josie had already received two considerable pay raises.

      Josie's senior school year came and went and, after graduating with a 2.8 grade average, he again returned to the business of house building. With each paycheck Josie added new tools to his growing arsenal, kept a minimal of spending money, and socked the rest into a savings account. By summer's end a considerable nest egg had been secured.

It was not long thereafter that Josie descended dramatically to one knee and proposed to the woman of his boyhood dreams.

It was a small wedding that accommodated only family and close friends. After the reception Josie loaded his new bride into the limousine Greg had arranged as a gift. He handed the driver a paper containing the address to a place of which Adrienne knew nothing.

The single-story house offered a certain sense of humility as it rested on the small plot. Although the roof was obviously old and weathered, the home's exterior walls had recently received a fresh coat of white paint. The front yard was surrounded by chain-link, covered with neatly mowed grass, and offered two small trees. The entry was positioned at the home's center while at its sides were two large wood-framed windows that opened above an unkempt row of rose bushes. It was a modest blue-collar home.

In the driveway sat Josie's El Camino.

After pulling to the curb the smartly dressed chauffeur got out, circled the car, and opened the lady's door. Josie met him there then watched with held breath as his beautiful bride stepped out. Josie tipped the chauffeur handsomely and said he could go. After thanking him, the man turned toward the driver's compartment. A minute later the newlyweds stood alone for the first time that day.

From the moment she had seen the El Camino, Adrienne had known, and it had taken all her will to hold back the tears. Now, as they stood alone at the curb it was safe to cry. So, it was with bitter-sweet emotion that she turned tear-filled eyes on him and said, "Oh Josie…it's beautiful!" He held her close then. When she'd finished, he smiled into sparkling eyes as his thumbs wiped tears from salty cheeks. Josie led his new bride through the yard and onto the stoop...then carried her across the threshold.

It had been a perfect wedding day.

4

In the years that followed, Josie continued to climb the ladder of house building success. He became a journeyman carpenter, then a foreman. Eventually, using squirreled away money (Josie's unusual drive for success had prompted continual savings) and the good credit he had established with the purchase of his new 4-by-4 truck, second car, and extravagant home furnishings, Greg and Josie became partners. Together they built one spec house…then another…and another…and still another. In time Josie started his own construction company which grew almost overnight into a veritable monster. With each new foundation poured, Josie knew he was doing the right thing. For was he not building a better life for his family? Was he not gaining the respect of his peers and becoming somebody in the eyes of his community? *Yeah,* he thought, *more money, more luxury, more respect…even power! That's what life's really all about. Dirt farmer indeed.*

Time passed. Bowdon continued to grow.

Josie's desire was to pursue success before parenthood and, to the dismay of his wife's ticking maternal clock, he had made this intention perfectly clear. So, it was not until after Josie's 30th birthday that his son Mosaic, (Moze for short) was born. Although the child brought his father considerable joy, it was also around this time that Josie received the greatest business proposal of his life.

A group of investors had targeted the town of Bowden with intent to begin a tract house project. From their masterplan, entire neighborhoods and communities would be erected in a massive melee of machinery, labor, and sawdust.

The investors sought the services of reliable local talent and Josie was already a major contractor in the area. When they approached him and learned that, to their surprise, he was a man who slept on a mattress of squirreled away money and a substantial reserve of bank credit, they invited him into partnership. Josie requested a few days to think on it.

For three long days and restless nights Josie contemplated hard upon the proposal facing him. It would be the biggest decision of his life. In order to gain a position as standing partner, Josie would have to exhaust the entirety of his every resource. If he did not commit and sought instead the rout of safety, he would still gain the building contracts, which would change nothing since his company already enjoyed all the work it could handle. If Josie did commit and the tract house project was successful, he would go on to make millions. If the endeavor failed however, bankruptcy would become the only option. He would be ruined. Yet if he did nothing, he would neither gain, nor lose. Financially Josie would remain stagnant and this option seemed almost as bad as ruin.

After talking with Adrienne, whose advice was that he follow his conscience, Josie decided to seek the advice of her father. "I'd take the safe route," Greg said, "Look at it this way Josie: You're 32 now and if you keep on the way you've been, you'll retire by forty-five. But if you stuff all your eggs into this one basket and the deal falls through, you'll have wasted the last ten years of your life. To risky. Take the sure thing. Retire young. Go fishing."

The more Josie thought, the more he could not accept Gregory's advice. After all, this might be his one big chance, and if he did not gamble, he would always wonder what might have been. *Besides*, he mused, *most remarkably successful men had, at one time or other, taken big risks to acquire such greatness*. And he was right.

Josie's mind was made up.

The great project required almost all of Josie's time as, besides the seemingly endless business responsibilities, he had hired extra men and the new crews needed more supervision than might have been expected. Employees could be such a pain. And new problems just seemed to come from everywhere and nowhere. As soon as Josie had solved one, ten more were waiting. There just weren't enough hours in a day.

Days passed into months, and the months into years as Josie's son grew into a young boy. Since Josie's schedule did not allow much, if any, time for family (he had moved on to other tract projects), he barely noticed. Although Josie would eventually buy his son an air gun like the one his father had given him, the forests were rapidly disappearing, and the city allowed little freedom for a boy to hunt rabbits or seek communion with the land.

It mattered little however, since the tract houses were bringing in huge profit. With each penny gained, Josie continued to reinvest. Josie made his first million. This financial triumph was exhilarating, and it rekindled his desire to push harder. Redoubling his efforts, Josie made new investments—some were successful. The family moved to a mansion. Fine cars were purchased, and servants hired.

Everyone called Josie Sir.

Men from all walks of life began to pay homage to the great man. Everyone, it seemed, vied for a piece of Josie's attention. He made a host of new friends who kissed his ass and massaged his ego in effort to shorten the gap between themselves and his money. And they jumped when he told them to. This kind of power was intoxicating. As his arrogance grew, Josie convinced himself that, in the light of such outstanding achievement, God must have endowed to him the gift of being a natural leader. Josie began to exude an air of importance. He became bossy in business, often looking down upon those of lesser accomplishment. After all, any who were fortunate enough to receive advice from a master should consider themselves lucky indeed.

This attitude did not go over well at home and with the added insult of his constant absence, Josie's know-it-all poise seemed only to drive a wedge between himself and his family. Of the things that made up Adrienne's personal life he had not shared for a long time and Josie often felt as though he barely knew this woman. To Mosaic there had been little time for fathering.

But it's for them that I do it! He reminded himself, *For I must work in order to build a better life for my family!*

Occasionally Josie's attention was drawn to Mosaic by notes from school telling of the boy's increasing fits of anger and propensity for fistfights. Josie's stern reprimands had little affect and only seemed to drive the boy even farther away. *It's just a phase,* Josie had thought, o*r maybe he's a bad apple.* But Mosaic's lot was a regrettable inconvenience that fell under the shadow of greater occurrences. For the taste of success was intoxicating; and Josie's life was about money. If, in fact, there was more Josie no longer remembered, or perhaps had never known.

Profit was his only God.

THE SPIRIT OF A WOMAN
Chapter 10

1

Tall for his age, Mosaic was growing into adolescence. His dark hair was short above a well-proportioned face with strong brows and eyes of such dark brown they appeared almost black. His young body was lean yet muscular. In truth, Mosaic was becoming a physical presence that was hard to ignore. Although Adrienne tried to seek a relationship with her son, Mosaic had always been a sullen and distant boy. But now a posture of teenage rebellion settled over him and this attitude only drove the boy even farther from his mother's affection.

To her credit, Adrienne remained faithful throughout the years of Josie's absence, but in her aloneness, she was forced to explore other avenues of fulfillment. After experimenting with a few ideas, Adrienne ultimately found within herself a natural love of horses. Expanding upon this interest, she purchased a young Palomino mare named Chelsea. To Adrienne, she was the most beautiful animal on earth. Although sometimes the victim of a nervous disposition, Chelsea was a gentle horse and before long a special bond had formed between them.

Because new city zoning ordinances would not allow a horse kept near the mansion, Adrienne was forced to board Chelsea some distance away. But this inconvenience would ultimately prove a blessing.

The Double-S horse ranch belonged to an older couple named Ben and Irma Sutton. It resided in the gently sloped mountains of forests and meadows some 23-miles beyond the expanding city of Bowdon. No pavement existed anywhere on the property. Its main house was single story, dark brown, and appeared in need of maintenance. The barn was about the same. Chickens ran freely while a lazy old hound-dog often lay motionless on the porch. Wooden corals held all manner of horses and the place always smelled of them. Old bathtubs were used for watering troughs. Beyond the dirt parking lot, a row of horse-trailers, including Adrienne's, were parked against a wooden fence. The ranch was surrounded by vast countryside, and its nearest neighbor was almost two miles away. Adrienne loved it here, and before long her blue-jean clad figure became a common sight to the Suttons.

Although her own home seemed lonely and unbefitting, Adrienne found great contentment amid the country air and horses. And for this she settled. Adrienne's work at the ranch was voluntary, and she sometimes thought it ironic that she should be performing the same kind of labor that had originally attracted her so passionately to Josie. In time, Adrienne learned a great deal of ranching and horses. As this knowledge grew into confidence, she and Chelsea began venturing much farther from the ranch.

Adrienne learned that many shared her passion. Among them, picnics, get-togethers, campouts, and other events were not uncommon activities. One day Linda Carpenter held out a flyer to invite Adrienne on a campout that she and her husband Chet would be attending. *Campouts,* Adrienne thought, *I love camping, and I can go with friends.* She looked at Chet, who stood nearby checking the hoofs of the black stallion he called Lightning. He was 6'2", with thin build, dark hair with streaks of gray, clean shaven, and when Chet smiled his teeth seemed almost too white behind those slightly pronounced lips. He seemed a good match for his wife who stood 5'9" and had dark features as well, except without the gray. Adrienne had grown fond of both.

Adrienne looked back to the flyer. *Best of all,* she thought, *everyone will bring horses.* The leaflet promised that, among other activities, a country band featuring the famous (so claimed) fiddler "Country Joe" would be in attendance. All at once Adrienne's mind was made up. She would go. The event would not take place for two weeks and that, she reasoned, was plenty of time to make the necessary preparations.

As the days passed, Adrienne prepared for the trip with real enthusiasm. But as the final day of departure drew near, the adult voice of responsibility began to talk…and it spoke to her in her own voice, *"You shouldn't do this Adrienne. It's not the responsible thing you know, and probably isn't safe. What if the truck breaks down? You might blow a tire and be killed. You're not going to have fun anyway, so why not just stay home? There's a lot that needs to be done here. You could make an excuse to Chet and Linda…"* In her head this incessant talk rambled on, but in her gut, there seemed some deep need to take this chance.

Adrienne was torn.

Excitement brought her quickly from slumber on the morning of departure. She looked to the adjacent pillow. Josie was already gone and, as was common, Mosaic had not come home last night. She was alone. Well, not quite alone, for the responsible voice still chattered loudly. But there was more to it today, for along with this babble was a very real sense of fear. No. Not fear exactly, it was something more akin to terror. It seemed the incessant voice was now showing its true self. A strange sense of detachment settled upon her then. Feeling more like a robot on autopilot than a human being, she set about the familiar tasks of showering and dressing. Her one-ton diesel-dully had been packed yesterday and after two cups of coffee and a bagel, Adrienne made her way to it. She pulled to the street, the freeway, and eventually the small country road that led to the ranch.

As Adrienne passed beneath the wrought-iron Double-S sign she saw Chet and Linda's truck parked beside the stables. Their horse trailer was already hooked up. She was late!

Quickly finding her own trailer, Adrienne began to back her truck to it as Chet stepped behind to guide her with hand signals. When satisfied, he cranked down the tongue and began attaching the safety chain. Adrienne appeared at the tailgate. "You're already hooked up!" she cried, "I thought you said to be here at nine."

Her nervous edge caught Chet off guard, and he looked up to note Adrienne's uneasy stance. She seemed a bit freaked out. Chet smiled and said, "You ain't late young lady…we're early. Just figured to get a jump on things. But don't get your feathers in a tiz girlfriend, there ain't no hurry. Take all the time you like. Besides, we still gotta load the horses."

Chet did have a beautiful smile, and his mellow manner helped…some.

With trailer in tow, Adrienne drove to the stable and, as she set about the task of loading saddle, bridle, alfalfa, etc. into the extra compartment of her twin-horse trailer, that strange feeling of otherworldly disconnectedness deepened. She was numb now and felt very little of anything at all. This was preferable to the sense of panic she had experienced earlier. Chet and Linda seemed fine, but this was not their first event.

When all was ready, engines were started, and Adrienne followed her friends to the little highway. Fifteen miles of twisting mountain road later, the pavement straightened abruptly as it ran almost arrow straight across the open desert. Although she had, on rare occasion, visited this place before, today the seemingly endless brown land of low brush, cactus, rocks, and occasional Yucca trees seemed different. They felt like an adventure.

Two hours passed.

Tiny desert towns came and went and at one of these the little convoy stopped for an early lunch. Back from the small desert highway set a quaint little breakfast and lunch place and both trucks parked upon the rather large, paved front lot. On the establishment's wooden front deck a few vacant tables and chairs rested in the shade of large sun-umbrellas and the trio took seats there. A young waitress arrived. She was a bubbly thing who chatted pleasantly as she filled coffee cups. After glancing over the menus, Adrienne ordered a French dip while her companions went for burgers and fries. The girl buzzed away and the three were left to sit alone again. Not surprisingly, conversation soon turned to talk of horses, travel, and camping.

2

As Adrienne tossed the last bite into her mouth, an old Ford Fairlane pulled into the lot. With the meal finished, Adrienne leaned back to allow a moment's digestion as she sipped steaming coffee from the cup their waitress had recently refilled. Looking over the mug held to her lips with both hands, Adrienne watched as the Ford backed into a space against the porch. Once parked in front of the two horse hauling rigs, a young couple and their daughter stepped out. With the little blond headed girl clinging to her mother's hand, they started up the deck's four steps. Adrienne could not help but notice the girl's incessant interest in the trucks. In fact, she could not take her eyes from them.

When the young family reached the top, the slightly pudgy woman turned green eyes on the trio and said to no one in particular, "Do those rigs belong to you guys?"

"Sure. They're ours," Chet gave his friendly smile. Adrienne and Linda smiled too.

Encouraged by their seemingly easy approachability, the woman continued, "Where are you going?"

"To a campout in Spearhead Lake," Chet answered, then began to tell something of the scheduled event.

When he had finished the woman said, "That sounds simply wonderful! What do you think of that Karen?"

The girl looked up to her mother and nodded.

"Do you-all like horses?" Adrienne asked.

"Oh, we do," said the woman, "Especially our daughter. Say hello Karen." The girl waved bashfully as she clung to her mother's dress. "Hi," her voice came softly. Little Karen seemed uncommonly shy.

"Horses are all she ever talks about," the woman continued, "Of course she wants a pony for her birthday and Evan and I hope to get one as soon as we're in a position to do so." Her husband nodded his agreement. "Karen's bedroom has horse print curtains, a horse print quilt…."

"My bed has a picture of them kissing," the little girl interrupted, "…and a baby too."

"That's right Karen," the woman petted her daughter's blond tresses affectionately. And she hates Barbie. The only toys she ever asks for are horses. Horse dolls, rocking horses, Black Beauty videos, a riding stick with a head on it, swing set…. I think she has them all. I don't know where she gets it, but Karen just loves horses."

"Would you like to pet one?" Adrienne asked the girl.

Seemingly unsure of whether to be frightened or excited by this proposal, Karen looked to her parents for approval.

"Well Karen," said the girl's mother, "what do you think?"

Then, sensing the child's fear she added, "I'll come with you." With that Karen looked back to Adrienne and, seemingly unsure of herself, slowly nodded her little head.

Adrienne stood and walked around the table. When she'd arrived near the top of the steps, she squatted to meet the child's eyes, stuck out her hand, and said, "I'm Adrienne, I don't think we've been formally introduced."

For a moment the child only gazed silently at the fine lines that had begun to adorn Adrienne's middle-aged face. Then, as if having come to terms with some insoluble decision all at once, she took the stranger's hand, smiled a little and said, "I'm Karen."

"Pleased to meet-chu Karen. I'm a horse lover like you. They're mostly all I ever think about too. My horse's name is Chelsea and she's a palomino. She's really friendly so let's go meet her."

With that Adrienne started down the steps with the little family on her heals and Chet & Linda bringing up the rear. After walking past both trucks, the little entourage stopped behind Chelsea's trailer. Karen stared in startled amazement at the seemingly giant, especially from where she stood, horses butt pressed against the trailer's rear door with long blondish tail that hung outside and swished occasionally at invisible flies.

Adrienne dropped the tailgate, which made an easy loading ramp, and walked to the front of the empty stall beside her horse. She turned to look at Karen and said, "Come on."

Still clinging to her mother's hand, both stepped into the trailer then stopped. Adrienne's eyes beckoned silently. Her mother released the girl and, after a glance up to receive a reassuring nod from mom's round face, Karen turned attention to the big adventure ahead and walked forward on her own. Chelsea snorted and the girl froze. But Karen had decided to trust this strange lady who seemed so kind. Besides, she reasoned, her dad was close, and he wouldn't let anything bad happen. Karen's fear was soon overcome by fascination as the huge animal twitched and shifted its enormous weight beside her.

Adrienne held out her hand…and the child took it. She then squatted on pointed cowboy boots, looked into Karen's blue eyes, then turned to pet Chelsea affectionately on the foreleg. In a moment, Karen did too. As Adrienne looked into the face of this little girl's deep concentration and utter fascination at so simple a task, she found herself overcome with warm emotion and, although she did not understand them, Adrienne fought to hold back tears.

When Chelsea lifted her leg to stomp several times, the startled child withdrew her hand quickly and looked to her new mentor for reassurance. Adrienne smiled…and Karen smiled back. Feeling more confident now, Adrienne reached for the girl and lifted her. Karen calmly allowed this. Once standing, Adrienne shifted her to one arm. After looking into Karen's eyes to offer another reassuring smile, the horsewoman reached to pet the magnificent creature on her muzzle. Chelsea snorted, bobbed her head up and down, and fidgeted slightly at the cramped quarters of her confinement. When Adrienne withdrew her hand, Chelsea hung her massive head over the railing that separated them and snorted once more.

Again, Karen was startled, but this time she did not look to Adrienne for reassurance and instead reached to touch the actual face of the animal she had been dreaming of for so long. Chelsea did not seem to mind. After a moment, Adrienne bent to pull a handful of alfalfa from the bail on the floor. She gave a portion to Karen then held the remainder out to Chelsea, who at once began munching the green offering. When the horse had finished Adrienne turned her face back to the child and said, "Now you try. Do it like this Karen," and she held her own hand out to demonstrate, "Keep your palm up and fingers straight so she won't bight them when she takes the alfalfa."

Karen contemplated the idea of a horse-bite—it made her nervous. Seeing this, Adrienne added, "She won't try to bite you honey. It's just that she can't see her own mouth and if you stick a finger in there she might bite it by accident. So just keep your hand flat and you won't have any trouble at all. That's how everyone does it."

Again, the little girl decided to trust this strange woman and held out her offering as instructed. Chelsea glutinously accepted the treat. Although Karen did find the feeling of horse-lips against her palm a bit disconcerting, Adrienne saw that the child's face wore an expression of delighted surprise. Karen finally withdrew her empty hand.

Although she knew it would be a hassle, Adrienne just couldn't help herself. So, she said to the little girl, "Would you like to ride her?"

Looking a bit shocked at this idea, Karen just stared into the woman's eyes. Then, as fear was again overcome by excitement she said, "Could I?"

"Of course, you can," Adrienne replied while setting the girl to the ground, "Let me get her ready and we'll ride together." Then the voice of a responsible adult entered Adrienne's mind to quell the child she too had momentarily become. Adrienne looked to the girl's mother and said, "Would it be okay if I take Karen for a little ride around the parking lot?"

Lines of concern creased the woman's forehead, but in the light of such an unusual opportunity, Karen's mom could not bring herself to say no. "It will be her first," she said, then added thoughtfully, "Are you sure it's not too much trouble?"

"No trouble at all," Adrienne lied, "It'll be my pleasure," she added truthfully. Looking to her two companions, Adrienne asked, "Do we have time Chet?"

"Sure," he answered, unable to be the bad guy who would spoil everyone's fun, "We're on vacation ain't we? But if you break out the camping gear we're leaving you behind."

Adrienne reached for a hackamore that hung from a hook on the wall and fitted it to Chelsea's head. Next, she slid between the rails and stood to face the big animal. Placing one hand on the horse's muzzle and the other against her shoulder, Adrienne backed the mare from her trailer.

Karen again clung to her mother's dress and watched in frozen amazement as the great beast stood before her twitching at the annoyance of occasional flies and swishing her tail lazily from side to side.

Strong legs pushed Adrienne easily onto the horse's bare back. Once positioned, she reached both arms to again beckon the little girl.

In her fear and excitement Karen almost began to cry. But her strange love of horses was much too powerful to allow that, for she knew tears would only shatter this opportunity. No, she thought, I'm going to ride this horse. Then a deeper realization came and again she thought—**I'm gonna actually ride a horse!**

Karen's mind was so preoccupied that she had not noticed her father's approach. When his hands clamped onto her little torso the girl's head spun quickly to face him and dad noted the sheer terror that contorted the child's pretty face. Momentarily, she calmed a little.

"Are you ready honey?" he asked.

Even though Karen's mouth seemed much too dry for talking, she tried anyway, "Yes please," she said, and even these simple words had required big effort.

Karen was lifted from the ground then set in front of Adrienne. Once there, she looked down to contemplate the situation. Karen noted the warm back muscles that moved slightly between her legs, *It's alive!* she thought. She'd never sat atop anything beyond her parent's lap that was alive before. The sensation was exhilarating. Karen ran excited eyes from where she sat, up Chelsea's long mane, then to the back of two twitching ears. Karen also noted the woman's single arm as it came around her right side to hold the reins.

"What should I hold onto?" she asked.

"Take hold of her mane," Adrienne answered.

"But won't that hurt her?"

"No honey, not at all. You just hold on tight as you like," and with that Adrienne kicked Chelsea lightly and the horse started forward. Karen took hold of the long golden mane.

From her place behind the trailer Karen's mother watched as the horse walked in large circles around the lot. She saw Adrienne give the reins to the little girl and took note of Karen's clumsy handling of them. But Adrienne was patient, and the child's skill quickly improved…at least a little. She tried to turn Chelsea and had some success. Karen's delight at this small achievement was so big that her smile could easily be seen from the place at which her parents stood. When sufficient time had passed Adrienne took control back from the little girl. Chelsea was led off the pavement then and proceeded into open desert. Mom nervously clutched the small amulet that hung around her neck and watched as the rider threw one arm around her daughter and kicked the horse stoutly in the ribs. Chelsea broke into a full gallop as a thin cloud of desert dust stirred from beneath pounding hoofs to leave a smoky trail that fanned out behind. Adrienne's love of this sport and natural aptitude for all that is woodsy had made her a quick study at this game and Karen's parents noted that the rider was very skilled indeed.

Upon their return Karen was lifted from the mount by her father who then carried the girl to her mother's side for closer inspection. Aside from an almost comically wide grin, the child was no worse for wear.

Adrienne led her horse back into the trailer, removed the hackamore, exited the stall, and re-secured the gate. She turned to face the small entourage and noted that Karen again stood beside her mother's dress. Both parents expressed their gratitude and Adrienne accepted this praise graciously.

When the '*thank you*' session was finished, Adrienne watched the little girl release her mother's hand and walk forward on her own. As the gap closed between them, Adrienne squatted on her haunches to meet the child's eyes. For a moment, the girl only stared at her and said nothing. Then, without warning, she stepped forward and threw little arms around her mentor's neck. As Adrienne returned the hug, she realized they had just shared one of the most important events of Karen's short life.

"Thank you," she heard the girl whisper into one ear, "I'll never forget you." And again, Adrienne fought against a wonderful surge of emotion.

"I won't forget you either," she said.

Finally, the girl loosened her hold and, after one last smile into Adrienne's sparkling blue eyes, turned to rejoin her parents.

With the pleasantries completed, the little family turned to the restaurant where they would order lunch. Adrienne watched them go. But, while she had been busy galloping across the desert, Chet had paid the tab and their business here was finished.

She climbed into the cab. Again, the open desert rolled calmly past. As she traveled, Adrienne could not stop the flashes of Karen's big adventure from rerunning through her mind. Each time they did, a warm smile crept across her lips.

As the miles passed, Adrienne began to see a tall line of mountains looming in the distance. Seemingly humongous, she had been told that in places they climb to a peak altitude of 7,000 feet. Once near, the little mostly deserted highway turned left to parallel the mountains as Adrienne admired their sheer mass through the windshield at her right. When 15 miles had passed, Chet turned into a canyon that ran rather steeply up and into the mountains. The road cut higher into the hillside rather than through the rough canyon below.

    Pavement ended; tires crunched onto dirt.

    Although not exceptionally treacherous, on her right was the steep desert mountain, and left a sharp drop. No guardrail existed. Caught between feelings of fear, awe, wonder and the concentration needed to guide her truck, Adrienne's mind ran the gamut of emotion. But this small adversity called for strength, and there was no one to turn to but herself. And it was there that she found it. With this new power came an unexpected gift. Adrienne felt alive! More so than she ever had before.

    The road eventually left the canyon to level off and, before actually reaching the thick pine forests higher up, they came to a strange place where desert and green mountain terrain seemed to exist as one. Here, pine and oak trees grew above a desert floor of needle-covered dirt, brush, rock, and occasional cacti. Such land is called 'high-desert-mesa'. For Adrienne, it was amazing.

    The campground was not far now, and at its entrance a jovial man exchanged their fees for a single page schedule of events.

2

    They proceeded on. As with most campgrounds, this place was a small maze of dirt roads and camping slips. A variety of rigs, tents, and people already occupied many. Camp-stoves, coffeepots, and other equipment sat atop wooden picnic tables while men and women lounged in lawn-chairs. The only common theme seemed to be horses; and those were everywhere. Of all descriptions, they stood tied to trees, trailers, and even bumpers.

    Adrienne's excitement was renewed, as was her apprehension.

Chet picked a slot beneath the shade of trees and Adrienne took the space beside. Horses were released and tied to trees before all began erecting their tents and equipment. And although Chet offered Adrienne assistance, she would not take it.

No longer really afraid, Adrienne still felt nervous for she knew not what to expect here. She calmed her unease with busyness by making the camp perfect. Next, she took brush, water, and alfalfa to her horse. As Adrienne worked the brush across Chelsea's flank, a husky voice came from behind, "I see ya got yer-self all set up there honey. How 'bout a cold Coors as yer reward?"

Startled, Adrienne turned to find a woman standing there. Notably short, she was big-boned with thick blond hair that fell from beneath a black Stetson cowboy hat to just below her shoulders. The woman wore a set of old pointed toed cowboy boots, jeans that seemed too tight against her plump figure, and a de-sleeved flannel shirt covering extra-large breasts. She stood with arm outstretched and two cans of Coors held one atop the other by a single pudgy hand.

"No thank you," Adrienne said, "It's still a little early."

"Good point. How 'bout a Pepsi then?" and the other hand came up with two sodas held in the same manner.

"Why thank you," Adrienne smiled as she reached for one. Both popped their tabs and took a drink.

The woman belched without so much as a blush, stuck out her empty hand, and said, "Name's Molly. Me and Mack are from over Stern Valley way. We're really from Texas, but we been in Stern fer better'n 18 years now."

"Adrienne," she took the woman's hand, "From Bowdon."

"Glad to make your acquaintance Adrienne. Ain't been to Bowdon in a coon's age, but I hear it's growin' like a dill-weed."

"It is shocking," Adrienne momentarily forgot herself, "When I was a girl there were just trees, fields, and farms. Mostly gone now," she looked a little sad then.

"Yeah, I heard it's become quite the thriving metropolis." Silence fell for another long moment and again the women stared at each other. But Molly was not one to be at a loss of words for long. "You ain't much of a city person are yuh honey?"

Adrienne considered that. Although she was extraordinarily

rich, in her heart she had never wanted for anything more than a simple country life. It seemed ironic that in her youth she'd shunned the rich kids in favor of a country-boy, then ended up with a money-man just the same.

"No. Guess I'm not."

"Then why do yuh stay?"

"It's my husband's business. Seems like that's all he ever thinks about. I tell yah though Molly, looking at this place I think he's missing something."

"Yeah," Molly said steering the subject away from Adrienne's husband, "Sure is beautiful. Me 'n Mack come up here a lot in summer. That's us over yonder," she pointed to a nearby camp and Adrienne noted the old Chevy dually with huge cab-over camper. Beside it a balding, potbellied man sat in a folding lawn chair with beer held in his porky hand as he stared seemingly into space.

"That's my husband Mack. I guess this makes us neighbors. Say, I never seen you at one of these gigs before."

"This is my first. I came with Chet and Linda. Well, I followed them here," Adrienne pointed.

"Yeah," Molly stared at the couple, who'd just finished saddling their horses and appeared ready to mount up, "I've seen 'em around, but never been formally introduced."

"Want to? They're wonderful people."

"Looks like they're gettin' ready for a ride but…sure honey, I'd like that. How 'bout you lead the way?" Adrienne did, and then made introductions.

"Makin' friends with the natives already I see," Chet offered a grin, "Guess we won't have to play mother-hen to you-there Missy." His smile broadened at Adrienne's slight embarrassment. "Well, we're off. Hope to see more of you though Molly." Chet swung onto Lightning's back.

"You two comin' to the shindig tonight?" Molly asked.

"Wouldn't miss it," Chet replied. "Have fun now kids." With that Chet tipped his imaginary hat, and then started along a trail that wove into the woods. Adrienne, noting she had not been invited, assumed rightly that the couple wished to be alone. She thought of Josie. Where was he now? But she already knew.

"What say I introduce you to some of the folks around here?"

Molly's outgoing nature had a way of overcoming the shyness of others. Besides, what else did Adrienne have to do?

For the afternoon's remainder, they visited a variety of camps. Everyone seemed to know Molly, and Adrienne was introduced to a variety of friendly folks.

The last camp offered a host of people sitting in lawn chairs around a cracked concrete fire-pit. Evening's twilight was already dimming the landscape as a fire crackled there. On vacation now, all seemed happy and their smiling faces were eager to welcome the new arrivals. Adrienne was offered everything from coffee, pop, beer, hotdogs, burgers, toasted marshmallows, and S'mores. Laughter was abundant as jokes filled the air. After a while, the mood seemed to mellow. One thin man in white cowboy hat began to strum his acoustic guitar. A young woman joined him in song, as did some of the others. Adrienne watched firelight flicker across the man's face as it contorted with the emotion of his song. The mood, the land, the night, the fire, and especially the guitarist's passion, all moved her deeply. Before long, she too joined in the songs.

3

So preoccupied was she, that when a trim woman walked up and dropped into the lawn chair beside hers, Adrienne barely noticed. But Molly did, and it was from the other seat that she leaned across Adrienne's lap and said, "Hey Carrie, ain't yah even gonna say hi?"

Adrienne turned to appraise the new arrival. Carrie looked to be about 35, wore brown square-toed boots, Wrangler jeans, a belt with large oval buckle, and dark blue tee shirt. The long, straight hair that was tied in a ponytail that ran almost to her ass and its deep brown matched her eyes almost exactly. She was a robust, good-looking woman who seemed to somehow exude an aura of strength and independence.

"Oh…Molly," Carrie's tone seemed too feminine for the

tomboy air she carried, "Didn't see you there. Been quite a while. What's new sister?"

"Same old shit, Carrie. Just hangin' with the horses when I'm not busy babysitting that lump uh Jell-O I married."

"You've got a great way of making the single life seem better Molly. Thank you very much."

"Well, you got the right idea there girlfriend. Take it from the voice of experience and stay that way. This here's Adrienne. It's her first shindig and I sorta been shufflin' her around."

"Pleased to meet you Adrienne," Carrie offered her hand.

"Glad to meet you too," Adrienne accepted. "Did you come with friends?"

"Not Carrie," Molly interjected, "Miss Independence here's a lone wolf. A free spirit. Some of us around here call her 'The Wind' 'cause she just kinda blows wherever she wants. Sure, there's been lots o' men come 'round tryin' t' nail her boot-straps down, but Carrie won't have none of it. Oh, she plays with 'um all right, after all she is only flesh and blood, but…."

"Alright Molly!" Carrie interrupted.

Molly's cheeks flushed with embarrassment. But she'd been unable to help herself. To Adrienne however, Molly's admiration for the younger woman seemed quite obvious.

"But she is right about one thing Adrienne. I did come alone."

"Told yah," Molly said weakly.

Adrienne was instantly intrigued. She too had come alone. Well not exactly alone, she had followed Chet and Linda. But she had driven her own rig and, having come with no man, had wondered at the soundness of this brave move. But, sitting beside her was a woman who made such ventures as though they were a simple trip to the corner store. She'd had no idea women did such things. In that instant Adrienne's interest in Carrie was set. She hoped they would become friends.

"Where you from Carrie?"

"Barkley."

Adrienne knew the place. It was 35-miles from Bowdon, and even closer to the Double-S. "I'm from Bowdon," she said, "Came alone too. Well, I followed friends, but it's still just me and my horse."

Now Carrie took notice. Of all her friends, she was the only lone, traveling, horse-woman she knew. Everyone else came with family, friends, spouse, or whatever. A few men showed up solo, but seldom women. Oh, she didn't mind, and it was true what Molly had said about here being a lone wolf. But it isn't always easy to be the only of your kind, and it could get lonely at times.

"What about your husband?" Carrie asked, "I see you've got a wedding ring."

"He's a workaholic. Puts in about a thousand hours a week and I almost never see him. Might as well be married to my goddamn horse!"

"Tough," Carrie said.

The screech of an amplifier rang in the distance...then died. A few notes twanged from an electric guitar...and stopped. Someone dragged a bow across a fiddle...then quit. A drummer tapped his sticks four times, and the music came to life.

"What say we grab a spot at the stage before they're gone?" Molly said. All agreed, and the women started off.

Stars glittered in the blackness above. Scattered campfires threw off shadowy light that flicked into the sparse trees. And a mystery called from somewhere beyond in the form of live music. This dream-like place seemed so distant from Adrienne's daily life. She felt as if she was experiencing the world for the first time.

As they passed her camp, Molly picked up three folding chairs, handed one to each woman, and grabbed a six-pack of Coors.

"Where's Mack," Carrie asked, "You finally leave him home for once?"

"Naw. He's around somewhere, if he ain't already passed out in the camper. Hell, he was drunk when I left him. I'd bet he's probably out somewhere talkin' shit with the boys though."

"Adrienne remembered something, "I'll be right back. Will you wait?"

"A'course, dear," Molly's said. "Just don't take all night."

In a flash, Adrienne returned with a bottle of red wine and paper cups. "Ready," she picked up her chair and the walking resumed.

At campground's end, a clearing sat in the midst of this strange desert/forest. Through the night's deep shadow, Adrienne saw a large flatbed trailer/stage with an animated three-man band positioned atop as their country music drowned the drone of a gas generator set nearby. A small crowd had already assembled. They sat in folding chairs or stood gawking at the band while talking with one another.

    The girls set their chairs and dropped into them. Molly cracked a Coors while Carrie and Adrienne went for wine.

4

    Dancers began to take the floor and within minutes the clearing moved in a blur of colorful clothing, big hats, giant belt-buckles and happy faces. The uneven dirt surface was a challenge and Adrienne laughed as she watched the more drunken participants tip this way and that. But her laughter turned to delight when she saw the swing dancers perform in seemingly prefect unison with their partners. There was line-dancing too.

    Linda appeared from the crowd and plopped into a chair beside Molly's. "Well," Molly said, "where's your hubby?"

    "He's over there talkin' with some guys," Linda pointed to a group of men standing in the distance. Mack was among them, "They started off with horses, but the conversation turned to football and went downhill from there."

    "Boy talk huh?" Molly said, "Well, welcome to the girl's club honey. Care for a beer?" she held up a can.

    "Don't mind if I do," Linda popped the top, chugged half the can, wiped wet lips with the back of her hand, then let out a loud belch.

    Adrienne was a little shocked.

    "To bad men ain't more like horses." she said, "You know, just take them out and ride 'em, then give them some hay, brush 'em, and put 'em out to pasture till your wanna ride some more. Now I know horses ain't exactly that fuckin' easy, but at least you don't have to listen to their bullshit!"

"What's crawled into your panties?" Adrienne said. She noted that Linda was already pretty well lit.

"He ain't all that bad I guess. It's just that he can be such a jackass at times."

"Lady, you got nothin' t' bitch about," Molly interjected, "Least your man's half purdy—and seems well mannered to boot. Hell, just look at that old goat I gotta crawl in 'ta bed with every night."

All eyes turned to Mack.

"Bald head. Pot belly. Drunk half the time. Even if he was a horse I wouldn't wanna ride him."

Carrie's hand flew to her face as she laughed through a mouthful of wine. She was, after all, the only confirmed bachelorette present and this kind of talk always renewed her resolve to stay that way.

"Then why do you stay with him Molly?" Adrienne asked.

"Well, I guess it's 'cause we been married for over 20-years now an'…hell, I wouldn't know how t' leave him anymore. Besides, after all these years we kinda got each other figured an' don't get under one-another's feet no more. He just leaves me to do whatever I please…same as I do him. 'Sides, you ain't one to talk there missy; how come you stay with yours? Sounds like he ain't no walk in the park neither."

"Well, first off Molly, he's handsome…very handsome. And he's not a bad man. Josie's got a big heart. It's just that he's so caught up in his job it's almost like not having a man at all," Adrienne was annoyed that her sadness bled through even as she tried to hide it.

"Well," Molly went on, "maybe we outta all take lesson from 'ol Carrie here. She's the only one does exactly like Linda was sayin'.

The spotlight was on Carrie now. In her uncommon strength and insistence on honesty, Carrie was not one to justify her actions. She was just Carrie, and if you didn't like it you could go fuck yourself. "That's right," she said, "I just ride 'em a piece, and when they get to irritating me, I turn them loose. Keeps life simple. Besides, variety is the spice of life."

Just then, a man stepped from the crowd and asked Adrienne

to dance. She looked up. He was tall and thin with muscular build, light hair and strong jaw-line. Aside from a crew cut that accentuated slightly protruding ears, he was not an unattractive guy. But he was so young.

"Oh no, I couldn't," she replied, "But thank you anyway." Thwarted, the man started away.

"Why don't you dance with him?" Molly scolded.

"I'm married," she pointed to the ring.

"My god child, he asked you for a dance…not a blow-job. Come on girl. Everyone deserves a little fun now and again, don't they?"

Adrienne gasped at Molly's directness. But the wine had begun to do its job, and a slightly sinful grin crept slowly onto Adrienne's face.

"Hey Billy," Molly yelled, but the boy didn't hear. **"Hey Billy,"** she tried again. Billy had stopped nearby to talk with friends, but the music was too loud. Molly picked up an empty beer-can and threw it hard at the boy's backside, but it bounced soundly off the back of his head instead. Billy's hand shot up and he spun around to eye the crowd suspiciously.

Molly cringed. "Ooo," she whispered, "That must'a hurt."

"Great shot Molly," Carrie struggled weakly to contain her laugh. Linda snickered, then they all bellowed in unison.

Having gained his attention, Molly motioned the boy back. "Molly, I didn't see you there," he said, "Was that you beaned me on the noggin with a beer-can?" Billy's hand came up to rub his head some more. The girls snickered again. Billy pretended not to notice.

"Sorry 'bout that Billy-boy. I didn't mean t'… Awe, hell, you probably had it comin' fer somethin' you done anyway," she smiled at him.

Molly's brassy ways had always commanded Billy's respect. He liked her. Besides, he couldn't believe this any less than an accident.

"Listen Billy, this here's Adrienne. She's new around here and don't know many folks. Anyway, after you left she changed her mind about that dance. The offer still stand?"

"It's a hell of a way to get a dance but, what the hey, let's give 'er a whirl," and he held a hand out to Adrienne. She took it, shot an unsure smile back to Molly, then moved onto the floor.

At first, she was a little stiff in such unfamiliar territory. The moonlight seemed very bright as it washed over the crowd. Music thundered through her ears. Flashes of clothing spun in a prism of moving color. She could feel the crowd's heat. The uneasiness passed. Adrienne got into it.

As the night wore on Adrienne spent a lot of time on the dance floor. So did Carrie. Linda got Chet out there a few times, and Mac didn't care who Molly danced with.

It was late when the girls finally said goodnight and went their separate ways. Adrienne crawled into her sleeping bag. She was drunk but could not remember when she'd had a better time.

The following day passed Adrienne in a blur of new adventures, ideas, emotions, and friends. Again, she hung with Molly and Carry. The trio ate breakfast together, participated in a group ride, and tried their hand at the horse games—which were silly things played only for fun. In the *Balloon Toss* Adrienne laughed hysterically when a water balloon exploded onto one competitor or another as he or she tried to catch the squishy thing from a trotting horse. Adrienne won a second-place trophy in that one.

Sunday morning finally rolled around and, because most had to work Monday, the little campground was a blur of motion as folks began to repack and clear out. Adrienne knew she would soon fall in behind Chet and Linda for the journey home, and she felt an unsettling sense of loss. It had been a wonderful experience and she knew she would do it again.

The girls exchanged phone numbers, talked of good times to come, and promised to keep in touch. Hugs were exchanged and Adrienne even cried a little.

On the ride home, Adrienne thought of the wonderful time she'd had. Full lips curled into a pleasant smile as she recalled each detail of the weekend. But the smile vanished when she remembered the terror that had accompanied her here. Of what had she been afraid? The fear had been only a hollow specter after all. A lie that sought to keep her in the bondage of only that which is familiar and deny her the opportunities, experiences, and joys, of all that lay beyond. If she ever had to face this demon again she knew now that she could, and would, defeat him. Although she knew it not at that moment, Adrienne had just granted herself **The World**.

With that, she went home.

TIME MARCHES ON
Chapter 11

1

Adrienne and Carrie did become good friends. They kept in almost constant phone contact and, since Carrie lived less than 10-miles from the Double-S anyway, Adrienne visited her often. Although Carrie's house was intentionally kept small and inexpensive to better devote her slender resources to other interests, the place resided on county land and Carrie was able to board her horse at home. The girls schemed often of the new places and events they would visit and the adventure that awaited them there. Carrie's knowledge, experience, and capacity for new ideas, was so extensive it often left Adrienne shocked. Carrie was truly a mover and a shaker. But Adrienne gathered her courage, followed in her mentor's footsteps, and learned quickly. Sometimes they traveled together, but in Carrie's seemingly ingrained, and Adrienne's growing, strength and independence, the women most often met at their destination instead.

Mosaic grew into a young man. Although he had possessed a mean streak in the past, as he aged, this attitude mellowed. Unlike his father, Mosaic had not known fulfillment in his youth. Although Moze would never find peace in this life, he was not a stupid boy. Since he could find no other worthy reason for existence in this insane world, Mosaic decided to follow the example of his father. *Power* and *Profit* were obviously the only reason for life, and because fits of anger would only hinder this ambition, Moze learned to control his temper.

Mosaic took interest in the family business. This delighted his father and Josie experienced real pride in the educating of his son into the business he himself had worked so hard to build. *Some day,* Josie thought, *Mosaic will rule this empire.* This idea added even more fertilizer to the tract-house king's already booming ego. Moze learned quickly. He and Josie became an unstoppable force.

Mosaic moved into a home of his own. In a year he was married and, to the delight of his parents, the new couple soon bore a son. They named him Alexander.

Adrienne was elated with this new arrival. Never one to be neglected by his grandmother, her cooing and showers of affection became a familiar event to him. In time the boy would sometimes accompany his grandmother to the Double-S—her personal world beyond the city lights—and it would suit him fine. But just now grandma had a life of her own. Through her diligence Adrienne had found among the horses a road that was right for her. So right in fact, that for a joy and fulfillment she had not previously known existed, Adrienne would never falter.

Immersing ever deeper into the world of horse and bridal, Adrienne's horizons expanded dramatically. She and Chelsea became involved in barrel racing. Rodeos held her interest too, as did any event that attracted horses, horse people, and her growing arsenal of friends. Long journeys—now often traveled alone—became common. Having become familiar territory in recent years, the trips no longer scared her. Instead, they brought only excitement.

Josie continued to work.

As did that of her husband, Adrienne's empire also grew. As Josie tallied his gains in money, possession, and power, his wife counted hers in friends, passion, fun, tranquility, and the love of God's land. And just as Josie's empire had been forged of persistent effort and commitment…so then was Adrienne's.

Again, the years passed.

Josie collapsed in his office. His secretary called an ambulance, then his wife. Adrienne drove straight to the hospital, as did Mosaic. And although old age had taken Josie's parents from him years ago, his brother Jacob showed up with his wife Ellyn.

Josie had suffered a massive heart attack. The doctor informed the family that if the patient did not undergo immediate bypass surgery his chances for survival were slim. Josie was 52-years old.

The surgery was scheduled. It lasted many hours.

His recovery would not prove an easy one.

Before her, Josie slept amid the late-night hospital sheets. *As never before he needs my strength now*, Adrienne thought as she looked down upon him, *and with God as my witness, I will give it gladly.* And with this conviction the beautiful woman allowed herself the passing luxury of tears.

After the surgery, the first thing Josie noticed was his wife who seemed always to be at his bedside. He needed her now. And there she was, strong, beautiful, and radiant. He had not considered her seriously, he realized, for many years. There had simply not been time. He'd been too busy, *Josie had convinced himself*, working to build a better life for her.

He considered her now.

She's so beautiful, he thought, *and intelligent. She's really a pleasure to talk with. But then*, he remembered suddenly, *she's always been like that.* Josie thought of the day they had met on the bus, of the feelings she had stirred in him, and the need she'd unwittingly awoke within his loins. He smiled at her as these warm memories washed over him. She smiled back. But there was something different about her. What was it? She had changed. He looked more closely. She was older of course, but that was not it… At once it hit him: Adrienne carried a new strength, a kind of magnificence. Her eyes…they sparkled with a fire not present before. Her spirit glowed through them. Even in her weakened state of dismay at his uncertain condition, it was there. She exuded confidence, vitality, and strength in her every movement, her every gesture. Josie was astonished! From where had this change originated? When had it happened?

Standing (or lying) in the light of such a woman, Josie fell in love again. *Look at her*, he thought, *in all her beauty and radiance she still loves me.* **She loved him!** How could a creature such as she care so for a dirt farmer—millionaire—and now a broken man—such as he? He saw then that it mattered not what he did in the world, her only wish was to spend this life with him; and for years he had denied her the only thing she'd ever asked. And still she loved him. Josie felt sadness then. He was ashamed.

Although Mosaic made regular visits to the hospital, he spent most of his time out running the business. To his father's inquiries the young man made only superficial reports. Although the two often disagreed on many things, Mosaic found that he cared very much for his dad and did not wish to bring him stress at a time like this. No, he would bear the company's burdens alone. After all, he was quite capable. His father, Mosaic knew, now needed only rest. The boy would do his part.

    Jacob was there too. Long ago he had taken a wife then finished school to open practice as a family dentist. With the passing of time, coupled with his family of a wife and three children, Jake had made his own peace in this world. The childhood rivalries between he and Josie were long passed. Jacob loved his little brother and had come to offer any support he could.

    Josie was truly a fortunate man.

    Josie had been in the hospital for just under a week when a very strange thing happened. It was in the wee-hours of the morning that he came suddenly awake from a mildly drug-induced slumber. But he did not feel drugged. In fact, Josie's mind seemed uncommonly clear. Adrienne was not at his bedside and it had taken considerable argument to convince her to go home and get some sleep.

    Uncommon wealth had granted Josie a private room and it was there that he now lay staring at the ceiling. The hospital was unusually quiet at this late hour. Aside from a pale beam of moonlight that glowed weakly through one thinly curtained window, the room was dark. He was alone.

    Josie truly was a broken man. For all his power, strength, and notoriety he could not remember ever having been so frail. Josie felt his mortality then. The Great Man would *actually die* someday—maybe soon—over this he commanded no power. The idea came as quite a shock. In his helplessness and weakened state of body, so then was his mind and strength-of-will also weakened. In an instant, Josie's heart had shattered his ego to allow him the luxury of an open mind. From this new perspective he began to see things differently.

    He thought of the Great Man who enjoys the recognition, praise, and indulgence of the multitudes. Yet in his heart he was still only a man. Just a man; with all the same strengths, weaknesses, hopes, dreams, fears, feelings, loves, insecurities, emotions, triumphs, and failures of any other. Power and position had changed nothing. He was still only a man among men. *It was all a lie,* he thought, *my whole life...just a lie*. With that the Great Man hung his head to cry. And his sobs were so strong, and so heartfelt with the anguish of the human spirit that even God heard them from the splendor of his meadow. And in that moment, He too shed a tear for the child he called Josie.

2

Josie emerged from the hospital a changed man. Although his recovery came slowly, under the codling of his wife Josie's strength began to return. The doctor had warned against excessive stress and this caution granted him good excuse for not returning to work. In truth, Josie no longer wished to return. After all, life is short and he desired to spend the entirety of its precious remaining moments in the company of people he loved, and the things he enjoyed—though he was no longer sure what those might be. Besides, he had already worked a lifetime's worth. But it did not matter. He was different now. And as he was, so then would he act.

There seemed so many things he had not noticed before and each demanded his attention now! Like a young child, Josie examined his surroundings as if seeing them for the first time.

He was fascinated.

Josie watched a spider work diligently with a fly caught in its web at the corner of a bedroom window.

He was captivated.

The Great Man sat on the swinging chair in the mansion's manicured backyard and watched Merlin, the family's pet German Shepherd, carouse the grounds. First, he sniffed here, then he sniffed there. Finally, Merlin found the right bush and lifted his leg. Still unsatisfied, he found another and repeated this ritual. This simple activity seemed of profound importance in the life of a dog.

Again, Josie was fascinated.

Bees buzzed busily over flowers and birds sung in the trees. Even everyday colors seemed more vibrant than he remembered.

And the sky was so blue—the air so warm. Josie felt awake, more so than he ever had before.

Eventually Merlin found his ball and brought it that his master might play fetch with him. Josie took the slimy toy with one hand and scratched his pet behind the ears with the other. Merlin crooned. When Josie stopped, the big animal laid his massive head into the man's lap. *He loves me too,* Josie thought, *I am certainly a lucky man to have a friend like him.* With that he threw the yucky ball and the dog bounded after it.

Josie's sex drive returned! Although it was out of concern for his health that Adrienne attempted feebly to thwart his initial advances, Josie's playful seductions won her over easily. In reality, she had not put up much of a fight; for this man still stirred a flame within her womanhood. And Josie was just so frisky all the time! Adrienne began to enjoy a sex life far better than she could remember. God how she had missed him. Now he was back! And sometimes, in the solitude of night, gratitude leaked from her eyes and she thanked the Almighty for Josie's return.

The doctor had suggested that his will to live was of great importance now and, in order to assist the recovery process, she should take whatever action seemed appropriate to that objective. To her however, Josie's will to live seemed stronger than ever.

In effort to liberate him from the confines of home Adrienne began taking Josie on short outings into the world. It was on a happenstance drive at the outskirts of the expending city that they came upon Cactus Lake. Although Cactus Lake had been converted into Cactus Park, it was still the same place Josie had spent so much time with his father and brother in his youth. In contrast to days past though, the grounds were now green with closely cropped grass. Some trees had been removed and those that remained were finely manicured. There were picnic tables with steel barbeque grills. A playground with a swing set and slide had been added along with a cement walkway that encircled this quiet little body of water. Some jogged while others lounged and still others watched their children at the playground on this beautiful Saturday afternoon. At one table a large family sat busily to their picnic lunch. But it was the boy and his father who stood with poles at water's edge that inspired Josie.

Fishing! Josie had not thought it for years, "Let's do some fishing baby." and Josie turned a wide grin on his wife. She grinned back; for his childlike fascination with the world had become infectious these days.

"Okay," Adrienne replied, glad of his interest in anything that was not work. "Tomorrow. We'll get some poles and a license…"

"No." his interruption was firm. Tomorrow might never come, Josie knew that now and wished to do his living while he still could. "Let's do it today. Right now!"

So, they did.

Two hours later both Stevenson's stood on the shore of Cactus Lake. Josie began to string his new line then added hooks and a bobber. Adrienne took off her shoes and rolled up the cuffs of her jeans. She
strung a bobber and three hooks to her own line. Josie watched with wide amazement as this strange girl added a live worm to each hook. With concentration complete to this task, she did not flinch.

Forever, it seemed, they had basked in the glow of extreme wealth and Adrienne had been a lady of business parties and her mansion. Now Josie remembered: *She's a country girl. She's always been a country girl!*

Adrienne waded into the water, cast her line, then sat upon a large rock near the shore. Josie felt as though he was experiencing this woman for the first time. Unable to control himself, the predator began to stalk his pray. With stealth born of the powerful panther who crouches in the deep jungle, Josie slunk forward. Sharp concentration spurred the huge cat's paws to break the surface of calm water and sink soundlessly to the bottom. His breath became shallow, quiet. Closer…closer… The unsuspecting pray shifted a little. The panther froze! Had he been discovered? No. The hunt was still good. Closer…closer… Now! In a violent melee of claw and carnage he snatched the unsuspecting doe from behind and dragged her kicking and laughing from her perch. The powerful panther deposited his prey onto the shore, pounced upon her, and tore viciously into the soft and vulnerable neck area with his gentle teeth. It would all be over soon… It tickled, as he had known it would, and the victim writhed and giggled beneath him. But she soon threw remarkably strong arms around his body and pulled his weight down upon her shapely form. The panther was shocked! She kissed him then, and the couple necked passionately for a while. Like children they laughed, played…then fished all morning.

Although neither had knowledge of it, there was another Great Man who had once said, 'In order to enter the gates of heaven one must approach with the heart of a child.' That man's name was Jesus Christ.

They caught many perch and a few trout too. Adrienne attached her fish to the stringer, then scaled and gutted them at day's end.

Again, Josie was fascinated.

That night Adrienne Barbequed fresh trout in the back yard while Josie occupied a lawn-chair, scratched Merlin's ears, and sometimes stared at the night sky. For all this time life had been going on right under his nose and he had not even known it. Josie looked into the big face of the panting shepherd. He felt kind of stupid gawking at such simple things. What would his associates say? Probably that he was losing his mind or going senile. But what did he care? Josie could not remember when he had ever been happier.

Simple things… It seemed a storehouse of wealth could be amassed from them. Josie had formerly believed that wealth could be obtained only through the acquisition of man-made objects. He now realized that a vast degree of life's best rewards lay in God's creation as well. One of these was his grandson. Josie resolved to spend more time with the boy. And so, he would.

Josie knew that Adrienne loved her horse thing—whatever that was. How could he not? For some time now their house had been permeated with horse memorabilia: pictures, statues, painted bedspreads, and the like. And had she not spent almost all her spare time at that Double-S Ranch in recent years? And what about all the weekends, and sometimes entire weeks, of traveling to one "event" or another? Oh, he had not minded her absence so much. Josie trusted his wife. She had never given him reason not to. He had sometimes wondered where she went and what she did on these outings, but for serious inquiry he'd simply had no time or interest. There had always been much more important matters to demand his attention. But busy was something Josie no longer was, and he thought of her strange interest now. Josie also knew that her original confusion, trauma, and fear over his heart attack had turned to one of happiness, relief, and contentment in recent months. But she had not left his side since the illness and he knew she missed those damn horses. Missed them a lot. He could see it in her eyes.

"Why don't you take me horseback riding?" he asked one morning.

Adrienne's head spun quickly to him and Josie felt, more than saw, her surprise. "Do you... Are you... Sure. I'd love that Josie! When?"

Life is short. Josie knew that now. Wishing to miss no more of it he would not put the good things off. Josie would live for the here and now—for the *moment*. Some say that God lives only in the moment. If this is true, then He and Josie were destined to spend a lot of time together.

"Today. After breakfast. Is that okay?

Silence hung in the air as she contemplated him. For a moment it was only her jaw muscles that moved. Slowly then, full lips curled until the smile reached all the way up to her sparkling blue eyes. "Okay," she grinned, "After breakfast it is."

It was one of those rare, perfect summer-days when Adrienne's truck left the city for the twisting two-lane that led into the country and the Double-S. Josie sat contentedly gazing through the open passenger window. It had been quite a while since he had ventured beyond the city. Eventually the truck turned onto a dirt road, passed under the arched Double-S sign, and stopped at the stables.

It was a weekday and customers were scarce. Ben was gone for the day and, aside from Irma who was busy giving antibiotic shots to a sick mare, Josie and Adrienne had the place to themselves. Adrienne saddled Chelsea then tied her to a fence while Josie's fascination led him to explore the area, pet dogs, and talk to chickens. Knowing that Chet would appreciate the exercise of his horse anyway, Adrienne saddled Lightning. Next, she called to Josie and handed him Chelsea's rains. Both mounted and rode into the mountains.

The countryside had a calming effect, and the ride brought Josie back to the days of his youth. He had loved the land so: the sounds, the smells, and the freshness of its open spaces. It had brought him such tranquility as a boy. How had he forgotten?

The day was long, as summer days are, and they rode for hours. Along with a canteen of water and thermos of hot tea, Adrienne had packed lunch into the small daypack now tied to Lightning's saddle. The couple dismounted beside a stream. They watered the horses, tied them to a gnarled tree, then sat to cold sandwiches, tea, and red apples. A gentle breeze blew across the land. It tugged at Josie's hair. For a while, all the world seemed perfect.

It was late afternoon when they finally left the Double-S. On the way home Josie took his girl to dinner and a movie—just like old times.

3

In the months that followed, Josie began to accompany his wife on campouts and other horse-oriented events. Josie purchased a Black Arabian gelding called Chump (so named for his sometimes-stubborn disposition). He met Carrie, who seemed a little standoffish at first. Secretly, Carrie feared for the loss of her friend. Close friendship did not always come easy to one so free and she worried that Josie's arrival might drive a wedge between this one. To some extent, it did; but Adrienne had never known anyone like Carrie, and she would always love this unique woman. It did not take long for Carrie to realize this. Besides, Josie was easy to like. And Carrie did. In fact, she soon grew very fond of him. From then on, Carrie's enthusiasm at his arrival never failed to brighten Josie's day.

Molly thought Josie was a "hunk", and he made a host of other new friends too. The world his wife had discovered in his absence amazed Josie. And she had gained so much for it. She was truly a magnificent woman these days; so confident and filled with vitality. Josie counted his blessings some more.

Josie loved the campouts, the smell of horses, the camaraderie of the people and, of course, the land. But the world of horse and bridle did not call so deeply to him as it did his wife. Josie wondered if anything ever would.

Although occasionally briefed on business by his son, Josie faded farther into the company's background with the passing of each day. His power withered. Mosaic became the new "Money King". Oh, they still called Josie "Sir", but no one took him too seriously anymore, or came to pay homage to "The Great Man". Josie could care less, for now that his life was truely great, he no longer needed anyone to tell him about it.

To Mosaic, this new power seemed a license to kill. After all, the world of big business is a battleground. And all's fair in love and war, right? Moze began to take actions that often crossed the line of morality. Oh, he kept within the confines of legality. Mosaic did not wish to see the inside of a prison cell. Still, some were hurt, and a few ruined.

The company's profits soared.

Josie was sickened. For even in the throes of ambition he had always been a fair man. For him, watching prosperity grow in the lives of all involved was one of the greatest rewards of being the Money King. The idea of doing things any other way had simply never occurred to him.

Mosaic did not see things that way. For had not Josie himself taught his only son that the world means nothing in the light of material gain? That profit is the alpha and the omega, the only true reason for existence? In fact, this was perhaps the only real thing his father had taken time to teach the boy.

Josie became sickened with himself.

It was at about this time that Josie acquired a nasty cough. Adrienne filled him with chicken soup and medicine but the cold persisted. Josie began to complain of chest pains, but it wasn't until he started to hack up blood that Adrienne insisted he see a doctor. Tests were taken. The patient had lung cancer. More tests were made, and the diagnosis showed that the cancer had already spread to other parts of the body. The doctor informed him that any therapy was useless now. The cancer was terminal. The best he could do was offer prescriptions to help keep him comfortable. The doctor advised that Josie remain in the hospital under professional care but did not argue when Josie said he wished to die at home.

Unlike some he had known, the cancer was merciful and took him down quickly. Josie lost weight at an alarming rate. For each day that passed he seemed to age a year. Josie became gaunt, pale, and weak.

The time was close now and Josie's family stayed near. In the last days Mosaic and his son moved into one of the mansion's spare rooms. Jacob came everyday. Friends visited often. Adrienne's strength had left her now and she sometimes wept openly at Josie's bedside. Sometimes they cried together. But mostly they tried to enjoy the time that remained.

The day arrived. Although he knew not how, Josie was well aware that this was his final day on earth. Josie lay in bed at noon staring out one of the mansion's big picture-windows. His eyes strayed from the tract-houses that lay beyond the sill to focus upon his young grandson who stood with the rest of Josie's family beside the beautiful, gold-laden deathbed. And he thought, *What have I left for you my grandchild? For you will never know the oak and apple trees, clean waters and golden fields that can bring such happiness to the heart of a child and are your God given birthright. For in its place, you will be surrounded instead with the greed of artificial comfort, and frantic pursuit—even corruption—into the disease of **"more"** and the accusation of only greater material gain within this stressed-out world of debt, smog, and concrete that I have worked so hard to create.*

A tear fell from Josie's eye and his grandson, seeing this, mistakenly believed that his grandpa was only sad because he was so sick.

How can I tell him, Josie thought, *for my words will mean but little to a six-year-old boy, for he sees only my actions now—as did my only son. And will he not follow in my footsteps? For have I not taught my own son that the world means nothing in the light of material gain? Oh God,* Josie thought as the tears began to flow. *How can I tell him what I've learned?*

But the boy already knew. In fact, he had been born knowing. With that Josie closed his eyes and he died.

THREE NIGHTS IN THE MEADOW
Chapter 12

1

Again, Josie found himself in the meadow and again he met God. "Oh God," he cried, tears still streaming from his eyes, "Did you see?"

"Of course, I did Josie."

"Then you know that I have bought and owned your land. I then killed your trees, bulldozed the hills, and ran the animals off. Where there was beauty and harmony I built hideous structures bringing with them tension, anxiety, and pollution. I'm so ashamed. Are you mad?"

"You cannot own the land any more than the moon or the stars my friend. But look at it this way, when your child plays in the driver's seat of your automobile pretending he's all grown up and owns the car, do you mind? Of course not. Likewise, when my children play in the fields pretending they own the land I created four and a half billion years before their birth, should I be upset? They're only children; let them pretend. In time they'll come to know better."

"But," Josie retorted, "I and others have pillaged that land in the name of profit and power. In the end I fear man will use his machinery and growing power to destroy the earth! Why, if we don't…" He was ranting now.

"Have you ever looked at the night sky?" God's interruption was abrupt.

"…Of course, I have," Josie bellowed with annoyance, "But what does that have to do with…"

God's voice cut him off again, "And you know that each star

is a sun like your own, only many are much larger. And each star glows with the power of massive nuclear reaction and explosion. And, the number of stars in the heavens seems infinite doesn't it? Now that, my friend, ***is power***. And from where I sit, it's only a small display. Good thing I'm a nice guy huh?" God's grin was sly, almost devilish. "Now look at the power of Mother Nature," he lightened, "No matter how hard he tries, man has *never* been able to sway her sometimes flighty whims in even the slightest way. No Josie, man has no power. But is it not necessary that I allow him the elusion of power? If I didn't would anyone take life's pleasures, hardships, and lessons seriously? For the world must appear very real; don't you think? But let's face it, if man really did have power we'd all be in deep trouble wouldn't we? It would be like giving a six-year-old a bazooka—look out universe!

"But what of the pollution and weapons of mass destruction?" Josie blurted impatiently, "Could we not pretty much wipe out life on earth?"

"Oh, come on Josie," It was God's turn to be exasperated, "Do you really think that no matter what people do I could not put the world back into whatever state I cared to in only 5,000 years? Less, if I felt like it. "Look at it this way my friend: when you put a kid in a playpen do you not expect him to not mess his little world up? And if he does will you be mad? Of course not, for he is only a child; and it will take only a few minutes to clean up after him anyway. But the child is confined to the playpen—just as you are to the earth my friend—to protect the world beyond from him, and himself from the world beyond. When he is mature enough—and as it will eventually be for all my children—he will be allowed out of the playpen—and beyond the earth itself—to explore the real world; or that which is known to some as heaven.

These extraordinary ideas took Josie by surprise and he stopped to contemplate them.

When the moment had passed God led the conversation in a new direction, "In any case Josie, I know you feel you've done me a serious wrong with your tract house thing. In reality though, the only one you've harmed is yourself. For although man tends to believe he can build a better world than I, in truth he usually tends to build confusion and disharmony instead. Man's wish to become God is, to some extent, natural. It's just that he often goes about it in the wrong way. He must simply learn to coexist with, and even enjoy, that which is rather than destroy it and build something he can rule over. God does not rule, but seeks only to live in harmony with all that is an extension of himself.

"So, yes, I forgive you for being the Tract House King. Now, can you forgive yourself? And, more importantly, did you learn anything?"

Josie fell silent again to consider these words. God's bright eyes, remarkably relaxed manner, and easily forgiving nature always had a calming affect on him. It seemed that nothing had the power to disturb The Almighty. This, Josie thought, was the most wonderful part of God's magnificence.

"Come on Josie, let's sit beside the stream for a while. With that, Josie shouldered his bundle of yet unsettled emotions and followed his friend to the oaks. The two men then sat to bask in the vast beauty and calmness as fine shade fell from the old oaks to grant cool sanctuary from the warm sunshine.

In a moment, Josie said sheepishly, "You know God; I had all the money, all the power, respect and even worship of my peers. They said I was a Great Man. Sometimes I felt powerful. This was exhilarating and I often took to power, and even ego, tripping." Feeling ashamed, Josie looked to God for his reaction. It was an embarrassing subject, but he wished to get it off his chest. God only gazed calmly across the meadow as he listened. He seemed unaffected by the subject's nature, so Josie continued, "Yet in my deepest moments I did not feel that way. I felt only as a man like any other. If anything, it seemed that my status often provoked fear in others and this only helped to separate me from my fellows. It was sometimes hard to know who my real friends were, for there were so many who came only to massage my ego rather than reveal their true feelings. Only after the heart attack did I...." Josie ran out of words then.

After a moment God turned his magnificent eyes to Josie and began to speak, "You see me here in the meadow and you think that I am God, and so you are right my friend. But God does not exist only here in this meadow; God is all encompassing. In all the sea, land, plants, animals, and people, you will find a piece of 'The Almighty', as you are so fond of calling me. Therefore, to separate yourself from your fellows is to separate yourself from me. And alone Josie, your spirit will wither and die; for even you are a very important part of the whole. It's for this reason that I do not sit in judgment of you my friend, and although I may be your teacher and command much greater power, I consider you my equal. For without you, I too would be incomplete.

"So, you see that to willfully injure another, or even the world around you, is only to shoot yourself in the foot. For these things are all part of you; and you will only live well when you learn to take care of yourself. To enjoy a fulfilling existence, each must learn to accept those around him, as I do, for what they are. The idea of status means nothing, as I love the wino in the gutter just as much as the king in the castle; for they are all on the same journey, and they are all my children. Besides, in time they may simply trade places.

"You may be only a child now but someday you will grow into a fine man Josie. Hell, you are well on your way now and I am very proud of you."

With this statement Josie fell to a profound sense of comfort, accomplishment and well being. God loved him, was proud of him; even liked him and valued his companionship as would a good friend. Josie's heart warmed, he felt whole and content. Josie began to fill with gratitude. In a moment it leaked from his eyes. Josie felt embarrassment and sought rather weakly to conceal his emotion. But God seemed not to notice, and again he only gazed across the gently blowing fields.

2

In a moment God said, "Shall we build a pit and gather wood for the evening fire?"

So, he would be staying the night here with God…The Creator of All Things! Josie nodded excitedly and both men rose to the task. A pit was quickly assembled from rocks gathered at the water's edge. The men began to pull dry wood from the surrounding forest. In short time a large pile occupied the ground nearby.

God chose two poles from the others. One was four-foot long and forked at one end; the other was nine feet and straight. He began to assemble these while Josie sat upon a large rock at the nearby fire-pit and watched with ardent interest. Using the old bone-handled knife always worn at his waist, God stripped any small branches from both poles. Next, he sharpened the strait end of the forked branch. Using a large rock, he beat the pointed end of his forked pole into the ground then fit the longer pole into the fork and set its other end on the dirt. When finished the work resembled a large roasting spit with one of the Y-poles missing.

Josie was fascinated.

When this was done, God began to break shorter branches then lean them against either side of his long ridgepole. When finished, the thing looked like the discarded skeleton of some prehistoric creature. God stood back to admire his handiwork. So did Josie.

"What is it?" Josie's calm demeanor failed to muffle his ignorance.

"My house," God's explanation was pretty thin. "The nights can get chilly around here. Might wanna build one for yourself."

Without another question, Josie did and in short time a second wooden skeleton stood beside the first. With frames complete, the men gathered brush and other forest debris to pile over them. When finished, this insulation was four feet thick. Next, they lined the insides with pine-needles, grasses, and any other suitable forest debris available. These would act as both mattress and blanket. The idea seemed to be that the wooden frame above would hold the thick layer of bedding-insulation atop their bodies so it would not fall away as one repositioned himself throughout the night. When complete, Josie eyed the primitive structures skeptically. He had doubts. But the fact that both entryways faced the nearby fire-pit was of some consolation at least.

The sun was at its zenith now. The day half-gone. "You hungry?"

"Yup," Josie answered.

"How about blackberries?" God pointed across the meadow

and Josie's eyes followed. There, past the wildflowers, tall, dried grass, and one particularly big bolder, sat a large ribbon of bushes—a berry-patch. Both men set off in its direction. Bees buzzed all around as they walked, and an occasional hummingbird swooped close to suckle nectar from a flower. Warm sunshine pelted Josie's skin and he began to sweat. They reached the destination. The swollen berries were juicy-sweet and for half an hour no human sound beyond the rustle of leaves or snap of a twig disturbed the air as both men became lost to their private worlds among the thorny bushes.

When hunger was sated to some satisfaction, both again met before the berry-patch. Josie stood looking at the purple stains on his hands and wondering if his lips were the same when God said, "Lets walk," and he moved off along the meadow's perimeter.

Josie followed.

Along the way, God stopped to regard a small grove of birch trees gathered at meadow's edge. He picked up a short slab of the curly bark then motioned that Josie should do the same. When this was done, God tucked his slab under one arm and continued on. Before long God stopped again to admire what looked to Josie like a simple weed growing low to the ground. After a moment's contemplation, he pulled this weed from the dirt to reveal a small carrot attached to its other end. God offered his prize a warm smile, then set this wild vegetable into his birch-bark tray and looked for another. Josie soon engaged keen interest into the search for carrots as well. In short time each man had a little pile gathered upon his tray.

They moved on.

Next came wild garlic and the same ritual was repeated. There were wild onions, rosemary, mustard flowers, chickweed, purslane, and others. An apple tree offered fresh fruit. Their gathering continued methodically and without hurry beneath the warm afternoon sun. For Josie, this was the best of times he had yet spent in the company of his unusual friend.

When finally, the men returned to their camp beneath the oaks and near the water's edge, both bark slabs were filled to nearly overflowing with wild edibles. After setting his tray near the newly built fire-pit, God picked up a long shaft he had previously cut from a young sapling while gathering firewood. With this item in hand, he took a seat against the old oak to whittle in the shade for a while. With a sigh of contentment Josie plopped down against the tree beside him. It felt good to be off his feet. A gentle breeze cooled sweaty skin as he relaxed in the deep shade the ancient oak provided.

For a time, conversation remained simple, and although Josie watched with curiosity the item upon which God worked, he made no comment.

In a while God said, "See that thicket of bushes near those trees at the edge of the meadow?" he pointed.

Josie saw them.

"Just to the left of that dead pine is a rolling snare-trap and I believe a cottontail is caught in it now. Would you go fetch him please?"

"Sure," Josie got to his feet.

"Take this," God handed him the knife, "and clean him." Josie took the tool. "I'm going downstream and do some fishing." Josie noted that the end of God's sapling-shaft had been split into two expertly barbed and finished points now held apart from each another with a wooden wedge lashed between them using cordage made from the strong fibers of dogbane. It seemed a finely crafted spear. "Meet you back here in a little while, okay?" Josie nodded, as the older man got to his feet. As both walked in opposite directions God said over his shoulder, "Wish me luck."

"Good luck God," The statement seemed somehow ridiculous.

The rabbit was where God had said it would be. Josie paid extra attention to the cleaning process taking gentle care to not pull the rabbit's calf muscles from the bone as he tugged the hide over its hind legs. Josie wanted everything just right. Never before could he remember having made camp in such a manner as today. With exception of the steel blade in God's bone-handled knife, every aspect of this endeavor had been accomplished entirely from the wild landscape—off the grid and completely primitive. To Josie, such activity stirred an excitement seated so deeply that mere words seemed inadequate for description. But was not passion more important than understanding anyway? In any case, this time spent with his friend and mentor seemed of infinite importance and Josie wished to display those few woodsmen's skills he had learned as a boy with some confidence here. Silly as it seemed, Josie hoped to impress his Creator.

The day had waned into late afternoon as Josie walked back to camp with the cottontail dangling by hind legs from his left hand and God's knife held loosely in his right. God had not yet returned and in his absence Josie began to break twigs and assemble them into the pit for the evening fire. When this was done, he picked a few green branches and began whittling them into the thin skewers he rightly anticipated might later be used to cook the rabbit and fish—if, in fact, God did have any luck.

Afternoon was ebbing toward evening as God came walking home along the streambank and Josie watched him. As always, his straight-black hair cascaded around fair-skinned face to land atop the dull-red Pendleton shirt which in turn fell slightly over brown pants that ultimately ran to sandal-clad feet. But it was his stride and stature that demanded admiration. For, with spear in one hand and two large rainbow trout suspended from cordage in the other, he moved with magnificent strength and agility. The flow of God's stride blended perfectly with the natural beauty of water, meadow, forest, hills, and fading sky, around him. The God-of-all-things moving through a world of his own creation. And even from were he sat Josie could see the almost supernatural glow of those florescent blue eyes.

As God approached Josie said, "I see you had some luck."

"Yeah. Fishing was good today. Could maybe have caught more but I think these two and that rabbit," he pointed his spear to where the cottontail lay, "will be plenty." God held out his hand and Josie gave him the knife. The older man moved off to one of the flatter rocks atop the fire-pit and began to clean and scale his catch.

By now the sky offered only a hint of its former blue and the surrounding forest was a darkening silhouette in the distant background. Two stars appeared in the heavens and Josie noted the sound of crickets. It all seemed so perfectly unreal. He looked to the wood piled so meticulously in the fire-pit and a funny thought occurred. How would God light the fire? Lightning bolts? Stick matches? An eternal Bic lighter? This last mental image brought a snicker and Josie almost laughed out loud. Still, it was a curiosity.

In a moment God reached for the leather pouch that always hung at his side. From it he produced a single rock. God held it in one open palm and looked down in what appeared to be a moment of silent meditation. Next, he reached to the thong tied around his waist and produced a tuft of extra dry moss. God placed this moss atop the fire-pit's wall then took the rock in one hand and knife in the other.

Josie watched in silent fascination from the growing shadows of his place against the old oak and squinted harder through the darkness to better witness this strange ceremony.

After bending one knee to the ground beside his mossy bundle, the Almighty then struck the rock with the back of his knife-blade. A large blue spark illuminated the immediate area for a split second—then died.

Josie ebbed forward for a better view. He had read of ancient fires being ignited in this manner but had never bore witness to such a thing. The process intrigued him.

Again, God struck his knife to the rock, and again the pit flashed with light. The spark caught and a small wisp of smoke rose from the moss. God picked the moss up, cradled it in his palms, and began to blow very gently. A tiny flame soon came to life and the moss was then placed with great care beneath Josie's kindling. Minutes later a fire crackled in the pit.

Josie looked with new wonder at his strange friend. God had made the kindling of fire from only flint, steel and moss look almost easy. Josie had always assumed the making of fire from rock to be a difficult art that required practice and skill. Had God learned through hours of patient persistence? Did God make fires in heaven using stones or was this simply easy for him because he was, of course, God? Josie was then struck with an odd revelation. Here he sat in the presence of *The Creator of All Things* wondering how *The Almighty* had made fire from flint and moss. He felt kinda stupid then.

As if on cue, God held the implements out and asked if Josie would like to try them. Josie took both rock and knife. Then, while God returned his attention to the fire, Josie struck them together—they sparked. He tried again—a larger spark.

"It takes some practice," God said as he turned to again face his friend, "But it sure is exciting the first time you're successful."

"You had to practice to learn this?"

"I experience many things through the eyes, actions, and emotions of my children Josie. I'm the culmination of all experience."

Josie contemplated this as he stared into the shadowed face of God. The firelight crackled beyond. "Then you possess the talents of all who live?"

"All who live, and all who *have* lived my friend.

"Can you play guitar like Jimmy Hendrix?"

"Yup."

Josie fell silent. This was too much.

"Don't sweat it man. No one can understand God. It's really only important that one try to trust him instead."

This was a far more attainable ideal and it put Josie's mind at ease. After all, although he did not always like the things God did, Josie had learned long ago to have at least some trust in his creator.

3

God turned his attention to the food and Josie helped. Three of the skewers Josie had whittled were seared in the fire to keep the wood flavor from tainting the meat. Both fish and rabbit were then run through with them. The rabbit was stuffed with rosemary and garlic while both trout got garlic, bay leaf, and sorrel to add a slightly lemony flavor. When finished, the meat was set aside and both men turned attention to the greens. After these had been cleaned thoroughly at the stream, the tender leaves of chickweed and pulsane were torn into bite-sized sections then set into the birch-bark bowls to act in place of lettuce for the salads. Next was added carrots, onions, mustard flowers, water cress, mallow flower buds, and stems of the thistle plant (much like celery), which first had to be peeled. For utensils they would use whittled chopsticks and their bare hands.

Once the fire had mellowed into glowing coals, Josie set the three skewers across the higher rocks surrounding the pit then sat to tend the meat as it cooked. With his mind now virtually enmeshed into the proper preparation of this meal, Josie engaged only halfheartedly in conversation. He wanted everything to be just right.

He was, after all, cooking dinner for *God*.

God could have cared less. In the light of Josie's preoccupation, the older man moved off to the sanctity of the mighty oak so he might rest against its trunk and watch Josie from the deep shadows. From there God noted Josie's silhouetted outline set so intently to his work against the flickering background of firelight. In his fascination, God thought to himself...

Josie has come far. He is becoming such a kind, caring, considerate, strong, capable man. He's such a pleasure to be around! And a single tear fell from the Creator's eye. Although God had seen his efforts come to fruition countless times before, each child was so different—and each one he loved so much. For his part, Josie remained unaware of this observation as he stared into the flames and tended the food. For him, the evening was somewhere beyond magic.

The meal was remarkably satisfying, and when it was finished both men leaned upon their trees and stared contently into the fire. As the minutes passed, Josie's mind wandered to his wife. Already he missed her. So he asked, "Has Adrienne ever come here?"

"Many times," God replied, "She loves it here. This place seems to bring out the kid in her. When Adrienne's here she often teases me about the flaky way the meadow has been 'thrown together', then says I need a woman around to help with color coordination, cute curtains, and certainly classier furnishings. Then she talks of where she'd put the sofa, hang the pictures and, of course, install a dishwashing machine so I could stop washing my bowls in that nasty old creek. Sometimes she dances around then flops upon her back to stare at the sky. Then she'll call me to her side, and we'll watch clouds and talk of the things we see in them. She's a wonderful woman Josie. She speaks of you often and she loves you very much. She tells me all the time."

Josie's heart warmed and he smiled radiantly. In a moment he asked another question, "Does everyone come to this meadow?"

"No, Josie. Passions vary and everyone is different. For instance: there's a girl I always meet at the Louvre Art Museum in Paris."

Josie contemplated the idea of God staying in the Louvre

with a presumably dead girl and wondered how that worked. He decided not to ask.

"This keeps life spicy," God continued, "and I truly enjoy experiencing the quirks of each individual. Working to understand how they see things and staying with them through even the worst of times when they may become such an extreme example of human degradation that no other is able to tolerate them. For only I posses the foresight to love them always for the unique jewel I know they will one day become. Never have I given up—and not once has a child failed. It's an experience I never tire of."

Josie thought hard on these words. They said so much to him. But his mind soon wandered to another question, "But God, what of those born crippled, crazy, or just plain unfortunate?"

God let out a long sigh. He leveled piercing eyes into Josie's and again began to speak, "It's important that man has free will and I never interfere with this. But even through all the calamity that this ideal brings, I'm always there to provide comfort and strength to those who seek. And although it's a daunting task at times, the bringing of divine order to chaos is still within my capabilities Josie. I'm sure you've heard it said that God moves in mysterious ways his wonders to perform. But rest assured, that everything I do is in the best interest of my children. I *can* tell you one thing however: insanity, unfortunate birth, bad circumstance, and even pain itself, are only temporary—as is life on earth."

Josie fell silent as he contemplated these things. Amber-light danced in his eyes as Josie stared into the fire's eternal glow. Crickets trilled lightly in his ear, as did the sound of frogs emanating from the water's edge. A billion stars twinkled in the moonless sky as Josie sat beside his friend. In this man's company, life seemed so worthwhile, and with him, Josie felt contented, unafraid, and even happy. When conversation did return it remained casual and unfettered with the need of contemplation.

In time both men retired to their simple lodges. Although the temperature had dropped considerably, Josie slept so warmly inside his leafy bed that it was necessary to shed a few articles of clothing during the night.

For two nights more Josie stayed here in the meadow. But on the fourth day the young man found himself again contemplating his own reflection in the water's surface…

THE CALLING
Chapter 13

1

The great American city was a place of many people and much industry. Streets lined with a seemingly constant flow of auto traffic separated the tall buildings of this concrete jungle and there wasn't a single tree that had not been planted by man's own hand. At the river's dirty edge, a smelly dog food factory sat some distance from a large paper mill. Ribbons of crowded multilane freeway cut through, separated, circled, and often rose a hundred reinforced-concrete feet above this booming metropolis as an endless stream of automobiles shuffled the multitudes to and from their very important business. In the surrounding suburbs pretty houses lined narrow neighborhood roads of tight cul-de-sacs, streetlights, and sometimes small-marauding gangs of children aboard bicycles or skateboards.

For many, the city was a wonderland of entertainment and opportunity the likes of which no small town could hope to duplicate. But for the young Josie McWaters and his soon-to-be bride, the poor air quality, fast pace, and seething crowded-ness of this concrete jungle affected both as only a barren wasteland of high-stress insanity and spiritual ruin.

The oldest of four siblings, Adrienne had been raised in a household of seemingly constant activity. Although never a violent man, her father had spent the majority of his years in a semi drunken stupor. Her mother, a woman of nervous disposition, seemingly neurotic fears, and paranoia, had always seemed a little on the psychotic side to Adrienne. *What a pair,* she had often thought, *they certainly do deserve each other*. And so, upon her high school graduation, it had been with enthusiasm that she had accepted Josie's marriage proposal then moved into his small apartment by the railroad tracks. For not only would she gain a husband, but the move would also bring sudden escape from the strangely disturbed household of her childhood. But it really had not mattered, for she'd have married him regardless. Oh yes, Adrienne could still remember the day she had first laid eyes upon Josie's fine features, and this memory still seldom failed to evoke that dreamy look whenever she thought of it…

It had been in line at the high school cafeteria that she had first seen him standing there talking to the counter girl. Oh, she'd tried to look coy as her eyes had taken him in, but Adrienne had known that her observations were quite obvious to anyone who'd taken notice. But she had been unable to help herself. At a modest five foot nine inches he had seemed so wonderfully tall from her-own height of only five-three. His shoulders were strong and, like the rest of his body, heavily muscled. He had worn a medium-length shock of dark brown hair that, upon closer inspection, she'd noted, matched his deep and dreamy eyes almost exactly. His nose was straight and rather chiseled above a strong chin-line. At the risk of seeming sleazy, Adrienne followed him to the metal tables then sat nervously to face him.

Josie's initial reaction had been most pleasing…*thank God*. And why not? What with her compact yet shapely frame, Adrienne was about as fine a dark haired, blue eyed, beauty as any young man could hope to catch. When the awkwardness had passed and, to the delight of both parties, it had become almost immediately apparent that the personalities of each complimented the other in a most intoxicating way.

The rest was history.

For almost three years now they had lived in the cheap, one-bedroom, ground-floor apartment that resided near the railroad tracks. And although the passing trains had at first awakened her during the night, Adrienne had long since learned to sleep through them.

As do many parents, Josie's mother had wanted more for her son than her own life had produced and had repeatedly pressured him to pursue a college degree. However, the boy took little interest in school. Besides, he saw no use in spending so much time and money on education unless inspired by a solid objective such as a career interest of his own preference. But Josie could find nothing that so tickled his fancy, for in truth he did not know what he wanted to be when he grew up. So, to his father's delight, Josie had been inducted into the family business. Like his father before him, Josie's dad worked in the plumbing business and Josie, enticed by the prospect of a solid paycheck, had taken to the trade with only mild enthusiasm. In the end, it was from this work that Josie took little to no satisfaction at all.

Adrienne had taken work as waitress at a local breakfast place serving coffee, spuds, and sausage to the often hurried, and occasionally grumpy, customers that frequented the greasy spoon. Although the boss genuinely liked her (as did most everyone) and the workplace offered a certain comfortable familiarity, the job itself seemed to suck the very life from her soul and she sometimes wondered if this existence would not drive her to imminent madness one day. But the sacrifice would soon be worth it. For more than two-years the couple had been secretly saving toward their big plan… She could hardly wait!

2

The wedding had been postponed for these past years because both wanted their marriage to matter, to be the start of something new. Something better. And it was to this end that the greatest of plans had been secretly made.

It was a rather large wedding for such a small church as, besides their respective families, both Josie and Adrienne had acquired a good standing of friends over the years. And although few knew of the changing tide, both newlyweds were fully aware. At the reception Adrienne cried often as she spoke to those for whom she had grown close. Her emotion, as did Josie's, seemed excessive even for the occasion. Most shrugged it off as the nervous happiness that generally accompanies one's big wedding day. Newlyweds could be so sappy.

They were wrong.

Most of the wedding presents consisted of camping equipment or cash as the couple had repeatedly reminded everyone of the month-long honeymoon vacation that would be made from the meager comfort of Josie's old copper-brown Ford van.

There had been plenty of time to consider and execute interior ideas for the van and the couple had often shared Adrienne's little Honda car while their traveling vehicle underwent its many changes. Josie had always been good with his hands, and the application of this talent when applied to the Ford with such passion, had produced truly wonderful results.

After acquiring the carcass of a smallish wooden rowboat, Josie had removed the vessel's twin bench seats then sanded its interior to a fine finish before adding two coats of clear varnish. He had then set the boat upside down atop the van with bow facing forward. Josie cut a hole in the van's ceiling to accommodate the new boat-roof exactly. Next, he attached it with a liberal amount of silicone caulking and flat-head bolts then finished the transition with mitered strips of varnished wood. The end result was much nicer than he had expected. With exception of the driver's compartment, it was now possible to stand upright anywhere in the van. The effect was one of greatly improved spaciousness in a fine wooden finish.

Josie had then turned his attention to the van's interior, and Adrienne helped.

All interior walls had been insolated then covered with a light tan wooden paneling. Against the rear doors, a doublewide mattress was laid atop a sturdy plywood frame. Built diagonal to the van, the bed now looked fine with its beautifully handcrafted patchwork quilt and two fluffy flower-print pillows set against the headboard. Above each pillow a small 12-volt spot-lamp had been mounted to provide for reading. Beneath the bed, a few cardboard boxes would hold all their simple wardrobe, solar shower, and a few other possessions. The floor lay covered in low, light brown carpet. Next to the bed's footboard was a large Coleman ice-chest, while beside its headboard a wooden table waited to hold coffee cups, or whatever. Beside that stood a taller counter that held a three burner Coleman stove (used for heat, as well as cooking) and one small sink with drain-hose running through a hole in the floor. Above the sink was a small window, while below it two cabinet doors hid shelves containing food, cooking utensils, and a couple of gallon water jugs. For the van's few windows, Adrienne stitched sheer white curtains. To provide greater privacy, she had also added a second set of heavy black felt curtains behind those, and two larger felt curtains that hung just behind the driver's compartment. These had been cut long enough to be draped forward of the driving seats, which could be reversed to serve as living area furniture. A small steel platform had also been attached to the rear bumper. Here was stored two bicycles, one large water cooler, a pair of folding lawn chairs, and one seven-gallon propane bottle with hose running to the stove. Mechanical needs had also been considered and the van was now in the best running condition it had known while in Josie's possession.

In the end, the small sanctuary offered a charming air of comfortable efficiency and even compact luxury. To Adrienne it was beautiful—in a hippie sort of way—and the combination of freedom and security it offered brought a wonderful sense of excitement. As the big day drew near, her young mind indulged all the more into wonderful fantasies of extraordinary adventure in far off lands. But as the time of actual departure drew close Adrienne's emotions had taken a shocking turn…as had Josie's. Yet it was not until their wedding day that the full implications of such an extreme decision burned so brightly within her.

The reception was held at a local park and it was a simple deception to claim the truth of their own home being too small to support such a crowd. But the ruse had actually been fabricated to draw attention away from the newlywed's empty house.

Little by little the things of their home had gone. Some given away, some donated or sold, but most simply made their final debut at the local garbage can. It was the termination of a life whose time had passed; now it was time to die. For a new life can only begin from the death of the old. And Josie did not mind, for he regarded the satisfaction of material desires as only the means by which one could live and function as a human being. For him, these satisfactions were *not* the final end and aim of life. And he believed that the burdens of unnecessary possessions would now only hinder, or obstruct completely, the journey of spirit that awaited.

As she looked into the faces of old friends Adrienne tried to control the mess of emotions that threatened to break her. She might never see them again. Oh-my-god! Her home, her family, siblings, school, job, even the city itself—all she had ever known—were dissolving so quickly now. Anticipation, anxiety, excitement, sadness, and above all else…fear! No, not fear exactly, it was something more akin to *terror* now. Yet, even in the face of such stormy emotion, Adrienne held her head high and offered the world only the best new-bride's poker face she could muster. After all, Adrienne had always known that she did not belong in this city. How she knew did not matter, and she did not question. And it was to this truth that she offered the blind trust of a child. Although she looked to Josie for his strength, and he smiled reassurance to her in return, what Adrienne did not know was that inside him a tornado of emotion identical to her own also raged.

For they would not be returning.

The rouse of a month-long honeymoon had been concocted only because neither wished to hear incessant babble from their parents (especially Adrienne's mother), or anyone else, of how college and settling down was the next right step and that they should not waste their lives this way. And it was just as well; for it is also true that all the world will at first seek to hinder or belittle those who move toward the dreams that they themselves are afraid to follow. Sometime later they would call home from the safety of a payphone and drop the hammer.

Except for a few rather drunken, comical episodes, performed for the entertainment of all by a couple of Josie's buddies, the reception came off without a hitch. In the end the bride and groom hugged old friends and said their goodbyes as people began to filter out. Josie and Adrienne went home.

3

The van rested in the parking lot of the rundown apartment by the tracks that night and it was here that the couple slept in their new home for the first time. After all, the apartment was completely empty now. Even the key had been returned.

There was nothing left for them here but this parking lot.

The phenomena of shock had settled over both occupants and there was little talk. Fear seemed a very real thing with only these thin metal walls between themselves and the big world outside. To deny this demon forever, one need merely to avoid stepping beyond the comfort of all that is familiar; but all who seek new destinies must invariably do so against the fear of it. For to simply "*feel the fear and do it anyway*" is the very definition of *courage*. And on that first night, even the smallest of noises seemed amplified by ten while each occupant lay awake with ears ardently attuned to the coming of his or her imminent doom. At least that's how it felt. Each sought comfort in the other's embrace, and sleep seemed a very hard thing to find.

What a way to spend one's honeymoon.

The season was early spring and by eight a.m. warm sunshine filtered through the van's rear windows to gently wake Josie from the deep slumber that had seemed so impossible only hours before. At first the unfamiliar décor threw him. But his senses soon came to reality…and reality came to him! They were in the van. *Oh-my-god!* Dressed in only skivvies, Josie arose to sit upon the bedside with head hung low as he gripped its edge to await sleep's foggy departure.

Josie heard Adrienne stir behind him. In a moment she crawled up dressed only in one of his old blue T-shirts. When she was beside him the pretty young girl dropped her butt to the sitting-dog position and cocked her head sideways to look into his eyes from a rather strange angle. Josie gave her the serious look his churning guts demanded. *What am I doing?* He thought, *What about our future? Am I mad giving up all the security we've worked so hard for?* Anxiety gripped tighter now. Josie considered calling the trip off.

She stared back at him with her strangely cocked head and only returned his own expression of trepidation. Then, just as the words 'Let's don't go' were forming at the tip of Josie's tongue, Adrienne's face broke into such a mischievous grin that he could not help but grin back. "We're free," she said with such happy radiance that his heart actually skipped a beat, "Now let's get the fuck outta here!"

Josie's senses returned. Of what was he thinking? Of course, they could not stay. Was he mad? Mad with panic perhaps. Hard earned security my ass. What a lie that was. Adrienne was right. Freedom was what they had worked so hard for…and now they had it.

Josie brightened.

The City fell behind and the road opened up ahead as two nervous travelers watched through the windshield of their changing world. For a destination, Josie knew only that he wished to see the Rocky Mountains, and Adrienne the Grand Canyon. South and west. That's where they would go. After that…who knew? But it mattered not really, for what Josie did know was that he could not stay in the city for even another moment and nothing short of divine intervention would stop him now.

Wishing to put as many miles between himself and the city as possible, Josie just drove. But emotion haunted him. Sure, his resolve was strong, and excitement loomed; but trepidation was still the most prevalent of feelings. Josie's body sat rigid behind the wheel. Adrienne felt it too and there was little talk as both endured this internal ache in relative silence.

City gave way to suburb, then suburb succumbed to the green countryside of forest and rolling hills that lay beyond. But the change brought little solace, for this place was familiar since there had been numerous camping or holiday excursions made here with family throughout their youth.

Still tension remained.

Some hours later the forests began to subside as the Great Plains spread out ahead. Wide-open prairie with its skies that seemed never ending was something both newlyweds had previously seen only in pictures, but those had seemed small by comparison to the real thing. With the reality of such open space also came a very real sense of freedom. This element brought a feeling of wonder. As this new emotion grew larger, their nagging apprehension lessened accordingly.

Both relaxed a little.

Josie took a desolate off-ramp then stopped the van to check his map. It had been decided long ago that super-highways would be avoided whenever possible. Back-roads and slow days were their intention. Well, the city was four hours behind. Might as well start here.

The lonely little two-lane led away from the crowded freeways of hurried travel. It rose and fell across the slight grades of mostly arrow straight pavement that lit out across an endless sea of greenish-gold prairie. Josie reduced his speed. In the distance, bushy little trees grew in small groves spread sparsely across the plains. Occasionally there were huge corn and wheat fields, or those that held vast pastures of hay now cut and rolled into the massive wheels that dotted the hillsides. A fine meadow of sunflowers—their huge yellow faces turned in unison to the sun—came and went. Sometimes herds of cattle and even a few horses were fenced upon the plains with long miles of barbed wire, their troughs filled mostly by windmill powered pumps. Many of the tiny towns that came and went were little more than a few small businesses and scattered houses. The miles fell slowly past as morning's light faded to afternoon sunshine. It was still early when the van was put down for the night in a larger town that offered a campground.

On the grill that sat under a short shade-tree beside their wooden picnic table, Josie cooked two T-bones while Adrienne prepared rice-pilaf and a salad inside the van. After dinner there were showers. That night Josie lay in bed sipping hot tea as Adrienne read to him from an old Jack London novel titled "Into The Wild". It was a story of escape from captivity. Josie liked it.

Sleep was better this night, for it felt as though they were simply on a camping trip.

Neither Josie nor Adrienne were morning people and, although both had awakened just after 8am, it was closer to 10:00 when they had finally crawled out of the sack. Screwing around also took time and it was not until shortly after noon that the journey was resumed. Although neither knew it then, this lazy scenario was destined to become routine. Traveling would thus be, to the bafflement of most they were destined to meet, insufferably slow.

Neither cared.

As the campground faded from the rearview mirror it became impossible not to remember that this was *not* a simple camping trip. No. The future was now unset…unknown. A nagging panic returned. But today its bite was less. Josie's knees were more relaxed, and Adrienne seemed improved as well. There was more talk.

The van soon topped a little rise that offered an even greater view than before. "Unfuckingreal," Josie muttered as he looked about. The entire horizon—*only the horizon*—had become laced with a thousand wispy clouds. Although the tops of every one was billowy white, the bottoms were arrow-straight and very dark thus giving the elusion that each had been hung in the air with a single brush stroke. Beyond these clouds the sky's hue was a light fluorescent blue, while directly above him it was a much darker cobalt-color and held absolutely no clouds at all! Mere words could never convey the experience of such a neon spectacle suspended above so open and desolate a land. And as he would time and again from this day forth, the young city-boy wondered at the often-astonishing displays of Nature's eccentric beauty.

The mood lightened some more.

By the fourth morning fear had diminished almost completely. *Fear,* Josie thought, *it is so often like a seemingly solid wall of black mist that appears impenetrable, but once one has walked through and is looking back he sees that, in reality, it was only hollow air after all. Nothing really there.*

The journey continued.

Josie repeatedly pulled random roads from the map and the days of this new adventure wound through places like: Sac City, Clarkson, Utica, Friend, and Holdrege. Sometimes a second night was secured in a campground for an extra day of relaxation, or time dedicated to exploring the area and its people. Days became filled with wonder, and nights with the sanctity of campgrounds.

Then came the night when there simply was no campground. Oh, they had looked; but the lonely backroads of western Nebraska were just that…lonely, and no town offered camping on this day. Although a voice in his head screamed that he should not do it, there really was no choice. A dirt road led away from the pavement to quickly disappear across a small rise. Calculating correctly that there were no fresh tire-tracks, no mailbox, and therefore probably no house back there, Josie took it. Once beyond sight of the highway the tiny road trailed off to nothing. Josie found a level spot and parked.

The same demon that had spoken from inside his own head, *and in his own voice*, on that last morning in the parking lot of the apartment beside the tracks, came to talk some more: *"This land belongs to someone else,* it said. *What if you're found out? You'll be arrested for trespassing. They'll impound the van.* This seemed the responsible voice of an intelligent adult, but when Josie did not obey it shifted into higher gears, *"What if a crazy farmer runs you off with a shotgun? What about snakes! Scorpions! Terrible things could happen!"* The voice became more desperate. *"My god man, you could be killed!! Your wife raped!! Think of your new bride for God's sake!! Don't dooo thisss Josie!!!"* Fear showed its true colors now. But it mattered not, for these thoughts were destined to haunt that first night on the land. They seemed an unavoidable visitor who insisted on attending the unveiling of *anything* that was new in his life. And it was so often throughout history that this same demon had brought defeat to the dreams of so many.

    But not today.

    After dinner, the van doors were locked, and Adrienne again read aloud from her book. Eventually the lights were extinguished, and the pair huddled together in the darkness of a vast and unknown land. The silence that had always lived upon the Great Plains permeated the metal hull of their four-wheeled sanctuary and its sound was deafening. Noises of the city were familiar, almost soothing, for they had always been there. But not this! How often the darkness of night brings such strange amplification to the shadowy demons that can lurk in the depths of one's mind. And so, it was tonight as Josie lay awake with ears supernaturally attuned to any slight rustle of the wind, shuffle of a rodent's tiny feet, or the minute flap of a field bat's wing; for each surely brought the terror of imminent doom.

    Above, a billion stars lit the never-ending sky as the Milky Way stretched far across eternity in a brilliant display of tranquility that can never be observed amid big city lights.

    Morning brought blue skies and warm sunshine as Josie sat in the open side doors staring out at the day. The demons were mostly gone now. They had been replaced with the friendly rays that warmed his face as he sipped coffee. A playful breeze cooled him while a deep calm laid claim to his quiet mind. Josie had never known such a thing. *Could it be that practicing extensive safety that prohibits new experiences deemed dangerous by one's own mind did not equal responsibility at all?* he thought. *Was it instead an act of irresponsibility to be afraid of one's own life?*

These thoughts were interrupted by Adrienne setting a plate of bacon, scrambled eggs and pan-toasted bread into his lap then taking a seat beside to address her own breakfast. There was little talk this morning.

Eventually dishes were rinsed, loose objects repacked, and the journey resumed.

4

Although the plains had their appeal, the couple had spent nearly two weeks wandering across them. It was getting old. Josie consulted his map for a change of scenery and a course was soon set for the Badlands of South Dakota.

That evening Josie stood at a counter in the little office of the hitching post, which was billed as a "Campground/RV Resort". He asked the fat proprietor, "How much for one night, one van, and two people?"

"Twenty bucks," the guy seemed friendly.

Josie glanced at the glass counter that offered a variety of candy-bars for sale beneath its scratched surface. He gazed back at the man, "What do I get for that?"

The man pointed a pudgy finger through the side window, "Any of the primitive spots along that fence. If you want hookups, it's ten-bucks more."

Josie's eyes followed the man's hand. A few fancy motorhomes sat plugged into some of the nearer spaces. Beyond them, against the chain-link, sat one economy car with orange tent flapping in the breeze beside it. Looking past the fence Josie noted that, aside from the campground's few little trees planted to offer meager shade, the thousands of square miles beyond were *identical* to those within the chain-link. So, what was he really paying for? Hot showers? Sure, but the van already had a solar shower; and a showers were not a daily necessity anyway. So, what then?

Security.

That was it. One must pay for the promise of security. Josie thought of a quote by Helen Keller he had once read and, having been somewhat moved, committed to memory. It went: "Security is mostly a superstition. It does not exist in nature, nor do the children of men, as a whole, experience it. Avoiding danger is no safer in the long run than outright exposure. Life is either a daring adventure or nothing."

Josie turned on his heal and walked out the door.

By nightfall, the van was again parked on the plains. Although apprehension again hung in the air, its weight was lighter by nightfall, and even expected to some extent.

The following day they entered Badlands National Park and the adventure was renewed against a background of such surreal land formations and flat hues of outrageously colored terrain that Josie felt like he was on the moon. The park offered three days of paid camping amid the army of tourists who vacation to such famous places as this.

It was the last campground Josie would ever pay for.

After Badlands came the Black Hills of South Dakota and time was spent exploring Mount Rushmore, Crazy Horse, the Needles highway, and open pine forests or grand meadows filled with deer, groundhog, buffalo, porcupine, wild turkey, and others. Josie and Adrienne marveled at a forest so dramatically different from those they had known back home. The world held so many wonders.

Nights were spent parked along forgotten dirt roads or in other sorted places and it was with a slight sense of paranoia that Josie searched so diligently for, then thoroughly enjoyed, the many private and well-hidden spots in which they stayed.

More and more, Josie was stepping beyond the confines of the normal. The agreed-upon standard. The way things are usually done. This was scary, but also necessary. For if one simply does what others do, then he will get what they get. Yet if he desires something different, then he must do something different. This was simple math. Although Josie gave no conscious thought to this idea, the concept was, for him, indispensable. Considering the astonishing life that lay ahead, these first few risks, these baby steps into the extraordinary, were but a tiny beginning.

Next came the ride across Wyoming, and the famous Yellowstone Park. Mother Nature had long ago built this land atop a subterranean bed of molten lava that in turn superheats the underground rivers to produce a spectacle of geysers and other above-ground burning-water phenomena. The result was breathtaking.

Josie learned of a free campground located three miles beyond the park's south entrance. Upon arrival, both noted that this area was almost devoid of campers. It seemed that most tourists, so readily abundant in the other campgrounds, did not wish to camp where they could not pay.

Situated along the edge of a wide creek that rested beside a vast forest, the campground offered no more than a flat piece of land with barbeque grill and chemical toilet. Yet it was only a short walk from camp to a primitive hot spring of almost perfect bath-water temperature.

Through the steam that shimmered skyward from the glassy surface on that first night, they sat naked and immersed to the neck in the naturally heated water while gazing at the thick forest that stood as silhouette against a backdrop of star laden sky. A three-quarter moon glowed steadily to bathe the heavens above, and maybe those below, with its milky light. Aside from their sporadic talk, the only sounds were those of trickling water and the not-so-distant cries of coyotes that periodically beckoned in unison to the waxing moon.

For almost a week the couple enjoyed the park's incredible spectacles by day, and hot spring by evening.

The time spent in the Wyoming Mountains was certainly an eye-opening experience, but this particular range also runs far into the south where it eventually climbs to the much higher elevations known as the Colorado Rocky Mountains. When the mood eventually moved them, Josie and Adrienne left the spectacular park of camera obsessed tourists and continued south. They passed the Grand Tetons and yet another Indian reservation before the mountains smoothed again, temporarily, into high-altitude plains of rolling hills and yellow grasslands. The trip took a few days. For no longer were there schedules to keep, timeclocks to punch, bills to pay, or the pressures of what must be accomplished in a day. The past was only as a fading dream and the future a blank canvas. The old life was slipping away as the new became real and with this change a new sense of calm, wonder and even peace began to take hold.

It was late afternoon when the old van passed Colorado's state line and began its climb into the higher altitude of mostly pine forest with a spattering of oak, fir, spruce, poplar, select groves of aspen, and a few others. Yet unlike the heavily congested woods of close-nit trees and tangled brush so common to the east, this forest-floor was uncluttered and roomy amid the tall pines and steep mountain grades. There were many unmarked-dirt roads that led into the forest, only to end quickly at an old fire-pit, fishing hole, hunting trail, or whatever. As his eyes searched calmly for a suitable place to set in for the night, Josie had yet to learn the significance of this day.

5

Josie removed his elbow from the driver's window then set both hands upon the wheel to better swing the van to the left. There was a momentary drop as front tires left pavement and began to crunch loudly upon the gravel surface below. Almost immediately it became apparent that this road did not lead to any camp or fishing hole—for directly ahead stood an old house. Josie stopped the van while he and Adrienne strained their eyes to discern whether the tattered place was occupied or not. The front wall had been built of wood then painted brick red. The front door hung open over a covered porch with its four steps leading to the driveway.

However, things were not as they had once been.

Like sentries on a mission, the forest had moved close to nestle itself against the structure. A tangle of trees grew so near the porch-steps that passage would almost require a chainsaw. Farther on, a small army of branches scratched with wind-powered persistence against the wall. From *inside* the front door, Josie noted that two young ponderosa pine trees grew up and through what should have been the roof. The people were long gone and in their absence the forest, with its mighty powers of weather, plant, and animal life, was moving in to reclaim its hold upon this place. Mankind was losing this battle...

...The house was being systematically destroyed.

Directly ahead, the road became a Y with either fork running off to circle the house before coming back onto itself. A circular driveway with house in the middle. Josie took the right fork. As the van passed alongside, Josie stared through his open window to see that the place had once been a large structure built above a big basement. But that was over now, for all that remained standing was that front wall; everything else had crumbled and fallen to become an unruly heap of wood and debris strewn at the bottom of the basement.

When Josie had reached the home's far side, he threw the van into park and shut its motor down. Quiet came again to the forest. Josie opened the door and stepped out. The house-in-the-hole was an interesting spectral and he walked slowly toward it. But other debris were strewn about and Josie watched closely lest he trip over something. A brass doorknob protruded upward, and he stepped over it. The skeletal remains of a child's tricycle lay half buried as it slowly lost its battle with the earth. Josie stepped around it. Bits and pieces of the tale were everywhere. Part of a bathtub poked up through the undergrowth, an ancient refrigerator lay on its side. A long stairway, its dirty white carpet still wrapped over wooden steps, sat as silent mystery upon the ground.

Josie reached the basement's edge. He gazed in.

Studs, beams, and other boards lay in an unruly pile of rotting lumber down there. An antique furnace poked partially through the mess, as did an old water heater. There was a propane-stove, porcelain sink, toilet, wasted furniture, old canning jars, and other bits of litter. Josie turned and sat upon the low rock wall that had once served as the home's foundation. He pulled one foot over his knee, then paused to look at the white picket fence still surrounding the yard.

Adrienne had wondered off to do her own exploring and Josie was left alone with his thoughts. He reflected on the family that had lived, dreamed, and raised their children here. Of the man, or couple, who had worked so hard to keep up the mortgage, pay utility bills, insurance, and so on. How they had labored to maintain the yard, clean the carpet, cut back advancing trees, fix the plumbing, and more. Christmas by the fireplace; presents under the tree; elementary and high school; good times and bad; feast and famine. But that was over now. The play was finished. The actors had moved on or died…

…and now the stage was being systematically dismantled.

Soon, not a single sign of man's creation would be left to tell the story.

Josie thought of a science documentary he had once seen on television. They had said that the earth was four and a half *billion* years old. *A phenomenal stretch of time!* The documentary had stated that if it were possible to have run a stop-action camera and condensed this entire event into a twenty-four-hour movie, the *entirety* of man's existence on the planet would only occupy around thirty-seconds. *Thirty seconds!* For modern man the timescale would be less than one second. *A single second!* And if a person closely observed the single second, in hopes of catching even a glimpse of this house—and if he did not blink—there would be no chance of ever seeing even a blip of its existence. Josie marveled at the power of Nature with new respect. For in her eternal shadow even the all-important business of the world's Super Powers was as only the flailing of children playing momentarily in a sandbox. In short time she would wipe the slate clean of *all* they had ever touched. For in her shadow even the seemingly eternal pyramids of Egypt would soon crumble helplessly and the eons for which they had stood be recorded in her ledger as less the blink of an eye.

That's how important it all really was.

Then what was anything a man did in this world actually worth? Was life that hollow? The thought was terribly disconcerting.

A memory from high school's senior year popped into Josie's mind. It had been a good friend who had died in an auto accident and Josie had attended the open casket funeral. He had gazed down upon the corpse that someone had worked so diligently to disguise as only a young man sleeping. The ruse had failed. It was keenly apparent that his friend was no longer in there. Where he had gone no one knew for sure, but one thing was certain: No longer did he reside in that body. And now that he had gone, it—and everything else the young man had ever maintained in this world—would immediately begin the transformation back into dirt.

In that moment, beside the disintegrating house, Josie realized that when he left this place the *only* thing going with him would be that which resides in himself, what actually makes him alive, and that which resides in everyone else to make them alive as well. We would all be leaving together, while everything left behind fades back into dirt.

So, the only thing actually real here was the spirit. What was of true importance then, really, was how his own spirit was changed and affected, and how he affected the spirits of those around him. Everything else was only a momentary backdrop; that which is necessary to produce the human movie. Josie thought of his own van then. The reality of its true value was only in the way it affected his spirit and that of the woman he loved. In this capacity, it was indispensable. But, when the time came that he needed it no more, it would simply return to the dirt. So, the true value of things might only be in their ability to serve his human need while he, in turn, sought to serve himself, his fellow man, and, hopefully in so doing, God as well.

This revelation seemed somehow disturbing. But there it was—baby science—obvious and undeniable.

Adrienne stepped from the van's far side and Josie's eyes followed the back of her tight white tank-top as she disappeared down a small trail and into the heavy forest. He got up and followed.

The trail dropped slowly down an embankment to finish at the sandy shore of a little creek. Adrienne was sitting there now. Josie plopped down and threw an arm around her. He smiled. She smiled back. For a moment both relaxed to take in the sights.

There was little, if any, level ground here and although tall trees blocked much of the sunshine at this late afternoon hour, the air was warm and alive with the sweet smells of early summer. Ferns and other vegetation grew along the stream's damp bank. The water babbled around protruding rocks, then past one tiny island and the green foliage that grew upon it. Dragonflies and other airborne bugs flew above, or dipped low to quickly contact the surface, as all reveled in the liquid life. Aside from birdsong and trickling water, no other sound existed.

A deep calm enveloped him.

Curiosity came next and Josie arose and walked to the water's edge. He squatted then peered at the shimmering surface. There were small fish, he could see, and strange bugs that skirted upon the water's thin crust. He picked up a small stick to poke at the murky bottom and was delighted to watch the current carry his churned-up silt downstream. Josie examined this tranquil day with the enthusiasm of a boy at summer-camp.

The sound of a small splash disturbed his play and Josie turned to see the shapely form of Adrienne's naked body as she stepped into the water. Her face had always bore an unusual mouth with extraordinarily large teeth set below beautiful blue eyes and he had often kidded that her dentist should charge extra. But far from being a thing of embarrassment, this characteristic added a dramatically stunning quality to her otherwise dark features and when she smiled the effect could be radiant. As sturdy legs carried her farther into the water she turned and smiled at him. Once immersed to the waist Adrienne sat to breathe hard at the slight chill, then relaxed and closed her eyes to better experience the sensation.

So fully had the girl's show captured his attention that, without knowing how it, the young man found himself standing. Her eyes opened and she regarded him thoughtfully as long brown hair floated in a half-ring around her head. Then the smile again, "Come on in Van Man. The water's good and the company ain't too bad either!" she goaded.

"Jeez Adrienne, you're naked!"

"Ah…yeah…I know."

"What if the cops come?"

"What…think they'll get turned on?"

"Nooo…," his tone seemed pained.

"Oh, so you're sayin' I'm not hot enough to turn a cop's head now huh? Boo hoo, my honey thinks I'm fat. Boo hoo hoo," Her lame effort at sincerity was only comically effective as she teased.

"Nooo…" he repeated, "You know what I mean."

"Oh, come on old man," that smile again, "There ain't no one around here. Go on, take a chance. Come play with me," and she pushed her lower lip into a pout as one arm stretched to beckon him.

It was not long before he joined her. For a time, Josie let himself float belly down with hands outstretched to the sandy creek-bottom to pull him slowly forward. But Adrienne soon interrupted this mission of exploration with a gentle arm across his back. Josie fell under her spell. He took her in his arms, and it was there in the cool clear water that the young newlyweds necked for a while. Josie carried his new bride to the beach then and, after kicking their strewn clothes into a makeshift blanket, set her down and took her right there upon the sandy garments. As they passed through a selection of favored positions, Josie came at one point to be upon his back and staring up through tall trees at the open sky. Never before had Josie been laid beyond the confines of four walls. The experience was erotic. The session lasted a long time (Josie had always liked to drag sex out, stating that he came to see the whole show, not just the encore) and its finality left them both exhausted. And although they had been married for some weeks now, both newlyweds decided that this experience should be remembered as their *official* honeymoon romp.

It would be dark soon. They decided to stay the night.

6

Two folding chairs were set around a small fire-pit quickly thrown together just beyond the van doors. As the sun set upon the dying house and its visitors, Josie sat in the heat of his little fire and watched soft interior van-lights glow through the open sliding door as Adrienne cooked thin slabs of roast beef and sliced-potatoes upon the stove. Later, van lights were extinguished, and both lounged at fireside while amber light flickered across their faces and then moved on to the nearest trees before dissipating into the forest.

With small flashlight in hand, Adrienne read again read from her book. Tonight, it was an old publication titled "Jonathan Livingston Seagull" by Richard Bock. It was the story of one bird's flight to freedom while the others used their gift of wings in only the daily fight for scraps of food.

Josie drank tea as he listened. In his other hand was the

wooden pipe he sometimes reserved for special occasions. This was, after all, the official day of his honeymoon romp.

From a nearby bush came a rustling sound and Josie turned to note a raccoon stepping from the shadows to barely notice him as it went about its nocturnal business. Josie offered only mild interest as smoke puffed rhythmically from his mouth. There were other forest-sounds too. None of them human. *How strange,* Josie thought. Only weeks ago, an identical scenario had almost thrown him into a frenzy. But he had soon decided it was okay, for there were many besides himself who called the forest home. And if he wished to spend so much time in the woods then it was necessary that he accept, tolerate, and occasionally enjoy the company of these neighbors. Josie was also learning well to discern the difference between animal noises and the footsteps of approaching men.

He was changing so quickly now.

The side-door was left open that night and the newlyweds slept amid clean mountain air. Within the safety that she imagined while beside Josie, Adrienne was out almost as fast as her head hit the pillow. It was not so for Josie, and he lay for a long time beneath the beam of his overhead light and tried to read. He was alone with his thoughts…and it was a good thing. Josie paused often to look through the open doors to the bramble of shadowy forest beyond. He listened to the constant trill of crickets as it mixed with the sporadic frog song emanating from the nearby creek. This life was so different from anything he had known. But, he was adjusting now and the more he did, the more things began to feel…right. For the first time in his few years upon this earth Josie felt serenity.

When it came, sleep was the best that night.

Josie was up by 8 a.m. Adrienne's late rise to obvious drowsiness inspired him to comedy and Josie promptly declared it "Queen Shoegoo Day".

"What's that?" Adrienne asked sleepily as she sat at the bed's edge with only Josie's big green T-shirt covering her small frame.

"Oh, it's a Celtic thing. An ancient tradition handed down from my great, great, great-great-great-great grand cousin twice removed, Earl Shoegoo," he said while setting a cup of coffee into her hand. "He was a great man, in an ordinary sort of way. And he will never be forgotten, although I don't think anyone's heard of him. Oh yeah, Earl Shoegoo. He was married to a striking woman of

285 fabulous pounds who went by the name of Helga. Legend remembers Earl for his unshakable sense of chivalry; although there were those who just thought he was extraordinarily pussy-whipped. But I think it was the small whip Helga wore at her belt for style, and the four long scars across Earl's face that made them think that. Anyone could get the wrong idea you see."

    Josie looked to see if Adrienne were still listening and found that she had set the mug down to rest her chin upon both hands and elbows atop her knees. And she wore an expression that said, 'You're so full of shit'. But she *was* listening. So, he continued:

    "Anyway, it's the account of the day after their honeymoon that prompted the legend. For you see, even though it had rained the day before, it was exceptionally warm that evening as Earl walked his new bride to the restaurant. Suddenly, they came upon a large puddle. Instinctively Earl knew what to do and he reached for his coat to throw over the offending puddle. But…oh no…he wasn't wearing one! Earl's mind reeled. Oh, what to do, what to do." Josie's manner of animated theatrics was becoming a twitchy dance as the bullshit thickened, "And worst of all everyone was watching! Earl came quickly to the idea of carrying his new bride across. However, after eyeing her fine features for only a moment, thought better of it. Fortunately, though, Earl's exceptional brain possessed uncommon intelligence and, thinking fast, the new groom threw himself face down into the puddle that his beautiful wife might not have to get her tiny feet—size 12—wet. Earl thought he heard laughter then, but the sound was soon muffled beneath the crack of breaking ribs and, for a moment, everything went black."

    Adrienne burst out laughing. Josie cleared his throat as if she had just interrupted something sacred. When she had calmed, he continued:

    "Later, with the front of Earl's dripping clothes forming a pool under his chair, which pissed the waiter off, the new groom offered a painful smile. As he held his ribs with one hand, Earl rather whimpered his love for the beautiful woman…*cough*.

    "But being as he *was* a man of uncommon intelligence and sophistication Earl knew instinctively that a husband must listen to his wife if indeed, he truly loved her. So, he did listen as she talked incessantly of all the things she would soon buy with his money.

This made Earl happy, for he had recently been able to bully his way into a really good night job of shoveling in the stables and this would help augment the ten-hour days he was already putting in elsewhere. For you see, although he may shovel it, Earl didn't take shit from anyone. Did I mention that Earl was also the person responsible for the term, 'Don't let 'em walk on you?' Yup, he was a great man all right."

Adrienne was holding her gut as the laughter had taken her breath some moments before and her ribs hurt as she convulsed almost silently. Her face was contorted into what looked almost like pain.

Josie laughed with her.

"Anyway," he finally continued, "as the legend spread it was ultimately declared that "Shoegoo Day" become a national institution. So, the five rules of Shoegoo were written and put into law. It was also declared that on that day the 'Declaration of Shoegoo' would be strictly adhered to. The bill reads like this:

"On the day immediately following the evening of a man's wedding consummation, and for that day only, he will therefore treat his new bride in this manner:

"1: He will bring her coffee in bed.

"2: He will make her breakfast…if he feels like it.

"3: He will see to the satisfaction of her every sexual desire."

"Oooo…" Adrienne swooned.

"Please, no interruptions," Josie snapped.

"4: On this day, and only if she weighs under 200-lbs, she may walk on him if the need so arises; and he shall allow it.

"There were severe penalties for noncompliance too," Josie added, "Failure to adhere could be punishable by flogging, imprisonment or…and far worse…a bitchy wife!" Josie finished with a smug smile.

When a minute had passed, Adrienne said, "What about rule number 5?"

"Wha…?" Josie stammered.

"You said there were five rules. *What about number five?*"

"Oh yeah. So, I did. Ah…" his formerly full tank of bullshit seemed to be running low now. "Ah…don't tell me. I'll get it. Oh yeah! 'On this day, the new bride will be deemed Queen Shoegoo by morning and will therefore be entitled to all the privileges and luxuries that shall accompany that prestigious title." With that Josie descended to his knees, stretched his arms out, and began bowing to the floor before her. And he chanted, "Oh virtuous Queen Shoegoo, mother of all that is good, I offer my humble and unworthy self to only the task of thy funky, estrogen tainted bidding. Your wish is my command…" and again "Oh virtuous Queen…"

Adrienne was quite amused. She tried not to giggle. So, she said, "On your belly slave!"

"What?" Josie really was surprised.

"I said, on your belly, face against the floor. Now don't argue with your Queen. Just do it!"

He did.

Once in position, she hopped bare feet upon his back and said, "Any wife under 200 huh? Well, I'm only a buck and a quarter sucker," and with that she did a little dance.

Josie found it hard to laugh and breathe at the same time.

When she had finished, Adrienne returned to the bed's edge and picked up her coffee. Josie got to his feet and began the task of preparing his famous vegetarian omelet with Swiss; the thing he cooked best. The van soon filled with savory aroma. When finished, Josie cut the omelet to fill two plates. He reached behind to fluff Adrienne's pillow then patted the bed there to signify the need of his "Queen's" return to her throne. Once she had complied, he placed one hand against her chest to push her gently back against the pillow-padded wall. Josie then set a wooden cutting board with her breakfast plate upon it into her lap and handed her a fork. He sat beside her and both enjoyed their food amidst the wooded solitude of this bright morning. When the grub was gone, he returned the cutting board to the sink, then himself to her side. She looked at him in silent wonder of what he might do next on this special "Shoegoo" day.

Josie positioned himself below her and smiled before spreading her bent knees to place his head between them. Josie then licked his new bride to imminent satisfaction as she clutched the quilt with both hands. It was an event she had always favored.

When the session had ended, dishes were carried to the creek and both sat to clean them at the sandy shore. Afterwards, two cool baths were taken, and clean clothes donned before their simple possessions were again secured for travel.

It was high noon when the van's tires again touched hard pavement.

7

As the twisting two-lane climbed ever higher, the Rocky Mountains became a fantastic spectacle. So vast and imposing. So tall, steep, and even jagged in places, yet also laden with the many creeks and rivers nestled amid heavy pine forests in others.

It would take more than a month for the newlyweds to explore this place, its towns, and its people.

Small dirt roads leading short distances into the forest seemed always available here and it was in these secluded spots that the couple spent their nights. The creaks and rivers offered suitable bathing, while at other times water was heated by stove or fire for use in the solar shower.

They visited towns like Steamboat Springs, Breckenridge, Creede, Telluride and others. Almost all had a woodsy, outdoorsman feel about them and most catered in large to the tourist trade, because economic opportunity was limited up here.

They met fishermen, hunters, hikers, painters, photographers, hippies, and locals; attended a few parties, concerts, and even one hiking trip. Sometimes the couple sat high atop a riverbank to applaud the whitewater rafters as they paddled furiously past. Twice they stopped to watch mountain climbers work the ropes that secured them to the side of jagged cliffs. Occasionally, a road led the van to such altitudes that the trees grew shorter until they eventually disappeared altogether to leave only bald ground streaked with long patches of dirty snow. Many creeks were clogged with beaver-dams. There were deer and coyote too. They saw a black bear.

Eventually the mountains were left to fade from Josie's rearview mirrors as the western deserts opened up ahead. At times, this land was so vast and empty it made even the mid-western plains seem fertile and lush. Yet in other places the desert offered such vivid color and fantastically enormous natural anomalies that it was easy to feel as if one had been transported to another planet. In Las Vegas they stayed for five days. Next came the Grand Canyon, and Death Valley too.

Initially Josie had worried that the van would attract unwanted attention from weirdos, concerned citizens, police, and the like. Occasionally it did. It was, after all, an unorthodox spectacle. But it was on the contrary that more often people seemed attracted to the odd sanctuary on wheels. Many simply brought their curiosity. Some talked of their own similar adventures. But in others, the van seemed to awaken something inside them. Sometimes Josie watched the light flicker in a person's eyes as they learned the nature of this journey. Often the visitor was moved to talk excitedly of his or her own dreams and this input helped. For in his decision to walk such an unusual path, Josie had begun to question his own sanity; however, it seemed he might be alright after all. Josie also began to experience a refreshing new sense of purpose in the inspiration that many gained from him. In time a few lives would even change as result of touching his own. The McWaters began to enjoy a certain notoriety and even small fame.

In the high mountain town of Lake Tahoe two guys invited the newlyweds to park in the side-yard of their big house for as long as they liked. The place was a bachelor pad with four young men in residence. It was a party-place. Here people came and went almost constantly, bringing with them all the fun and drama (especially amongst lovers) deserving of such a setting. Of course, there was the common attraction to almost all who are young, the comedy, drunkenness, and crazy antics which brought to both Josie and Adrienne a wonderful time.

When a month had passed, they moved on.

The western coastline was explored for some time as the list of towns and cities they visited continued to grow. Yellowstone had inspired in them a mutual love for the hot springs, which are common in the west, and a course was set to visit as many as possible. Most of these offered a variety of often-breathtaking land, unusual people, and interesting events.

When the chill of fall began, a winter course was set for Southern California. Beaches, bikinis, and bicycles; it was all the Beach Boys had promised. It was also amazing how warm the southern winters could be, especially when one had previously known nothing beyond the frigid north.

For two and a half years the couple traveled. In time, and although always an adventure, the road slowly became a lifestyle. As it did, Josie was forced to accept new ways, new ideas, and certainly new and sometimes very unorthodox methods. He was, after all, embracing a way of life for which there was no real blueprint. For there were few who had gone this way before to blaze a trail he could follow. Adaptation became Josie's second nature. His watchful eye began to miss almost nothing that might aid in his plight. He listened to, and observed the ways of, almost any traveler, snowbird, vacationer, freight-train hobo, boy scout, or even bum that might offer information. In time he met others like himself. Mostly though, Josie learned from trial and error.

There was a lot to know…

Josie learned to use the terrain for his advantage. Heavy tree-coverage cut down wind and offered better concealment. Mountain peaks were colder, while valleys warmer. If one learned position of the rising sun by noting the North Star the previous night, he could place camp in the comfort of morning shade by summer's heat, or catch the warmth of early sunshine by winter's cold. He found that "truck stops", sometimes called "travel plazas", could offer free 'sleeping' in their big parking-lots. These places usually included a restaurant, television room, laundromat, companionship among truckers, and even free showers if one knew how to get them. Towns generally offered racket clubs, gyms, or YMCAs. These brought hot showers, saunas, hot tubs, swimming pools and exercise equipment into their lives.

Josie found that to roam meaninglessly for long periods could often be an empty affair that left one feeling a nagging need to set down roots somewhere. But he also found that if one were experiencing a barrage of new and interesting adventures then settling down would be the farthest thing from his mind. But most adventure requires other people and therefore the couple began to attend many events. Nearly all offered an extensive social scene. They visited art shows, folk and jazz festivals, campouts, concerts, sporting events, drag races, auto rallies, the Mardi Gras in New Orleans, Burning Man in the Nevada desert, and even The Calgary Stampede of Canada.

The list went on.

The couple learned that amid those who came to enjoy these events there were also the many that came to make them happen. Some were vendors who lived in trucks, hotel rooms, and the huge tents that served as their mobile storefronts. They came to sell food, art, accessories, clothing or any other such snake-oil that their customers were willing to pay for. This was the world of the modern-day gypsy. Among them Josie and Adrienne made many friends and often found temporary employment. A rather convenient job it seemed: work long hours for a week or ten days, then gather your pay and move on.

Both Josie and Adrienne loved their home-life and genuinely enjoyed the natural environments in which they stayed. To this end Josie began to seek better, if not more private, acreage on which they could live.

Josie learned that almost always there were secluded and seldom visited plots of land all around him—sometimes even in towns and cities. Most people never took note of these places simply because they had no reason to. Besides, few would consider making camp there even if they were of such a mind. The idea was far beyond the accepted norm. It was the unknown again, to which Josie had become familiar. It was now the *known*, and no longer did he fear it. For a man's life is only a product of his conditioning—of what he is used to. And as this uncommon stile of living slowly became normal to Josie, it was the normal that began to feel alien to him.

It came naturally then that Josie began to question the wisdom of why one man should have the right to burden another for his need to live upon the land to which he was born. If man is of God, and the land is of God, then how was it that another man should interfere with this communion? Was mankind really the rightful owner of the earth? Josie wondered. So many wars had been fought over this subject. But he could not see it. Slowly, this question was growing into a conviction.

Josie learned *so many* other things as well; each of which

helped to better his rather eccentric way of life. And as he progressed, Josie became even more open to new ideas, regardless of how unconventional they might seem, and he was quick to implement them. Josie was becoming a bold, strong, and even rugged individualist. With this new wisdom he would gain freedom; the freedom to follow the path of not another…*but that of only his own heart.*

    People noticed.

SMOKY MOUNTAINS
Chapter 14

1

That third winter was spent in the semitropical islands of the Florida Keys. By springtime however, the van was again on the road and heading north.

Their travels led through some of the Georgia's most beautiful countryside, but it was not until they entered the Smoky Mountains of South Carolina that Josie became so affected.

These mountains in no way resembled those of the west. The western Rockys often soared to altitudes of over 14,000 jagged feet with uncommonly long winters that were frequently brutal. On the contrary, the Smokys were gently sloped with moderate altitudes that seldom rose beyond 1,700 feet. And, although undoubtedly cold, winters here would never be brutal. However, it was the forest itself that took Josie's breath from him. So thick, so green, and so diverse! The hills were remarkably suffocated with trees such as Dogwood, Sycamore, Maple, White Pine, Red Oak, Elm, Cherry, Fur, Cedar… The list went on. These strikingly green hills and valleys were also just as rich in a wide variety of ground vegetation that probably exceeded even the countless species of trees. Animal species varied almost as widely.

It was a melee of life.

With so many creeks, the occasional river, frequent rains and mist, life giving water seemed abundant here. It was not uncommon to see low clouds that move like puffs of ghostly smoke against the treetops therefore giving credence to the name 'Smoky Mountains'. The Appalachian Mountain range itself (of which the Smokys are part) stretches across five states from Georgia to Virginia and contains the greatest concentration of federal and public lands and the largest remaining expanse of wilderness left in the eastern United

States. So much protected land guaranteed that these mountains could never be overbuilt.

Josie drove roads that climbed over mountain peaks and across hillsides, but most often ran through valleys. Little towns came and went.

Eventually, they arrived at the Great Smoky Mountain National Park, which receives millions of tourists per year and their abundant numbers were clearly apparent. Nestled at the park's south entrance is the town of Cherokee. Set largely in a valley and beside the Ocanaluftee River, Cherokee's heritage stems from the once dominant Cherokee Indians who still occupy this region in large numbers and now cater mostly to the thriving tourist industry for their livelihoods. As with everywhere in these mountains, the distinct green forest dominates the background of shops and businesses that line Cherokee's roads. Clad with names like *War Eagle Trading Post*, *Little Bear Leather*, *Ambush Graphics,* and *Heavenly Fudge*, these places seemed almost ridiculous in their repetition as so many sell rubber tomahawks, mass produced moccasins, ice cream, fudge, etc. Although many Native People work in shops, others simply stand in the streets selling their wares. Some, self-proclaimed genuine War Chiefs dressed in feathers and buckskin, sell photos of themselves posing with the tourists. Others offer face painting, Native dancing, and even storytelling to the many gawking visitors. Both newlyweds found the local population quite friendly, and this beautiful place certainly held its appeal. At the town's eastern end stood a large Indian casino that dropped half its earnings (a considerable sum) back into the individual hands of its people. For all their historic years of trial and suffering, it seemed to Josie that these Natives now lived in relative peace and prosperity.

The couple moved on.

There were many other small towns that dotted the landscape throughout the southern region of these mountains. Although most catered at least in part to the tourist industry or wealthy summertime residents, there were still so many workers, ranchers, and other common people that these mountains, at least to Josie, began to feel like home. But in truth, it was the land itself that called to him with such ferocity.

They passed through places like Sylva, Bryson City, Robbinsville, and others. Sometimes two days were spent in one location while another might get a week. As usual, they camped in sorted spots. For better than a month they traveled these mountains and even though the countryside required frequent rains to maintain its vibrant green beauty, the sky remained mostly clear and sunshine was the order of most days.

    Flowers bloomed, birds nested, and animals bred as springtime ebbed toward early summer. Never before had Josie's heart held such calm and Adrienne noted with some amazement the ease that had recently overtaken his features to offer a younger, almost boyish, appearance. Josie's manner had also calmed, and he had become so much easier to live with inside the confines of their little home. *He's happy,* she thought. And so, he was. Thoughts of travel began to fade as the sun-filled mountains tightened their grip on the spirits of both van-occupants. It was not long before Josie could no longer imagine being anywhere else. Although neither had made a conscious decision, the couple would settle here.

    Located at the base of a large valley set far from the mainstream tourist track, Andrews had once been a thriving little community. With its economy built on the revenue of nearby factories producing things like jeans, furniture and a few other commodities, Andrews had gotten along pretty well at one time. But most industry had left the area long ago, taking with it the town's economic mainstay. Andrews had slumped into decline. People left. Along the outskirts many empty houses stood abandoned to the elements, while others simply sat vacant. Yet there were still plenty of well kept, *and* run-down, homes that were occupied. For economy, Andrews now subsided mostly on small business, the two factories that remained, revenue from those who had retired here, construction or maintenance of houses, and simple living.

    Among the numerous working businesses of Main Street were probably almost as many that sat empty. But within those that functioned, the spirit of this town still lived. Although it had changed, Andrews was nowhere near dead and the couple looked on with delight as they strolled past places like: Sister Sophisti's Cuts and Tannery; Dean's Music, C.D.s, records, and tapes; The Burger Basket; In Nonnie's Attic (quilting supplies, etc.); Galloway's Auto Repair; and the Mission Thrift Store. On the modern side was a McDonald's; KFC; Subway Sandwich; Family Dollar; and even a small Cinema. After all the glitz and tourism lately, both Josie and his wife found this place refreshing, honest, and just plain down-home. Although the surrounding mountainsides were covered with the usual blanket of forest, this valley offered its share of meadows too. Many of these held small herds of horses; a thing that seemed of genuine interest to Josie's wife.

    The land upon which Josie chose to make camp was six miles from town.

    Leading away from the pavement of a small and seldom traveled two-lane, the gravel road angled up a mountainside. The gravel eventually ended at a tiny dirt drive with weeds growing tall enough to indicate that this passage was seldom, if ever, used. From there the narrow dirt road twisted upward into the trees and was lost from sight. A half-mile farther it ended at a small clearing that had obviously been cut into the mountain's southern face long ago. Although the clearing was surrounded by forest on three sides, the fourth was not and instead dropped quickly over the mountain's edge to offer a panoramic view of the surrounding hills that rolled on to the horizon. The clearing's far end had once held a small house and the road was its driveway. That was over now; for all that remained was the home's rock-and-mortar foundation. Nearby, what looked like a small pump house, still standing, though it leaned heavily to one side. At the clearing's center lay what was left of a more recent bonfire. Around it was strewn several empty beer-cans, while beside the ruined home someone had dumped a few loads of construction refuse. But the clearing was large, the area nice and except for the sound of birds it was quiet here. This place would do.

    Josie and Adrienne began to settle in around Andrews. Friends came quickly since it was much too small a place for everyone not to know most everyone else. Days in town were made of long walks, bicycle rides, restaurants, socializing, and an occasional movie. At home it was lazy mornings, longer walks, cooking, lounging and exploring the area.

    Days passed into a week. Then two.

2

It was 10 a.m. Beside the van set two folding chairs in which Josie and Adrienne sat contentedly sipping morning coffee. Only a few clouds marked the sky, and the ground was still damp and sweet smelling from the previous night's rain. No fire burned in the pit before them, for today would be sunny and warm.

Josie and Adrienne heard the sound of tires crunching against dirt long before the vehicle came into view. Both stared in that direction. A chrome grill became visible as the car peaked the rise then moved slowly into the clearing. Rather stunned by the prospect of a visitor, the couple held their position. Carrying only the driver, the old Lincoln Town Car stopped, and Josie noted its dull white paint with scratches and bits of rust.

His heart quickened.

After a moment's contemplation, the man stepped out. He was tall and thin with the lines of one well into his 50s etched upon a chiseled face that hung below a crew-cut of heavily graying hair. An old white T-shirt, faded jeans, leather belt, tan work-boots, and silver wristwatch, was his statement. The man had a haggard look about him. It spoke of the hardness that sometimes accompanies a life of skepticism and dreams unfulfilled. Josie recognized him. Roy was one of the older men who came almost daily to sit at the tables inside the Texaco gas station/convenience store to drink coffee and shoot the bull with others who came for like purpose. Although Josie had made short conversation with him on two occasions, he was still quite unsure of this guy.

The man turned his gaze slowly over the area. He noted it seemingly without emotion. But eventually his eyes settled upon the couple. "Josie…Adrienne," he said tipping his hatless head in the Southern manner of respect for the fairer sex.

"'Morning Roy," Josie replied.

"What're you two doin' out here?"

"Well…we've been staying the night," Josie's report was nervous. "Is this your land sir? If so, I hope you're not upset. We ain't lookin' to cause no trou…"

"Don't call me sir," Roy snapped. "Make's me feel old."

Josie fell silent.

Roy looked to what was left of the old foundation. Josie followed his gaze. "You know," he began, "that little house belonged to my grandma before she passed. Place went through my family for some years after, and by the time it ended up in my possession the house was in pretty bad shape. Well, I didn't have no money to fix it up. Probably wasn't worth it by then no how, so I just left it be. Gone now. Oh well. The taxes ain't much so I just pay 'em. Don't really know why. Guess I just wanna keep the property in the family is all."

He looked back at Josie then. "You two like it here?"

"Yes si…ah…yeah Roy, we think it's a great place."

Roy rubbed his chin with one hand as he regarded the couple for a moment's contemplation. "Planin' on staying for a while were ya?"

"Well…we really like Andrews if that's what you mean. So, I'd say…yeah…we might like to stay a while."

Roy's right index finger pointed purposefully to the ground. His face was hard, "I'm talkin' about right here on my land. That's what I'm sayin'."

Josie only stared at the man as a loss for words came over him. Of course, they would like to stay here, but he couldn't just say that…could he? Roy was eyeing him expectantly now. "Sure," Josie finally managed, "We'd love to stay." He opened his mouth to say more; then closed it again. It was an awkward moment, but at least it was out.

Roy's gaze left Josie to again scan the lot around them. He began to speak, "Damn kids like to come in here and party now and then you know. Guess I don't really mind much, 'cept the little bastards throw their trash everywhere. Now and then I also get some cocksucker…" Roy looked to Adrienne as his words trail off, "Pardon my French mam. It's just that I get so god-awful mad when I think about it. My grandmother was a good woman you know. Madelyn was her name and I use-ta come visit when I was a boy. Christmas, Thanksgivin', family gatherin's, other times too. She was a great cook. Ma tried to match her, never could though. Sometimes I'd even just stay here a day or so for no good reason." He looked directly into Adrienne's eyes then, "I loved my grandma you know…in the way a boy does…think of her now and then still. Miss her sometimes." His emotion came strong now, Adrienne's intuition told her. But Roy held his feelings like a jailer. There was something cold in him. Cynical. Almost mean. Adrienne could feel that too.

Josie remained oblivious.

Roy turned back to the young man. "Anyway, as I was sayin', every now and then some…person…gets the idea this here's the city dump and comes in with a load of trash then piles it wherever he pleases." Roy pointed to a mound of construction refuse now mostly covered with grass. "Guess I'd probably shoot 'em if I caught 'em," he aimed a hard stare back at Josie. "Tried puttin' a chain across the driveway but someone hooked a truck up an' yanked it loose. Probably them damn kids."

Did Roy have enemies? Adrienne wondered.

Josie: oblivious.

Roy walked a few paces away. He looked to the wispy clouds for one long moment before returning to again face Josie, who was now standing. "Tell you what young man; if you'd like to stay on this here land, I might have a deal for you."

Had Josie heard right? This could be interesting. "What's your proposition Roy?"

"Well, if you clean this place up—I got a truck you can use, you pay for gas and dump fees of course—then I'll give you the power of "caretaker" so you kin run anyone out comes in here causing trouble. Then you just stay a while, an' we'll see. How's that sound?"

Josie looked to the still-seated Adrienne, who offered him a slight nod. He turned his stare to the ground for only a moment before again raising it into Roy's gray eyes. Josie stuck out his hand, "Guess you got yourself a deal mister."

The men shook.

"When kin you start?" Roy asked.

"When would you like?"

"How 'bout right now? You and me kin ride to the house an' I'll give you the truck. Don't need it for nothin' right now so you kin keep it a few days while you work."

"Okay," Josie said. He turned to Adrienne then, "Be back in a while baby. Need anything?"

She shook her pretty head, "Have fun."

"Oh yeah."

Josie turned and almost ran into Roy, who had stepped closer. Roy's voice came low and hard. "You're gonna be havin' my own truck right here on my own property young man. Now you and me don't know each-other too good and for all I know you're a fine boy so I'm gonna say this as polite as I can. Don't fuck with me on this one Josie. If you do there's gonna be bad trouble between us."

Roy's statement did not have the impact he might have liked, for Josie knew the old guy was just trying to protect his interests as best he could. He offered humility, "No problem Roy. You're not gonna regret this…I mean it." *Hope I don't regret it either*, Josie thought.

Roy noted courage in the young man's eyes and a moment of respect passed between them.

"Alright then." and he turned for the Lincoln.

Josie followed.

The couple soon learned that Roy had, in reality, offered very little to lose. The old Chevy half-ton work-truck was beat to death. It smoked, coughed and all around ran like hell. But run it did, and for three days they worked until Grandma's place was once again pure. Josie held true to his bargain and kept undesirables off the property. Roy seldom visited after that, but Josie did see him in town regular enough. In time, Roy grew fond of Adrienne, and especially Josie. It was not a difficult thing to do. Roy was a man of arduous temperament, scant social skill (not that he really cared), and a seeming contempt for humanity in general. He enjoyed only few acquaintances and even fewer real friends. But, no man is an island and Josie's ability to look beyond such shortcomings impressed the older man. Josie kept a genuine interest in the lives of those he knew, and people felt this. His integrity in such matters was undeniable.

So, Roy liked him…liked him a lot. Though he never said as much.

3

Stability settled in. Josie's eyes began to regard Grandma's land in a more permanent way. It looked like home.

He made changes:

Not for the first time, Josie entered the wooden pump-house. Inside and towards the back, he again found the round water well that was ringed with a three-foot rock and mortar wall identical to the home's foundation. The well had been capped with a steal lid now notched at one side to make way for the copper pipe running into it. It appeared the well had long ago offered water by means of rope and bucket before an electric pump was later installed to supply the home's new indoor plumbing. Josie heaved the lid aside and gazed in. Ten feet below, the dark water shimmered. What a score. A plastic bucket was soon lowered by rope and Josie deemed the water good. Even drank a little. Cooking and cleaning became easier after that.

Josie nailed a large brown tarp around three small trees that rooted close together to act as curtain for his makeshift shower-stall. Over the ground between them he placed a wooden pallet as floor then roped his solar shower to the branches above. Again, water was heated over the fire or Coleman stove then poured into the shower-bag.

Holes were dug farther into the woods to be used as a toilet and Adrienne did not mind. To such trivial inconvenience she had simply grown accustomed. Really, she seldom even noticed anymore; for man is the most adaptable animal on earth and Adrienne had done just that…adapted. Besides, these past three years had been the best of her life and that was a thing not to be taken lightly. Trivial inconveniences were just that—trivial.

Adrienne had her eye on the bigger picture.

With a mind wired more like a modern-day hunter/gatherer these days, Josie's senses were always attuned to the necessities of their simple needs and Adrienne was often impressed with the efficiency of his eye and seeming genius of ingenuity. So often he spotted an inexpensive, free, or discarded, tool, chair, sofa, grill, device, slice of wood, or whatever, that, when applied to his sometimes-unorthodox ideas, became such a useful item in their simple lives. It has been said that: *If one does not want what the multitudes have, then he should simply watch what they do and not do it*. Josie had become a living example of such philosophy.

Over the grass that lay trampled before the van's sliding passenger-side door a section of brown low-rise carpet was thrown to hold down dust and ease the plight of bare feet. Atop this, an ugly yellow couch Josie had acquired for nothing somewhere was placed against the van. Adrienne was quick to cover it with a blanket depicting the face of a lion in brown and white across its surface. A small wooden coffee table was also added. The existing fire-pit was moved, improved, and set just beyond the table.

"It's a…living room with fireplace!" Adrienne exclaimed with some admiration for the nutty, off beat virtue of her hubby's crafty ability. "And what a view!"

Josie replied, "And the noble knight McWaters declared, 'For the virtue of thy beauty and thy grace fair Queen,'" he bowed gallantly to her, "'thy cup shall runneth over with the luxury of fine chattels.'" Again, he bowed and this time paused to kiss the back of her hand. Adrienne put the other hand against her face to stifle a smirk. She tried not to giggle, but his outlandish theatrics never ceased to crack her up.

She touched his shoulder then and spoke with tones of lofty authority "And as your reward fine knight only the *best* of fair maidens shall be sent to your sleeping chambers this evening."

"Oh, thank you my Queen. Your generosity is without limit," and a boyish-grin crossed his face as Josie backed away, clenched one fist, and made like a sports fan. **"Yes!"** he cried while performing a stupid little victory dance.

Both got a good laugh.

There were probably those who would, or maybe did, say that Josie was poor-white-trash, and that it was anyone's guess why such a nice girl as Adrienne would live in relative poverty with him. Surley she could do better! Josie figured he probably wasn't impressing anyone—except maybe himself. But it was too late for amendment. For the influence of what others might say, although of slight consideration, had little affect upon his actions anymore. Josie thought for himself now.

The new place came to be affectionately known as,

"Grandma's".

Back in the city, Josie had been unable to sit still and simply be. His insides had seemed perpetually squirrelly there. There were always so many things that needed his attention in the alleged "real world". The all-important pressure of endless responsibility and drive for "success" had haunted his days and sometimes even his sleeping moments. That was over now, for there were few responsibilities left, and the care of what remained was a simple job. Simple living. It suited him well. For him, the city's hustle and bustle no longer existed. It had gone in a rush leaving behind only the luxury of a quiet mind. So often now Josie found himself content to simply watch time pass as he relaxed to let the day unfold.

The change was profound.

There were those who complained to him of boredom and lack of opportunity in the small towns and mountains of this place. Josie wondered why they stayed. Then he remembered the terror that had accompanied his own departure from the city. There was also the consideration of family. But if one's spirit were dying in a place then what good was he to anyone anyway? Did loved ones really wish to witness such a thing? But Josie had persevered. His heart had called…and he had followed. The payoff now seemed beyond measure.

Interest in the land grew quickly and Josie began to make long forays into the woods. He walked game trails, ridge-tops and valleys too. A beaver-dam held back the water of a nearby spring to create a large pool filled with gently flowing water and an array of so many different bugs in motion. Some swam while others flew. And there were fish. Animals came to drink and Josie saw them often. It was a melee of life. Everything interested him now. Bees at work over a million flowers. Animal tracks. A hunting cabin abandoned to the woods until the ever-encroaching powers of nature closed in to reclaim it. Clouds in the sky. Deer that Josie sometimes tried to follow but would always elude him with ease. It all seemed so enchanting. To another man this life might bring only boredom, but for the young Josie McWaters it seemed magical!

4

Upon the storefront of Mary Joe's Feed was a bulletin board filled with a variety of business cards and paper scraps advertising everything from houses for rent, handyman services, baby sitting, autos, and even an ATV for sale. Curiosity brought the young Adrienne McWaters to stand before this small wealth of local information and it was here that she found a flier advertising the need for a hired hand at the nearby *Kelly Ranch*. The note stated that such duties would include the exercising, feeding, brushing, and other general care (including shoveling Adrienne guessed) of boarded horses. Kelly's was a horse ranch. Adrienne decided to apply.

The next day Josie drove under the arched *Kelly Ranch* sign to navigate the quarter mile of dirt road leading in. Kelly's was a moderately large affair set into a valley surrounded by the rolling mountains. The ranch itself lay across a big clearing cut amid thick forest. Ahead, a handful of slightly worn corrals came into view and Adrienne's heart quickened as she took note of the many horses that munched alfalfa, nipped playfully at each other, or just stood seemingly staring into space. They came in so many colors. They were so…beautiful!

And just like that she knew. Adrienne knew! Excitement gripped her. *Oh-my-god*, she thought, *what if I don't get the job?* Her stomach tightened. Adrienne began to pray.

Without a word, Josie piloted the old van onward. Had he taken notice, Josie would have been puzzled at the indiscernible array of emotion that held in his wife's face as she leaned slightly forward while unconsciously increasing a death-grip on the doorhandle.

The wooden corrals came in a multitude of shapes and sized. One was little more than a fenced field, while two others bordered either side of the van as it passed. Ahead, was a large barn with one small Ford tractor and two, smallish travel-trailers parked beside it. Upon the hill at the barn's right sat a wonderful little ranch house. In its gravel driveway was a late modal Cadillac and old Chevy pick-up truck.

Adrienne struggled with herself.

A tan colored mutt and his shaggy black companion came barking happily to the van. Like a pair of snaggle-toothed, K9 tugboats, they turned to accompany the big vehicle's arrival.

At their left came the sight of a middle-aged woman who stood at the center of a smaller round corral to turn in slow circles while holding a rope leading to the Black Arabian that pranced around her. She had fair skin and green eyes that seemed, even from Adrienne's seat at roadside, to blaze from beneath a shock of long-blond hair tied into ponytail. The woman wore a white T-shirt tucked smartly into tight black jeans that were covered to the knee with leather riding boots. Although she was big-boned and large breasted, the moderation of waist and ease with which she carried herself told Adrienne that this woman was anything but lazy. To Adrienne she seemed so majestic…so strong.

A knot crawled into Adrienne's throat as she realized this was probably Jean, the woman she had spoken with on the phone. Her pulse quickened. *Fear. Oh-my-god!* Adrienne hoped, even pleaded with God, that Jean would like her. Could she do it? Could she talk to her? Adrienne had to try.

Josie sat oblivious.

"Park right here!" Adrienne's voice betrayed too much emotion as she pointed to roadside. Josie saw something was up. He decided to keep quiet. He pulled over, killed the engine, then sat to look at her. Josie saw the importance in her deep blue eyes then, and he offered only silent, if not submissive, regard. It was her call now. From here on, he would offer only support…and do as she asked.

For Josie loved her as no other.

Without another word Adrienne turned to consider both dogs through the open window. After deciding the wagging tails meant only a friendly welcoming committee, she opened the door. "Wait for me here," she said while simultaneously wished the fucking van looked more like an average pick-up truck than some hippy freak show.

"Yes Ma'am," he replied to her backside as she slid from the seat then squatted to address both dogs. Once introductions were completed, Josie watched as the mutts escorted her across the short field to the round corral and trotting Arabian. After making a slow approach, Adrienne leaned against the fence to watch for a while. She felt the horse's wind as he passed. For a long time, Adrienne only observed.

Eventually Josie saw the black horse begin to slow and, once it had stopped, the blond woman released her hold and approached the fence to address her visitor. Josie watched the two women shake hands and begin to talk.

For almost forty minutes they carried on in the way women do; at least that's what Josie saw. But eventually the blond girl turned to regain her work while Adrienne walked quickly to the van. As she approached the driver's window Josie noted the heavy air of disappointment etched into her face. And he felt for her. But just as he opened his mouth to express his regret, she blurted, "I'm hired," and her grin bloomed like flowers after spring rain. "I'm hired Josie," and although he knew not why it should be, Josie watched as clean tears welled in sparkly blue eyes then spilled down smooth cheeks. Women could be so emotional about the littlest things sometimes. But this was not one of those times…he saw. No. Something here was of great importance to her now. He knew not what, nor did he really care. She knew, and that was all that mattered.

"I'm so glad," and he reached through the window to brush dark hair from her face with both hands then wipe salty tears from her cheeks with his thumbs. "I'm so glad for you baby," and his smile brought yet another little bout of waterworks. Josie almost cried himself.

"I can start right now!" the smile returned. "Oh Josie, could you come back and pick me up at five?"

"Be my pleasure ma'am," and he reached to hand her light denim jacket through the window, "Take this in case it cools off. See you at five."

For one whole minute she hugged him. Then, and without a word, she turned and walked away. Josie watched her go. He started the engine and, after finding a U-turn, Josie left the ranch.

Weeks passed.

5

    Josie and Adrienne came to know many of the townspeople. Although the inescapable gossip often belittled their offbeat lifestyle, small towns tend to take care of their own. Employment found Josie—especially once word had spread of his background in plumbing. But, he flatly refused to work full time. For as the ways of Nature's world tightened their grip on the young man's spirit, his refusal to forsake its call for the gain of virtually *anything* escalated into a powerful conviction. He would not falter.
    It became quickly apparent that another vehicle was necessary, and Josie bought a used truck. The old four-wheel-drive Ford F-100 offered a short-bed, four-on-the-floor, and six-cylinder engine. The original paint had been red, but years of oxidation had long since reduce it to a dull brownish hue. But the price was right.
    Adrienne now generally drove herself to work while Josie slept in. Sometimes he drove her then kept the truck for his own use.
    In Adrienne's absence Josie indulged farther into his own interests.
    The land again.
    Josie found that if he were to voyage into the woods then sit very still for some hours the animals would eventually resume their daily business around him. This fascinated him. In time he began to recognize those individual animals he saw repeatedly. One jay bird had a crooked foot as the result of an injury that had not mended well, while another's unusually aggressive nature, even for a jay, distinguished it from the rest. Josie saw that mammals are habitual creatures who set up routines they seldom stray from. He began to recognize some of the rabbits who came to forage in the same areas everyday. Deer were no different and it surprised the young city-boy to learn that so many animals, as was also common among people, spent most of their lives in a small area.
    By day Josie attended to what few chores remained in his life, relaxed at home, observed the natural world—*and grew bored.*

By its nature, ranch work brought little pay, but to Adrienne's compensation came far more in the form of satisfaction. And for this she offered service gladly and in return received earnest friendship among her employers, the freedom to ride as much as she wished, and a good feeling of belonging to a place among those who shared her passion. *Passion*…what a wonderful addition to her life!

At work Adrienne saw much more of Jean than her husband Ed because his real estate business often kept him busy elsewhere. But she liked him very much. And he liked her. In short time Jean designated to Adrienne one of the small camping trailers. It had complete hook-ups and even hot running water so long as its propane tanks held fuel. Adrienne began to stay the night on occasion, but generally preferred going home to Josie. She was scheduled to only four days a week at the *Kelly Ranch*, but it was common to see her there on off days as well. Sometimes she came simply to ride.

Things were pretty good for the young babe from the city.

On occasion, Adrienne still thought of that fearful night in the parking lot of Josie's old apartment building. So much had changed since then.

The air grew brisk and cold as fall came to the mountains. Trees turned a riot of colors and a chilled wind began to scatter neon leaves across Grandma's land. The air became crisp and icy. Frost glazed the truck's windshield some mornings, and rain was cold. Snow would be next. Squirrels acted squirrelly as they sprinted in seemingly senseless circles that sometimes brought them quick deaths beneath automobile tires. Other animals seemed nervous too.

So did Josie.

He had known the harsh bite of frozen winter months all his life, but always in the sanctity of a house in the large city with so many people and resources close at hand. This was different. It frightened him. Action must be taken.

Josie's first concern was *heat*.

Brought from the frigid northern city that had once been their home, long underwear, wool socks, beanie-hats, gloves, insulated boots, and heavy goose-down jackets were retrieved from boxes beneath the bed. Although a window must be left cracked to alleviate the stuffiness it created, the cooking-stove served as adequate heating. But it used too much gas. Josie replaced the van's passenger seat with a tiny old wood-burning stove and ran its flue through the passenger window. When in use the stove put out far more heat than needed. But it required wood, as did the fire-pit outside which was still used regularly to escape confinement inside the van.

Josie became a wood-hound. His chainsaw buzzed all over Grandma's property and the search extended to places far and wide as well. His watchful eye seldom missed a downed branch or tree and if Josie thought he could take it with minimal trouble, he pulled the trusty chainsaw from his truck-bed and went at it.

Josie shored up the old pump house, re-shingled its roof, then insulated it. Next, he installed an old propane RV water heater that now received its water from a jerrycan suspended above. A small propane heater was also set on the floor inside and a mirror hung on the wall.

As the season deepened snow came to the mountains.

At first, the change of lifestyle that must accompany the season, had seemed a frightening event. On the other hand, as had become common in recent years, the couple simply adapted.

6

A person's heart may call him or her to any of a thousand things, but for the young Josie McWaters it had always been the land. Josie lived closer to the earth than ever before, but still his deepest desire was to go farther. *The land will provide...if only I knew how.* For so long as he could remember, this idea had been with him. Yet, in days past it had existed only in fantasy. Overshadowed by worship of other things, by belief in opinion of the masses; by ignorance; and by an idea that he was simply not good enough to achieve such dreams, it had been banished to the secret chambers of his mind—a place reserved only for fantasy and ridiculous ideas that held no footing amid the realities of this world. Adulthood had brought maturity and with it the dream had grown small—*but it would not die.* And although once a warm and sustaining virtue, its voice had then become only an irritating haunting. That was changing now. Like a ship emerging from the mist, it grew more prevalent with each day's passing. The dream again. Was it still possible in this modern age? Josie had to know. Nature's ways…he must learn them.

George was 50-years old, and a close friendship between he and Josie had seemed to come quite naturally. George lived some miles east of town and had been a confirmed bachelor for many years. He was an eccentric dude who loved little more than his house in these mountains; of which he thoroughly enjoyed showing off to Josie. The place was completely off the utility grid and reflected George's passion with an excess of mostly homemade amenities that seemed a strange mix of woodsman, Indian, and even hippie-type origin. Three large skylights let sunshine into his living room. A wood-burning stove, made from one steel 55-gallon drum, was set atop four cinderblocks. Thick firs and Indian blankets covered most of the furniture. Oil burning lanterns hung everywhere.

The kitchen offered a three-burner camp stove and one small propane-powered refrigerator with fuel bottle sitting at its side. Water came to the sink by means of a water-tower, made from another 55-gallon drum that was gravity filled from a hose placed into an uphill creek. George's colorful, handmade pottery adorned the house while the backroom held his manual pottery wheel and the back yard a homemade propane kiln for the finishing of his work. There were other unusual amenities too…all very ingenious. One of these sparked Josie's desire. He had to have one! Josie decided not to tell his wife. It would be a surprise.

These mountains offered hundreds of thousands of public acres open to hunting, and George was a hunter. Josie was invited and he contemplated this offer. He had never killed an animal before. To this matter Josie had never even felt a desire. But it was only natural that one takes sustenance from the earth in this way. So, it had been since time beginning.

The decision was made.

Although target practice started with the usual awkwardness, Josie's aim improved quickly. He seemed a natural. George loaned Josie a rifle and the two men soon took to hunting the forests together. The killing of small game bothered Josie far less than he had originally feared, and in time he graduated to larger animals and found that his feelings did not change. Josie bought two used rifles:

22 and 30.06 caliber.

With jubilant excitement and true joy in the kill, George often maxed out the legal bag limits then gave the excess to friends. Josie did not; for once his own needs had been met the young woodsman took no more. For him, keeping lesson of the natural way was all that mattered. As for the love of the kill, Josie simply did not have it.

Some hunters brought their kills to town for butchering, but George never would since he took too much pride in the ability to dress his own kill. And although George did keep some of his own take in the freezers of friends he had offered excess to, George had also fire-dried his own meats for years. He was a man far closer to the natural way than anyone Josie had known, and the younger woodsman paid close attention to the lessons his friend was happy to offer.

Adrienne began to experience a variety of wild meats.

Spring came to the mountains. New leaves overtook the branches of previously naked birch, dogwood, hickory, white ash, red oak, and others. Forest green returned to push the bleak white days of winter aside. Migrating birds returned while slow moving rivers became skinned over with yellow pollen and the fallen blossoms of tulip trees. It was a time of renewal for all the forest.

Josie planted a garden.

Fishing was a pastime to which Josie brought some passion and he began to spend many hours at the water's edge. Sometimes Adrienne joined him. It was an event that both came to favor.

Although fishing suited him, gardening did not, and it took little time for Josie to realize a complete lack of interest in farming. Hunting and gathering was his game. *The land would provide…if only he knew how.* But Adrienne found real solace in botany and the garden soon became her territory. By season's end, many plants would flourish under her care.

These mountains offer the greatest assortment of herbs and edible plant life in the country and, after retrieving a few library books on this subject, Josie began to harvest a variety of these. He found this activity exceedingly satisfying.

Summer passed to fall and again the trees turned a riot of fluorescent colors.

7

It was early afternoon as Josie pulled excitedly into Grandma's with the beat-up object in his truck. His prize was almost identical to the one he had seen at George's and Josie had been lucky to find it. But he must work fast to have the project up and running in time. Adrienne would be working late today, and this was a good thing. The object was heavy and sweat glistened on Josie's brow by the time he had worked the awkward bastard past the tailgate and allowed it to hit the dirt with a muffled thud. The thing was then lifted, one end at a time, and four concrete blocks pushed beneath with his foot. Once suspended at the proper height Josie paused to consider his work. Next, he placed many large rocks in a circle below and added fuel. And there was more. It was a lot of work.

Evening was close when Josie picked his wife up from Kelley's and a restaurant was chosen to kill off remaining daylight.

Night's darkness filled the air as Adrienne peered from the passenger's seat to watch the truck's headlights illuminate the familiar foliage of Grandma's road. It had been a long day and she was tired. Bed sounded nice. Once the truck had topped the rise the surrounding forest gave way to the clearing that was their home. Adrienne gazed ahead with small interest.

Josie worked to conceal his stupid grin.

No moon hung in the sky to bathe the world with its pale lunar radiance on this fine evening. In its absence, the clearing appeared as only a shadowy outline of their strange home. Beyond, the tall tree line appeared as silhouette against the eternal background of a star filled sky. Beautiful though it was, Adrienne had seen it all before and took little interest now. The coals of Josie's earlier fire smoldered red from the usual pit near the van. But there was a second fire! Was there a problem? Adrienne perked up. She leaned forward to peer harder through the windshield.

"Josie. You see that?"

"Yeah."

"What is it?"

"I don't know," he lied, "Think it's something bad?"

His answer was not right. Something was up.

As the truck grew nearer, headlights lit the shadows, and the object came into view. Adrienne's jaw hung slack as she stared in stunned disbelief. It was an old cast-iron bathtub set atop four concrete cinderblocks. From its surface steam swirled lazily up and away while below it the fire that had burned down in the absence of its caretaker still glowed.

Adrienne closed her mouth with a light click. "Are we having soup?" she jeered, never taking her eyes from the strange aberration.

"No, we're having a bath…If you're up for it I mean."

Adrienne looked at him. Those stupid, guilty, prankster's eyes; like she'd never seen that before. Time for theatrics again. Well, she could certainly play along. Her gaze returned to the tub. Without another word she opened the door and stepped out. In full character now, Adrienne walked to the carpet that encircled their usual fire-pit. Josie watched through the windshield with mounting interest. Oblivious of his presence—as though she were the only person on earth—the young woman began to undress. Josie stepped from the cab then stopped to rest knuckles under chin and elbows atop the hood.

The silent voyeur.

Orange firelight illuminated her body as the girl continued to remove pieces of clothing and place them atop his favorite recliner chair. Leaning to remove the last piece—her tight jeans—she turned a strong backside to him. The voyeur's interest peaked. The girl neither knew, nor cared, that he was there.

Standing naked against the night, Adrienne threw long dark hair back with a flick of her head then walked to the water's edge. She pushed one hand into the brew and withdrew it quickly. "It's fucking hot, Josie! Sure, you don't wanna make soup?" Adrienne broke character.

Appearing quickly, Josie pushed his own hand into the tub then added one of the two plastic buckets filled with cold water he had set nearby earlier. Josie stirred his concoction with an old wooden boat-paddle. He tested the temperature again. "Perfect," he mumbled. Then, "Yeah. We're gonna make soup. Clam soup. Now slide your clam in there."

"Ooo, so forceful," she swooned with mock sincerity. "Yes master." Adrienne slid into the tub. Josie disappeared momentarily but quickly returned to stand at attention beside her. A red towel lay folded neatly across his left arm while a saucered cup of hot chi tea was held in his right. Josie stood ridged…eyes straight ahead. For clothes he wore *only* skimpy red Fruit-of-the-Looms…and nothing else.

The vision was so ridiculous that Adrienne burst into laughter.

Josie's features remained stern.

Adrienne caught herself and promptly regained composure. Her face became rigid. "Thank you, James," she said, "Now be a good dear and fetch my dick for me would you?"

"Yes m'lady. Right away."

"And while you're there, fetch yourself some tea as well."

Again, "Yes m'lady," and he was gone.

Josie soon returned with cup and towel to resume the exact position he had occupied only minutes before. This time he was naked. Once in place, eyes straight ahead, Josie thrust young hips forward for her inspection, "Here is the item you requested m'lady."

Adrienne grabbed the thing and inspected it thoroughly. "It'll do just fine James," she said. "Now place it into the water for me, will you? We can't have this running around dirty, now can we?"

"No m'lady." Josie set the towel down and climbed in.

The show was over now, and each relinquished his or her character. The water was hot, as was the tea, and steam rose to mist one's view before disappearing into the moonless night. Josie raised a toast, "To the good life," he said.

Adrienne raised her cup above the steaming knee she had thrown over the tub-rail and clinked it to his. "To the good life Josie," and tears welled in happy eyes then.

Josie smiled back.

8

    The first two winters had been a challenge. A thing of beauty. But as the third deepened into cold white monotony, time became the culmination of deepening boredom for Josie. Depression spawned. Just a little at first, but it grew. Then more. Much more, until eventually the young man sometimes found it difficult just to get out of bed. He read books, took walks, fished, hunted, jerked meat, cut wood, and tried with real effort to regain his former state of reverence. These attempts failed. He had come so far, done so much. What was left? What had he missed? Josie wondered where his playful spirit had gone.

    Adrienne's life had steadily improved. Her job—her passion—took her to new heights. She gave lessons now and often led groups of paying customers on tours as well. A fine quarter horse, sorrel in color and black of mane, had come into Adrienne's possession and along with it had also come an aging twin-bay horse trailer. Cinnamon was only six years old. Spirited and agile, yet soon very much in love with her new woman, this horse/human team soon became preferred barrel-race and pole-bending contestants at the rodeos they attended. Josie loved to watch these events. Oh, he had eyed the others. Many were damn good. But Adrienne was one of the best! With the horse's movements her body seemed to flow as one; little hands held tight to the reigns in front, feet kicking in hurried movement yet still in perfect rhythm. It was quite erotic. There were other horse-oriented assemblies too. The "Wagon Train", a local camping/riding event, was one of his wife's favorites. And there was more. Adrienne's world was expanding.

    By winter's end Adrienne had come to fear for the condition of her husband's declining mental state. He had grown lethargic, gained weight, become pale and unhealthy looking. Josie's eyes were dull, his mind slow, and indecision plagued him at almost every choice now. Nothing she had thought to try had restored his former tenacity. Maybe it was only the gray days of winter that had him down. Well, warmer weather was around the corner and only time would tell.

    Adrienne felt helpless.

Spring came to the mountains in a rush of new color and life. Leaves refilled the trees as the chill relaxed its grip. Skies became blue and inviting. Josie tried to regain his former lust for life, but it was no use.

His life had been painfully stagnant before the road-trip, but the change that had led to these mountains had been the most profound and uplifting experience of his life. Now here he was again; back to a similar, if not worse, mental funk. What was the use? Maybe it was time for another change. That was a thought. Should he leave this place and resume the journey? But what of the job Adrienne loved so much? This life seemed to be working so well for her. Josie's, however, was not and he was alternately happy for his wife and jealous of her too. She was excelling, while he slowly lost his mind. Failure. It hurt badly. Josie feared for his own sanity.

While alone on one of his deep woods forays Josie paused to look up. In a moment of torrid anger, he began to scream to whatever God might be listening, "What's wrong with me?" he began, "To the best of my ability I've tried to follow my dreams, as is only what I believe you'd have me do. And this is my reward? To live in heaven while I suffer like hell? What have I missed?" Josie shook his fist angrily at the sky, "**What do you want from me you fucking bastard!?**" But there was no answer, only the sound of birds and a gentle wind. "**Damn you!**" Josie screamed some more. Still no reply. So, he ranted again until his anger peaked and eventually diminished. When his energy was exhausted Josie slumped to the ground in an uncontrollable fit of sobbing. For a long time, he sat upon the dirt and cried. But eventually the tears, as did the anger, subsided, leaving him with only the quiet of his moment. He felt spent now…his mind a thoughtless blank. The silence that replaced his mental turmoil was soothing. Then, in the still of his mind, Josie found two small words:

The land.

If that was God's answer it was bullshit. He *was* on the land. Had *been* on the land. Built a *life* on the land. Had *hunted* the land. What was left? Ah…it was just two little words floating in his head anyway, not the word of God. Get a grip. *You're fucked up,* Josie told himself. Besides, in recent months he had begun to doubt there was a God.

Resigned to his fate, Josie climbed to his feet and walked

home a broken man.

Two days passed.

It was on a semi-clouded Saturday that Josie found himself in the town of Cherokee to attend an event called The Festival of Native People. The show would take place at the fairground and promised theatrical performances by Native Americans from across the country.

Adrienne was occupied elsewhere, and Josie had come alone. For him, this event was a chance to get out and hopefully shake a few cobwebs from his brain. God knows he had been alone too much lately.

After paying the fee, Josie entered through an iron gate. Vending tents lined either side of the concrete walkway and he admired the many Indian works of leather, paintings, and other crafts for sale. It was a good crowd today. Not too big and not too small. Many white tourists with cameras hanging from their necks mingled among the numerous Indian locals. A strange mix. A heavy-tarp roof held high above by a permanent structure of aluminum framework shaded both stage and bleachers. Very nice. Josie bought a coke then took a seat near front and center stage.

The show began. Decorated in bright costume, different Native groups, representing one region of the country or another, alternately took the stage to perform ancient dances and ceremonies. The theatrics were often very well played, and Josie enjoyed the show immensely. He stayed for its entirety.

It was three p.m. when Josie finally exited through the main gate. Gazing into the crowd, he noted an odd-looking couple sitting upon a low rock-wall. Josie knew them. Sid, a young man in his mid 20s, was a big Native with round face and the usual longish jet-black hair so common to his race. His girl Pam was small, thin, wore dishwater blond hair, and was obviously not of Indian descent.

Josie approached.

"Josie!" Sid's greeting came with his usual high spirits, "Where you been hiding man? Ain't seen you since…hell…last year? How's the ol' lady?"

"She's good," Josie pumped the man's hand, then addressed his girl, "Pam. Nice to see you again." Turning back to the big Indian Josie said, "Same old shit Sid. She's out doin' the horse thing today.

Never seen her happier. But I just ain't been getting out much lately."

"Still hiding back there in the sticks huh? Well, that always seems how you like it best. Still makin' jerky?"

"Yeah. How's your mom Sid?" her diabetes and poor health was common knowledge.

"She's good," Sid looked closer into his friend's face and noted the dark bags under Josie's sunken eyes. An expression of concern creased Sid's round features. "You look like hammered shit. What's goin' on man?"

The comment shocked Josie. He recovered quickly. "Shows huh? Just been in a bad place lately I guess. Don't really know why. Can't seem to shake it though."

Sid turned thoughtful for a moment. Finally, he said, "When I'm down I always double up on the lodges. Helps a lot. Why don't you come sweat with us this weekend?"

Again, Josie was a little shocked. Of course, he had heard of the '*Inipi*' or '*Native Sweat Lodge Ceremony*'. It was a ritual that dated back beyond the eons of recorded history. A sacred practice of the ancients. Of the truly natural man. Never before had Josie been invited to such a thing. He wondered that it was happening now. Could this help him? It mattered not, for wild horses could not keep Josie from an opportunity like this.

"I'd like that Sid. Just tell me where and when."

Sid did tell him.

Josie was instructed to bring one towel, a pair of shorts, and his appetite. He was to arrive by noon on Saturday.

9

It was 11:30am when Josie pulled his truck among the fifteen or so other vehicles in the parking lot and killed the engine. Grabbing his rolled-up towel and shorts, Josie exited the truck. Two houses stood ahead and at one of these two Cherokee men were engaged in conversation on the porch. It was beneath a clear sky that

Josie crossed the lot to stand just beyond the handrail from them. One sat in a rocker while the other leaned against the rail. The standing man went by the name of River Otter while the other, an older guy, Josie had not seen before. With no idea what to expect, Josie just stood there feeling kinda stupid. Breaking conversation for a moment, River turned to the newcomer and said, "Over that way and to the right," he pointed to a small driveway that dropped quickly downhill before becoming lost into the trees. "You'll see the lodges." Without another word, the Indian re-engaged his former conversation. Josie felt no less confused than before.

Some 150-feet down, the pavement hung a hard right then ended at a dirt trail. Fifty feet farther on, Josie stood at a footpath that led down to a smallish clearing. He paused to look it over. At the clearing's right was a short trail leading up a steep hill to a small house with covered porch. The clearing's remaining perimeter was hemmed-in so completely by a wall of thick forest that it seemed the surreal event, now taking place below him, might be all that existed in the world.

With both doors facing him from the clearing's far end, two sweat lodges stood side by side and Josie squinted at them. They were the first he had ever seen. Shaped like huge turtle shells, both were covered with thick green military tarps and strips of old carpet. Before each lodge stood a low dirt and rock alter that held a collection of sticks, feathers, tobacco, and other objects. In the foreground, a large bonfire blazed in a big pit while a pile of roughly cut wood, and one gasoline-powered log splitter, waited silently nearby. Woodchips littered the ground.

But it was the people that brought the scene to life and, spread in a half-circle around the intense flames, fifteen or twenty sat in small groups talking or simply staring into the fire. Some drank coffee, bottled water, or even soda pop. About a third were white men and women. Josie soon spotted Sid and his girl and made his way to them. After the greeting, Josie sat into a folding chair to enjoy the fire's heat and quietly await whatever happened next. For a long time, nothing did, and Josie was content to simply observe. It was immediately evident that the Indian loved to laugh. He seemed to find humor almost everywhere and for the duration of Josie's dealings among them this trait would reassert itself again and again.

As the fire burned down, many large rocks, formerly concealed within the blaze, became visible. They glowed red.

Eventually the time arrived, and Josie followed the men to change clothes behind a tarp curtain strung between two trees. Upon their return, all wore only shorts and carried a towel. At one side of the fire pit the men formed a line to face the woman who stood in line at its other side to face them back. At the head of both lines the door of each sweat lodge faced the fire burning between the men and women. Josie felt the air's slight chill now and a small nervousness prompted him to pick at the towel held at belly height with both hands.

Both lodges were smudged with sage before a medicine man took his place at the altar of the men's lodge while a graying medicine woman knelt before the other. Each held a colorfully long-stemmed pipe adorned with feathers. Josie watched in silent fascination as each ceremonial leader made his or her offering of tobacco to the Great Spirit before filling the pipes then carrying on in prayer and other ritual.

Oh-my-god, Josie thought, *A fanatical religious ordeal. What have I gotten myself into?* He stood rigid. But the men beside him were talking and even laughing in low tones. And although quiet and respectful, there was other activity among the ranks as well. Josie saw that the vibe remained relaxed, friendly. It would seem fanaticism held no place here.

When the ceremonial leaders had finished, both pipes were passed along the now quiet ranks. Josie noted that ritual demanded one hold the bowl in his left hand.

Eventually the altar-ceremony ended, and the men turned their backs in respect for the woman as they entered the far lodge. When this was done the men walked around their own lodge to enter from the other side, consequently taking care not to cross before the altar. More ritual. But it was to ritual that the event owed its wonderful air of authenticity.

Once inside, the men sat in a tight circle against the dome's round wall. Below them strips of old carpet provided insulation from the dirt. Sitting between two big Indians, Josie's apprehension grew into wonder as he noted that the framework holding the tarps above them was little more than a skeleton of saplings lashed together. Colorful prayer-ties adorned the ceiling and Josie wondered at their significance.

The Medicine Man settled into his place beside the door-flap. More ritual was performed before a five-gallon water bucket was placed at his side. Then, retrieved by a man who would remain outside for the duration of this sweat, rocks from the fire were pushed through the door at the end of a pitchfork. Once inside, they were repositioned in the small pit at room-center by the man sitting beside Josie who moved them with the antler of a deer.

The rocks glowed red.

Immediately the air became heated, and with it Josie's stomach knotted. Could he endure this? He wondered. They'd let him out if he freaked, but Josie would not do that. He would remain seated regardless. The door-flap was closed then adjusted until *absolute* darkness fell. Josie could no longer see his hand before his face. Trapped in complete blackness now, butterflies danced frantically in his stomach. In the language of the ancients the Medicine Man began to pray. Louder…then still louder! until finally the sharp sizzle of water bursting into steam as it was poured across the hot rocks momentarily drowned the chant. Instantly the heated vapor brought a sting to Josie's shoulders as it settled upon his skin.

He sat rigid.

Abruptly the men burst into song. But it was the Cherokee language, and Josie understood not a word. Still, the power moved him. A true ceremony of the ancients. The natural people; and he was a part of it! Steam and sweat soaked him. His skin burned. Josie's composure began to break. This event would prove unlike anything he had experienced before. But the intimate details of the Inipi ceremony are sacred and should therefore never be told.

With three short breaks wherein the door-flap was opened to allow cool air to sweep briefly across hot sweat-soaked skin, the ceremony lasted almost two hours. Eventually it concluded and the men filed out. Still bound by the propriety of ritual, hugs and handshakes were exchanged by all before the men broke protocol and moved to redress themselves then lounge casually around the fire again.

The ceremony was over.

The true nature of all religious practice is to seek a closer relationship with one's Creator, and the effort of these native people was no different. Their belief that The Great Spirit exists in *all* things—plant, animal, human, and earth—worked well for Josie. Although by no means a cure for his depression, the ordeal had left his spirit very much uplifted, which was a most welcomed respite from his recent state of unrest.

A woman soon called from the little house upon the hill, and all made their way up for the usual feast. Among the food and conversation new friends were made. Later, Josie climbed back into his truck and it was with a sense of tranquility and wonder that he made the 20-mile trip home.

So, began yet another 'journey of spirit' for Josie.

DANCING DEER
Chapter 15

1

The sweat lodges were a nice addition to Josie's life, and he began to frequent them weekly. His face became known to the Indians. On occasion, Josie arrived to find a white stallion with black spots tethered to a tree and he soon learned of the man who rode him. For, to many of the Cherokee he was something of a living legend:

Dancing Deer or "Buck", as he was often called, was probably 60-years of age; although it was hard to tell from his lean physique and ease of agility. High of cheekbone and full of lip, his black eyes regarded the world from below a thick shock of graying-black hair that cascaded partway down his back. Dancing Deer was obviously full-blooded Indian. More often than not, he arrived in a well-worn cowboy style shirt, blue jeans, and what appeared to be handmade moccasins. He seemed a quiet man, Josie noted, and although Buck took to laughter as easily as the others, he seldom engaged in lengthy conversation, choosing instead to sit quietly and watch the people or simply stare into the fire.

Dancing Deer was somewhat of a mystery.

But there was talk of him and Josie soon heard myth of the man's history. Curiosity coupled with latent interest in these people also prompted Josie to a little historical library research on the Cherokee Nation in general. Such historical accounts fascinated the young woodsman and, as the pieces of Buck's rumored origin begin to fit into the pages of written history, Josie's fascination with the man redoubled. Josie studied and he learned...

Long ago the Cherokee were the dominant force within these mountains. Their many villages spread across the western Appalation mountain range then poured onto the northern and southern foothills where they were mostly isolated by this mountainous homeland. A typical Cherokee village consisted of 30 to 100 individual homes and one large council house. Homes were constructed of a circular framework of interwoven branches (larger versions of the sweat-lodges) that were then covered with mud. The land teemed with game and food was plentiful in this veritable Eden. From it the Native took no more than he needed and saw no reason to expand upon that which he already knew. And if there were a happier people anywhere, the Cherokee could not imagine it. So it had been, it was said, since time beginning.

But it was not to last, for in 1540 a Spanish expedition visited the region thus leaving behind a handful of European diseases for which the Native's bodies had no natural immunities and in short order 75% of their population was wiped out. Fifty-five years later a series of smallpox epidemics cut their remaining numbers in half.

Trouble for the Cherokee had only begun.

In time more whites began to imigrate from across the sea and the number of their settlements spread slowly across the land. These new foreigners had so many wonderful and useful things of which the Indians had not seen before. And they wanted them. Why should they not? Almost from the beginning trade had commenced between the Natives and their white visitors.

After the founding of the Carolina colonies a treaty was struck naming the British as the Cherokee's allies and sole suppliers. For the commodities of cloth, steel pans, kettles, knives, drills, whiskey, firearms, ammunition, etc. the Cherokee traded the wagonloads of mostly deer-hides, other skins (raw material for the booming European leather industry at that time), and Indian slaves acquired through raids on neighboring tribes.

Indian slaves! Their own neighbors! Josie was shocked.

As the desire for these new possessions grew among the Native People so then was its influence reflected in major changes within their leadership. Power shifted from priest to warrior, and warriors became *hunters for profit*.

Material desire had come to the Indian.

As Native dependence on these new trade-goods increased, so then were the Cherokee drawn into the British wars against the French and Spanish. Countless Cherokee died. Yet, even before the arrival of white men there had always been conflict, raids, and occasional wars between the Cherokee and their Indian neighbors. But the rivalry between these new European factions aggravated traditional Indian hostilities dramatically and the fighting became almost constant.

The conflict continued for so many decades. The English, British, Spanish, French and Dutch, all vying for control of Native trade interests. Caught in the desire for trade goods that had now become incorporated thoroughly into his daily life, the Indian would continue to fight his neighbor, side with his allied supplier in wars that were not his own, and commit atrocities unlike any he had seen before.

However, the Native had underestimated the whites. The white man saw the Natives as only an inferior creation that must ultimately be exterminated to make space for God's superior race. Long ago the white man had decimated his own Eden and now he sought the Indian's. As the white's numbers spread steadily across the land it became increasingly apparent that they cared little of what method need be exploited to acquire possession of it.

Although the Native people could no more understand the white man's idea of land ownership than that of claiming to own the moon or stars, at times land was gained through purchase or a signed treaty with Chiefs who complied mostly in hope of preserving good relations, averting war, maintaining prosperity, and protecting their families. But the whites often broke these treaties, took the land by force and, to the Native's horror, wiped out entire villages of men, women, and children.

Wars broke out. The Indian fought valiantly and won many battles. Countless lives, many innocent, were lost to both sides. But in time, the whites began to prove too powerful and slowly yet steadily many Natives were forced from their homeland to retreat farther west and ultimately into territory wars with other Indians as well as the whites.

A change was coming...

In the year 1806 Chief Doublehead signed a treaty that awarded the whites a staggering ten million acres of Cherokee land. Not long thereafter, Doublehead was assassinated as a traitor. His murder was most likely realized with sanction from the Cherokee Council.

In the wake of his death, John Ross (only part Indian) was elected Principal Chief by the Cherokee people. He and a man known as Major Ridge (also part Indian) were revolutionaries and brought many new ideas to the Cherokee think-tank. It seemed apparent that the ways of the traditional Indian were rapidly becoming extinct, as was anyone who chose to live by them. Chief Ross's radical proposal was to adapt the Cherokee to the ways of the white man's world. It was Ross's dream that one day a new star representing the State of the Cherokee would be added to the American flag. These new leaders established a capital in the hills of northern Georgia. It was called *New Echota*. The traditional clan system of government was replaced with an elected tribal council and a written constitution modeled after that of the United States was incorporated. In less than 30 years the Cherokee underwent the most remarkable adaptation to white culture of any Native American people.

Many Cherokee became wealthy farmers, cultivated beautiful fields, owned large herds of livestock, and lived in fine houses. Chief John Ross himself resided in a $10,000 home. Invitation brought Christian missionaries and an alphabet that provided the Cherokee a written language was soon created. They built schools, established a court system, and published a newspaper. One historical record proclaimed that in 1826 an inventory of *New Echota* property represented: 1,569 black slaves, 22,000 cattle, 7,600 horses, 46,000 swine, 2,500 sheep, 2,488 spinning wheels, 762 looms, 2,942 plows, 172 wagons, 31 grist mills, 10 sawmills, 62 blacksmith shops, 8 cotton machines, 18 schools, and 18 ferries. In fact, many of their white neighbors were becoming more and more envious of the "civilized" Cherokee's thriving prosperity.

This transformation seemed inconceivable, and Josie wondered in awe at what kind of man John Ross must have been. Yet, it was here at *New Echota* that the legend of Dancing Deer had begun. Josie fit the pieces together:

At *New Echota* the poorer Cherokee lived in log cabins. In one of the cabins a Native named Bow had taken residence. Bow's first wife had produced not a single child before her untimely death at the hand of sickness. Shortly thereafter, he had arrived at *New Echota* as a latecomer. Bow had then taken a new wife and was almost 30-years of age when his first son, and later two daughters, were born. Bow had lived by virtue of entirely traditional method before his introduction to civilization and, although enjoying the modern luxuries so many quickly adopted, he had never truly embraced these new ways.

Bow was a skeptic.

Some distance north:

It was around the same time as *New Echota* was being founded that Chief Yonaguski and 400 of his people had chosen through treaty to accept 640-acres at the nearby base of the North Carolina Smokey Mountains and along the Oconaluftee river.

While still a young boy, William Holland Thomas had come to this region as a white trader who would operate a small store. Shunned by his own family, it was not long after Thomas's arrival that Chief Yonaguski had adopted the forlorn young man and William had found a home among them. In time, William became a prominent businessman who also owned and operated several other enterprises in the area. Eventually he would serve as spokesman for all the Cherokee in this region. Named after William's Cherokee wife, the settlement would come to be called Qualla Town...

...and much later, the town of *Cherokee*.

Meanwhile, in *New Echota*:

With the election of Andrew Jackson to the presidency in 1828, the Cherokee Nation was doomed. It was in that same year that gold was discovered on Cherokee land in northern Georgia and a melee of miners fell upon the area. Crimes against the Cherokee increased dramatically.

With Jackson's support, the Indian Removal Act was introduced to Congress in 1829. One year later it passed, and John Ross came quickly under heavy pressure to relocate his people. In the meantime, Andrew Jackson refused to enforce the treaties that protected the Cherokee homeland from incursion. Now freed from federal interference, Georgia and Tennessee rained like Black Death upon the Cherokee. Ross was arrested. The Phoenix newspaper building was burned. The largest Cherokee mansion was confiscated, and the Moravian mission and schoolhouse was converted into militia headquarters.

Upon his release, John Ross went to Washington with the goal of signing a removal treaty which surrendered the Cherokee

Nation's homeland in exchange for $5,000,000 plus 7,000,000 acres in Oklahoma and an agreement to relocate within two years.

Back in *Qualla Town*:

William Thomas also visited Washington where he argued that, unlike those of other regions, the Oconaluftee Cherokee were North Carolina citizens and individual landowners. Perhaps it was because their numbers remained small, unobtrusive, and located in the isolated western North Carolina Mountains (some distance northeast of *New Echota*) that aided in William's success. Or maybe it was guilt. Whatever the reasons, the Oconaluftee Cherokee were granted a rather tenuous (as was everything Cherokee in those days), exemption from the Indian removal process. William had also noted an unusual stipulation in the *New Echota* treaty that allowed certain Cherokee to remain in the east and still collect the same payment as those being removed. He argued that this article applied to his people and eventually won these annuities. The federal government appointed Thomas as agent and trustee of all the remaining Oconaluftee Cherokee thus giving him complete control of their funds. Thomas used this money to buy more land for his people.

It seemed to Josie that William Holland Thomas brought a notable element of integrity and human kindness to a world that offered very little of either. He was immensely impressed.

New Echota:

Bow had foreseen the changing tide early. For the whites and Indian as well—for mankind in general—he had turned away in bitter disgust. He had tasted the modern way of musket, luxury, property, and possession. It was an easy thing to become used to. Bow had witnessed the enslavement of the black man to the Indian and whites as well. He also knew that many Indian slaves had been traded for the *procurement of material gain*. Bow understood that all men want for their needs. This was natural. What he failed to see was how so many could become so seduced by this disease of "*more*" that they would commit such atrocities against one another. Was it true that the acquisition of property and power justified the creation of hell in the life of another? For himself, Bow could not choose this path; for were not all destined to soon leave this place anyway? How many possessions could one take? In the totality of things a man's life is, after all, only as a single raindrop upon the surface of a still pond…its ripples could so profoundly affect those of another. And did not all enter the same pond anyway? One thing was certain; life in this world did not last long. Bow would do his best to enjoy the beauty.

He was a man ahead of his time.

Bow's resolve was to leave the world of men forever. While some set out for the Oklahoma reservation, Bow had been among the first to take his family and flee far to the north. Avoiding Qualla Town, they had passed deep into the mountain wilderness beyond. Later, others would follow.

In times past, the Great Spirit had provided for all his creatures in these mountains—including the people. The essentials of living had most often been a simple matter then. But the once plentiful game was now gone. And no matter how one prayed, seldom did the deer, elk, coyote, or bear come to offer himself to the people anymore. Much of what little meat remained came from small game now, and even that was scarce. The mountains seemed eerily dead. It was a fearful thing indeed and Bow's gut often ached with a dread even greater than hunger.

Fortunately, their minimal numbers were easily concealed and required only small provision. Still, in the interest of elusiveness and hunting, they moved often. And although the Cherokee had always supplemented their hunting with agriculture, Bow's little entourage was forced to adopt many ways of the nomadic hunter-gatherer. Bow taught his children the ancient ways and, with the help of his son Walker, they had survived.

New Echota:

When the relocation deadline finally arrived, 7,000 soldiers—the entire American army—marched into the Cherokee homeland. The Cherokee's reward for embracing the "white man's way" was thus to be driven from their homes at gunpoint. Starving and long ago beaten, the Indian's spirit and ability to fight no longer existed and the army encountered little resistance. Entire families were forced into hastily built stockades while soldiers scoured the countryside collecting outlying bands of Cherokee. As this process continued throughout the summer, unsanitary conditions at the stockades created an ideal breading-ground for measles, whooping cough, and dysentery. Suffering was catastrophic. Many died.

Josie saw that no matter what approach they took—accommodation, war, surrender, or flight—the Indian's fate was always the same.

In October of that same year, departing in large groups under guard of the mounted military escort who held them at gunpoint, 16,650 Cherokee set out into the approaching winter with little food and no real shelter. On this 800-mile journey the soldiers did nothing to protect the Indians from the whites who repeatedly attacked and robbed them of what little they had left. Ice, wind, and snow froze many to death. Disease, exhaustion, and malnutrition took more. Over 4,000 (along with the wife of John Ross) died en-route. Most could do little more for the emaciated bodies of their friends and family than leave them unburied beside the trail. On this journey the Cherokee endured hardship and humiliation unlike anything they had seen before.

History would remember it as The Trail of Tears.

Eventually, the 12,650 surviving Cherokee arrived at the Western Oklahoma reservation where some 6,000 Cherokee had already been established for 11-years. These western people maintained their traditional system of three chiefs and no written laws; while the new arrivals considered themselves superior for their intricate government, court system, and written constitution. None would compromise and violence soon erupted. For the following six years, civil war over boarders and jurisdiction prevailed.

Unbelievably, several hundred Cherokee had escaped along The Trail of Tears to regain the mountains of their homeland and live as smaller groups in hiding. Four years after their escape into the mountains, the army gave up its effort to find these fugitives and those Cherokee that remained in the Appalachians were allowed to stay in "unofficial" status. Many left their places of hiding to join William Thomas's people along the Oconaluftee River.

Things relaxed a little.

Bow was not impressed. There had been many individuals he had liked very much, but for humanity as a whole Bow held small esteem and even less trust. Although he made periodic visits to the outlying villages located within the Qualla Boundary, Bow remained true to his resolve of living much farther into the mountain wilderness. To him, exile seemed a far better choice than the havoc that all humanity seemed destined to reap upon itself with such predictable regularity. His reasoning seemed sound, for in time the Cherokee would fight among both the Union and Confederate armies in the American Civil War. One third would perish. And for almost all Native Americans, trouble, prosecution, and death would persist throughout most of the following century.

Eventually Bow's daughters grew, married and were seldom seen by him again. As for Walker, he journeyed to live in town for a time but ultimately returned to the mountains with his new wife Water. Sharing the most in common with his father, Walker would spend the rest of his life deep within these mountains. Of his three sons and single daughter, all would eventually make their way to the more modernized ways of Qualla Town. All except one son. His name was Smoke, and for him this place, this life, had always been the way of his heart. He knew the forest cared for him. It would feed him, clothe him, and look after him as one of its own. His father had said this, and so the boy believed. And although he sometimes complained of the hard times, Smoke did not mind. The young Cherokee had found peace here—all the peace he had ever known. Smoke's forays to civilization had only confirmed this and he would not trade his ancient ways for all the modern conveniences in the world. And for his remarkable passion a great hunter came to pass. Of Smoke's children would be born one son who shared these feelings. That man was Dancing Deer's father.

2

It was Friday at the Cherokee sweat lodges and Josie again found himself sitting beside the roaring fire that concealed rocks within its center. He stared without expression into the flames as they warmed his knees and face. As usual, subtle commotion carried on all around, but Josie took little notice today. His gaze was soon interrupted by the peripheral image of a single rider entering the clearing. Turning to look, he noted the spotted stallion.

Dressed as usual, Buck sat his mount to take in the small crowd and Josie was struck by the majesty of this ancient sight. Buck dismounted and, after tethering his horse to a dogwood, walked to the fire and took the seat directly beside Josies. The younger man held his breath. Some bayed Buck greeting, but Josie remained silent. He wanted to talk with this man. Wanted to say *something* but knew not of what to speak and was afraid he might say the wrong thing. A humbling experience.

Minutes passed.

"I've heard talk that your choice is not to live like the others," Josie looked startled as the old man addressed him. He had never done this before. "They say you've spurned the modern city from which you came and now refuse even to live in a house. Is this true?"

Josie stared blankly at the old Native he had thus only admired from afar. Seldom had he heard the man speak. Was Buck really talking to him now? Josie uttered two words, "It's true."

"Is it also true that you take little from your town, choosing instead to gain most of your needs from the earth and its animals?"

"Yes…to the best of my ability," Josie added. He felt small in the light of this man—this legend—and the things he undoubtedly knew. Humility overwhelmed Josie some more.

"What calls to your heart Josie?" Buck paused. Then, "What is your deepest desire?"

Josie's heart leapt. Buck knew his name! A question…it required an answer. Josie contemplated. Only honesty would do. "The land," he offered, "That it will provide…if only I could learn how," Josie turned both palms up in a gesture of resigned inadequacy.

The old man paused for a long moment. His impassive stare suggested contemplation. Again, he spoke, "Look at the people here. Most are my ancestors…my blood. Many still embrace the ancient religion, and this is good. Most however, decline the old ways of earth and wind in favor of modern conveniences like television, gas heaters, and air-conditioning. It is not for me to judge the actions of another, but although the lineage of all who walk the earth came at some point from the natural world, mine has only recently abandoned it and I marvel at what this has done to them," Buck waved one gnarled hand in a round motion to indicate the others.

It was true. Most were now as "*civilized*" as the white man. For this, their life span had shortened, and many were fat, sick, or both.

For a long moment Buck became silent and Josie humbly returned his eyes to the fire. Then the old man spoke again, "I would be honored if you'd care to make a visit to my home. We could smoke for a while."

Josie could hardly believe his ears. He looked quickly around to make sure the invitation had not been meant for someone else. "Are you serious?" Josie almost blurted.

Buck's full lips curled into a slight smile. He said nothing.

Although his insides screamed **yes!** Josie offered only a more restrained, "I'd like that very much."

"We will meet here again in one week," Buck held Josie's eyes captive in his own, "You should come prepared to stay for three days."

"I will."

As the day of his rendezvous with Dancing Deer drew nearer, Josie made preparation. Although the early spring weather was unseasonably warm, days were often cool, and nights could be downright chilly. To the metal-framed backpack, Josie tied his down sleeping bag. He added a change of clothes, socks, jacket, matches and flashlight. For food Josie brought two bags of home dried fruits, nuts, some of his jerked venison, and two bota-bags filled with water. Josie purchased tobacco to bring as gift for his host. As a sort of dressing, he took the tobacco from its plastic bag and placed it in a small leather drawstring pouch.

He was nervous.

3

Again, Josie helped cut wood for the lodge-fire—all the while keeping discreet watch for the spotted stallion. But it was not there. The young white man then sat as he had the week before while the fire again warmed his hands and knees. His loaded backpack rested against a nearby sycamore. There were friends here and Josie made the appropriate engagements, but his eyes seemed far away as the flames flickered in them.

Still no stallion.

Josie wondered if Dancing Deer had forgotten. But he had not, and when Buck finally did arrive it was from the trees that he *walked* rather than sat his mount. After shaking a few hands, he took a seat some distance away. To Josie he neither spoke nor acknowledged.

The sweats went as usual. Then the feast, to which Josie added some of his jerked meat. Afterward, a small crowd gathered upon the porch to tell tales, smoke cigarettes, and lounge as the food settled in their bellies. By ones and twos, they eventually wondered off until only Dancing Deer and Josie remained. Buck offered Josie a wide smile showing two relatively straight rows of large yellow teeth. "Ready?" he said.

Josie nodded, "Where's the horse?"

"I left him home. Today we walk,"

Josie got to his feet.

The tiny residential streets snaked past sporadic houses for only a while before Buck and Josie left the pavement in favor of a heavily wooded trail. Before long this faded to little more than a game trail and they walked below a canopy of tall trees. The forest floor became a bramble of brush, leaves and tree trunks that lay in varying degrees of decomposition. Flat ground was almost nonexistent, and their movement varied from up, down, and across, these steep mountain grades.

Josie was amazed at the old man's stamina and lightness of foot as he worked to keep up. Of course, Josie carried a 30-lb pack while his guide wore only a water bag (which appeared made from the stomach of some animal) that hung from a strap thrown over his shoulder. Still, Buck appeared to be almost 60, yet he moved with the agility of a cat. Josie's admiration grew a little more.

Eventually they crossed the Blue Ridge Parkway; a fine road built for hundreds of miles through the Smokey Mountains to accommodate the automobiles of tourists. As they started down the other side all signs of man were soon lost. The road behind could no longer be seen nor the occasional swoosh of a passing car heard.

Again, the paths they followed were little more than game trails and Josie wondered how Buck found his way. Although Dancing Deer moved fluidly, the pace was relaxed, and Josie genuinely enjoyed this forest and all its beauty.

On occasion, a break was called and Josie would set his pack against a tree then sit to lean against it. Buck sat too. The old Native paid his visitor small attention now, choosing instead to drink from his bag and gaze distractedly into the forest. Josie felt his nervousness then. Buck's relaxed contentedness in these intervals of stillness seemed a marvel and the young woodsman envied it.

Birdsong echoed through the trees.

Josie guessed they might have crossed onto the National Forest. Off limits to the building of houses and highways, it was a place set-aside for only animals, birds, plants, and other natural things. Although the law might have seen otherwise, Josie thought it the perfect place for his host to reside.

A dark canopy of overcast moved in to cover the sky, while below it pale clouds floated like ghosts across the treetops. A gentle rain began. Dancing Deer seemed unaffected as Josie watched his lithe form move fluidly ahead. They traveled upon a well-marked trail that led gradually down a secluded mountainside into the valley below. As they neared the bottom Josie heard the babble of water before he saw a large stream that passed to the right. Dancing Deer turned left to walk upstream along its shore.

The air was fresh, and rain fell harder.

Josie knew not how much time had passed for neither man owned a watch, but they had no doubt been on the trail for hours. Eventually the men crossed a fallen log to continue upon the opposite shore. In time a smaller creek came to intersect from the right and Buck turned to follow it.

The rain had lightened. Now it stopped.

Very soon they came to a left curve in the stream and Josie noted a small clearing at its right. As if guarding its territory, the spotted stallion stood near the water's edge, head down and munching on what remained of the closely cropped grass. The horse raised his head and trained both ears to the approaching men. For a moment, his curiosity seemed to mount at the sight of two rather than the usual one. But interest faded quickly, and he turned back to the grass. Josie noted that the horse was neither tethered nor fenced. It did not wear a bridle or even a rope. Buck's stallion stood naked.

As they drew nearer, the small clearing opened up and a fire-pit surrounded with smooth rocks came into view. A sooty stand of lashed together branches had been fashioned over it and Josie recognized this for the drying of meats and some cooking methods. Beside the fire-pit were two small wooden tripods that passed for chairs. On the side facing the pit, each of these had been upholstered with a row of smooth sticks also lashed together, while the ground before them had been padded with a mat made of woven reeds. One simply sat upon the mat then leaned against the tripod. Nearby stood an unruly pile of broken branches and log firewood, a small pile of rocks, and some cooking utensils. Beyond the fire-pit, where it was sheltered from wind by surrounding trees, stood an oval shaped structure that appeared to have been coated with mud then insulated with a thick layer of brush and other forest debris. Its door was an igloo shaped entryway covered with a deer-hide.

Both men crossed the stream at a place where large rocks allowed for dry feet and Dancing Deer stopped to greet his horse for a moment before moving farther into the clearing. Josie followed. Once arrived, Buck set his water bag down and settled into one of the chairs. Josie took the other. For a time both relaxed in the relative silence of only birdsong, bugs, and other forest sounds.

Josie tried to conceal his excitement. It all seemed so unreal. But here he was, in the very real world of a truly natural man. Josie could hardly believe his senses. He looked up to note that the horse was gone.

It would be dark soon.

Finally, Dancing Deer got up to retrieve kindling then returned to build a teepee of small twigs in the fire-pit. The old Indian then sat at the edge of his mat to face a small fireboard as his right fingers held a long thin mullein stalk loosely while both hands rested on the knees of his crossed legs. For a moment he closed his eyes and seemed to offer prayer. Next, Buck placed the end of his little spear into the fireboard's notch and, with long downward strokes, spun it between both palms. At the end of the seventh stroke a puff of smoke arose, and a small coal was produced.

Josie was riveted.

Dancing Deer flicked his coal into a bed of dry-moss tinder

then picked the little bundle up. He wrapped the tinder carefully around his coal then blew on it with a thin stream of air. He seemed to be talking to it. He coaxed and encouraged with little gestures and expressions. It seemed the kind of affection one might lavish upon a living thing. The coal grew under his care. With each breath it expanded and brightened until it was eventually consumed by smoke. Finally, the tinder burst into flames and Buck placed it under the kindling in his fire-pit. Within minutes a good fire crackled there.

Amazement filled Josie's eyes.

Once the fire had matured, Dancing Deer set a few stones into the coals then covered them with more wood. With this task completed, the old Native resettled into his seat. Again, he regarded the forest.

Twilight was fading.

For 20-minutes Buck said nothing while Josie wondered of the necessity for heated rocks, and even more so at what ancient secrets waited inside the rounded home only a few feet away.

Eventually Dancing Deer arose and turned to enter the house. When Buck returned, it was a long handmade pipe that he held in one hand. Josie reached for his pack and retrieved his gift. Holding out the tobacco, Josie appreciated the foresight of a leather pouch for it seemed far more appropriate now. "I brought this for you," he said.

The old man regarded him for a moment, then he smiled, and Josie noted a kindness in those old eyes that he'd not seen there before. Dancing Deer reached for the pouch, opened it, then held it to his nose. Approval was evident in his gesture and, without a word, he took some of the tobacco into his fingertips, held it before him, and again uttered silent prayer. High above, the evening's first stars could be seen while firelight flickered across Dancing Deer's leathery face.

Once the pipe had been filled, Buck pulled a light from the fire and began puffing. In a minute, he handed it to Josie. They smoked for a while.

Time had again passed when Dancing Deer pointed to a clay pot and asked Josie to fill it half-full of water from the stream. Josie complied and, upon his return, Buck plucked a glowing rock from the fire and held it between two sticks. Regarding it for a moment, Buck seemed to offer the same reverence he had earlier professed for the little coal that had given him fire. Again, his lips moved. Then, using a ladle made from animal skull, Dancing Deer dipped water from the clay container to wash the soot from his rock with a loud hiss. When this was done, he placed it into the pot and repeated this process twice more before sitting back to wait for a while. Above him, the moon was waning tonight and offered only weak illumination that allowed starlight to dominate the sky.

The water began to boil.

Dancing Deer again arose and walked into the darkness. In a moment he returned carrying a woven basket filled with roots, wild vegetables, dried meat, and what appeared to be small stalks of leafy plants—probably seasoning. Using a knife that appeared made of glassy black stone with handle wrapped in rawhide, Dancing Deer began cutting his bounty into bite sized sections and dropping them into the pot. Upon seeing this, Josie reached for his pack to offer some of his jerky.

Buck added that too.

When finished, Buck resettled himself beside the fire and again grew silent for a moment. Then, "It's going to be a late meal," he apologized, "But the trip was slower without the horse. Hope you don't mind."

Are you kidding, Josie thought, *I wouldn't have missed this for the world!* "Not at all," was all he said.

When minutes had passed, Buck asked of his new friend without looking at him, "Tell me the story of how you came to the mountains my young friend. Until now I've heard only gossip."

Josie was slow to honor the old Indian's request, but once started, the tale seemed to run away with him. Every pertinent detail from city-boy to woodsman was then illuminated in story. Without so much as a glance in his direction, Dancing Deer listened and even thought Josie a pretty good storyteller. It took a long while and at times Buck moved to stir, taste, and add more rocks to the stew. Still, he listened…and missed nothing.

It was with an exhausted feeling of emotional nakedness and even embarrassment that Josie finished his tale. He hardly knew this man—and Buck's ways were so very different. What would he think? As reward for Josie's effort, Dancing Deer offered only a subtle grunt.

Josie was perplexed.

The food was good and both men ate their fill.

Josie knelt beside his host at the water's edge and washed his clay bowl and spoon made of bone. When they had returned to the clearing, Dancing Deer pulled a burning branch from the fire and invited the visitor into his home.

It was necessary that Josie duck to accommodate the doorway. Once inside he paused in the heavy darkness as Buck moved forward to place his flame into a fire-pit at room center, which had earlier been fortified with wood. The flame licked slowly up as Josie squinted into the din. The home seemed roomy for its size.

He heard Dancing Deer's voice, "Come in my young friend. Have a seat." Josie saw his host seated upon the ground with back leaned against his bed as he motioned to yet another tripod seat beside the fire. Josie entered then sat. It was quieter here, for thick walls now muffled the incessant chorus of tree frogs and only the crackle of fire dominated. The flames grew. Josie's eyes adjusted. He looked again:

Around the hearth were a few cooking utensils and earthen pots made of clay. There was also a stool, workbench, and Buck's bedframe which was suspended by sturdy sapling legs in front then attached to the rounded wall behind. Even sized sticks had been lashed on top to provide a platform covered with hides and topped with what appeared to be the skin of a black bear.

One old Indian sat comfortably against its front.

At the wall, across from Dancing Deer, stood another platform—possibly used for sitting—that offered only one thin, hairless, hide. Beneath both platforms were stored a variety of baskets and other goods. Beside the doorway sat two lidded clay vases and Josie rightly assumed these for water storage. Also near the entry was a neat pile of firewood. As the fire's light brightened, Josie could see that the home's structural frame was like that of the sweat lodges; but its floor and walls had been so thoroughly covered with mats made of reed and cattail that a close look was required to note this. Herbs, roots, and tools hung from rawhide cords or beams and a bow with quiver of arrows was lashed above Dancing Deer's bed.

The place smelled of smoke and sage.

Again, Dancing Deer filled his pipe, and again he made praise of the tobacco, and this time to the man who had given it to him as well. Talk was light…when there was any, and the night grew late. Eventually Buck declared his bedtime and offered Josie the adjacent platform, or anywhere else he wished to sleep.

The old Indian banked the fire as Josie unrolled his sleeping bag over the platform. Both men climbed into bed. Excitement kept sleep at bay for a long time as Josie watched the fire's amber shadows dance across the walls and ceiling. But when sleep finally did come, its quality was the best.

4

Morning brought the crackle of fire to Josie's ears and his eyes opened to find Dancing Deer already up and adding heated rocks to a small caldron of water. Josie arose to a seated position before making his "Good morning," through sleepy eyes.

The tea was brewed from a mixture of pine needles, oak buds, and sassafras root. When it was ready both men sat as they had the night before to enjoy its pungent flavor from cups made of thick bamboo stalks. Josie offered his home-dried fruits and Dancing Deer seemed quite pleased; though Josie would later learn that Buck seldom ate breakfast. Both cups were eventually refilled, and the men went to sit outside. Although still slightly brisk, warm sunshine filtered through the trees as both sipped their tea in silence while birdsong told story of the awakening forest. Branches rustled above as a lone squirrel foraged. The presence of honeybees, ants, and other insects told that spring had indeed sprung. The horse was back. Josie could see him standing beyond the stream's far bank.

In a moment Dancing Deer said, "Raccoons came last night—three hours before sunup, I think. Two adults and one adolescent. There were once two more, but both were taken by a crafty weasel while still very young. The mother has a lame hind foot…on her right side. They came from downstream and paused to note the hide, then dismissed it as a useless mystery before moving on. Once away from the water, both adults paused to sniff the strange scents here; but they were not really strange because all live nearby and have visited before. Their noses brought the odors of man, smoke, and *food*. So, they focused keen night vision ahead and trained ears as well. When there was no one to be seen or heard, both adults assumed us sleeping and came forward. But the youngest had been momentarily distracted, by nothing in particular really, and, failing to make his own assessment, only came when he noted the others had gone. But his elders had split up by then: she to scout near the fire-pit, while the male came to the cooking pot. He stretched on hind legs to gaze into the pot...but found nothing. The female however, had circled your seat to find a bit of jerky that had been dropped last night when you reached for a sample to show me."

Josie remembered that. He had simply disregarded the tidbit as dirty and lost to the darkness. *But Buck's attention was busy then*, Josie thought, *He could not have seen me drop it. How does he know?*

"When the others learned of her score there was a scuffle," Buck continued, "But she would not share. She retreated to the trees while her kin—quite aware of her temper I think—did not follow. They looked some more, found nothing, and finally departed through those trees," Dancing Deer pointed. He settled both hands back into his lap then.

"But the ants had better luck because they did not need our food. For, of the many moths that committed suicide into the flames last night, one managed the fall of his charred body to the dirt beyond the coals," Buck pointed at a spot beside the pit. "Big score. The ants simply dragged their roast moth off that way," his finger traced a path. "Probably wished we'd a seasoned him up a bit huh?" he offered that big, yellow toothed grin again. When the smile faded, he looked toward the water and said, "There were others too," then fell silent.

Josie was speechless. Was it really possible to know all of this so early in the morning? Or at all for that matter. "How do you know these things?" he asked.

The old Indian's gaze never strayed from the distant forest, "The earth told me." His tone stated clearly that Josie should ask no more.

Silence fell between them, as Josie's mind struggled with the answer given him. Then it hit him: *The earth…the tracks. Of course!* He had learned something of tracking on previous hunting forays. Josie set his skill to work. He looked for the spot upon which the jerky had fallen…but could not find it. Josie's eyes then scoured the area for tracks, but the dirt was packed here and its marks were few. Only a handful of scuffs could be seen. Or were they from his own feet? Josie looked to the moth's resting-place…and still saw nothing. He kneeled beside it. Still nothing. Closer he focused, then finally stood to follow the trail Buck had indicated until his eyes passed across a sandy spot. Tiny drag-marks. That was all. Fascinated, Josie arose to retrace the steps of raccoons. Again, there were only scuff marks and it was not until he had reached the water's edge and started slightly downstream that Josie found a few complete prints near the muddy shore. They were fresh. But how was it possible to know all the things Dancing Deer had told of? Josie did not believe the old man a liar. Later he would know this. Obviously, Buck had ways unlike any he had seen before. Josie longed to learn them.

From his squatting position beside the mud, Josie heard a voice from behind, "Look into the water my friend." Josie turned his head. "Do you see the deerskin?"

Yes. Right beside him, just below the surface and tied to rocks by rawhide cord with the hide's hair-tips facing upstream so the water's flow might help to loosen them. How could he not have noticed it before? The tracks, he had been too busy studying them. Josie's cheeks flushed with embarrassment. "Yes," he said, "I see it."

"Would you bring it to camp for me?"

"Sure," Josie said, as he stood then turned to find the voice's owner gone.

As Josie carried the wet hide into the clearing, he saw that the old man now stood with hands stroking the stallion's neck as he talked gently to the big animal. The horse returned his gesture with obvious affection. Buck turned to regard Josie with a big smile, then led him to a four-sided rack made from lashed together branches which lay upon the ground. Buck motioned that Josie should place the skin at its center. When this was done, both men knelt. Using his knife, Dancing Deer began punching holes near the hide's perimeter. Josie watched closely. Once five punctures had been made, the old man handed this work to the younger and prompted him to continue. Asking no questions, Josie simply did as he was told.

The skin was from a buck Dancing Deer had taken while on a winter hunt. Although butchering was attended to at once, the hide had been stored for tanning at some later date when better weather granted greater ease of workmanship. That time had come. Looking closely over the skin, Dancing Deer pointed to a single arrow hole just back of one shoulder.

Josie squinted.

"This area is weak," came the gruff tone that could only be Indian, "It must be stitched or will surly rip as the process is continued." Buck poked more holes then laced the weak place together with fine thread made of sinew. Once completed, Dancing Deer began to string the hide's edges to the rack with rawhide straps. When this was done he tightened the straps until the skin was suspended just off the ground. Both men then lifted the rack and leaned it against two nearby trees. For a moment Buck stood to contemplate his work. Then, as Josie watched, the ole man reached forward to stroke the fir as his lips began to move. But it was the language of the ancients that emanated in such low tone and Josie understood not a word. In a moment Dancing Deer switched abruptly to English,

"My brother, I regret that I should have to take your life, but without this gift I could not survive. You and your kind are lucky to have been born with such beautiful pelts to wear upon your backs for all your days. We people have not been so blessed and without your gift could not survive for long. Do not think that I don't appreciate it. And even though you leave this world, a part of you will live on here as I work your coat into a thing of lasting beauty then wrap myself with it to take refuge from the winter cold. And I will not forget you. Thank you, my friend."

The old Native reached for the coat then and began pulling hair from the hide with his hands. Josie watched closely. The skin seemed resistant to this idea, and the work looked tedious. After a few minutes Dancing Deer turned to his visitor and asked if he cared to take over.

Josie would have stood on his head should this man have asked.

Before allowing him to begin, Dancing Deer stressed the necessity of prayer and appreciation for the deer's presence in one's life. "The deer's sacrifice of flesh for the survival of his two-legged brother is the greatest of gifts that can be given. Would we do as much for him? There is little appreciation adequate to honor such a thing, but we must always try…and never forget. If the deer's gift is unappreciated and used poorly then his spirit will tell those of the others and no longer will they approach the bow. The connection with all things will be broken and future hunts will go bad." It was the first of a rare practice wherein the old man explained a thing so fully.

    He looked expectantly at Josie then, and the younger man knew of the importance of the things Dancing Deer had spoken—at least to the Indian. And although these beliefs were new to him, Josie wished to learn. Besides, for his time spent with this land and the slight, by comparison, connection he had made with it, these new ideas just felt right. So, he would try.

    Josie nodded, then turned to place his hands upon the fir. He stroked it and quietly made a prayer of his own. At first, he felt stupid. But then he did not. So was the young, X-city-boy's first attempt at a spiritual connection with the naked hide of a buck.

    Seemingly satisfied, Buck returned to his seat and took up the weaving of a basket. Just as birds returned to build new nests or refortify old while neighboring plants put forth new shoots and leaves to replace those lost to the frigid winter, so then was Spring a time of renewal for the Indian as well. To this end certain effort was put to the repair or replacement of many a garment, furnishing, leaking roof, weapon, cooking utensil, or other tool.

    At first Josie found this ancient tanning process fascinating. After a while, this labor brought his body to sweaty dampness. It would be hot today. Clouds were scant and there was no rain in sight. Josie took off his shirt.

    For hours the young man labored in the sun while his host sat in the shade and doddled with far less strenuous tasks attended to between many breaks. Occasionally, Josie made it apparent of his wish to join in these pauses; but Buck's stern looks kept him at the tanning rack. The Indian would not even speak to him now. Resentment spawned.

    Josie kept working.

Eventually Dancing Deer came to offer water and a wooden pincer tool that served as large tweezers. With these Buck pulled a few hairs from the back and neck areas where the fir was especially thick and tenacious. He handed the tool to Josie and, without a word, regained his mat for a little nap. Josie's resentment mounted.

And still he worked.

By midday the job was done, and Dancing Deer was again making stew. Taking an adjacent seat, Josie announced that the hide was now hairless. Josie thought he hid his antipathy well, but also suspected the old man knew of it. Buck only nodded then pointed to the stew-pot indicating that Josie should help himself. Returning this silent treatment, the irritated city-boy addressed the food. Once finished, Josie walked downstream and threw himself into the water; since he did not wish to sleep in that rancid sweat and hide smell now emanating from his body.

The afternoon passed uneventfully, as did evening. Again, Dancing Deer said little.

5

By morning, Josie awoke to find his host dressed in well-worn buckskins and he noted the garments with much interest. The supple texture, tight stitching, and beautiful fringe that hung from back and arms was most intriguing. Having never seen Buck dressed in such fashion before, Josie decided that cloth was probably simply a better choice if one wished to blend in while moving among the modern public in town. But Buck's appearance today, Josie thought, held something of an ancient magnificence.

By late morning Josie was again set to the tanning rack. The hide had shrunk to pull tightly at the straps that suspended it. As it had dried, the surface formed a dull, glassy, sheen of hard cuticle coating. After running through the process of prayer again, Dancing Deer pointed out the hide's occasional scar or weak spot. With a scraping tool made of cannon-bone lashed tightly to a wooden handle, Dancing Deer made long downward bulldozing strokes that stripped off bits of the cuticle. He warned about the danger of pushing through the weaker areas, but also stated that enough pressure must be met to accomplish the task. Buck then handed the scrapper to Josie and, as the day before, strolled off to regain the shade of his sitting mat.

It would be hot again.

While some hides are cooperative and allow themselves worked into a thing of usefulness rather quickly and easily, others take the opposite demeanor and fight this process all the way. Unbeknownst to Josie, this skin would assume the latter attitude.

Josie soon found scrapping to be much more labor-intensive than the de-hairing of yesterday. As before, Dancing Deer offered no breaks and only brought water on occasion while pausing to scrutinize the work and offer suggestion. Josie endured this criticism quietly…

…and still he worked.

His arms began to ache

…and still he worked.

The sun burned his winter white skin

…and still he worked.

Resentment grew

…and *still* Josie worked. But so did his mind. It started to say things: *Is this what I've been invited for...to work like a slave? Dancing Deer's getting old. Maybe he's just tired and looking for help in his daily struggle against Nature. That's probably it. The old bastard.* Josie began to have second thoughts about the wisdom of this man.

Yet still…he worked.

As the shiny, rather nasty, coating began to come clean and Josie scraped his way to the softer, suede-like fibers below, his spirits lifted a little. Through his effort, the formerly grizzly looking, and smelly, animal hide was becoming a thing of suppleness and beauty. Josie found himself intrigued by the skin, but increasingly angry with the old man.

Again, Dancing Deer doddled. Then, after outfitting himself appropriately, left camp for a few hours and returned with four trout. Fishing. Josie had missed it. Had not even been invited.

Dancing Deer inspected Josie's progress. Josie had hoped the old Indian would be pleased, but Buck's expression registered nothing. Instead, he took up a smooth rock and worked it in circles over a small section of the skin. In short order this spot became almost as smooth as velvet. Although exhaustion was evident in Josie's eyes, his interest was revived for this new procedure and result. Josie brightened. The old man regained his seat while the younger set to the new task. Although for a time Josie's interest was in fact rekindled, its color faded quickly and resentment returned.

Again, the old man's glare kept Josie at the rack. And again, Buck maintained silence.

He's gone crazy out here all alone, Josie thought.

And still he worked.

That night firelight flickered in Josie's weary eyes as the cup of tea dangled loosely from one hand laid across his bent knee. His thoughts were quiet and deep. Resentment, even anger, festered there. Josie fought to hold his feelings at bay. This task was made easier by the absence of much talk. The mood struck him as rather grave this night and Josie wondered where the magic of his arrival had gone…if it had, in fact, been a thing of reality at all. But at least he had eaten well. Buck had seen to that.

6

The following morning Dancing Deer de-racked the skin, then cut a small section from the thickest shoulder area and set it aside. Next, Josie was set to work upon the braining process. Aside from a slight repulsiveness to the feel of raw brains (acquired from other, smaller, animals) squishing through his fingers, at least the labor was less intensive today. But the process created almost magical changes to the hide and Josie's feelings were often torn between his former resentment, and a growing wonder for the work.

The hide was set to soak for a while.

The next morning Josie staked and worked the skin as he was

shown. More hard labor. But the sunshine was again good and with its help the drying process was shortened to only three hours. Next came buffing. Then, ultimately, the smoking and rebuffing of his hide. This work lasted into the following day.

When finished it was a thing of rare beauty. Soft, supple, and brought to a shade of fine dark brown by the hickory smoke. Josie stroked it longingly. Sure, he had seen plenty of leather goods in his day. Hadn't everyone? But this was different. Brought to such fine finish by the labor of his own hand, it seemed infinitely more beautiful. He thought of the animal that had died to offer such prize. Josie felt something then.

Dancing Deer took the hide and inspected it with blank expression. Josie thought he saw approval there, but the old man said nothing and simply set the skin down. Next, he informed the visitor it was time for him to leave. He had, after all, stayed a day beyond his invitation.

Why you slimy, ungrateful bastard, Josie wanted to say, *A day extra to do your fucking slave labor. Screw you!* But what he did instead was move silently to gather his things from within the earth-shelter. "I'm never coming back here," Josie mumbled almost silently as he stuffed the down-bag violently into its sack. But when he turned to look around Josie was again overtaken with the rounded walls of woven mats, herbs, and earthen smells of dirt, wood-smoke, and sage. Emotion overwhelmed him then and Josie almost cried. On a whim of unknown reason, Josie took what was left of his own food and set it on the bed. He had no appetite for it anyway. When finished, he grabbed the backpack, turned, and stormed through the door.

Once outside, Josie stopped to note the squat backside of Dancing Deer who stood at the clearing's center as he stroked the horse affectionately. His left hand held the rains of a rawhide hackamore now fashioned to the animal's large head.

Josie approached from behind then swung around to face the old Indian with his best stance of defiance. There was so much he wanted to say. So much emotion. Most of it bad—some of it good, but all of it jumbled. There was little sense there so Josie only stood in his silent defiance. This was the best he could do. Buck regarded him through seemingly cold eyes.

"How will I find the way?"

"Can you ride?" Dancing Deer answered with a question.
"I can."
"Take the horse then. He knows the way. When you reach the road let him loose. He knows the way back as well. From there you're on your own." Buck held one hand toward the backpack and Josie gave it to him. In return he was handed the rains. Josie mounted the stallion, and Dancing Deer handed up the pack, which Josie then settled upon his back. He looked down at the old Indian, but said nothing. Setting his eyes ahead, Josie kicked the horse gently and it started forward, but Dancing Deer grabbed the muzzle strap to stop him. Josie glanced down to see the old prick staring up. "If you wish to return be at the lodges next Saturday," and with that he let the horse go. Josie offered an almost imperceptible nod then spurred the horse on.

The trip, he guessed, took three hours or more and for most of it Josie's mind oscillated between reverence and despair. It had been a most disturbing experience after all.

Time helped to assemble his thoughts and within a few days Josie had resigned to not take another date with the disturbed old Indian. It had been too painful. Yet, when Dancing Deer stepped into the clearing the following Saturday, he found the young Josie McWaters sitting with the others. But it was the backpack leaned once more against a nearby tree that gave him a thin smile.

For three visits more Josie was put to hard labor amid the home of his mentor Dancing Deer. Sometimes it was hauling firewood from long distances. Other times, he was sent with gathering basket to collect cooking-rocks. Whatever the job, it was *always* hard labor. Josie's sweat poured as Dancing Deer lounged in the shade and attended to the much lighter and more interesting chores of basket weaving, attending to arrow shafts, repairing his many tools and, all to often, simply lounging. Talk was kept minimal, and the Indian's vibe emanated a distant coolness or even contempt toward his visitor. No longer was Josie offered the stallion to make his way home. Now he was set by morning to walk upon work-weary legs that strained to carry the steel-framed backpack.

Always Josie vowed never to return. And, *always* Dancing Deer arrived at the sweat lodges to again find his young visitor seated upon the log, his pack resting nearby.

Always, Josie brought tobacco to his host. And *never* did he complain.

7

It was the fifth sweat Josie had attended since his first stay with Dancing Deer. Today the old Indian did not walk, but instead rode the spotted stallion into the clearing. For his first few returns to this place Buck had been sure he would not again see the face of his young visitor. Now he was not so sure. But today, more than any other, it was the sight of the young Josie McWaters once again sitting with the others, his backpack leaning against a nearby tree, that brought not a thin smile to Buck's full lips, but a broad grin instead.

For the entire ceremony both men again ignored each other until, as before, they were the last still sitting upon the porch. Buck had plucked a long grass-stem from the ground and now placed it between his teeth while Josie stared off to no place in-particular. For ten minutes the two men sat in silence. A gentle breeze ruffled the leaves. A squirrel sat high in a pine while pulling apart its cones and dropping their petals to the ground. As usual, birdsong seemed incessant.

Finally, Dancing Deer began to speak:

"There are many here who would gladly come to waste my time for a while before returning to the air conditioning. I do not wish my time wasted. But I am old and have no children for which to pass on my empire," Buck paused to chuckle at that. "I have found all the satisfactions of my life in these old ways. Mostly they are a thing of the past now…lost to the world of modern men. One day though, I believe they will be of importance again. Anyway, as my final days near, I find it increasingly necessary to pass my legacy on," this time he did not laugh. "Yet still, I do not wish my time wasted, nor my knowledge taken as only interest for someone's amusement."

Was Dancing Deer thinking of him? Josie dared not dream it; dared not bring hope so high lest this be only a misinterpretation on his part. For if the latter were true, he would be crushed. Yet if not, was he then worthy? Sometimes the mind can be a terrible thing and Josie's tortured him now. He waited for more words, but all Buck said was, "Shall we go?"

Dancing Deer walked ahead with reins held loosely in one hand, as the spotted stallion plodded behind, and Josie behind him. No words were spoken. Eventually they crossed the highway and at its far side Buck removed the crude hackamore, placed it over his shoulder, and set the horse free. It lumbered ahead, sometimes pausing to pull green shoots from the rich ground before moving on again. But for the entirety of this trip, seldom would the stallion be beyond sight for long.

The air seemed easier today…friendlier. Josie could feel it. Something had changed.

Again, they traveled steadily down the mountain and again Josie noted the sound of moving water as they neared the small river. Dancing Deer stopped abruptly to squat and inspect the ground. Josie knelt beside to better note the source of Buck's interest. He saw prints and scratches upon this rare spot of bare dirt but could not properly make them out. Dancing Deer said, "He was an average sized bobcat. Male. Medium size. I've noted his progress along this trail for some time now. He came from the smaller stream of this canyon," Buck pointed down and to their right. "His hunt had gone poorly this night for his track speaks of hunger. It was early dawn and, resigned to his fate for he carried his head low, the cat was returning to his den for the day's sleep. But the sound of fluttering wings caught his ears and the great cat crouched low," Buck's gnarled finger pointed to a spot upon the ground. "Do you see?" Josie looked closer. Yes, there was a smooth place where the body's bulk had settled into the dirt. Buck's finger traced the outer edges to expound upon areas where fur had brushed ever so lightly to leave small marks. The nail imprints left in the dirt by one fore-paw and made more pronounced for the flexing of claws, and the elbow placed slightly aft, were also made point of. The other paws had landed in fallen needles to leave only scant trace and Josie could hardly see them at all.

"It was a lead quail that had flown from the brush to sit upon the trunk of that fallen birch," Buck pointed again. "The cat knew it to be only the lead bird and if he waited more would soon follow; for the wind was with him and moved his scent behind and away. So, they crossed before him—and there were many. Knowing well of their keen eyes and quick bursts of speed, the cat also knew his chances for a successful kill were scant. Scant, but still possible if skill held and luck was with him. He also knew the quail to be small and only a half meal at best. So, he contemplated these things. Finally, he decided that a half meal was better than nothing, and a slim chance was still a chance. So, he moved forward a few steps then left the trail in pursuit." Again, Buck pointed and Josie noted the small ridges pushed up at the paw-print's right side as the animal had swung its weight off-trail to the left. Some steps farther Dancing Deer made note of the markings left by many quail as they had crossed the path.

Josie looked perplexed.

"I hope he got his dinner," Buck continued, "But I doubt it. We could follow and find out, but why dishonor him by sharing in his failure. I think we will just continue on."

Josie could not believe what he was hearing. He opened his mouth to speak; then closed it again. Finally, he said, "You learned all this from just walking down the trail?"

To which Buck replied, "You did not?"

After a long pause Josie looked to the ground and said, "No."

"Did you not then also see the Horned Owl who sleeps high in the pine? Or the tree squirrel who barely paused from his lunch of delicate mushrooms to note us, while three groundhogs—far more curious of the horse than us—watched with interest and amusement from their home below the spicebush as we passed?

"No," Josie's tone was humble, "I didn't."

Dancing Deer looked briefly into his companion's face and offered a warm smile that reached all the way up to his eyes, "One day you will." Buck turned his gaze ahead then started forward, "I believe you will."

Although momentarily stricken with a small, self imposed embarrassment, Josie felt no belittlement here. And so, he followed.

It was along the river's left shore that Dancing Deer stopped near a line of heavy thicket and turned to face his guest. "We will wait for a moment," his tone was low as one hand reached innocently for a stone resting near his feet.

The rabbit's eyes, as do most animals, see differently than those of humans. They are adept at noting things in motion, but often cannot discern the differences in shapes that do not move. Therefore, if a predator sits perfectly still, he will often be missed to the sight of his prey who must then rely solely on scent to warn him. The rabbit believes this to be true of humans as well, and will often sit unmoving even though partly hidden by brush, he may still be in plain sight. So, it was today.

Dancing Deer knew of these things and he did not seek to be still but remained casual in his movement. Then, in one fluid motion, he turned and flung the rock hard into the bush. The rabbit let out a single squeak and fell to its side. Dancing Deer quickly pulled his prize from the brush then cut its throat while the heart still pumped its last beats to free the meat of blood. Removing one of the leather straps seemingly always tied around his waist, Buck bound the hind feet then hung his catch from a low branch as blood dripped from its muzzle. Josie watched with fascination as the old Indian offered yet another prayer in the ancient language. Switching to English then, he again offered thanks to the Great Spirit for the gift that would help sustain his life. Dancing Deer promised to use it well.

Once cleaned in the river water, Buck tied the rabbit to his waist and both men continued on.

At a place where the waters grew wide and slow, Buck stopped to cut a good stalk of cattail. The season was early and these new shoots would still be tender and succulent. When enough had been gathered, he offered a prayer of thanks to those taken and those that remained.

That night the men lounged again on reed mats and tripod backrests beside a fire that slowly spit-roasted rabbit stuffed with garlic, dried-crushed spicebush berries, and toothwort root, while cattail shoots boiled in a cauldron of rock heated water. As before, talk was infrequent, but the vibe of Josie's Indian host had changed this night. Gone was the heavy air of inflexible disdain or even seeming contempt of past visits. Buck offered smiles, laughter, encouragement, and a certain tolerance of Josie's ignorance for the land of his origin and the harmony of her ancient ways. Josie sat with a friend now—and he knew it.

When the food had been eaten, both men relaxed to smoke for a while. Josie's belly was full, and the pipe mellowed him. When this was done a time of quiet settled in. For Josie it was almost as meditation. He listened to the fire crackle and watched its sparks of glowing wood-ember rise steadily skyward before they fizzled to ash then fell to reacquaint with the soil. Soon they would live again in the trunk of yet another tree. But to the eye these rising sparks seemed only to seek union with the black canopy of stars that hung so close Josie felt he could reach up and pluck one from the heavens. Connection. It enveloped him. Yet if the sky seemed quiet, the forest seldom was. Tree-frogs croaked loudly while crickets joined, and a locust trilled somewhere nearby. In the distance a coyote yipped. A chorus of others erupted, and their screams filled the night. But the song ended as abruptly as it had begun.

Contentment. It was such a valuable thing.

Josie slept well that night.

8

It was barely dawn when he awoke. Without movement Josie opened his eyes to note that the fire had been stoked and Dancing Deer was gone. Slowly he arose then moved to pour a rather pungent coffee substitute made of chicory from the clay pot at fire's edge. He added a sweet kind of sugar made from the stalks of reeds. That was better. In a moment he went to the doorway and, much taken with the sight beyond, Josie squatted in the igloo shaped passage to watch…

It was the eerie time of dawn's first light when the last stars twinkle weakly above, and blackness gives way to the first shades of pale gray. As is so common in these mountains, mist lay heavy upon the early morning earth. Small clouds kissed the outlying treetops as they moved slowly across the mountainsides. Dew dripped from leaves and all the world seemed wet at this early hour. There, by the water's edge, Dancing Deer stood naked, his back to the lodge and arms hung loosely at his sides. For a long time, he stood motionless. Finally, Buck knelt to reach forward and run one hand lightly across the water's surface. He pushed both in then and seemed to be feeling gently of the cool texture. In a moment he stood and inserted one foot…then the other. Folding legs beneath, Dancing Deer sat between smooth rocks and into the first few inches of calm water that resided near the bank. Again, he remained motionless for a time. Very near him, three raccoons—two adult and one adolescent—sat drinking and preening themselves in the clear water. Buck paid them little mind. He reached with one hand and drew a small portion of the liquid into his palm, lifted it to his face, and seemed to take in the scent of its fresh aroma. In a moment he tilted palm to mouth and placed the small portion on his tongue. Like an aristocrat sampling fine wine, the old Indian savored the liquid for some time before finally swallowing with a look of contented approval. When this was done, Buck drank his fill.

Native people believe water to be the earth's blood; for does it not pass through cavernous veins only to emerge as streams that flow to the sea before eventually returning as rain clouds to begin its journey again? And wherever it goes, life flourishes—yet wherever it is not, things die. And the very same liquid that flows through one's own body will ultimately pass through the squirrel, boar, deer, ant, lizard, bear, human, and every other living thing on the earth. Water must truly be the blood that binds us all.

Dancing Deer slid further into the water and immersed himself. When he surfaced again it was to the far side that Buck faced. "Josie," he said without turning, "would you come here please?"

The raccoons did not stir.

How did Dancing Deer know he was there? Josie gave the question little thought though, for by now he was becoming almost used to such oddities. He started forward.

The raccoons scattered.

When Josie arrived at the bank, Dancing Deer offered him a morning's greeting served with a rather serene smile. Josie returned the "Good morning," before the old man asked a thing of him, "Would you come have a bath this morning my young friend?"

Then, "Have you any clean clothes with you today?"

Josie did.

"Good. It would be wise to smell as little like men as is possible. Our endeavors will undoubtedly fare better this day if we do not stink."

For a Native of the woods, Dancing Deer sure has an impeccable vocabulary, Josie thought, *Intelligence is certainly something not lacking in him.* Then it hit him: *Necessary to remove our scent? To what purpose?* The question gave birth to excitement. Josie removed his clothes and entered the pool.

When the bath was finished both men readied themselves for the half day's journey that Dancing Deer had promised, but mentioned few details. As directed, Josie rinsed his body with a solution of boiled birch-bark that, he was told, would help to nullify the sent of man. Buck dressed himself in buckskin leggings, breechcloth, and moccasins laced with woven strands of horsetail strung through eyelets cut from the quill ends of bird feathers. From the waist up he wore only beads and two feathers tied into long black hair further decorated with streaks of gray. Around Buck's neck a leather thong held a single bear claw as pendent. Pushing his head and right shoulder through a thick rawhide-strap, Dancing Deer hung a deep forage basket, which had been woven from oak splits, across his back. To his waist the Indian tied a small pouch filled with ash from the fire. In his hand was carried a long, river-cane blowgun with darts whittled from buckeye wood and tufted with thistledown. Josie wore cut-off jean-shorts, dark brown T-shirt, light hiking boots and, as instructed, his empty backpack.

So equipped, the two men set out.

For a while they walked beside the creek but eventually turned away and up the crest of a small mountain. Here, where the sun's rays were more prominent, they came upon a large grove of blackberries. Setting his burdens down without a word, Dancing Deer moved to the thorny bushes then paused for a moment of what Josie knew was silent prayer. When finished he eyed the thick bushes and their swollen fruit with delight, then reached forward and began to dine. Josie followed, and it was for a long time the men gorged.

Once satisfied with this breakfast both regained their possessions and moved on. Talk was scant.

The squirrel's presence in a tall pine was given away by the sounds of a cracking pinecone as its petals were pulled apart by strong arms so he might dine upon the small seeds beneath. Dancing Deer loaded his blowgun, raised it to rest both elbows firmly upon his chest, arched himself backwards, and placed the tube's larger end over his mouth. A quick burst of air brought the squirrel tumbling to the ground.

Josie was astonished at such a shot.

Dancing Deer readied the body, offered the appropriate prayers, then attached it to his waist. Without a word the men moved on.

Although Josie knew it not, the men were moving in a roundabout way towards the last in a series of animal traps set two days earlier. The traps had been positioned some distance apart for Dancing Deer knew of the fear and confusion that would spread rapidly among the local animals when one had been tripped. For a time, they would be on the alert. The Indian knew these habits well and, since most sought the best vegetation available, they tended to forage in areas where these grew in abundance and so Buck's traps had been set accordingly. But animals and humans are not so different in their food choices and therefore it was only natural that today's wanderings would take the men through areas of the best vegetation this forest had to offer.

In a while Buck made a small detour then paused before a smallish grove of light tan and rather rubbery looking mushrooms. The sight stirred Josie's appetite but little. Looking to the short, fungal offering, Dancing Deer said, "Ah. You return this year." Turning to address Josie he added, "We are in luck today my friend, for these…morels…I think the white man calls them, are some of the finest and most elusive of delicacies. Such a treat!" The usual prayers were offered before a fare portion was harvested with special care taken to hopefully assure the welfare of those that remained and the survival of their species. The take was wrapped in large green leaves and placed gently into Buck's basket.

The journey continued.

As it is for animals and man in the wild as well, spring is also a time of renewal for plants and these mountains offered some of the most diverse vegetation species of any place in the world. Second only, it was said, to the Amazon jungle. Dancing Deer seemed infinitely attuned to this fact and his watchful eye and seeming sixth sense missed little, if any, of the varieties useful to man. To this end many things were added to the basket and backpack as they walked. Fresh garlic was pulled from the ground. Sassafras was taken—the leaves of which would be dried and later used to thicken and season soup. There was Spring Beauty—whose root-bulbs could be prepared like potatoes. Wild Onion, and others for which Dancing Deer could neither recall, or perhaps had never known the white man's names, were also taken. They nibbled often, and Josie experienced a variety of new tastes. Although perhaps lacking much real flavor, miner's lettuce was one of his favorites and Josie dined heartily at a large grove of them.

Whishing neither to forewarn the presence of man through sight nor scent, Buck approached his traps from the least used direction of heavy thicket, rather than walk the more heavily used game trails or transitional places most often trodden by animals.

Dancing Deer crouched low as he began a slow, silent advance. Josie tried to imitate. When they had moved close enough, the old Indian motioned they should kneel and Josie did as told. Buck pointed then, and Josie strained his eyes through the thick forest. At first the lines of tree and vine seemed to blend as one jumbled collage, but Josie's eye soon perceived the object of Dancing Deer's interest. There, in the distance, one motionless turkey hung by its neck from a stout sapling. A snare! It was an ancient and obviously quite lethal (also illegal in most places) trap that had fooled the large bird into being caught! Josie's lips curled into a smile.

Setting his basket down, Dancing Deer motioned that Josie should not follow, then stalked into the woods and was soon lost among the trees. Although Josie's eyes searched with ardent interest, he caught not a glimpse of movement until the Indian stepped out to remove the large bird then inspect his trap. One of the pegs that held the trigger mechanism had been damaged when tripped and Dancing Deer quickly whittled a new one. When finished, the light tan of newly carved wood offered an unnatural appearance and Buck rubbed it to a dark bark-brown using the wood-ash brought from camp. Buck also dusted his trap with more ash to cover the scent of man, for the smell of burnt wood is so common in the forest that most animals generally ignore it. The Indian reset his snare with extreme attentiveness, for its snap must be quick and lethal to bring minimal pain upon those who shared this land with him. This particular trap was designed to take one who passed upon a common trail unaware and therefore Buck used no bait. When finished, Dancing Deer sprinkled more ash lightly over the area. He offered the appropriate prayers then backed out as invisibly as he had come. Upon his return, Buck handed the large bird to Josie, who placed it in his backpack. Without a word, the men moved on.

Although ardently amazed, Josie held his emotion at bay.

To those traps that had not yet sprung, Buck offered only a glance as they passed, for it seemed the old Indian had known of their inactivity even before they had arrived.

It was said that a correctly constructed deadfall was capable of killing a bear. To the validity of such claim Josie knew not the answer, but he did know that it could take a wild boar, such as the one Dancing Deer retrieved from just such a trap.

The sun had fallen to early afternoon when the heavily burdened men returned to camp. "The hunt was good today," Buck said after setting his load down, "But this should never be expected because it is not always so."

There was work to be done. Herbs and some greens were hung from walls and ceiling within the shelter while others were sliced, or set whole, to dry in the sun. A fire was struck. Animal carcasses were cleaned and skinned; much of the meat was sliced thin and hung on racks to dry between the sun's rays above, and smoking coals below. Hides were fleshed then stored for scraping and tanning at a later date.

Although most Native Cherokee meals are kept simple, Dancing Deer deemed this a special occasion and he cooked accordingly. The turkey was skewered then set on a spit to roast over hot coals. Later, a salad of fresh greens would be added along with the root-bulbs of Spring Beauty (set near the coals to roast), and sautéed mushrooms too.

Time passed uneventfully that evening. After dinner, Josie's belly bulged with the satisfaction of his feast. Again, he sat at fire's edge with the old Indian, and again they smoked the pipe. Talk was small—of what little talk there was. But no awkwardness crossed his path this night, and again Josie enjoyed his contentedness in this wilderness place and amid the company of such an extraordinary man.

But, he felt something more too. For Josie had unusual interest in all things natural, and it was to each of the things they had gathered today that he had directed this passion. Before, he had seen them mostly as only pretty things that helped to paint a vista of beauty meant only for the eye, but now he began to see the direct relation each life offered to his own. For each thing they had pulled from the ground, Dancing Deer had told of its properties, benefits, harms, or even poisons. He had talked of the ways in which each approached life, and of the assets given it by The Great Spirit to assure survival and prosperity. Sure, Josie had cooked with garlic many times, but never had he considered it a living being. That was over now, for from this day forth garlic would always be as one who lived from the soil to share this world and enhance his life with its beauty, taste, healing properties, and even sustenance. And whenever he sat in a meadow beside its tall stem and small white buds Josie would consider it as friend.

To the animals, Josie's own hands had pulled hide over glassy eyes that had been keen and sharp only hours before. He had cut meat from bone then brought it to the sustenance needed for his own survival. Never again could Josie think of meat as something only from a package. The earth provided, and in this place where *nothing* was processed or packaged, the circle of life was undeniable. All things were truly connected, and never again could Josie squash a bug without wondering of its life and the ways in which it affected those who depended upon it.

For the first time Josie felt as though the world truly fit him. There was a certain rightness about it all. But this was only a beginning.

Dancing Deer arose, then disappeared into his home. Upon return, his gnarled hands held a drum built from a log hollowed with fire and skinned tightly with thin rawhide. The straps at its sides held a variety of bone beads—many dyed different colors—and an assortment of bird feathers. As he sat before the fire, with face turned up and eyes closed, Dancing Deer began to play. And as it had been 10,000-years before him, the drum's deep rhythm radiated through the dark forest. But it was in the language of the ancients that

Dancing Deer sang, and Josie understood not a word. The scene felt so unreal. So beautiful. Josie felt his goose bumps rise. In a while he stood to dance around the fire.

The celebration continued long into the night.

9

The following day started rather late. The men lounged beneath a blue sky drinking the chicory brew, talking, and letting time flow past. For food they would eat leftovers and nibble dried fruits and meat (Nuts such as hickory, walnut, and chestnut, would have to wait until their season in early autumn). Today there was little to be done.

So, they loafed, talked, and ate.

Josie asked of the traps, for he wished to learn of their construction and use. But Dancing Deer only replied, "If it is knowledge of hunting you wish my young friend, then first you must learn the ways of stalking. For only when you can move with invisibility will farther hunting skill be of any real value." With that Josie had dropped the subject. He would do as instructed. Stalking. The art of moving unnoticed. Of sneaking upon ones pray. Of course. Most ancient weaponry was effective only at close range.

Josie would practice.

The morning passed and Dancing Deer seemed not to notice. It was mid-afternoon when the old Indian arose to enter his home. In a moment he returned with a deer-hide. Josie recognized it at once. And why shouldn't he? He had seen it more than he cared to remember.

As Josie watched, Dancing Deer spread the skin over a hard patch of earth then knelt beside it. Buck had a simple template cut from old rawhide and he laid it atop the skin then traced its pattern with the knife-tip. When finished he reversed the template and traced another. These impressions were made upon the softer leather Josie had tanned himself. Dancing Deer then laid out the smaller patch of rawhide he had cut from the hide's thick shoulder area before the tanning process and made two impressions on this much heavier material using the soles of his own feet. Josie smiled as recognition hit him: Moccasins!

As instructed, Josie removed his hiking boots and Dancing Deer held the template to one foot. Compensations were made for the slightly larger size, and a second pattern was traced. Buck cut his pattern with ease then handed the knife to Josie, who struggled with his first cut but did better on the second. Dancing Deer showed his apprentice how to make cordage from a circular section of rawhide, then waited patently beside the fire-pit as the novice struggled with this seemingly simple task. Holes were then made in the appropriate places using a pointed bone awl before the men took leisurely seats upon their reed mats to stitch for a while.

Josie's concentration was so complete that he barely noticed as the old Indian began to speak, "In the time of my ancestors the taking of life was a sacred matter. If not hungry already, the hunter often fasted for days before the hunt so the spirits of those he sought would know his need was true. Prayers were made for the spirits of all who offered themselves so the people might live. In gratitude, all parts of the body were used. For if one offends the spirit of his brother then that spirit will tell the others and no longer will they offer themselves to the bow."

Josie had heard this before.

"In time the white man came with his steel knives, pots, pans, cloth, steel drills, sewing needles, whiskey and, of course, guns. The people had never seen such things, and they liked them very much. Why should they not? Almost immediately trade with the whites began. Among other things, the Native traded skins—fox, raccoon, bobcat, squirrel, bear and especially *deer*—for these were what the whites wanted. The Native became very used to his new luxuries."

Josie's interest perked and he paused to listen.

"Trade increased until eventually some Natives considered themselves quite wealthy. Hides were as money now and they piled high upon the trade wagons. Deer were killed in staggering numbers; taken for only their skins with much left behind to rot. No longer were prayers offered to the spirits, for there were none adequate to forgive such an act.

"Although seldom good, relations with the whites eventually deteriorated completely. From there, things became worse until finally the red man was faced with the very real threat of extinction. Some of the people sought refuge in these mountains, but food was scarce now and no matter how he prayed, no longer did the deer—or any others—come to offer themselves. And so, it was for his crime that the Indian was made to watch his children starve, sometimes to death, even as his enemies closed upon his heal." Dancing Deer fell silent then; the leathery age-lined skin of his Indian features showed pain. In a moment he began again, "I think it's a thing that will in time come to the white man as well."

Another pause. Then great conviction:

"Never will I trade blood for metal, land for luxury, or water for whiskey. Stone and bone are good enough for me!" With that Dancing Deer returned to his work.

Much moved by this story, Josie was a long time in returning full attention to the moccasins. For although he had read of this matter in history books, it was quite different to hear it from one whose ancestors had been there, and whose life was so affected. To feel the emotion of this man for whom he had grown so fond so fast. Buck's story offered ideas to which Josie would reflect upon for many years to come.

These new moccasins were of the simplest design and, by the time Josie was still struggling to finish the first, Dancing Deer's work was done. He left them with Josie for reference then moved off for a bath in the stream.

As had those before, the evening passed beside the crackle of hardwood burning in the pit. Tonight, there was storytelling. Josie had little to tell so he listened instead. Buck spoke of great hunts; some seemingly impossible. And close calls too. Of times when flood, or a stubbornly long winter, had brought famine. Of childhood accounts, family (all gone now), and vision quests so extraordinary that some might not have believed them. But Josie did. These stories captivated the younger man so completely that the hours passed without notice and it was late when Josie finally pulled the sleeping-bag across his body and settled in for the night.

10

The wee hours brought a storm and by morning it was still raining. But by midday the rain had stopped, air warmed, and humidity hung thickly again. After offering prayers, Dancing Deer resumed work on what remained of Josie's hide. Two simple patterns were cut. More time was taken to add beads made of bone and some coloring prepared largely with berry juices. In short time both men wore new loincloths.

The loincloth and the moccasins were the first authentic natural clothes Josie had ever owned. Of the deer-hide he had been so angry about, Josie felt foolish now…and grateful. But he did not voice these feelings for Josie knew the old man had little stomach for such sentiment. Instead, he would show it.

Dressed in only his new garments, Josie stole alone into the woods for he wished to begin the practice of his first skill…stalking. To anything that had eyes to see him and nose to smell him Josie sought to approach without being noticed. However, most knew of his presence almost immediately and fled when he moved too close, or simply chose to leave.

Anywhere else he would have felt foolish, even stupid, dressed as he now was and sneaking up on birds, squirrels, and dragonflies. But not here. For Dancing Deer lived in a different world. Moved to a different drummer. Here different was good. Different was necessary. Mostly Josie felt stupid for being new. For his own inexperience. Although this discomfort was necessary, he did not like it. Determination spawned and Josie vowed to hone his skill as quickly as possible.

Some days later, Josie returned to Grandma's. Seldom had he been happier to see Adrienne. Yet still he practiced. Josie stalked dogs, cats, butterflies, frogs, bees, common house flies, and even his wife. It was his new obsession.

Soon Josie was back with his mentor and he even tried to stalk Dancing Deer, but the old Indian always knew of Josie's move seemingly before it had begun. He laughed at such attempt then offered demonstration. Josie watched with resolute concentration as Dancing Deer began in a forward slouch toward a doe that grazed in the distance. Rather than turned slightly out as is the way of the white man, his toes pointed in the direction he was moving. For each carefully placed step he first set the outside ball of his foot gently to the ground. Then, through thin moccasin soles Buck rolled his foot toward the arch while feeling for any twig that might snap under his weight. Only when satisfied did he commit to the step. Rather than placing his feet side by side, Dancing Deer put one foot directly in front of the other. In this manner he seemed to glide unobtrusively across the undergrowth rather than trample it. Buck chose his path carefully and seemed to blend almost perfectly with the foliage. Josie noted that Dancing Deer often waited for the cover of sound—the squawk of a jay or rustle of leaves in the wind—before moving again. Some sixth sense seemed always to warn him just before the animal looked his way and Dancing Deer either froze or sought cover when possible. Often Josie found him hard to make out even when in plain sight. Before his eyes, a man had become all but invisible. Josie realized he had seen this same phenomenon among many of the forest creatures, but until now, had never witnessed a man achieve it. Josie felt his inadequacy then, but Buck later soothed his foreboding by reminding him that one must always start at the beginning.

Josie began to divide his time almost equally between Grandma's and Buck's home in the mountains. And it was with real hunger that he practiced his new skill while also making ardent note of almost everything Dancing Deer did. When Buck was sufficiently impressed with Josie's progress, he added more:

Dancing Deer said that many modern hunters must often wait until they stumble upon their prey almost accidentally. This method would do no good in a world where a missed kill could mean the difference between prosperity and famine. So, it was of vital importance that one perfect "*the art of tracking*", and Dancing Deer made this practice seem almost easy. From just a few marks on the ground he could discern what the animal was; something of its size; whether it was male or female; hungry or fed; hunting, loafing, rutting, afraid, being pursued, or simply playing. He also knew where it was going and, most importantly, *when* the track was made. Josie saw none of these things and for him the trail usually seemed to disappear only inches beyond any tracks that were clear. Yet,

Dancing Deer had the ability to rebuild, to see in his mind, almost exactly what had previously transpired in almost any given place. It was uncanny.

A zealous interest in tracks soon became Josie's second obsession. He began to see them everywhere and followed almost all to the conclusion of his limited ability. He tracked dogs, cats, deer, coyote, turkey, mice, snakes, people, his wife, and even Dancing Deer. Constantly he tried to remember what his own moves had been then examine the marks left by them. Josie tracked himself.

Dancing Deer showed that, although the earth will generally record for some time what has transpired in a given place, its clues are not always written in dirt. "Notice everything," Buck said, "See where the deer chewed new buds from a sapling, or the rabbit hid on its run from the fox. Make note of broken branches or grass laid down. See every stone or pebble turned from its resting place." When Josie found a set of prints, Dancing Deer asked him questions: "In what direction is your brother moving? What is the age of his track? Does he travel to or from his home? Is he eating, running, walking, or fleeing?" Seldom did Josie have answers. He vowed that one day he would.

"When the track is lost," Buck said, "look ahead. The habit of his kind will tell where he may have gone, and where you might reacquire his track."

Josie gave him a dumb look.

Dancing Deer went on, "As important as knowing the track, is it also essential that one know the habits of those he tracks. One must know his brothers and sisters well."

Josie became a passionate animal watcher, and he began to offer countless hours of sitting motionless to observe the actions of one species or another. Always he made note of their movements then went to check the marks each specific action had left upon the earth. Sometimes, when he found a fresh set of prints, Josie made note of the shifting weather patterns then return periodically for an entire month to see what changes had occurred. To record the track's age in his mind. To date them.

One day he came to tell Dancing Deer of what he had learned, of how well he'd come to know the habits of his brothers and sisters. The old Indian laughed, then replied, "If one has a brother does he not live for a time in the same world with him…or does he only observe from a distance?"

Josie was confused. He thought to ask details but knew better of it.

It was at the edge of a field inhabited by many cottontail rabbits that Josie sat watching. With his new skill, Josie lay on his belly then stalked silently into the field. For some time, he stayed clear of the others and tried only to become a rabbit. He noticed everything a rabbit would notice. The world appeared so different when looking up at it. Josie licked dew from the grass and nibbled at young shoots and other grasses. He experienced the largeness of his natural surroundings and discovered many fears and abilities he never realized a rabbit might have.

When half the day was gone, Josie moved closer. So close in fact, that one rather large female actually brushed against his nose as she passed. For the day's remainder, through the night, and the following day, he moved little. For food he ate grass and for water he again licked dew from leaves. And Josie watched. He saw the young play and the old preen themselves. For the entirety of a day's cycle he watched them feed, breed, and avoid danger. In that short time, he learned more about the rabbit's daily life than a library filled with books might have told him. Intimacy enveloped him and Josie felt a connection with all rabbits now.

It took some time for the den of squirrels to become used to such a creature as Josie living in the tall pine so close to their burrow, and at first they were tremendously wary and scolded him verbally. For from them Josie could not conceal his presence. But his patience prevailed and eventually they came simply to accept him as benign.

And so, he watched them.

Josie observed their comings and goings, watched the storage of food, play, mating rituals and friendships as well. Josie peered inside the burrow and noted the way the sleeping space had been lined with leaves and moss then covered with twigs woven crisscross over the bed to better hold the forest debris that served as insulating blanket from the cold. He also noted the roof's construction. Dancing Deer would later tell him that there was no way to improve upon the wisdom of the squirrels. After some failed experimentation,

Josie would learn to make his own temporary camps using almost exactly those methods he had learned from them. He would learn many things from other animals as well.

Josie followed the squirrel's movements from ground as well as tree. He was astounded at their acrobatic agility and strength. They seemed almost supernatural. When this was done Josie knew the squirrel's daily summer habits from beginning to end. He would stay with them again in the fall, and then note them by winter and springtime too.

Josie lived with a doe and her growing fawn and slept for almost a month, and as it had been with the others, in time, they had come to accept his presence as simply benevolent. So, it continued with others. In time, loneliness amid the forest faded to an impossibility among the company of so many he had come to know so well. In the past Josie had at times felt an uncommon closeness with various people. Now he began to harbor such feelings toward *all* who shared this world with him. He felt as integral part of a greater whole. A oneness with all things and God too. It was an exhilarating sensation.

Josie's practices continued throughout the summer, but this was not all that occupied his time. Josie learned to make fire using a bow-drill. He wove mats and baskets, tried pottery, improved in the fine art of tool making, and caught many fish. By late summer Dancing Deer moved his camp, as he did periodically, to a lower altitude and Josie built his own home nearby it. He decorated the new place with reed-mats, baskets, and even built furniture. In the floor Josie installed a rock-lined catch for food storage and a fire-pit near the center. It was amazing how little one actually needed to prosper in the wild.

Throughout the summer months, leaves, shoots, and flowers were so abundant that both men ate little meat. But as fall drew near Dancing Deer's hunting forays increased dramatically. Traps were set, bounty claimed, broken parts repaired when necessary, and the traps moved then immediately reset. Often Josie accompanied his mentor to the sight of these, and although now invited to stalk in close and observe as the old man attended to such tools of ancient design, Josie was not yet allowed to touch them. So, he only listened as Buck spoke briefly of why the trap had worked, the reasons for its particular design (he used a wide variety) and why it had been chosen for this place and particular quarry. Josie hung onto every word.

Large game was hunted as well and although Josie was allowed to observe, again he was not permitted to participate. To this activity Dancing Deer offered few words, and Josie knew better than to ask. So he watched.

Unlike most white hunters, Dancing Deer never took the largest and most prestigious buck in a herd but picked instead a weak or lame animal that might not survive the winter anyway. Once selected, he would stalk his prey for hours or even days as might a cat or wolf. As was the way of almost all natural predators, Buck would take the weak and allow the strong to survive. In this way the Indian did not take…he gave. He gave to the herd a stronger future.

Josie was often amazed when Dancing Deer would locate animals without seeing or hearing sign of them. He could not help but ask, and the old man had only replied, "Can you not feel a fly walking across your back? Is not the body of Mother Earth the same as your own? Are you not a part of all the things of Her creation?" There were mysteries here that lay well beyond the parameters of Josie's present ability.

To the preparation and drying of meat Josie worked. He tanned hides, fished, foraged. and made new clothes. The leaves began to change color. A cold wind blew from the north. The geese and blue jays left. Rabbits ate fiercely to build their coats and layers of fat. Groundhogs sought hibernation, and turtles disappeared from the water. The blue bird lined his winter nest. The skunk and raccoon remained in their summer homes. They were capable of long naps and would sleep through the coldest of snow-covered weeks. The meadow grasses were heavy with seed and the men gathered much for their gruel. Roots and nuts came to season and many were taken then stored.

Josie had meat to last. His catches were stuffed with nuts, leaves, grasses, herbs, and roots for soups. He had buckskins, rabbit lined mittens, moccasins, and a heavy coat made from the hide of a bear that Dancing Deer had presented as a gift. There was enough wood gathered to warm his home and cook his food. He was ready.

Winter came.

Snow covered the mountains to bring a silence so complete it seemed almost eerie. It was a time of much meditation. Stories were often told beside the evening fire now. Josie learned even more of his friend's unusual history and was again fascinated by these tales. Although the days were slow and often idle, there was still a lot to be learned and by winter's end Josie would, in many ways, have become a different man.

Again, the season changed.

When Dancing Deer had deemed Josie's skill and attitude sufficient, he set to teach to the younger man use of the traps. For a long time, Josie had yearned to learn such things and he was excited. Josie was made to set these ancient tools *without* the lethal element (rendering their recoil harmless to his prey) until such time as he had perfected their construction and use. Once it was decided that Josie had mastered this skill, he was told to fast for two days before setting his traps. Thereafter he would eat nothing until such time as his effort provided food. For hunger did not only ensure special attention paid to the finer details of one's traps, but also conveyed to the spirits of those he would take that his need was true.

Josie readily complied.

It was not long thereafter, that Josie set out to take his first natural deer. As instructed, he would use only one knife and a short spear with fire hardened tip. The hunt required that Josie stalk directly upon his prey and thrust the spear into its heart.

It was a small buck that had been born with a lame hind foot that Josie had chosen. In fact, he had known this animal since its birth. Josie had watched its attempts at life. Its struggles. Its triumphs and failures. He had seen it at play with the others and felt its satisfaction when they had accepted him. Still, Josie did as Dancing Deer had instructed. But as the spear hit its mark the little deer turned to meet his gaze and Josie was made to share the astonishment, shock, and fear in the eyes of one he had come to know as friend. It was a terrible emotion that filled him then. But the deer did not die quickly. It fought for life and Josie was forced to throw his own body upon it and strangle the little deer with bare hands then watch as the life slowly drained. When the eyes finally glazed over, Josie hung his head to cry. It was for a long time that he lay upon the still body that way. When the moment had passed Josie realized that never before had he actually killed a deer—it was always his bullet that had killed it while he had stood in the distance.

But today he had shared the moment of death and it had changed him forever.

In the past Josie had paid lip service to many of the prayers deemed necessary by his mentor, but today his prayers for the little deer were given with new sincerity.

Again, time passed.

11

In the years that followed Josie began to make lone voyages into the forest. These often lasted a month or more. At first, he took only a knife and the clothes on his back. Later, he would walk into the mountains with none of these things.

Josie had once believed that to Nature the puny man must fight for survival against her immeasurable elements, unpredictable creatures, and fits of unprecedented anger. What a strange notion that had been. For in truth, Nature kept him as her own. She would feed him, clothe him, and see to all his needs if only he flowed with her ways rather than against them. For if he embraced the latter, she would surely eat him alive. Seldom did he use the word "survival" anymore when talking with friends, for this word had been replaced with the more appropriate "*prosper*".

To the Indian, the world of spirit, that lies just beyond what can be seen and touched, is as real as the ground upon which he stands. Dancing Deer seemed powerfully attuned to that place. And, although there was a day when Josie would not have entertained such ideas, now he was not so sure. For, so often did the old Indian see the un-seeable and know the unknowable.

The time arrived for Josie's own fasts and vision quests.

To the call of a dream, Josie walked into the mountains to spend thirteen moons—four entire seasons—alone there; reappearing periodically only for short intervals to commune privately with his wife.

When Josie emerged from the mountains the following spring, he was a hell of a sight. Barefoot and dressed only in breechcloth, he carried a finely crafted bow, quiver of arrows strung loosely across one shoulder, and a few basic tools. Across the right side of his ribs were three long scars that had not been there before. His hair and beard hung long and ragged and Adrienne might have been startled had she not become accustomed to such things in recent months. Yet she noted with some satisfaction that his body was clean, and he'd lost no weight at all. Josie's eyes sparkled with a new strength. Still, she sometimes wondered of his sanity. He had changed so much since the days of plumbing houses with his father in the distant city. What a misty and remote memory that seemed. But Adrienne knew this was something her husband must do. So, she had backed his play…and Josie was grateful.

Immediately, Josie picked up a pen and began to write the stories of his experience. Of escape from his old life. Of his many fears…and his struggle. Of his mentor. Of his teachers in the forest. *Of his journey.* For months he did little else for it seemed the pen possessed him. Such was this obsession that he often neglected to eat, sleep, or even venture outside. Although she said nothing, Adrienne worried. She had married such a crazy bastard it sometimes seemed.

Josie's words ran out in a day. He set the pen down and went straight to bed. When three days had passed Josie cleaned himself up and set off to the sweat lodges. His spirit now cleansed, Josie then went into the mountains to spend a month with Dancing Deer.

Adrienne had acquired some clerical skills back in high school and in her husband's absence she set with typewriter to put his chicken markings into print. It took time, but Adrienne was not only fast, she was also persistent.

Among those who boarded horses at the Kelly Ranch there was a local author named Rachel Gallin. Upon their meeting, she and Adrienne had become great friends almost immediately. Upon seeing Josie's work, Rachel was enthralled, and, after considerable editing, was able to assist in the publishing prosses.

Two years later Josie's story went to print in a series of short books. Very quickly these books began flying off the rack. Mail from those he had never met poured into Josie's P.O. Box. His work went on the best seller's list. Reporters visited Grandma's. Among others, National Geographic did a story, and Josie's face appeared on the cover of Time Magazine as well. An evening talk show asked him to appear as guest. Money flowed in.

It was overwhelming.

The couple bought a new truck, horse trailer, small jeep, and a few other odds and ends. That was it. For Josie's manner of measuring wealth differed dramatically from that most often presented by the modern society. Josie believed that:

When one finds he likes himself more often than he doesn't, and even thinks himself a very cool person, possibly one of his favorites, much of the time; and when he also finds that he likes his life more often than he doesn't, and is even excited about it often, then that man is indeed wealthy. No person is privilege to keep these two attributes at all times. But if one does not possess these qualities at all then it matters not if he is worth billions...that man is indeed poor. Statistics consistently confirm that the suicide rate among the monetarily rich is identical to those among the poor. Therefore, if a person is fortunate to enjoy these two attributes often then *it matters not how he acquires or maintains them*—that man is indeed rich. To Josie, this seemed the best yardstick with which to measure wealth, and by this calculation, he had been a very rich man for much of his short life.

The couple took trips both local and abroad to explore exotic places. These new sights and sensations were exhilarating, and new friends were made. Josie noted the huge number of things done so differently in other lands. One culture might agree that pets should not be allowed in a restaurant, while another paid the least attention to them there. One place might accept insects as a proper food, while another deemed them unpalatable. Tobacco, marijuana, and even opium smokers could be scorned in one land, while in another none paid them mind at all. One country's people might agree that public nudity was immoral, while for another it was normal. Among many ancient Indian cultures consensual promiscuity among females as young as twelve was perfectly normal, yet in Josie's own culture a person could be imprisoned for such practice. Josie also learned that in times past the Romans had accepted male homosexuality as ordinary conduct. To them, a younger man living with one older was commonly acceptable. In Josie's own culture however, all agreed that these things were a terrible taboo. The list of these discrepancies seemed endless. So where was the truth in any of it? Some called this phenomenon "*Agreement Reality*", and it blew even more holes through Josie's fading idea that the majority's opinion actually meant anything at all. So many things were, in reality, just "*made up*". This allowed even more flexibility for a man to decide what was right for *him* then pursue that idea no matter how unusual it might seem, while also allowing another freedom to do the same.

Freedom. It was such a valuable thing.

Josie also took solo trips into different environments where he lived from the land and learned new things. He traveled to naturalist meet-ups and campouts to interact with those of like mind. Josie gave talks. He continued to study books. With true enthusiasm, Josie immersed himself ever deeper into his passion; and as he did, so did his spirit become alive in a way he had never dreamed possible. Contentment filled him often now, and even the idea of depression seemed a distant memory.

More time passed.

GOLD MINE
Chapter 16

1

Better than two years had passed since Josie's first book went to print. Although an earth shelter had long ago been added to Grandma's, the van, and most everything else, remained as it had when the couple first settled here. It was the morning of an unusually warm spring day as Josie sat beside his wife upon the blanket-covered sofa just outside the van's side door. Before them, a fire crackled below one old wire refrigerator-shelf that sat atop the ring of rocks surrounding their fire pit to serve as grill for an old percolator coffee pot. Although Adrienne liked cream and sugar, Josie preferred his coffee black and steam rose slowly from their mugs as Adrienne talked of her previous day's foray into town and rattled on about some local gossip. Josie listened with only mild enthusiasm as his mind, now so accustomed as to continue even without conscious thought, also noted the movements of those animals who shared the immediate forest. Many he knew personally. And it was by their warning that he became aware of the vehicle's approach even before it could be heard. Turning attention to the road, Josie watched a spanking new, dark-brown, Jeep Cherokee emerge from the tree-line and make its way slowly toward the van as its off-road tires crunched loudly upon the dirt. Josie noted the clean-shaven and extremely well-dressed young man who sat behind the wheel, while what appeared to be an elderly woman occupied the back seat.

An intriguing mystery.

Once close, the jeep stopped and the big, strikingly handsome, chauffeur emerged from the driver's seat. Josie noted more closely the slightly wavy blond hair that hung loosely from under the chauffeur's cap to some distance below his strong shoulder-line. He seemed an interesting meld of both surfer and body builder all rapped into one finely tailored suit. Seemingly, without notice of his new environment, the man proceeded in a businesslike manner to open the rear door, then stand aside and at attention so his employer might pass unencumbered. The old woman stepped out. Slowly, she rose to her full height of 5'2", then turned to survey the property. She took in the wood-burning bathtub, earth-shelter, meat drying rack, strange hippie van, fire-pit, and coffeepot. When this was done, she cast a stern and wrinkled face to Josie and for a moment he thought he saw approval there.

    He studied her more closely. The old woman wore a simple, off-white dress that hung loosely over her plump body and she might have presented the air of a grandmother's lovability had her steely gaze not been so businesslike. Her left hand clutched a large white purse, while around her neck one heart shaped locket hung from a gold chain. The lipstick was too thick and red for such a round and pale face so heavily wrought with wrinkles. Pure white hair was pulled neatly into a bun while below, both lobes hung with busy diamond-studded earrings. All fingers—excluding the one traditionally reserved for wedding band—held an assortment of rings studded with even larger diamonds and other precious stones. It could all easily be taken as only the cheap costume jewelry sometimes worn by old women—except that it *was not*. For although obviously eccentric, this woman stunk of money. Looking to ground level, Josie noted her brand new hiking boots with their deeply treaded soles and wondered if, as might also be true of the jeep, they had been only recently purchased for just this foray.

    She started forward and, even through the rather off beat appearance, managed to carry very well the lofty air of power and importance so common to the filthy rich. The chauffeur moved quickly to open the jeep's rear hatch and retrieve one collapsing lawn-chair, a small wooden folding table, and little ice chest. After closing the door, he followed after her with these things.

    Josie never left the couch.

    The old woman arrived to stand before the couple, who were now well seasoned and not quite so young themselves. Looking into her wrinkled face Josie noted that the gray eyes were still sharp and spoke of keen intelligence. "Josie McWaters," she said and extended a rather frail hand. Josie took it gently and offered a welcoming smile. She turned then to his wife, "And Adrienne McWaters," Adrienne took the hand but only managed a slightly confused look in return. "My god," the old woman continued, "It's such a pleasure to meet you both."

By now the chauffeur had finished erecting the lawn-chair behind her and, setting the purse into her lap, the woman sank slowly into it. Next, he placed the folding table at her side. The strange visitor looked from Josie to Adrienne and after a moment's thought said, "I hope my coming unannounced is not too much of an inconvenience."

"Not at all," Josie answered still not to sure what to make of the situation but undeniably amused with this strange fiasco. "We were just having a little coffee. Would you like some?"

"No thank you," the woman replied as the chauffeur finished pouring a bottle of chilled Perrier water into a small crystal glass filled with ice. After handing her the cup he assumed a rather statuesque stance with one hand clasped over the other at his waist. The old woman took a sip then paused to eye them both. Finally, she turned to Josie and said, "Mr. McWaters, do you know who I am?"

"Please, call me Josie. And no; you've not yet introduced yourself."

"Good point. Well Josie, my name is Emma Hancock."

"Of Hancock Industries?" Josie snapped. His tone was sharp.

"I see you have heard of me," the gaze of her steel gray eyes remained steady into his own. In a moment they softened. "Please. I've not come on a matter of business or profit but am here rather on an errand of much more interesting importance. I think you will approve. Hear me out."

Josie relaxed a little.

"Do you mind if I smoke?" He did not. From her purse Emma produced a silver case filled with Benson & Hedges 100s. She slid one from the others and placed it between sticky red lips. The manservant quickly gave her a light then set a glass ashtray on the little table before returning to his statuesque pose. Emma took a long drag then exhaled the bluish smoke up and away. When this was done, she paused to look deeper into Josie's eyes. In a moment, her gaze averted.

Emma Hancock began to speak, "When I was a young girl I

often dreamed of a simpler life so much closer to the natural way. Somehow, big money and the concrete jungle never really sat square with me." Emma let her breath out loudly, then took a sip of her Perrier. She leveled sharp gray eyes upon Josie again, "But this is the hand I was dealt and I live with no regrets. Besides, I am old now and things simply are what they are." Her look softened, "I've read all five of your books and must admit to being moved very much by them. They took me back to the days of those dreams and I'm grateful to you Josie."

The power of the pen could, at times, be a truly amazing thing. Josie had seen it before.

Emma set her smoke into the ashtray. "At my age," she continued, "with all the days of business and profit done, and knowing that the time to leave this world is near, it makes one think and I wonder just what of it all I'll leave for the good of humanity. In any case Josie," her haughty rich air yielded even more now, "I've brought all my own copies of your work and was hoping you'd do me the honor of an autograph."

Josie was shocked. He consented.

Michael the manservant was sent to retrieve Emma's collection. When Josie had finished his endorsement, Emma thanked him then said, "You know; your third book, "Unlikely Friendships' was my favorite. But I was wondering, what ever happened to…" She began to prod Josie then and, at her encouragement, he talked of things that were not in his books and elaborated on some that were. She asked intelligent questions. Josie answered and found, much to his delight, Emma Hancock to be a very captive audience. When he inquired in return, the old industry mogul avoided talk of her family's business toils. The subject seemed to bore her. But of her personal life Emma spoke openly and it was soon learned that she had been a tenacious horsewoman all her life. This brought Adrienne into the conversation and more talk ensued.

In a while, Emma ordered Michael to bring more refreshments and a chair for himself. Conversation continued for almost two hours and by the time it began to subside, a friendship had been made. Then, as is common in conversation among people, there came a lull and quiet settled in. Seven seconds later it was Emma who broke the silence with an entirely new direction. "Do you know how my family made its money Josie?"

"Industry...I guess. No Emma. Not really."

"Well," the old woman paused to again wet her lips with Perrier, "It was my great grandpa Jack who made a little money during the gold rush of 1829. With this capital he invested in construction and my family began to build things. We built schools and courthouses. Government buildings of all kinds. *'Leave the little stuff to the little guy'* was our family motto. We built big. In time we began to construct factories, then skyscrapers. Next came roads, bridges, and overpasses too. In essence Josie, we built society.

"It was sometime back around the removal of the Cherokee from this area that Jack bought 2,600 acres of this mountain land that now lay with its backside against the National Forest. The original purchase was made in the interest of a mining operation that never panned out. But Jack so loved these mountains that he could not bring himself to sell the acreage. Besides, the fact of its remote location offered small chance of development for even minimal profit. Meanwhile, my family's busy involvement, in other more lucrative endeavors, had left this matter insignificant. But I fear that in time society will encroach and this will change. I share my great grandfather's sentiment and do not wish to see this place overbuilt or industrialized, but fear that there are those in my family who do not feel this way. But what am I to do? I am just an old woman now and possibly not to long for this world anyway. Therefore, I've decided to see to it that this land becomes part of the National Forest—or possibly a sanctuary of some sort—before I die. From what I see here, and having read your books Josie, I do not believe you are a sell-out for money. A very rare thing in this day and age. Tell me then," her tone seemed kinder now, "what would you do with a piece of land like that?"

"Emma..." Josie's voice went weak, "I..."

"Please Josie," she interrupted, "don't answer now," "Think it over a while, then get back to me." Emma's manservant held out a card and Josie took it. "My personal cell number is on the back. You can reach me there." With that she stood to make her goodbye while Michael gathered their effects. Josie also stood and, when the handshakes were finished, accompanied her to the jeep. As Emma sat into the backseat Josie noted that the white purse in her lap matched exactly the fine leather upholstery. Looking up she said,

"Goodbye for now Josie. I'll look forward to your call." He closed the door and watched the jeep drive off.

What a strange morning it had been.

2

In the week that followed Josie thought about Emma's proposal. All that land. Josie knew nothing of land ownership. Did not even understand it. But this is the way of the modern world—he knew. And reality is neither right nor wrong, it simply is.

At the end of five days Josie placed the call.

"Josie," Emma's tone seemed bright today, "have you come up with an answer for me?"

Crazy as his proposal might sound, Josie could do little more than tell the truth. What would she think? This big world industry mogul for whom, in the short time they had spent together, he had come to know and respect. Would she laugh at him? Scorn him? Think him a fool? Over the past days these questions had tormented him far more than the making of the answer to her question. That part had been easy. Josie took a deep breath then let it out, "Well," he began, "if I had a piece of land like that I'd live on it either entirely, or as close to the ancient ways as this modern world will allow. For as long as I breathe, and with or without your land, these methods will always live. Likewise, I'd allow all who share these ideals, and wish it, to come stay for as long as they like…." with that Josie's voice trailed off. For even these few words had seemed a grand effort.

There was a long pause at the line's other end and Josie held his breath. Finely, Emma's voice came on, "Well then Josie…the place is yours. I'll send my attorney over with the paperwork for you to sign. The contract will stipulate that the payment of any transfer fees, taxes, or other cost, seen and unforeseen, will become the sole responsibility of Hancock Industries for the next 100-years. But my lawyer believes it possible to have this land certified as a sanctuary and thus any cost incurred will become a tax write off. The land will then be an asset to Hancock Industries rather than a liability. There is however one small stipulation Josie. This being that you allow one small cabin, equipped only with only the *barest*," she emphasized, "of accommodations necessary for one old woman's visit on occasion, to be built on your land."

His land. Josie almost laughed out loud. What a joke. What a strange cosmic joke. Suddenly, Josie felt giddy. Although he knew not in what fashion exactly, his world was about to make a dramatic change. That was for sure. "Of course," he said, "That would be wonderful."

Josie hung up the phone. He pondered what had just happened. To him the motives of his industrial friend's actions in this matter seemed strangely convoluted. But what he had failed to see, as had she failed to mention, was that after a lifetime spent pouring countless miles of concrete into the very foundation of modern society, Emma Hancock wished to give back something that affected humanity in an opposite capacity. Something that helped to preserve those things for which they had so diligently worked to defeat.

Josie had been her answer.

3

Although it took only twelve miles of hard packed dirt to reach Josie's new home, this slow rode seemed much longer. But once arrived, the ride seemed infinitely worth it for, as is so common amidst these mountains, the property was uncommonly lush and beautiful. Some of the area closer to the dirt road had long ago been cleared leaving considerable meadow with scant trees scattered throughout. An unusual sight in a place made mostly of thick forest.

From work, Adrienne arranged a sabbatical. Next, she brought home two horses, her own sorrel colored quarter-horse, and a borrowed appaloosa, so that she and Josie could spend time exploring this new place by horseback. And so they did. It was mid-summer and although she knew Josie for what he had become, Adrienne was still amazed at the way he fed them from only those things that grew in abundance this time of year adding, on occasion, a small animal or freshly caught trout to the meal. At night they slept outside or stayed in a simple shelter built quickly from sticks arranged like a skeleton laid horizontally to the ground then covered with a layer of leaves and other forest debris. Clocks had no business in this place and time was measured only by the rising and setting of the sun. They became time rich. Play and, for Adrienne, learning was in abundance. Even the short hours of necessary work seemed enjoyable. Adrienne fell in love with Josie all over again. And to this land she soon deemed the name *"Gold Mine"*, after Emma's great grandfather's original investment here.

    When two weeks had passed, a spot was decided upon. Josie chose for his home a place in the most hospitable valley, near a wide creek deep enough for swimming, and not too far from the road. Josie took the base materials for his new house from an area of saplings spaced so close together that many would not survive to maturity anyway. This thinning-out prosses granted those left behind a greater chance for prosperity. In this way and others Josie would benefit rather than damage the land upon which he lived—and the lives of those who shared it.

    A large oval shaped earth-shelter was built with its entrance facing not only the creek, but the southern sunshine as well. Its outer skin was plastered with adobe then covered in woven mats for better waterproofing, and finally coated with almost four foot of leaves, moss, and other forest debris that would serve as heavy insulation. From the creek, Josie and Adrienne brought water to their new home through a trough lined with birch-bark halves. This allowed clean spring water to flow through one corner of the earth-shelter and provide all their indoor water needs. The sound of trickling water also brought a calming effect that Grandma's well never offered. The new home was lavishly furnished with simple Native furniture, reed mats, furs, and blankets. For a man's home is his refuge and Josie intended his to be among the finest and most comfortable. From Grandma's, they brought only a few small items and, of course, the charred bathtub. The van, and most everything else, was given away.

As the season grew late, they began to forage, hunt, dry, smoke, tan, construct warm clothes, and gather wood for the coming winter months. By the time this was done Adrienne had grown restless for the company of her peers and the pungent smell of horse flesh. She returned to work. And because of the long commute to Gold Mine, Adrienne began spending two or three nights a week in her little trailer at the Kelly Ranch.

4

Word of Josie's standing welcome to stay upon his land spread and, by the following spring, the first taker arrived. Mosaic was a young man with long black hair and thin face that matched his lean body. He wore old clothes and sandals. Mosaic had walked the entire road carrying only an expensive backpack filled with everything he owned, including a complete paperback collection of Josie's books. He hailed from the streets of Chicago and seemed high strung. Mosaic was searching, Josie knew, for he too had traveled a similar path not so long ago. But the younger man worshipped the ground upon which Josie walked and seemed anxious to do anything the older man suggested.

Josie was flattered and the two spent considerable time together, and it was through his efforts to help another with no thought of personal gain, that Josie often shared with his new friend a piece of heaven amid this wooded Eden. An even greater sense of joy enveloped him then.

Time passed. Things changed.

Mosaic would stay for two years but before he would leave others would come to take his place. And although most were transient, a small percentage settled for the duration. There was land to spare and therefore little need of overcrowding in the small villages of slightly varied earth-shelters, and occasional tent, that scattered throughout the valleys. Besides, few really care to live in such a fashion full time and, although many came and went, the stable population of Gold Mine would always remain small. As is true of anywhere people are gathered, there were problems. Josie ruled his land with a loose hand and was often amazed how things tended to work themselves out if he just let people be. It was also true that the remoteness of this location weeded out freeloaders and almost all who came were of like mind to this natural way of being. Here great passion was commonly shared and camaraderie generally prevailed.

Although some food was imported, gardens were also laid in. Adrienne's was among the first, and irrigation was brought to it from the creek through yet another birch-bark trough. Although Josie cared little for farming, he had long ago come to love the fresh vegetables often set upon the table by his wife. Some of the people raised pigs, chickens, and other livestock. In spring and summer women went out to gather berries and other wild vegetation, while by fall they took nuts and roots. Also by fall, and winter as well, small hunting parties sometimes set off into the mountains. Traps were occasionally used.

Emma showed up with a contractor in tow, and although this made Josie nervous, his foreboding was soon nullified when the little three-room cabin was built using indigenous logs and a minimal of imported materials. It would be the only house ever built at Gold Mine. The small yet cozy interior offered large pot-bellied stove, a wash basin, a tub that must be filled manually, candles, and an array of oil burning lamps. Emma imported large quantities of firewood and most of her food as well. Her latter years would enjoy much time spent in this place, for it must have been truth when she had first talked of youthful dreams and a simpler way. Josie felt that the old woman had received a long awaited gift here and it warmed his heart.

To Josie's delight, Dancing Deer came with the spotted stallion and put in a camp not far from his own. Although he feigned humility well, Josie knew the old Indian (quite the celebrity around Gold Mine) was truly pleased with the fruit his effort with a lost city-boy had brought to this day. Josie knew Buck's legacy had been realized beyond his hopes; for he saw genuine satisfaction in those old eyes.

Two sweat lodges were laid in and young men gathered rocks

and wood for the ceremonies Dancing Deer often led. And although seldom did he answer questions directly, Buck taught the ways of Native Spirituality through example, or answers formulated as questions stated to sate the hunger of anyone willing to ponder and pursue such wisdom.

Although the old Indian remained faithful to his nomadic ways for years, as age overcame him, Buck eventually settled at Gold Mine. Likewise, as they had done for Emma (less necessary for the sake of her frequent servants), the people looked out for Dancing Deer and many made gifts of the things they knew he needed. Dancing Deer's final years were some of the most rewarding he had known.

Adrienne started to hold a variety of horse events in the large meadow at "*Road's End*" (a name given the open place where the *road ended*). There were scheduled rides, measures of skill, bands of fiddle playing country and bluegrass music; dancing, camaraderie, and even a farrier who showed up to sell his services on occasion. These happenings were a great success.

As word got out that Gold Mine was not private land, and all who brought no trouble were welcome, people and their horses began showing up to ride these mountains and even make camp for a night or two on occasion. Some wanted to leave their mounts for short intervals and offered to pay for this service, so a few notched-log corrals were laid in and Adrienne began boarding horses. Eventually a large barn, built in the fashion of the ancient lodge house, was erected. Of necessity, Adrienne's veterinarian skills improved even more.

Seldom did she visit the Kelly Ranch after that; for the ranch had now come to her.

It was not unusual for Josie to spend days, or even weeks, alone in the mountains. For him, this manner of solitary communion seemed necessity for spiritual and physical wellbeing. Always, he learned more from the earth and its animals, but this did not hinder his time spent teaching and learning from those of like mind who came bearing new ideas and information. Josie knew that no man can ever know everything about anything.

There were others who came to *Gold Mine* in the same condition as had Josie's first patron—Mosaic. Although Josie seldom had all the answers, to them he offered friendship and served mostly as mentor. And though life is never perpetually wonderful, through the following of his own passion, pursuit of spiritual seeking, and the many hours of altruistic interaction shared with his fellow man, *Josie found a piece of heaven right here on earth.*

  Decades passed.

5

  Both Josie and Adrienne lived long lives and grew old and gray together. Of choice, they never bore children. There were plenty in the world anyway, and even a few at *Gold Mine*, to enjoy whenever they wished.

  Eventually, Adrienne left her husband to take a walk upon the wind. The two years following her death were the hardest Josie had ever known, and although he knew much of the circle of life, it was still for the longest time that he mourned. Some say memory fades for a reason. To this wisdom, Josie could not attest, but he did find that in time the idea came that he still had much to live for. And although he would never forget her, nor take another, Josie finally pulled up his bootstraps and continued on.

  For five years more he persisted. But no man may live forever and eventually he too took his final walk upon the land of *Gold Mine*.

HEAVEN
Chapter 17

1

Josie arrived at the meadow for the last time. But now, instead of remembering only one life, he remembered them all; and he wondered at what a journey it had been. Through his own experience Josie had learned so many of God's laws. Then he realized these were not really God's laws at all, they are simply the things a man must do if he wishes to *achieve heaven within himself*.

Josie looked ahead and there they were—*The Pearly Gates*! Twenty feet high with a wall of heavy stone running across the meadow at each side.

Josie approached the gates to await the moment they would open. Soon he would pass into heaven—God's most coveted of places! And although his excitement was unbearable, the mystery of what might lay on the other side was also freaking him out. So, Josie turned to God and asked, "Is there anything you can tell me about this place? Can you give me an idea, a clue…something?!"

"Well Josie, I can tell you this much. There are many who believe that once they pass the Gates they will become overwhelmed with such a profound sense of peace, serenity, and well-being, that it'll be like someone just gave them a shot of Demerol. '*Oh, I feel so wonderful and so high,*' they'll say, '*this simply must be heaven!*' It just isn't like that Josie. Heaven is not a place of drug addiction my friend." God's tone sharpened, "*You don't come to get a piece of heaven; you come to bring a piece of heaven. And you add your piece to the piece that he brought, to the piece that she brought, and to the piece the other person brought. That is what makes it heaven.* And that is why no one may pass through the Gates until they are ready. If they did, it just wouldn't be heaven, would it? Let's face it Josie, if everyone did exactly that in the place you just came from then heaven would be right there on earth."

The Gates swung slowly open. As Josie gazed to the other side what he saw looked exactly like the side he was on. With a beaming smile and uncommon sparkle in those neon-blue eyes God said, "You've earned this moment well my old friend, and it's your privilege to pass through alone. I'll be with you on the other side, but everyone goes through alone."

Josie looked into the face of his friend…but said nothing. Turning attention ahead he started forward. It was true what God had said, for once past the Gates he felt no different. Looking on, Josie saw a trail leading across the meadow, into the trees, and ultimately to a thin line of fire-smoke that wafted from somewhere beyond. He took it.

Josie knew not what to expect of heaven, God's most coveted of places, but he did know that heaven is a place of *complete freedom*. Here he need not stay with the land if he did not wish to, nor leave it either. In this place Josie would never really want for his needs; for no man would take more than his share therefore denying another. And although the needs of one might be greater, nothing would be hoarded or wasted needlessly. For greed has no place in heaven, and surely God had created enough for everyone—if only the bounty is shared. Here Josie would never be troubled for a place to be, for no man would pretend to own God's land then impose burden upon another for his right to be on it. Never again would Josie need to lock his doors—for none would steal from him. In this place Josie would not have to prove himself extraordinary, for he had already become a special man indeed—as had *all* who reside beyond the *Pearly Gates*. They would simply treat him as such—as would he them.

Josie's pace quickened with his excitement.

He was almost to the tree-line when a glance ahead brought a sight so startling that Josie actually stopped in his tracks. There, in the near distance, a woman stood alongside the trail watching him. Her right hand clutched the rains that led to the horse standing at her side.

About the Author

Seduced by past travels, it was in the spring of 1996 that Scotty set out to see if it was possible to create a comfortable, long-term lifestyle of living full time from the back of his old Harley Davidson. Over time he achieved that ideal to its fullest. In those earlier years his outrageous exploits and unconventional wisdoms were followed worldwide through the pages of magazines like: Easyriders; BIKER, VQ, V-Twin, Cycle Source, and others. Today, and seemingly by accident, he enjoys even more success though the outlets of various video platforms. Although he'd originally thought it was only the unusual stories people come for, Scotty was shocked to learn that it's actually his uncommon perceptions they seek most. And although devoid of motorcycles, Josie's is the culmination of such things. At this time, Scotty is still on the road and may one day pass through your own town.

Printed in Great Britain
by Amazon